"CLASSY ENTERTAINMENT."   —*Newsweek*

"POWERFUL, VERY TIMELY SUSPENSE. . . .
VERY LITTLE CAN PREPARE YOU FOR READ-
ING RICHARD LOURIE'S STUNNING NEW
NOVEL."   —*The Christian Science Monitor*

An agent in deep cover . . . a translator in deep trouble. The kind of suspense tale that makes you want to
shout out warnings to characters who are about to
walk into traps.

FIRST LOYALTY

"I WAS CAPTURED AND IN A KIND OF FRENZY
. . . UNABLE TO PUT IT ASIDE. LOURIE . . .
HAS WRITTEN A THRILLER AND, AT THE
SAME TIME, A NOVEL OF HIGH CALIBER."
     —Czeslaw Milosz

"AN EXCELLENT MIXTURE OF THRILLS AND
THE EXOTIC. . . . FRESH, SASSY, AND STIR-
RING."   —Saul Bellow

"ALIVE AND PASSIONATE. . . . I READ WITH
INTENSE ABSORPTION."   —Irving Howe

"FIRST CLASS!"   —*Booklist*

FIRST LOYALTY

by Richard Lourie

A DELL BOOK

Published by
Dell Publishing Co., Inc.
1 Dag Hammarskjold Plaza
New York, New York 10017

Dell ® TM 681510, Dell Publishing Co., Inc.

ISBN: 0-440-12572-3

Reprinted by arrangement with Harcourt Brace Jovanovich, Publishers

Printed in the United States of America

April 1987

10 9 8 7 6 5 4 3 2 1

WFH

To all its muses.

A poet . . . has no identity—he is
continually . . . filling some
other body.

—John Keats

So shall you hear
Of carnal, bloody, and unnatural acts;
Of accidental judgments, casual slaughters;
Of deaths put on by cunning and forced cause;
And, in this upshot, purposes mistook
Fall'n on the inventors' heads. All this can I
Truly deliver.

—William Shakespeare
Hamlet, act V, scene 2

PART ONE

1 "I'm being released tomorrow,"

said Najerian, who was
standing beside Evgeny Shar. That day they had both been
assigned to polishing television cabinets. The best job in T-52.
Grinding glass for picture tubes was the worst. The plastic
visors didn't help, and the fine spray of glass always ended
up in your lungs and glinted in the blood you spat.

"Congratulations," said Shar. "Exile or home?"

"Home. Leningrad."

Shar knew what Najerian was saying—it was an offer.
An offer to do a service. Some small, useful service.

Shar looked away from Najerian and out at the section
of T-52 he could see. One of the real criminals—a stubby,
neckless man with exophthalmic eyes—Venya the Swan was
wheeling a cartful of unfinished television cabinets which he

suddenly propelled at one of the political prisoners, a tall young man with fluffy brown hair who had once failed to hide his contempt for Venya. A serious error, which had led to others. Venya was first among the criminals and allowed no one's contempt to touch him. Even the guards were careful with him.

The cart slammed into the young man's leg and he immediately fell to the ground. Venya the Swan pulled a sharpened pencil from his pocket and jabbed it into the young man's kidney with the skill of a doctor.

Everyone would say it must have been in his back pocket. Those intellectuals, always with their pencils, they should be more careful.

The shriek of machines was so loud that only fine shavings of the young man's screams could be heard.

Venya began pushing his cart again, back at work.

"He was stupid," said Najerian to Shar. "I even told him myself, I said to apologize."

Venya swung his cart around the end of the polishing line and brought it to a stop a few feet from Shar and Najerian.

"Here's twelve more," said Venya with a smile, knowing they had seen.

"Thank you, Venya," said Najerian, who was not going to take any chances with one day to go.

"He was a friend of yours?" Venya asked Shar.

"He's only been here a month," said Shar. "He was lost here, Venya. He didn't know how to act. He insulted you without even knowing what he was doing. And that's a very different thing from a direct insult."

Venya pushed out his bottom lip as he stopped to think. "In a way you're right. But mistakes have to be paid for."

The alarm bell went off.

For a second Venya's eyes shot from side to side and his body tensed.

"Anyway, he may live," continued Venya. "And just so there's no bad blood between you and me, here is a present."

Venya pulled out another pencil identical to the one he had just used to puncture a kidney.

He handed it to Shar with a testing smile.

"I heard you saying your poems in the yard," said Venya. "I liked some."

"Thank you," said Shar, accepting the gift and the compliment at the same time.

Two Asian guards ran by, a blur of blue fur, black eyes, rabbit-white skin.

"I should get back to work," said Venya, beginning to unload the unfinished cabinets.

One of the Asian guards shouted something to the other, reverting to their own language in the heat of the moment.

"I would take something out for you, Evgeny, a poem, a letter. I have cigarette papers," said Najerian.

"And I," said Evgeny Shar with a pained smile, "have a pencil. All right. Let's do it right now and take advantage of the confusion."

Najerian slipped two cigarette papers out of his side pocket and handed them to Shar, saying, "I am personally very fond of your poem 'To My Daughter.' "

"Good," said Shar, "that helps me choose."

"You really know them all by heart?"

"Every comma," said Shar. "I'll be behind that stack of finished cabinets. Come grab me if there's a lineup."

The guards had ordered the machines shut off. As their screeching and howling died down, the prisoner's screams grew louder, and now there was a jagged hysteria to them as fear joined the pain.

Shar spread out the two thin pieces of paper on top of a gleaming cabinet that had a three-inch gouge in one corner. He told himself not to press too hard or the point would rip the paper. But the letters had to be as minute as possible, which required perfect control over the pencil. He wrote the title in capitals: TO MY DAUGHTER.

> Fifty men sleep under the state's blankets.
> I am one. In the hour of the dream . . .

More guards ran by. One of them gave Shar a quick, hard look. The Mongolian. He liked to hit.

The siren on the camp ambulance had just begun wailing as Evgeny Shar finished the first poem.

"Hurry up! Hurry up! There's going to be a lineup!" shouted Najerian, his eyes enlarged by terror and regret. If they caught him with Shar's poems in his pocket in the middle of something like this, it would be ten times worse.

"All right, all right, the second one is shorter."

But Shar had caught some of Najerian's panic, and he

could not keep his hand from moving faster, which made the letters larger. He wouldn't be able to fit it all on one side.

The screams were dying down, becoming moans, as they loaded the young man onto a stretcher.

"Not on his back!" someone shouted. "The pencil's still in there!"

The paper tore just as Shar was writing the last word.

"Come on, come on, it's a lineup!" cried Najerian.

Shar hid the papers in the cabinet and ran over to him.

"They're in the top cabinet, the one with the gouge," said Shar trotting beside Najerian. "The paper ripped on the second poem. The last word should be 'honor.'"

"Honor. I'll remember. Don't worry."

Shar took the place in the front row he had been assigned as a habitual disciplinary problem.

Camp Commandant Shemetyev, pacing furiously and barking orders to the guards, noticed Shar's somewhat tardy arrival.

The silence was terrible when everyone was finally in line. Only one machine whirred faintly in a far corner of T-52.

The Camp Commandant looked at the faces, checking that they were being offered up to him properly.

"I will learn exactly what happened here today," said the Camp Commandant. "Someone here is going to tell me the truth. The truth. Shar, two steps forward."

Savoring the containment of his own fury, the Commandant walked over to Shar and then looked at the other prisoners.

"Prisoner Shar, not only are you a poet and a lover of truth, but you had a clear view of the incident from your station."

"I was working. I didn't see what happened."

"What were you so busy doing—writing poems to be smuggled to the West to slander the Soviet Union? So that my fucking telephone can ring day and night with complaints from the center about security here! Guard, search him!"

The Mongolian guard who had given Shar the quick, hard look stepped over and began searching him with a style that combined violence with finesse. Finding the pencil in Shar's pocket, the Mongolian smiled happily, triumphantly.

The Commandant examined the pencil, which the Mongolian had handed him.

"The same as the other one," said the Commandant. "And stolen from us. We'll continue this conversation in the Special Block."

"Prisoners are allowed pencils!" protested Shar.

The Commandant nodded to the Mongolian, who moved closer to Shar.

"Prisoners cannot be taken to Special Block except for specific infringements of camp discipline, and I have committed none. I found the pencil on the floor."

The blow from the Mongolian's hand caught Shar right above the eye, at the bridge of the nose. The blood gurgled as it came out of his nose and ran down his lips.

"Escort the prisoner as ordered!" shouted the Commandant.

Catching sight of Venya's face as he was being dragged from T-52, Shar saw him give a shrug of sympathy and encouragement, but there may also have been a glint of mockery in Venya's eyes.

Shar felt less dazed out in the open air, though no less furious. He tried to struggle one arm free to wipe the blood off on his sleeve, but the guards' arms were like iron and he had to bend his head down to his sleeve. That offended the Oriental guards, who snapped him back straight before he had finished.

Shar could hear the Commandant behind him, puffing slightly.

A few prisoners stared at Shar as he was pulled across the yard, but most looked away. The guards didn't like it when prisoners looked, and they always remembered who had not averted his eyes.

The two guards at the door to Special Block I came to attention as they passed.

Shar, too, was held at attention, in the small office, while the basic information was taken down concerning his offense.

"Possible accomplice in a stabbing. Refusal to respond to questioning. Resisting discipline. Contempt of authority in front of other prisoners. Incitement to riot," droned Camp Commandant Shemetyev to the official at the desk.

As soon as the papers were stamped, the guards relaxed their grip. He was now the responsibility of the Special Block Police, who stepped forward to accept their prisoner. They were Russians. No non-Russians ever served on the Special Block Police.

They were less rough with Shar, as if to demonstrate their superiority to the Asiatics. The Camp Commandant returned their salute with a nod, saying: "I will return to question the prisoner in an hour and a half." Then the door leading into the interior of Special Block I slid open, and the guards marched Shar briskly down a corridor reeking of disinfectant.

Shar could not tell if there were any other prisoners, because all the doors were made of thick timber with only small peepholes in them.

They turned the corner. He knew the cell they were taking him to: the one at the end that was separated from the rest by an extension of the boiler room, the cell the prisoners had nicknamed "Happiness" because it was so very far away.

The cell door slammed behind Shar and ruffled the hair at the back of his head. For a moment he paid no attention to anything, wanting nothing but the relief of wiping the rest of the blood off his face onto his sleeve, which was unpleasantly damp.

They didn't have to do that, he thought, they didn't have to.

He shook his head and strode across the blue-and-red Turkish carpet toward the table, whose centerpiece was a plate heaped with chops and steaming sauerkraut. Before sitting down, he grabbed the carafe of vodka by the neck and took a long swig to wash the taste of blood from his mouth, then chased the vodka with a hunk of black bread he ripped from the fresh loaf beside the flowers, blue daisies.

He glanced with contempt at the magazines on the coffee

table, the Japanese video machine, the stereo. It wasn't enough! Though he sat down and began eating, it was without pleasure, only to feed his hunger.

He leaped up when the phone rang, knowing who it would be. Anton Vinias. Shakespeare.

"My apologies, Evgeny," said Vinias.

"They didn't have to do that."

"It was necessary, in my judgment. It's good for your legend. Four prisoners are being released this week. The story will get around. Besides, here's the good part: we're going to be forcibly exiling you quite soon, and the bruise will look romantic on West German TV."

"I don't need a bruise for that."

"Think of it as a combat injury, Lieutenant," said Vinias, resorting ever so slightly to the tone of the superior.

"So the exile is definite?" asked Shar.

"It is."

Shar said nothing.

"What are you thinking?" asked Vinias.

"That I'll be glad to be out of here."

"I'm sure."

"Will we see each other in Moscow?"

"Yes. Once."

"Good."

"Anything else?" asked Vinias.

"I am nearly out of my sleeping pills," said Shar.

"You'll be given more in Moscow."

"And when I'm outside the country?"

"We'll keep you supplied."

"Good."

"Again, my apologies," said Vinias.

"I forgive you," lied Shar.

Shar hung up the phone. As he unzipped his dark-blue coveralls, which stank of sweat and cabinet polish, he knew that he would never be anything if he did not some day free himself from Vinias, his creator, mentor, captor.

2 Nearly blind, Abram Luntz

pulled his chair closer to the television to watch the local news update on the whale that had been beached near Gloucester. Then he could make out the immense black body thrashing clumsily in the shallow waters, surrounded by young, bearded scientists in wet suits doing what they could for the whale, which was, in fact, practically nothing. Suddenly Luntz's chest became heavy with sorrow and his eyes damp with tears.

His wife looked over at him and said, "Now you're crying for the whales?"

"Not only for the whales," he answered gruffly, angry that she had not understood.

For a moment Luntz had seen a perfect image of his own fate as a poet exiled from Russia. That was him in Boston, in America, surrounded by well-meaning, intelligent people who could never understand the fate that had brought such a creature to suffocate there in those shallow waters. Their smiles, their science, their young, bearded faces, their cheerful, youthful ignorance.

He thought of the whale again the next morning, on his way to the mailbox in the lobby of his federally subsidized apartment building, and knew that he had been touched in that place where the heart heals its wounds with poetry. It was too soon yet, but he was sure that some day that poem would come to him, and he twitched recalling the cruel closeup of the gasping blowhole. Then his attention was distracted by the sound of his own slippers scuffling down the hall, which smelled of cats and floor wax. Music was coming from the apartment beside his, the one with the rainbow on the door and the sign NO MORE BATTERED WOMEN in English and Spanish. He had never understood the point of such a sign on one's front door—was it to warn prospective batterers? Now it had become even more important for him to understand such things, because the approach of blindness could suddenly strand him in an isolated terror, without even the consolation of hearing Russian speech in the air around him. But how could he understand this America, how could he not worry about the fate of the world, when its last hope seemed more interested in noise-music and drugs than in facing the great and terrible responsibilities that had been thrust on this country of well-meaning, intelligent people, so naïve it made you want to scream and strangle them a little, just so they would remember what life was all about.

"You are becoming too mean. Too mean and gloomy," he

told himself, running one finger down the wall to orient himself in the corridor. By squinting, he could create a small tunnel of light, where distorted forms moved as if seen through the fish-eye peephole on a door. "Why shouldn't I be gloomy and mean?" he continued the dialogue with himself. "Exiled like Dante, blind like Homer; one or the other is plenty, but, good God, both was too much. What did Dante call it? 'The bitter bread of exile.' It's a good thing Dante wasn't exiled to America, or he would have had to write 'the white, fluffy, tasteless bread of exile,' and that wouldn't have made for a very good line." His little joke improved his mood at once, like a shot of black-pepper vodka.

The mail had come, thank God. It was the main event of the day, most days. Small checks for long articles, invitations to give a reading or a talk, letters from friends now living in Germany or France or Israel, the mail was like a lottery that he always had a chance of winning. In the beginning he had even liked junk mail, because it was a product of the America he was trying to fathom, but now he examined it only when he was bargain-hunting. Today there was a phone bill (he was always afraid of the phone bill, the terrible reckoning, the hangover that follows every excess, the twenty-minute transatlantic gabfest turned into four stern and terrifying numbers), two Russian newspapers (he could tell just by the feel of the paper), a sample of hand cream, and a letter with a foreign stamp. He squinted down his narrow tube of sight and saw a rose-colored stamp, a very lovely color, fresh, almost moist, and he paused for a second simply to admire it. But what country was it from? He removed his glasses, letting them fall on their chain, and held the letter close to his eye, the muscles on the left side of his face distorted like a cameraman's. Österreich.

Just as Luntz had slit the envelope with his index finger, the front door opened and the black man and the blonde woman who lived at the other end of the hall walked in.

"Good day," said Luntz shyly, uncertain as to the etiquette of the situation.

"Yeah, not bad," said the black man, going over to check his mail.

Abram shifted his attention back to the note, which was brief.

Dear Abram!

These two poems were recently smuggled out from the camp in Mordovia where, as you know, Evgeny Shar is serving three years. We will arrange for . . .

The black man and the woman began arguing over something as they looked through their mail, and for a moment Abram was afraid that one of those stupid, violent

But then the arguing sudsided, they went in, and he returned to the note.

. . . We will arrange for publication in Europe. Could you help us in arranging publication in Russian and English in the United States?

All the best,
Fedya Glazanov

Luntz would save the reading of the poems until he returned to his study. Fedya's letter had been a little too brief and curt for his taste, even though he knew Fedya was always so busy playing the role of middleman in literature that he never had time for a little news or gossip. Still, what would literature be without people like Fedya to arrange the conferences, the panels, the readings, to think up new anthologies, found quarterlies, review books on the radio.

Luntz was not among the great admirers of Shar's first volume, which had created such a stir. Shar had been forced to pay the price of his convictions so quickly, so often, and so painfully that it had become almost impossible to speak of him in purely literary terms, and something of a sacrilege to criticize his works—especially among Americans, who were always fond of new heroes, no doubt because of watching too many stupid movies in their early youth.

He switched on his gooseneck lamp, shoved aside a stack of books and papers, and began to read the poems. He read with his whole body, which davened back and forth to the rhythm, his lips moving to taste the exact, flowing shape of the words, which, if they were good, would hum in his lips for a time afterward, like a kiss.

The poem about his daughter seemed better than the work Shar had been doing before he was sent to Mordovia. Plainer, more particular. Shar was one of the lucky ones: for some reason his poetry translated easily, which, to Luntz's mind, was always a little suspect. Perhaps it was the result of a general drop in linguistic culture as the necessary lies of Soviet life continued to erode the Russian language, but the new poets, and Shar especially, seemed to write something that was almost rhymed prose, and which, in any case, never dared to find its beauty in making the perfect choice of words, delighting in the Russianness of certain combinations. Pushkin had never been translated well, and he was, by common consent, the greatest. That somehow set the standard: the better the poet, the less translatable.

But, he had to ask himself, was he being entirely honest, was he absolutely free of rancor in thinking that? After all, his own poetry had proved untranslatable ("I'm sorry, Abram, but you take away the Russian and the poetry disappears," his friend David Aronow the translator had said to him on more than one occasion). That meant that he had never benefited from his exile in the way that other writers had; the major American magazines never, or almost never, asked him for an article, and he was rarely included in new anthologies of translations, rarely invited to speak at American universities. It wasn't the stupid pleasures of celebrity that he missed but the opportunity to be heard, to be read. Every time he saw an obituary in one of the émigré papers, he felt that he had lost another reader, and a poet with a diminishing audience was like a man going deaf. Some of the émigrés' children still spoke Russian, even quite good Russian, but it was no longer the language of their real life, and many of them were marrying Americans who considered their new in-laws outlandish and touching, and who grinned like idiots saying "good-bye" in Russian when they meant "thank you." Beached whales, they were all beached whales.

Shar might actually be a prose writer who had not discovered it yet. The camps were more suitable to poetry, since it could easily be memorized and written down later, after your release. Only Solzhenitsyn could compose whole volumes of prose in his mind while laying bricks. Solzhenitsyn had flirted with poetry, too, but he, at least, had had the good sense to see where his talent lay. In fact, poets were always scarcer than hens' teeth, and if a country had three or four at one time, that was a lot, that was a renaissance.

He would call David Aronow: Aronow would do the best job of translating the Shar poems, and he had good connections with the press. But what was his number again? 212 something.

3 No, that wasn't quite right either,

                                    thought David Aronow
the second before his pen would have touched down on the
legal pad and committed him to an imperfect decoding of the
text. Something was wrong, the Russian on the page and the
English within him were not meshing, he was not able to lose
himself in the flow of judgment that was translation.

He hunched back over the text and began reading the
previous lines to get a sort of flying start that would take him
over the snag point. The author of the memoirs, Irina Petrovskaya, alive and not too well in New York at eighty-five, was
describing what it meant to lose one's country, the land, the
sky, the people, and cities; but, as she herself pointed out, she
was not a poet, and she could not describe that feeling that
the center of her life was forever elsewhere. And so, in the

end, she had reverted to a single common Russian word, *toska*. And that was the point on which David Aronow had snagged.

He made an automatic movement toward his tattered dictionary, Smirnitsky's Russian-English, its blue-black cover the very color of seriousness. But he stopped himself; it would be a waste of time. He had looked that word up so many times, he could probably find it blindfolded. "Pining" was one of the choices, but you couldn't say "pining" —that sounded like something from a hillbilly love song, and he had never liked the word anyway, because of its accidental but nevertheless stupid association with pine trees.

But sometimes "longing" worked. "Longing" was nice in its way, containing the sense of distance, separation, and the effort to bridge the void with some great arc of feeling that had to fall short. But it, too, had a love-song sound to it. Longing for youuuu . . . That was his culture applying its patina. And a foreign language was a country unto itself: no matter how often you visited, there were always side streets, towns, and whole districts you never got to see, and you were always too aware of the great monuments, which the natives passed without a second's glance.

David Aronow got up from his desk and stretched until he heard the satisfying pop of cartilage in his neck and mid-back. Like schoolchildren hearing the recess bell, his legs were happy to be out from under the desk. The memoirs were taking more time than he had calculated, but, then again, what didn't. The problem was that the woman wrote simply yet with strong feeling, and that somehow had to be gotten in English or the text would be flat as a dish. Anyway, it was time for a break; he had made a few dollars, September's electric bill.

But he wasn't going to meet the publisher's deadline. He never did, and they knew to expect that, but, still, the deadline existed and generated a certain tension of its own. As the date approached, the editor would call—polite, friendly, just checking. Ordinarily, there would be no problem: one good rueful crack, a laugh, and the deadline would be moved ahead three months. He loved the slowness of the literary world—letters answered promptly two months later, books that were bought in a flurry when some situation was hot, appearing in print three years after the events were over. He had summarized all recent Eastern European history in three words: hopes, troops, memoirs. He dealt with the memoir end of things.

Unfortunately, a rueful crack would not be enough in this case, because the editor, Karen Cooper, had, until very recently, been his lover. It had been clear to him why he had loved his wife, but he had never been entirely sure why he had fallen for Karen. All her physical details were right, and that was important, for often he attributed spiritual qualities to physical faults. Large calves, for example, were a sign that the woman was somehow unfortunate. But that only meant she was the right erotic type, that was only lust filtered through a nervous system that hated truck backfires and the roar of New York steak joints. There was, of course, the Jew-Wasp attraction. Wasps—the mystery of those who have no mystery. At a party an older woman had once said:

"You know why you like Wasp women? Because we like to do the dirtiest things but we do them clean." There was something to that, too. Or had he loved her because she was sweet and square and ethical, three things he never allowed himself to be? Or was she some Jungian aspect of his female soul? God only knew about that. Or perhaps no fancy theories were required. There was a proverb he had always liked: "Marry a woman with your ear, not your eye." And he had loved her voice, clear, open, American, without the stain of any particular place. It was a pleasure just to lie on her couch and listen to her talk on the phone. And when she spoke to him directly it was diving into a New Hampshire lake.

He lit a cigarette and walked over to his bookcase. Squinting from the smoke of his cigarette, he let his gaze slide over the spines of the books, a hodgepodge of colors, always somehow harmonious no matter how they were arranged; he was looking for Morozov's wonderfully antiquated *Russian Idioms,* which was usually good for a laugh and occasionally even for an idea. Read me, read me, whispered all the books with their perfect silence.

But then he recalled that Morozov had been banished to the top shelf with all the other more or less useless books, including the gray cardboard carton marked in red letters *A Generation,* which contained his own half-finished book. He jabbed his cigarette out on a brick and then jumped up like a basketball player going for a rebound, hooking Morozov expertly with a crooked index finger. That made him smile; he loved every victory, no matter how small.

In opening the book, he was surprised to see a glossy

white sheet covered with technicolor rectangles, each containing the face of a child. As usual, one face shone brighter than the rest. At the bottom of the sheet were the words DELMAR SCHOOL THIRD GRADE 1966. Then he remembered why it was there. Years ago, in that other life, he had selected Morozov to flatten out a crease in the picture. He rubbed his hand across the crease, an old scar now.

In 1966 his son's baby teeth had been as even as the line of blond hair across his forehead. The clear eyes looked out happily at the new toy of the world, but there was already something impish in the smile, which later would turn into loutish adolescent sarcasm then ripen into an intelligent young man's irony. The boy's shoulders were so little that David Aronow felt something that was both tenderness and sorrow lurch in him. He remembered how his son would run to him at the end of a day, run to him across a room, across the lawn. And they would hug and kiss out of the natural happiness of love. And it had been the same with his wife, sudden glad embraces in the kitchen, the car, laughter for no reason that still made perfect sense.

He did not really know what had happened. He didn't know whether the garden of young family love was simply like any other garden: September came, the fruit was yielded and the flowers withered. If that was all it was, then he was merely lingering in a mixture of nostalgia and sorrow.

But there were other reasons why he had moved from Boston and was living alone in a studio apartment on Fourth Avenue between Tenth and Eleventh, making a living as a translator, secure in the knowledge that only a radical improvement in the world situation could hurt his business. The solitude had begun seeping in. As if his son's increasing height had somehow poked a hole in the dome that had enclosed and protected them from everything, and the chill of outer space and all the bacteria of history and existence had come streaming in. And he found that he was, in fact, alone, like a planet. In some ways he enjoyed the feeling of his new solitude— silky, metaphysical, luxuriant with reality—but at any moment it could turn into padded solitary for life.

In that period he reminded himself often of Chekhov's crack "Don't get married if you're afraid of solitude," telling himself that that feeling was inevitable, was, in fact, the feeling of being a grown human, that it would be perfectly possible to live out his solitude in the confines of his marriage. But that, too, proved to be a wish.

It proved a wish because of one particular quirk of his temperament—the inability to be moderate. Something that was subject to no further analysis told him that it was right to live as he had in the family years, and equally right to live alone in the solitary years. The two should not be mixed and confused; this was serious business. And he knew that sooner or later, probably later, he was going to heed that voice.

Wanting to make all the decent arrangements, he had not in the least intended an "interesting life crisis" to spice up his forties like a semitropical affair. He had not wanted all the drinks, the phone calls, the confessions, the tears. It was hard to tell people what he wanted. He couldn't say that he was, at heart, a philosopher who tried to solve riddles not by writing but by the way he lived. That would have sounded ridiculous, though it was pretty close to the truth.

On the other hand, his friends had plenty of ideas. One nudged him at a restaurant table: "Oh, are you going to get pussy. Guys like us—early forties, guys who have been married and know about them—can you imagine what kind of pussy you're going to be getting?" He had imagined and he had sampled. It was certainly good, generically good, like wine, though you did get a couple of sour bottles every now and again. He tried to explain to his friend that he wasn't heading for a romp. His friend didn't get it. David loved him anyway.

Another friend said he understood: "Look, we've known each other a long time; we've talked about these things. I understand. There's something ultimately humiliating about being married, about being so domesticated. The house always smells of the woman, even if she's never home, like mine. I saw her two nights last week; one she was exhausted, and the other night she was feeling vulnerable and needed support. What the fuck am I doing with myself, I ask myself, is this what my life is supposed to look like? You were smart, you married early, you had one kid, the kid's on his own, you're only forty, you were smart. I'll be fifty-fucking-four when Jessie's a freshman." But it wasn't quite that, either. He wasn't fleeing. He was leaving very reluctantly—if not against his will, then against his heart.

To help him through the initial panics of homelessness, he began writing a book about his generation, the one born in 1940. He abandoned the project as soon as he saw the conclusions he would reach: that his generation had been born under the old dispensation, under the sign of the flag and the Bible, but that, just as they were being formed, the future arrived. A new god was born in the desert when David Aronow was three, a god that spoke in nuclear thunder. In the beginning was the word, and in the end the number. So, his generation, born at precisely the moment when civilization changed its curriculum, was really an alumnus of neither school, a sort of Siamese twin. It was no wonder that his generation had made such liberal and inventive use of the word "freak." To freak, as a verb, that was something. And he could have gone on to trace why typical representatives of that generation, like himself, went from being good, bright children to sullen JD's, stoned on rhythm and blues, who began destroying American virtue, especially sexual virtue; and why those JD's, who were really not tough at all and were only playing a complicated social charade, then became beatniks, then hippies, who had to celebrate Life in general because there was no particular place for them in the world, and some of whom had to burn the flag they had so adored in their childhood. But history was the culprit, not America.

The last line of the book was going to be a variation on Joyce's line that history was a nightmare from which he was trying to awake. David Aronow's would have read, "History is the nightmare into which I have awoken."

He resisted the temptation to reach for the box containing his one-third-written book. Though he took a certain metallic pleasure in exercising his will, he also had to be honest about his heart. Some of his heart was still in that book, some of his heart was still with his family, and, worst of all, some of his heart was still with Karen Cooper. There was no question of that, because in the two weeks since he had told her that he could not see her anymore, he had dreamed of her several times. Odd dreams, clear, mysterious, undramatic, more like I Ching images than one-act plays. The emotions in the dreams were always clearer and fuller than they ever were in life. Not only that: in these dreams there were fine blends of emotion that he had never felt before, recipes of sorrow and exhilaration that he had never suspected could exist.

He had always had a sort of secret natural harmony with women, which he supposed went, like everything else, back to the beginning. He could be intimate with them, could really give what they seemed to want most—company. He was always feeling their smiles on him. But he could no longer give them, her, Karen, what she wanted. They were another tribe with their own religion, language, humor. But that wasn't quite it, either. It was the dynamic, the absolutely irrepressible dynamic of men and women, which he called quack-quack nature. Given the right complex of signals, curves, colors, emanations, a man followed his sexual impulse like a baby duck following whatever it believes to be its mother. And he knew where it led; he had gone the whole distance once. It led to life being born out of life, it led to happiness and unhappiness, and in the end it had led him to the brownish-yellow walls of that room, with Morozov and the school photo in his hands, and the telephone now ringing.

He took a last look at the picture, feeling a tremor of superstitious fatherly dread as he closed the cover over his son's face.

"Khello," said the voice he recognized at once, with a smile, as Luntz's.

"Khai," he answered jokingly in fake-émigré English, as he always did when they spoke by phone. "Khow are you?"

"Thank you. Not too terrible. You?"

"Fine."

"I am not disturbing your working?"

"No, I was just stuck on a word anyway."

"What word?"

"Toska," said David, stressing the last syllable, pronouncing the "o" as an "a".

"Difficult word. How you will translate it?"

"I'm still not sure. Maybe 'anguish.' "

"Listen, I-I-I . . ." sputtered Luntz, who sounded like a hydraulic engine starting up when he was excited or indignant, which was a good deal of the time. "Today I got a letter from Austria which contain-ed . . ."

"Not contain-ed. Contained. I keep telling you, we never say the *ed*'s at the end of words."

"And how about 'aged' and 'winged'?"

"Practically never."

"Never mind," said Luntz, switching to Russian. "The letter contained two new poems by Evgeny Shar. One of them, 'To My Daughter,' is pretty good. Personally, I am not the greatest admirer of his work—not that he pretends he is a genius, like certain of our émigré celebrities, and, of course, Shar's reputation was also created by terrible circumstances—but, in any case, these are important poems, and so if you could spare the time to translate them and help get them published somewhere in English, I would be grateful."

"Sure, no problem, Abram. Send them along." That was the only answer he could give, for he could not see himself explaining why he did not want to be in touch with Karen Cooper, who had edited Shar's first book and who was, of course, the right person to see the poems into print. Just before his attention returned to Abram's voice, David remembered the concluding couplet of his last conversation with her: "I can't love you the way a person should be loved." "You don't love me?"

"First I will make Xeroxes. The address is the same?"

"The same."

"Will you come to Boston?"

"I doubt it."

"Then I will come to see you in New York. But, you know, I make plans, I write poems and letters, but all the time I have this terrible feeling that the world is coming to its end, or that the little civilization we have left is going to be eclipsed and the world will enter an era of darkness, technological darkness, unlike anything seen before. And, frankly, every day I have less confidence in the West. Your leaders simply don't know who they're dealing with. Not because the Soviet leaders are so clever and tough—no, because in a certain way, they are madmen, lunatics, from a normal human point of view they are basically crazy. That is what I worry about, but now I must stop talking because it costs too much."

"I told you it was all right to call collect."

"I forgot."

"So, take it easy," said Aronow, switching to English.

"I hug you," said Luntz, staying in Russian.

4   The trolley car entered the forest

of birch trees.

Yuri Trofimovich Kovshin lowered his *Pravda* to look at the trees, as he did every morning on his way to the laboratory. They played a small but important role in Yuri's life, somehow striking the mood that would be with him through the day unless some serious turn of events created a mood of its own. At the very least the birches always wiped his memory clean of the long rows of raw concrete buildings he had just passed, particularly grim in the rain, and of the *Pravda* he had been reading, whose words were somehow like those buildings, row on grim row of them. Sometimes the birches produced a certain lyrical patriotism in him, a sense that there was something called Russia which had preceded the Soviet Union and, with luck, would outlast it. On other days Yuri admired the birches as a human decision, for it had taken a planning commission to decide that the trees should be spared and that they might even be an inducement to reflection, important in a community like Novorossisk, where so many of the scientists from Akademgorodok lived. He took it as a tiny instance of what science, planning, and taste could accomplish together, a balance point where nature and civilization rested in a graceful harmony.

Yuri Trofimovich looked once slowly down the trolley. People were yawning, reading the newspapers, half sleeping. They looked neither happy nor unhappy, just people beginning their day, but Russian people, with a certain shape to their noses, a certain way of looking at you, each one of them filled with the Russian language, which, in response to a word, would come flowing out of them. Down at the end of the car a red-faced, unshaven man sat bent forward with his head in his hands. He emanated poverty, alcoholism, black unhappiness. The bottom of the barrel. That was Russia too, a Russia he would not miss.

Why did he think that? he asked himself as he returned his eyes to the birch trees, which were blurring outside the window as the trolley accelerated. He did not want to answer his own question and could feel a lurch of evasion in himself. Then, when he saw what it was, there was a sort of sad relief in finally looking directly at it. Yes, for a long time now, some part of him had known that if the new work proved anywhere near as successful as he hoped, that could only mean that he would be presenting them—them!—with a gift that would become a weapon as soon as it touched their hands.

It was still only an idea, but even the idea alone was too fine and dangerous a thing for them to have. If the new requisitions were approved, the idea would be tested in the bloodstreams of lab animals and if those animals began to experience the expected significant increase in life span, there would be a strong new force in the world. It would be foolish to wait any longer—he would have to start covering his tracks, start today.

He thought back to the beginning of the project. It had really been Yasha Farb's idea to combine the pharmacological research being done in gerontology with their work on the varieties of extrasensory perception known as psi, and to form the psipharm unit. He missed Yasha. He missed his madcap Jewish effervescence and his refusal to accept any mental categories. "I work on the principle that everything we think is probably wrong, simply because it is we who are thinking it . . . and therefore . . ." was Farb's favorite way of demolishing an argument and opening up a new vector of possibilities. "Our very conception of man is crude beyond belief, a Krokodil cartoon compared with a Rembrandt. Of course all this ESP is a hazy area, but that's a good sign in itself. That's the look of the unknown." They didn't really need Farb after a certain point: he was the sort that had the original intuitions, the divining rod that pointed at the secret water, not the shovel that dug it up. Which was not to slight the quality of the original work he had done in setting up the psipharm division, and in establishing new procedures for blood analysis and chemical synthesis.

But Farb had chosen to leave during the heyday of Jewish

emigration, to leave with that odd sister of his, Raisa. Yuri always suspected that she was the force behind the move, that Farb had the scientist's gift of closing off the world and could have survived and continued there well enough. But who knows? Their family had suffered terribly at the hands of the Germans and again during the late forties. And though he had never spoken of it, perhaps Farb had been affected by the resurgence of anti-Semitism in the period of the emigration; perhaps he, too, had realized that sooner or later everything had to go bad here; or perhaps Farb had simply been beguiled by the lure of the West, where he felt he might have wider scope for his passions—theoretical pharmacology and sexual adventure.

They had been such unlikely friends. Farb—tall, clean-shaven, youthful, ebullient, angular, flighty—and Yuri—bearded, melancholy, gnomish, thoroughly married, his only extravagance a taste for jeans and cowboy boots.

Yuri remembered their last walk together, Farb's face wistful but radiant. Yuri had even been a little hurt that Farb had not been sadder to lose him. "Here's what it will be like, Yuri Trofimovich," said Farb, avoiding a puddle—the inevitable Soviet puddle. "It will be like that experiment where two people sit across from each other separated by a screen and try to think the same thoughts. That will be us. Just a quarter of Russia, Europe, and the Atlantic Ocean between us."

"But I heard that they're not so interested in psi over there."

"I'll get them interested. Or I'll do something else."

"Still, to leave Russia . . . it'll mean never being home again."

"I know," said Farb, after a moment of sorrowful silence, "but somehow even that seems right. We have to leave home, all those old ideas of home. We can't build a real human future with all those old, stupid ideas."

"You know the line from Shar's poem '1999'—'Our Savior, the Future Who art in the Heaven of endless tomorrows'?" asked Yuri.

"I know it," mumbled Farb.

Approaching the end of the birch trees, the trolley slowed for a curve, which made the trees more distinct and vivid against the clear morning air.

People were folding their newspapers into quarters and stuffing them in their coat pockets. The red-faced man at the end of the car was letting his head hang between his knees and vomiting. For a moment Yuri felt the panic and shame of a traitor. Not just to his country but to himself. For he was no longer quite himself, not the same man who had boarded the trolley twenty minutes ago. Now that person seemed incredibly distant to him, remote as the naïve young man he had been in his university years. Now he was enclosed in a new understanding, a new self, which no one could be allowed to see. Now he would have to imitate, not simply be the blinkered scientist, the high-minded research pharmacologist whose dissent was limited to an impatient tone when dealing with officialdom, and who returned home from work each day to eat dinner with his wife and daughter.

As Yuri Trofimovich was peeling off his galoshes with one hand while sorting through his mail with the other, his secretary came in with a cup of hot tea for him.

"Comrade Kovalyov would like you to drop by his office this morning around ten o'clock, but only if—and he stressed this—it in no way interferes with anything important."

"Thank you, Klara Ivanovna," said Yuri with a nod at the tea.

That was bad luck. He didn't want to see Kovalyov today, not now, not so early that morning. He still felt naked, transparent. And though Kovalyov would probably not bother to check on Yuri's activities, the fact was that he had nothing urgent, no meetings, no experiment scheduled, and unless something popped up in the next little while, there would be no valid reason for not going. He found Kovalyov's deference loathsome—"if it in no way interferes with anything important." That deference contained a certain irony and insinuation: Of course, I can wait, what is my work, the mere protection of the Soviet state, compared with the research of brilliant men like Yuri Trofimovich.

Yuri Trofimovich sat down at his desk and poured a little tea into the saucer. Pursing his lips in his snarly brown beard, where his daughter thought all sorts of tiny creatures might live, he blew on the amber tea, inhaling its fragrance with pleasure. He was a new person now, and he was the only person in the world who knew who he was.

The minutes passed, and no one came in with any serious problem; the phone was silent; the sounds from the outer office had nothing unusual about them. His mail included an invitation to speak in Amsterdam about his work on antistress pharmaceuticals, to which he would have to dictate a polite refusal. The psipharm unit had already produced a series of interesting results, which had apparently impressed someone far above them, and their work now received closer attention from both the Ministry of Defense and the KGB. Though their security status had not yet been officially upgraded, there had been informal but binding instructions: their travel was limited to Hungary and Bulgaria, which was both an indication of the new importance given their work and a measure of the limited trust they enjoyed. Their work was to be considered a "prior commitment," which meant, in that loathsome code of politeness, that foreign invitations were to be refused on the grounds of "prior commitments." Yuri was furious at himself for even succumbing to that one moment of shame and self-disgust on the trolley. In hell, treason was the work of angels. His heart stimulated by the scalding tea and the flare of his fury, Yuri Trofimovich decided that maybe it was even somehow appropriate and useful for him to be summoned in right away to Kovalyov, for there would be many such obstacles to overcome, and he might as well get used to them from the start.

Kovalyov was on the telephone when Yuri Trofimovich entered his office. Seated a quarter turn from his desk, he glanced up at Yuri Trofimovich in profile, his clear eye at odds with the rest of his face, which was crinkled in laughter at the remarks some crony was making at the other end. Kovalyov indicated a chair with a slight tilt of his head.

"So, wait, wait," said Kovalyov, "you mean Borya stood up to fire at the ducks and then—what? Right over backward? Into the lake? And the shotgun? What? Like a stone. And then he what? He made the local police dredge for it for two days. And his wife? Vanya, Vanya, no, stop, I have a visitor."

Trying to get comfortable in his chair, Yuri realized that it was all part of the same game they seemed to enjoy playing so much, the game of power. To keep him waiting now was of course somehow insulting; to chat intimately on the phone was to make him as invisible as a servant. It had been the same thing with "if it in no way interferes with anything important," the sarcastic politeness of the overlord. Perhaps that was even the way people were supposed to be; at least, that was the way most of them were, and people like Yuri and a few others were the exceptions that proved nothing. Yuri could not simply sink into his body and relax. His body felt like a collection of separate parts, a foot, a right thigh, a left shoulder, a head. But Kovalyov, his jacket off, his girth bulging against his white shirt, his hair trimmed high up the back of his neck, was cheerful and relaxed. Why was it, Yuri wondered, that they always seemed so comfortable?

"So, Yuri Trofimovich," said Kovalyov, swinging back around in his chair, "how is our work going?"

The word "our" had been stressed with a slight rise in Kovalyov's voice.

"If you've looked at the latest reports, you know that things are going rather well."

"I have looked at the latest reports *and* the latest requisition forms as well. You are asking the Soviet state for quite a lot of money."

"It will be money well spent."

"Possibly. But let us look at what we've already achieved and what it cost. The antistress pill—you will pardon me for calling it a pill—has been helpful in space travel, and I have heard that some members of the Central Committee swear by it. But so far this latest project has produced nothing but . . ."

"Interesting data, useful data."

"Useful for exactly what?"

"Very little serious work has been done by anybody on the mind-body border," said Yuri dryly, hoping his reticence would be taken for science's mild arrogance.

"I have here something Farb wrote way back when," said Kovalyov, opening a thin file on his desk. "Here it is. Farb wrote—let me see—'Mankind has always dreamed of transcending itself. The October Revolution was itself an expression of that urge. But historical changes are not limited to the battlefield, and it may well be that science, working in the uncharted areas where mind meets body, and using chemical means, will create a new and better sort of man.'"

Kovalyov looked up from the page and stared directly at Yuri Trofimovich in expectation of his reaction.

Yuri smiled fondly. "Farb was a great visionary. We wouldn't be here if it weren't for him."

"Yes, I know. And sometimes I think it was a mistake to allow him to emigrate. Wouldn't he, for example, be useful right now? Would we need all this money for computers, research animals, and so on?"

"We would. Because it's in the very nature of any project. Projects begin with an insight, an idea, a burst of enthusiasm, but there's always some point in the middle where things get bogged down and an extra burst of energy is very helpful."

"That means we are somewhere in the middle?"

"Yes, somewhere in the great middle."

"And since you've been working for about eighteen months, that means we could expect some definite results in about another twelve to eighteen months?"

"Statistically, yes, but in practice, as you must well know, anything can happen."

"Including utter failure?"

"Failure is a measurement that depends on the standard applied. If we achieve nothing in eighteen months, the lab could be shut down, and the experiment could be called a failure. Or the experiment could go for another ten months and succeed. In which case the previous eighteen could not be termed a failure."

"And what do you predict?"

"I don't predict. I do science."

"Well, I do predict. I predict, for example, that the funds you requested will be granted quite quickly, and before we know it there will be chimps and new computers among us. I also predict that your request for the special film magazines will be granted."

41

"Well, thank you very much."

"Oh, but don't thank me, Yuri Trofimovich. We all know to what all thanks are due."

"Yes," said Yuri.

"Yes, to the Soviet state. And yet, doesn't it surprise you a little that some people are so ungrateful? After years of protection, education, employment, how some people treat the Soviet state is simply amazing. Can you imagine, Yuri Trofimovich, people, supposedly even the best people, behave so badly. They lie to us; they say, 'We want to go to Jerusalem and be among our own people,' and the next thing you know they're in New York. Though maybe it comes to the same thing."

Yuri winced. He had an involuntary hatred for those little anti-Semitic remarks that some Russians treated as no more than salty tidbits to accompany their vodka, proof, like being a soccer fan, that they were one of the gang.

"Well, I'm sorry," continued Kovalyov, "but I am personally outraged that their press constantly speaks of the six million Jews and never mentions the twenty million Russian dead. As a Russian, Yuri Trofimovich, doesn't that make you indignant?"

"Yes, lies and distortions always do."

"So," said Kovalyov, his tone becoming more abrupt to indicate that the meeting was about to end, "you think that at this stage it is mostly a matter of rubles and long hours, and that, no matter what, we have a good head start in this field?"

"Yes, that's right."

"Very good, then, I won't keep you from your work a moment longer," said Kovalyov, rising.

Yuri rose in response. The moment he dreaded had come. He felt that his imitation of his old abstracted, irritable self had succeeded well enough, but feared that his own hand would betray him when it touched Kovalyov's. Fortunately, he was smoking and so could make a little show of transferring his cigarette from one hand to another, which might blur Kovalyov's perception of any electric quivering in his fingers or damp anguish on his palms.

Kovalyov's large hand enfolded Yuri's wiry, tobacco-stained fingers, and Kovalyov looked right at him with a smile and a nod of approval. Still, Yuri could not delude himself; something had leaped from hand to hand.

Or was that his paranoia? he wondered out in the corridor, aware that his heart was beating rapidly and that his thoughts were coming too fast.

5   His knee hurt.

A more or less constant dry ache which at any minute could jump with hot pain. The pain could come when he was sitting absolutely still at this desk and not bother him when he was taking the stairs. It could wake him at night in bed or cause him to curse at the dinner table. The doctors had prescribed various medications, but anything effective enough to dull the pain also clouded his thoughts and made him both lethargic and snappish. He could live with the dry ache and had even made his peace with it, worked it into the routine of his life. But the hot jump of pain was more than he could bear and always left him shaky with adrenalin for several minutes. The worst of it was not knowing exactly when it would strike. If he was not very careful, nearly all of his time could be turned into mere anticipation of the pain.

Anton Vinias considered the pain a humiliation, a personal defeat, and an ill omen reminding him of the limits of the will. Vinias hated the red-hot worm of pain, not only because he could not control it but also because it made everything he did seem trivial by comparison. In his worst moments he groveled before that blind, deaf god of pain and vowed to do whatever it wanted. But it wanted nothing, and Vinias would be left with the odor of a private shame.

Vinias was the head of SPETSDESINFORM, a special branch of the department of disinformation in the Committee for State Security (KGB). His particular genius was to orchestrate events in foreign countries so that they would appear to be a normal part of that society's functioning and not an artifice dreamed up thousands of miles away. It could be a soccer riot in Brazil or a cult murder in California. There was no one who could touch Vinias in this field, and he had risen to the top with a minimum of back scratching and back stabbing. Known to his colleagues as "Shakespeare," Vinias was treated with a certain reverence; though he enjoyed it, he was not a vain man in that sense. Besides, the admiration of the less gifted never seemed the greatest of compliments.

He had written a short theoretical treatise called *Authoring Events,* which existed in an edition of sixteen copies, fifteen of which were kept under lock and key in the department reading room and could be read there only. There was always a certain pleasure in seeing some young man reading his guide intently. He often wondered what they actually understood of it, for the concepts were about the very nature of reality and perception, which was a subtler business than shooting somebody in the street—though at times, of course, the point was to link those seemingly disparate things. Although Vinias recognized that objective reality existed, he saw time, space, and the mass of humanity as essentially colorless and formless and, locally at least, subject to a high degree of manipulation. Vinias laid the stress on perception, on creating perceptions through the manipulation of events and information. Reality was not much more than a mass of documentary footage, crying out for montage.

He had illustrated his ideas in his little book with the example of the memoirs of Horst Neidrich, an actual person who had lived in Heilbronn am Neckar in West Germany and had been a captain in the Wehrmacht during the Second World War. It was even true that Neidrich had served on the Russian front, had been present at the exhumation of the five thousand Polish officers' bodies at Katyń, and was identifiable in a photograph of the international investigation committee. In the early seventies, Neidrich had been secretly informed that his brother was alive and in a Soviet labor camp (where he had turned up as a prisoner of war and then been kept when his possible utility had been noticed). Once Neidrich was shown a movie of his brother appealing to him for help, he did not suffer many pangs of conscience before agreeing to write his memoirs, in which he would reveal the truth about Katyń—that it had in fact been a Nazi atrocity camouflaged to resemble a Soviet one and committed, of course, for propaganda purposes. Neidrich wrote that his conscience had tormented him all these years and that now he knew he must tell the world the truth because he saw the specter of fascism on the rise again.

The book was treated like any other book, because it was there, because it was made of paper and cardboard, and because the letters were the same as the letters one saw every day. It was regarded as real because its author had largely told the truth, the verifiable truth, about nearly everything, and because there was a picture of him at the site he described. The book was translated into several languages, reviewed, and, of course, attacked, but attacks were fine; after all, you don't attack something that does not exist. In most cases doubt was created; people were bound to think that maybe there was something to it.

In any event, since the Katyń area was under Soviet control, nothing could be proved one way or the other, and so the issue had to remain suspended, murky, irritatingly imprecise. This ambiguity was especially important in regard to Poland, which could be counted on to be periodically troublesome; Katyń was always a point of passion, a rallying cry for them. The job was to cloud Western sympathy for Poland—never much of a problem, since the West feared Eastern Europe the way a rich, fat boy fears the bad side of town.

After the publication of his book, Neidrich received a series of death threats, each of which was as fictitious as the key chapters of his book, and the threats were followed by the bombing of his car, credit for which was taken by a neofascist organization called Die Echte. Finally, cursing neofascist, capitalist West Germany and fearing for his life,

Neidrich took East German citizenship (itself a good propaganda antidote to the Wall) and moved to a suburb of Leipzig, where he had an emotional reunion, as planned, with his brother.

But Neidrich was nothing compared with Evgeny Shar, the dissident poet. An orphan raised in a Children's Home, Shar had been arrested at nineteen for organizing a little workshop that produced icons. He was swapping the icons with foreigners in exchange for their blue jeans, which he then sold at an enormous profit. Vinias had heard about him by chance, but two details about Shar had appealed to him at once—the icon workshop and the fact that Shar had been able to mingle with foreigners so easily. Vinias knew what that meant—that Shar had been able to read them well enough to put them completely at ease.

The search of Shar's workshop had turned up the usual items—Danish pornography, a tape cassette that had been stolen from a French diplomat's teen-age son (it was returned), hashish from Turkestan. But Shar, in the tradition of the Russian underworld, had also composed a whole series of ballads—high-spiritedly nihilistic, scabrous, ambitiously lengthy. Though the influence of Russian folk and underworld songs, as well as of Mayakovsky and Esenin, was all too apparent, it was nevertheless clear to Vinias that the young man had real potential.

Upon first interviewing Shar, Vinias saw that he also had the remarkable gift of immediately knowing what you wanted and adapting himself to you so quickly, so artfully, that he became essentially invisible. Certain women had that gift, the gift of those who seem to serve; unencumbered with personalities of their own, they could see right through into the personalities of others, others who were always so wrapped up in themselves, so blind. It was strange that when colleagues or critics wrote about Shar's poetry they always remarked on its selflessness and transparence, praising those qualities as if they were great virtues instead of spiritual failings. Even Shar himself had once mentioned this with a smile, and at that moment Vinias had realized that, of course, Shar had his own unique sense of humor, that no one but Shar could ever appreciate certain ironies, certain jokes. But how could he depend on Shar, who was not the least like anyone else? Or was he perhaps cleverer than everyone else and playing a master game invisible to all the other players? That was possible. But Vinias didn't really think so. Vinias believed Shar was like himself, a man who had risen to the exact position in the world that fulfilled him. Though some people suspected Vinias of wanting higher office, they were completely mistaken. Vinias had spent considerable time in the United States as a diplomatic attaché at the United Nations and had observed that, objectively, America was a better place to live, because goods were plentiful and nobody cared what you did. But for Vinias there was no question of any fulfillment of himself in America. What might he have become there? A frustrated man, a bitter confused person who never quite got hold of himself, a bohemian artist. No, only in the Soviet Union was there a place for a man with his qualities and ambitions, and Vinias occupied precisely that place.

As head of Special Disinformation, Vinias had been able to take a crude, gifted street hustler and turn him into Evgeny Shar, the poet who had won the heart of Russia in a way that no poet since Esenin had. Shar's language was simple and familiar; his visions were not the unique property of an elevated soul; his words became common property. His first book of poems had been called *Icons,* and there was always something much more Russian than Soviet about his tone and concerns. After a while his views, of course, clashed with those of the authorities, who did not like his vision of a Russia awakened to Christianity at the last hour, as set forth in his famous poem "1999."

Though even for Vinias it remained an open question whether Shar's talent was any more than a gift for infinitely subtle mimicry and an ability to second-guess the public, Shar was clearly intelligent and learned the intellectual history and vocabulary of both Russia and the West as easily as if it were some not-too-difficult foreign language. In any case, he was always to appear the natural, not the sophisticate. Vinias labored on Shar for years, and finally Shar's work met even his exacting standards. It was one thing, certainly, to create a poem, but something else to create a poet. Shar seemed content with his role, even though it entailed arrests and certain physical difficulties, and two years ago had earned him a three-year stretch in a labor camp. That, of course, had done wonders for Shar's reputation in the West, although their information indicated that it had done very little for the actual sales of his books. Apparently, you could attain celebrity status over there, simply by having the light of attention turned on you for a period of time, and after that you didn't have to do much of anything: your face and name always kept that special shine.

Shar was due to be launched soon. It was important that the Free Shar campaign in the West heat up a little more so they could think the Soviet Union was buckling under to the pressure of moral outrage, one of their favorite delusions. In fact, it was a foreign-policy question. The Soviet Union needed some positive points, because it would soon be initiating a new peace offensive, but that was not Vinias's concern. His task was to move the piece called Evgeny Shar from the camp to Moscow, from Moscow to Frankfurt, and from Frankfurt to New York. There Shar would quickly capitalize on his fame and establish himself as a Russian voice in exile. He would no doubt become exceedingly popular at once: he was good-looking, and that was very important there, especially for television; his English was decent; women would find him attractive, men admirable.

Shar would have several functions. He would serve as a deep probe, reporting to Vinias on the latest mutations in American social reality, which changed at a dizzying pace. His principal use, however, would be to counter the growing influence of the Russian exile community on right-wing politicians. Brezhnev and Andropov had made a mistake: it hadn't been such a great idea to boot all those dissidents out. They banded together in the West, published book after book, and the next thing you knew the Americans were talking tough and building bombs. It was really Andropov's fault, Vinias knew. Andropov was too much the chess player

—move Solzhenitsyn here, pin Sakharov in exile, take the Bishop of Rome.

And he, Vinias, had been called upon to correct the situation. That was all the applause he ever needed to hear.

Shar would arrive in America, publish the poetry he had written in the camp, rise to the heights, but then, at the appropriate moment, denounce America in a brilliant and heartbreaking book, *The Golden Calf*. He would appeal dramatically to Russia to allow him to return home, a chastened prodigal son. Russia would refuse. The Russian people would learn of all this from Radio Free Europe. Demonstrations would occur in the Soviet Union, which the police would, of course, break up. But Western journalists would hear with their own ears a policeman tell them that he was being as gentle as he could with the crowd because he himself and many of his fellow policemen were in favor of Shar's returning. The voice of Russia would speak and be heard. Evgeny Shar would be allowed to return home. Even more than a poet, Vinias had created a fate and a myth.

The phone rang, summoning Vinias to Colonel Malanov's office. On the way there he became aware of a certain irritation. Yes, Malanov could summon him, and Malanov liked to do it sometimes, as if simply to demonstrate to Vinias that no matter how great his abilities, rank counted for more, and the proof was in the obedience. What a diabolical paradox, thought Vinias: I am in the perfect position, imperfect only in that there are idiots above me who can give me orders. I could rise above them, but only at the cost of giving up my otherwise perfect position.

Malanov was very happy to see him, requiring no further proof of his own power than Vinias's presence in his spacious office with its bank of floor-to-ceiling windows.

"Tea?" asked Malanov.

"Thank you," replied Vinias.

Tea was brought, and they took their cups across the room to a large, low oval table made of blond wood.

"Swedish?" asked Vinias, glancing at the table as he sat down.

"Finnish."

"I like it."

"You do? I'm not used to it yet."

"The old one was in terrible shape."

"But this one, it sticks out. Maybe it's because the wood is too light."

"No, it's simply because you haven't gotten used to it yet."

"Could be." Malanov took a sip of tea. "Vinias, do you think there is anything to all that psi business?"

"Something."

"Once I dreamed clear as day that my grandfather died, and an hour after I woke they came running to tell us. But that was only once. Still, who knows?"

"It's not to my taste," said Vinias, "but you catch fish in murky waters, as the saying goes."

"It seems there are quite a few people who share that opinion. More money is being given to research, and results are actually expected in the not-too-distant future. But apparently one of the founders of the psipharm unit, a Jew by the name of Farb, chose to emigrate to the United States some time ago, before we really began to treat this sort of thing very seriously. Now, of course, the problem is that he is over there."

"But I didn't think they took that sort of thing very seriously over there."

"That's what they might want us to think. After all, you never know when you're being deceived."

"True."

"Farb is a point of weakness. Any leakage would probably flow to him, and he already knows a great deal. The logic is obvious. The file is on its way to you. Is there something wrong?"

"No, it's . . . it's just I sometimes . . . get this pain in my knee. Horrible."

"What do the doctors say?"

"Either exploratory surgery or drugs."

"You know, I've heard that they've had some remarkable results with healers down in the psipharm unit; maybe you should look into that. Call Kovalyov. He's our man down there; he'd probably know."

"I may just do that."

They shook hands at the door. Queasy in the aftermath of the pain, Vinias turned after a few steps to ask Malanov the name of the contact he had mentioned, but Malanov had already turned away and was staring across the room with a frown of disapproval at his new table.

6 "OK, places everyone, places."

The director ground out his low-tar cigarette with a grimace of distaste, as if punishing it for failing to satisfy him. He shoved back the sleeves of his army-navy-store turtleneck and moved toward the large chalked rectangle on the loft floor. While waiting for the blonde woman in the tan raincoat and the man beside her to take their places, he began:

"Now, remember, this is an argument that you've had many times before, but it's more than that. The argument is going on inside you both all the time. It's not part of your relationship, it *is* your relationship. But neither of you has come to that realization yet; you both still think there's something to fight about. Even so, somewhere inside you, you know that it's hopeless, and that's what gives the argument its special miserable fury, you see?"

They nodded.

"Achmed," called the director.

A small dark man peered out from behind one of the columns that supported the dirty tin ceiling.

"Are you ready?"

"I'm ready."

"All right," said the director, picking up a briefcase from the floor and taking a position about fifteen feet to the right of the couple. "I'll be him. Now, we'll take it from the line about a man's pride. And remember, you're still at the hissing, vicious state—there's no screaming or yelling. All right? All right, let's go."

The woman took a deep breath. In her middle thirties, she had sharp features and albino-blonde hair. The man beside her was fiddling with his posture to make a potbelly that would express all the aggressive touchiness of a defeated male.

"Don't you have any sense of what a man's pride is?" he asked.

"Not from living with you, I don't. That isn't pride, that's oversensitivity, and I'm sick of it. It's like living with a shut-in."

"Oh, sure, sure, sure, if I say one word you don't like then I'm a crude, insensitive slob, but it's perfectly all right, just perfectly all right for you to cut me down in front of a waiter. Did you see the look on his face?"

"Oh no, I can't believe it. You mean even that was too much for you? That's what I call truly incredible. Of course he was looking at you like that. That's how waiters look at people who can't make up their minds in restaurants, people who can never get the waiters' attention, people who are such babies that they can't take one drop of constructive criticism, and then they wonder why they fail at everything."

"Me? Fail? At what?"

"Try life, love, work, and whatever else's left."

The director nodded with satisfaction. They had the tone of self-pity down, that whine of hateful weakness. He closed his eyes for a second and listened to their voices as abstract sound, pure emotional tone, a trick he had perfected over the years. But it was just fine. He was retreating toward the violence in himself, and she, with all the stupid persistence of a rodent, was clawing him back to that hidden corner of himself.

Those cigarettes were horrible, he thought; you smoke one and two minutes later you want another one.

He opened his eyes. His left shoulder began bobbing in tune to some inner rhythm, as if he were counting with it. Then he called out, "Now, Achmed."

The small dark man came loping out from behind the post, crossed in front of the couple, who barely noticed him, and stopped in front of the director.

"OK, man, you give me your fuckin' wallet right now," said Achmed with a nasal, Hispanic accent, reaching inside his jacket.

7   The feeling kept changing.

First, Yasha Farb was the arrow and she was the bow that kept drawing back and relenting and drawing back farther, always on the verge on letting the arrow fly but never quite letting it fly. Then he was out sweating in the sun, and she, a stack of hay he made with his pitchfork. And then it seemed as if what they were doing was the perfect cooperation, more perfect and precise even than beautiful couples figure-skating on hissing, illuminated ice. Then he was a satyr, his legs running away with him as he tried to run through her to the other side. The other side. When she began to moan like a sleeper in a dream, a woman in labor, a person dying, the silvery mercury coiled and waiting to leap out of him became a silver pole on which he was vaulting toward the sky, every cell and nerve calling out: Clear the bar, clear the bar. He cleared the bar and hung in the air for a moment as she came flying toward him on her trapeze and let go, and he caught her perfectly in mid-air and they came tumbling down to the safety net of the sheets to the thunderous applause of the blood.

When the applause died down, they began to kiss and talk and search for a more comfortable position, their knees and elbows having suddenly become angular again.

"That was great," said Yasha. "And on a Tuesday."

Carolyn laughed and reached for a cigarette. "Beats lab."

"But the important thing . . ."

"Yes," she said with exaggerated throatiness, "yes, what's the important thing."

"The important thing is always to generalize from the particular."

"Oh no, you're not going to start generalizing already," said Carolyn, who was feeling the ease of a woman in her sexual pride.

"But listen, listen," said Farb, whose forehead had begun to corrugate with thought. "The particular is us. We make love. We feel benign toward existence. We don't want to go to war for abstractions. We love life. Correct?"

"Correct."

"Now, most people don't seem to be happy. This is not exactly what you would call the Planet of Happiness. If beautiful sex brings happiness and most people are not happy, that has to mean that most people are not experiencing beautiful sex, correct?"

"I think that's an understatement, Yash."

"And so, if most people could somehow experience beautiful sex, there would be a tremendous upsurge in human happiness. Who knows, perhaps it's more important to control the means of reproduction than production."

"What's that supposed to mean?" she asked, exhaling.

"Let's say, for example, that the twentieth century is the century of man's dreams come true. And his nightmares, too, of course, though that's another story. But man, for example, always dreamed of flying; for century after century he looked up at the birds and wanted to do that, too. Then, bang, twentieth century, up we go, and even off into space. But man has also dreamed of the perfect aphrodisiac. He tried everything, but nothing worked—they're still killing rhinos in Africa for their horns. Killing gigantic rhinoceroses so that man can have fun in bed! But if we can fly, we can also invent the perfect aphrodisiac. Everything is there, just waiting to be discovered! One little pill! It could induce sexual pleasure and also contain birth-control and antivenereal properties! Who wouldn't want it?"

"Me," she said. "I've got you."

An hour later, lightheaded, lighthearted, Farb strolled down Broadway, knowing that he was on the track of something. Oblivious of the crowds, he headed instinctively downtown, and gave himself over to his thoughts.

There was a great deal to think about. First, he knew that early sexological work done in Moscow had indicated that sex in the Soviet Union was even worse than the harvests. You did not have to subscribe to Reich's theories about the relation of the political system to the quality of orgasm to know that scared, weary, unhappy people will botch the sex act more often than not. And that will confirm their general sense that life is a grim and unsatisfying business, which in turn, of course, makes them better citizens of any totalitarian regime, whose greatest enemy is true human happiness, always inseparable from freedom and dignity.

Farb had always thought that sooner or later it would be some technological invention that would prove the undoing of the Soviet Union. For a time he had hoped this would come in the area of communications, for there was nothing the Soviets feared more than free and open communication, another sign of the healthy personality, the healthy social system. If someone could, for example, invent a tiny component that would turn an ordinary radio or television into some two-way means of communication, that might well have a revolutionary effect on the Soviet isolation.

On the other hand, the invention of a substance with genuine aphrodisiac powers could also have a nontrivial influence on the world situation, since in discovering the beauty of sex, people would simultaneously discover the dignity of being human. It was clear that the twenty-first century would be, among other things, a pharmaceutical century. Mankind would be taking more drugs than ever. Drugs were irresistible. Like television. Put a child in a house with a television that is on, and soon enough the child will find the television.

The situation with drugs was analogous. It was in the very nature of modern life, which was essentially boring.

Perhaps the Americans were right to scoff at ESP as a blind alley with no serious applications to espionage or defense. Perhaps the future would belong to the Americans, because they were making the right scientific choices or because they provided the medium in which the right scientific choices could be made. Yes, of course, science would decide the human future, which, in any case, would not much resemble the world they now lived in, with its hideously antiquated nation-states, the dinosaurs of history.

And it might not be difficult to get some capital for such a project. The universities would, of course, not be interested —it would offend their sense of propriety—but private capital had more flair, and it was obvious that, if successful, the project could yield an unheard-of financial reward. After all, millions of people would want it every day of the week. Every week of the year. What vistas, what vistas!

A cab honked angrily at Farb, and he stepped back up on the curb. For some reason, this reminded Farb that he had left his briefcase in his office when he had left the campus with Carolyn, who had suddenly found her lab canceled. So, preferring not to walk the same side of the street he had just covered, Farb crossed Broadway and began heading back up toward Columbia.

Yes, he continued his thoughts happily, America was the ideal place to do such research. First, because the society was sex-happy; second, because sex was used to sell everything, so why not sex itself; and, third, because a great deal of the preliminary research had probably already been done by all those institutes that measured orgasm and nipple dilation and God only knows what else. It was true that they were only interested in doing pure research, in accumulating data and drawing preliminary findings, whereas he had always believed in an *engagé* science, one that made choices and consciously strove to revolutionize the world—probably a genetic susceptibility to messianism common to both Jews and Russians.

America, America, land of screwballs and millionaires, he loved it more than ever. And now he could see that, for all his insistence on his premise "that everything we think is probably wrong," he had not been free enough in his own thinking. And that was why all his abilities had not gotten him very far in America. His academic position was actually two meager positions pasted together, and he might not even have received this had there not been pressure from the politically active faculty. There had been strong budgetary grounds for simply eliminating both of those half-time positions; his situation was shaky, the target of the accounting office, which was irked by the bookkeeping required simply to keep Yakov Farb employed, that is to say, alive. And now, for the first time in his life, he had seen the possibility of becoming rich. Splendidly, laughably rich. And why not? He was no fool; he knew how to live, it wouldn't be wasted on him. He would be a legendary patron of the arts, give parties people would remember all their lives, and continue to astound the world with the miracles flying out of his laboratory. And then maybe at last even his sister would be happy.

The thought of his sister cast a shadow across his mind. Her scorn, her fury. Even the way Raisa drove terrified him. Why he had allowed himself to be talked into buying that enormous Oldsmobile, instead of something sensible like a Dasher, he would never understand. Every time he heard her start up the car in front of their duplex in the Bronx, he felt a certain dread. And her on the West Side Highway, cutting in and out at seventy miles an hour, always rushing to be on time for her job teaching Russian at a junior college on Staten Island, was more than he cared to contemplate, let alone experience. Certainly they had lived through the worst of everything, but at some point that had to be accepted, at some point you had to realize that the work of all those human monsters should not be allowed to succeed to the extent of ruining your entire life. Certainly there would always be nightmares, and grief. Oh, he didn't know, he didn't know; he wished he had never thought of Raisa, for it brought back all those other questions. Perhaps it was always just a matter of their natures: she would have been full of shadow and fire even if she had grown up in some tidy American suburb, and he would have been happily curious wherever life had set him down.

Though he tried to switch his thoughts back to his new idea, he found that his mind had been too weighted by the memory of old sorrows to soar again. In any case, it was still able to consider some of the idea's more practical and immediate aspects. For a start, he could begin collecting literature on the subject, see who was doing what, where, and to what purpose. Hadn't he read something in the *Times* Science section about the aphrodisiac qualities of truffles? He could also investigate some of the financing possibilities. Which industry would be the most willing to fund the research— liquor, perfume, pharmaceutical? And did he have any connections that might prove valuable? Nothing came to mind. He had made very few friends in America, either among his American colleagues or in the Russian-émigré community, and for the same reason—he thought that America was rather a grand place to be. Except when it concerned cuisine, he engaged in no Slavic mooning for Russia, and he shared neither the American liberals' contempt for their own society, nor the émigrés' mistrust of American looseness. In his opinion, the émigrés' minds had been so stamped by the political and historical traumas of the twentieth century that they were unable to think in any other terms, and so, talented and noble though many of them were, he preferred to read their books and listen to their concerts than to engage in the inevitable arguments, which frayed nerves and soured friendships. As for the Americans, the conservatives were intelligent but prudishly dull, while the liberals, though better company, were infuriatingly softheaded.

He liked America because it was an open and dynamic medium, a laboratory where the most bizarre experiments were constantly being carried out. America was like television, an amazing invention with such lousy programs that people forgot how wonderful an instrument it was. All that was needed was to improve the programming. And America, like those new TV sets with dozens of channels, loved change, variety, choice. America had discovered that it was simply more useful to include than to exclude. Here, someone denounces American society, his book becomes a best seller, they interview him everywhere, and some of his ideas even go into circulation and start influencing the society at large. Everyone is happy. In Russia it was always either/or, whereas sharp-witted America had circumvented the problem by opting for everything.

Why should he suffer, why should he blame the world to his dying day, the way Raisa did? That was her specialty, he thought, opening the door to his office.

It was strange to think that just two hours before he had been standing there checking to make sure the door was locked when Carolyn came running around the corner, panting so hard she could barely get out the words: "My lab's been canceled." Who would have thought that such a statement could be so erotic? The grid of possibilities had shifted, and instead of a walk or a glass of tea alone in the student cafeteria, he had two hours of happy pleasure in her studio apartment, which had in turn produced a new idea. He liked everything about her, her voice, her hair, her choice of earrings and blouses, even her enthusiasm for science, though perhaps her mind did have too much of a practical turn for his liking.

Farb was engaged in a little pointless desktop straightening when there was a sharp but somehow tentative knock at his door. Carolyn? A straggling student?

"Come in," he said.

When the door opened, Farb saw a short, birdlike man, balding but with confused tufts of reddish hair, a sharp nose, and gray-green eyes. Their eyes met with the certainty and intimacy of Russian Jews recognizing each other.

"Sapozhnikov, Efrem Emanuilovich," said the visitor, introducing himself.

"Farb, Yakov Samoilovich. Please come in."

"I am sorry, but I can stay only a moment: my van is double-parked. I have something for you. Where is it?" muttered Sapozhnikov, reaching inside his leather jacket to withdraw a bulging wallet held together by a thick rubber band. Sapozhnikov pulled off the rubber band, slid it up on his left wrist, and began fumbling through the wallet. Farb smiled. He did miss Russian disorder. Even Carolyn had one of those click-open briefcases and always knew exactly where everything was.

"Here?" said Sapozhnikov with surprise and relief, but then was immediately crestfallen. "No. That's not yours. This I cannot understand at all."

He lay his wallet on Farb's desk and began searching his pockets. He had already been through his pockets twice when, by sheer force of will, he made himself stop and, looking somewhat sheepishly at Farb, said: "One moment. We will stop here and begin a scientific search. All right? All right. Left front pocket? No. Right front pocket? No. Inside left? No. Inside right? Wait, what's this?" Sapozhnikov pulled out an envelope that had been folded twice and perhaps driven farther into his pocket by the weight of his wallet. He blew a few specks of lint and tobacco off the envelope and unfolded it, peered at the name to make absolutely sure there was no mistake this time. "Here," he said, handing Farb the letter, "for you. Very good service, too. This letter probably only left Russia three or four days ago. Our mail service is six times faster than theirs, not to mention certain other advantages. My phone number is on the envelope; call me if you want to send an answer."

"Thank you," said Farb, taking the letter and gazing somewhat anxiously at it before laying it down on top of his desk.

"Can't you stay for a moment?" he asked.

"No, I'm sorry, I cannot. It took a long time just to find this office, and my van is double-parked. And between making a living and delivering these letters, I don't have a moment."

After seeing him to the door and shaking his hand, Farb returned to his desk and, still standing, looked down at the letter. He had recognized the feel of Soviet paper and did not like seeing his name typed in Cyrillic letters. Instinctively his eyes moved away from the envelope to the front of his desk, where he spotted Sapozhnikov's wallet.

Oh, my God, thought Farb, grabbing the wallet and running out into the corridor, which he found empty and bleak in the late-afternoon light. He listened for the sound of footsteps, but heard none. Which way would Sapozhnikov have gone? He answered his own question by running to the right, head down, fast as he could. He collided with Sapozhnikov coming around the corner.

"Sorry," puffed Sapozhnikov. "I forgot that damned wallet."

"Here, here," said Farb, handing it to him.

Sapozhnikov glared at the wallet as if it possessed a malicious spirit of its own, then rolled the rubber band down from his wrist and wrapped it twice around the wandering object, which he shoved firmly into his inside jacket pocket. "Things, always these things. By now I'll be towed."

"So go."

Sapozhnikov threw his hands out to the sides, a gesture that said that he was done rushing just to suit the world of endless aggravation and that maybe, if he had taken time to say good-bye like a normal person, he might not have forgotten the wallet in the first place. Understanding the gesture, Farb gave him a hug and a few good pats on his leather-jacketed back, and then stood in the corridor to watch him leave again.

But who was the letter from?

Having opened the onionskin envelope carefully, he unfolded the letter and saw that it was signed "Vanka-Vstanka," his old nickname for Yuri Trofimovich. Glad and apprehensive at the same time, he sat down to read this letter that had reached him from the other world.

Dear Yasha,

I am writing you for two reasons. One, to inform you on the progress of the work we began together here, and two, to establish a communication link with you that is not subject to any unwanted scrutiny. So, the first thing for you to do is to write back to me, using the same system. Also, please let me know exactly when you received this letter, because I want to be able to figure time. If you have any questions about the work, please keep them on the vague and general side for the time being. The main thing is for me to hear back from you and to know that I am not just talking to myself.

The work is starting to produce results. There is no hiding that fact from those who have the most practical interest in our successes, and, if the truth be told, they have been generous with funding and equipment, though that has also meant tighter control. I am now absolutely convinced that whatever we achieve should not be used to tip the balance in their direction.

We always knew that our work was looked upon with special favor by someone at the top who had a known weakness for healers and was probably entertaining grandiose notions of superspies who could read minds, hypnotize guards à la Wolf Messing, and project their thoughts onto film. But, without going into any details, let me say simply that now, even against my will, I am quite convinced that some of those phenomena do exist, though they are, by their very nature, both unpredictable and uncontrollable.

But the main thing is that your general notion that there might be some chemical or endocrinological substances related to areas of unusual human activity—the longevity of certain Georgians, and the extrasensory perceptions experienced by a small minority of the population—was pharmacologically correct.

I will furnish you with more information when I am certain that an unimpeded communication link exists between

*us. I only wish that such precautions were not necessary; it
is a tragedy, our tragedy, that they are.*

    Regards to your sister.

Vanka-Vstanka

8 For some reason, David Aronow

had agreed to hand-deliver the Shar translations to Karen Cooper. This errand had been magically transformed into a lunch, which was now only fifteen minutes away. David tossed the typed translations onto his desk and for a moment just let his memory of them echo in some chamber of his mind that had perfect pitch for the music of the vowels.

It had been a relief to do a little poetry; prose, no matter how symphonic, was always yard goods.

He decided to read the poem "To My Daughter" again; it was clearly the better of the two. Though he would be ashamed to be faulted, whether in the press or privately, for any lapse or error, this was not the real reason he took the pains that produced excellence. He loved excellence—the word, the idea, the thing itself. Certain people had that brilliance about them, and he had always been one of them: not only the A student, but the best of the A students. And he knew that the grading system they had all learned early in school would be with them for the rest of their lives. If someone asked you about a play and you said it was a C−, the rest would be mere detail, you had been understood. He had once heard a woman describe herself, with terrifying frankness, as a B+ person.

He picked up the poem.

TO MY DAUGHTER

Fifty men sleep under the state's blankets.
I am one. In the hour of the dream
we are all free men, citizens
of a world that, even in nightmare,

mocks this barracks knocked together
from planks and slogans, pain and nails.
The exact pressure of my daughter's arm,
her light six-year-old arm on my neck—

tell me what causes that perfect sensation,
more distinct than weeks of this other life,
this other life where fifty slaves are resurrected

from their sleep and the state's blankets,
white corpses yawning like root-cellar doors.
Some have dreamed of lakes and women,
while I held Katya, who was never born.

Some good sound effects had been achieved. He even liked "pain and nails" better than the original, because of the little repeated cry of "ai" in each word. "Lakes and women" was nice, too, though there it was the combination of ideas that mattered—lakes, women, and whatever associations chimed between them.

He vaguely regretted not having attempted a rhymed version, but English was so poor in that respect that it always made Russians, Luntz especially, shake their heads in dumbfounded compassion for a language where poems didn't rhyme and you could not call the one you loved "thou."

"Thou." It was too bad they didn't have the word "thou," which, though it could also be the bearer of contempt, was in every case intimate. So nineteenth-century, that toy century. The twentieth century would have rolled over it like a tank over toy soldiers. And he was from that century, a bad neighborhood. "Thou" is what everybody wanted to have said to them, what everybody wanted to be. Karen wanted to be his "thou," and he had felt it for her, a sort of glad freedom rising in the chest, turning the rib cage into thin air. But it was a serious business, he knew from experience. The feeling came with an oath. That was what he had been trying to tell her—not that he didn't have the feeling, but that he didn't want to swear the oath.

He wondered if they'd be able to skirt the whole thing at lunch. Intuitions would be arcing back and forth from them, of course, but the talk might stay on the surface—she Manhattan wise-ass, he cheerfully sardonic. Personaville, U.S.A.

In any case, it was six minutes to one, lunch was at one, he'd better get going.

He liked to walk in New York, though he hated to hurry. He always walked a little faster than he might have, but in New York it was a good idea not to amble, which made you look out-of-town, meaning vulnerable. The best thing about New York was that it incarnated some of the actual scope and density of history. There was a gigantic enterprise going on; it was just that our eyes were too puny to see it.

A toothless, mad black woman working her chin came down the sidewalk, ranting about Jesus Christ. The funny thing was that New York didn't just have everything, it had thirty-five of everything, and so that meant that right at that very moment, at thirty-four other points in the city, toothless, mad black women were working their chins and ranting about their sins and their Savior.

He loved the ranters, a ranter himself. They were a special tribe—those who could not stand it the way it was. Only the inhibitions of intelligence, he figured, kept him from ranting aloud. But to set him off all it took was one certain kind of face—future face, he called it, the flesh like Silly Putty, the features a genetic cartoon decal; they took seminars to learn how to be human. All the light and suffering of all the centuries had led to this. Was it a demonic joke, or had we cheated the cavemen and the Greeks by turning out like this? And he liked that mad black woman for another reason, too. At least she ranted about Jesus Christ. She was probably the only person on that block with a metaphysical thought in her head.

The restaurant's one window was curtained, creating a sort of peace inside, though a noisy one, for the bar was packed with ambitious men, their heads turning constantly, their eyes looking for the famous, the beautiful, the best. Some of their eyes rested on him for a moment. He knew why. It was the gray in his beard and at the sides of his hair —what he referred to as "the extinguished look"—and they probably mistook the mica glint in his eyes and his inward compression for the self-possessed wariness of a celebrity.

Now his own eyes were busy looking for Karen in the small dining room past the bar, where the fine weave of the linen tablecloths softened the overhead lights they reflected. Voices, clinking silverware, ice knocking on glass. She wasn't there yet.

The hostess held up one finger with a questioning look. He answered by holding up two fingers, a little victory sign. Now they were both happy. He was not alone in Manhattan, space would not go to waste, an extra lunch would be sold, the waitress's tip would double.

He ordered a glass of red wine and lit a cigarette after the first sip. That beautiful taste, like kissing a woman who smoked.

The kitchen gasped steam as the double doors swung open. He watched two heads draw closer while a confidence was shared. Allowed to roam at will, his eyes moved to a metal wristband on a hairy forearm and then skipped two tables to a woman's throat. The skin on her throat had started to go. Some days it would look fine enough, but on bad days, when she was tired or under some stress, it would look loose and sad. No one would want to kiss that throat any more. He would not want to kiss it, he knew, and this made him feel compassion for her, especially when he heard her laugh of intelligent desperation. They were all caught in time; somehow, amazingly, the one o'clock lunch appointment, the workday, the weekend were also the force that changed our bodies and took our lives away.

He looked at his own watch. Karen was almost fifteen minutes late. In New York, fifteen minutes late was still on time, given the general calamitous nature of things, but she would be walking to the restaurant and not have to contend with crosstown traffic.

Irritated by her lateness, especially since he had not wanted to be there in the first place, he began to count the reasons not to love her. He did not love her because she was that most driven and confused of creatures, the modern American woman, a combination in which the adjectives did not, he thought, sit well with the noun. He did not love her because she believed that long, arduous psychiatry would free her from the labyrinth of her neuroses. Twice a week, faithfully, at great expense, she brought her dreams and fears and little experiences to the Upper West Side to examine them with her woman shrink; he did not like being included among the life follicles and dream specimens. He did not love her because her beautiful body, so close to the ideal feminine erotic finely inscribed somewhere on his nerves, would in time begin to grow slack, the skin tone curdling ever so slightly, and he did not want to wake one morning and see that. He did not love her because she was an editor, which meant that sometimes she was snippy and schoolmarmish, and sometimes groupie-ishly gushing—a quality that, as soon as she detected it, she would flick away with a lash of irony, some sophisticated remark that took pleasure in its own edgy triviality. She had to do that, because she was not a city person but came from the Great Embarrassing Elsewhere, where Mom still lived and the *Reader's Digest* condensed volumes were neatly arranged at the base of the brass TV stand. He did not love her because she was earnest and in some ways had set about their love affair as if it were a kind of senior project. He did not love her because she saw everything as an "issue" to be discussed, and because she had no head for metaphysics. He did not love her because she always balanced her checkbook, took good care of her teeth, and could probably have a good time at a hootenanny. He did not love her because she loved him. And, finally, he did not love her because he loved her.

"Sor-ree," he heard her voice say with comically self-conscious apology.

He looked up and there she was again—as always, not quite as he remembered her.

She looked at him just long enough to see that he was closed to her and began removing her scarf, whose colors, a soft brown with hidden lines of red, pleased him. They did not use their lips in their kiss of greeting, only touching the sides of their faces, hers still cool from the late September air.

"Naturally, just as I was getting ready to leave," she said, sitting down and looking around for the waitress, "I got a long-distance call, from Paris, from an agent. I shouldn't tell you whose, so keep this under your hat; it was Kronsky's."

"Kronsky?"

"Kronsky who wrote *Notes from the Soviet Underworld*, about crime in the Soviet Union. Anyway, *Penthouse* picked up a first serial on it. Naturally, they're running the chapter about prostitution, and, naturally, now Kronsky's agent thinks he's got the hottest thing since Nikolai Gogol, and he wants fifty thousand for the next one, *Soviet Crime and Soviet Punishment*. I told him to stuff it. More or less. Miss, a Dewar's on the rocks, thank you."

As she ordered her drink, David thought that he had been right. They were being urbane, banally urbane, urbanal. But what he had not foreseen was how painfully constrictive that would be. And, of course, she was using it, too—what else could she do?—using it to say, This is how it feels when we don't love each other, when we are just friendly and intelligent and polite. Everything dimmed, everything matte finish. Is that what you really want?

"So," she said briskly, "how are Irina Petrovskaya's memoirs coming?"

"You don't have to worry about the deadline. I'm always three months late."

"No, really."

"The memoirs are fine. What can I tell you? The reviews will be good, and no one will buy it, and then it's on to the next one."

"Getting cynical in our old age, are we?"

He laughed a little at this remark, which she delivered

like a witty duchess in a period film. But it had its other intended effect as well. He was reminded of his age, forty-one, and hers, thirty-four. Reminded that if this separation, which was not their first, lasted too long, something terrible would happen: something that had been alive would dry and scroll up like the leaves that were already starting to fall.

Her drink came.

"What should we drink to?" she asked. "But think of something quick; I'm dying for this drink after Kronsky's agent."

He wanted to say something real to her, real and direct, but he couldn't get off the thin surface and heard himself saying, "Well, to Evgeny Shar for providing the occasion, and to Gander and Kuhn, who I assume is picking up the tab."

"Don't worry, it's business," she said, making a shorthand gesture of a clink before taking a healthy slug of her Scotch. "I mean, it's business if you brought me the Shar poems."

"I did."

"By the way, did I tell you that we might have a chance for the Op Ed with them?" she said, expressing a precise reverence for that piece of printed real estate.

"You did."

"You better give them to me now, or else I'll have to worry about forgetting them all through lunch."

"Here," he said, handing her the manila envelope.

"Thanks."

"What are you doing now?"

"Just checking to make sure they're in there."

"God, the anxiety level."

"You don't know. Last week I thought I'd lost forty pages of an author's corrections. Forty! OK, they're here, I see them. One with no title, and one called 'To My Daughter,' right?"

"Right."

"Which one is better?"

"The one to his daughter."

"Shar has a daughter?"

"He dreams about the daughter he never had. She's already six in the poem."

For a moment there was an odd pause, as when a city block suddenly grows silent. He tried to look in her eyes, but she would not allow him more than a glancing touch as she turned her head to the waitress, who had come to tell them the specials of the day. Karen's face, which had a scrubbed Scandinavian glow and eyes the color of evergreens reflected in still water, that face which never needed makeup except for an occasional lick of mascara or touch of lipstick which she was touchingly inept at applying, lost something in profile. The nose was revealed as a bit comically large at the end, the expanse of cheek was too simple, almost childish; but he could see her hair better, brown-black, well brushed, pulled up onto her head and fastened in back with a simple silver-colored barrette.

Somehow the mention of children unborn had made the air at the table raw with their own loss.

Why do you torture her, he thought, why don't you just love her?

She ordered sole, as he had thought she might; he took the London broil and another red wine.

Now that the waitress was gone and the flurry of ordering was over, they were somehow more alone than before.

"Look," said David, without quite knowing what he was going to say next. "Don't think I don't miss you."

"Are you trying to say you miss me?" she said with a smile too wide, like a clown's, with sorrow.

"Yes, of course, I miss you."

"I miss you, too. A lot," she said, underlining the last two words in a way that was all the more frank for including the childish.

"The worst thing for me," said David, wondering why the wrong words were coming out—they were true but not what he had meant to tell her—"the worst thing is to know that you're so close by."

"Well, I'm not moving out of New York just to suit you, buster."

They laughed together and suddenly were free of everything that had been said and done in the past. But he caught himself. One more step and he would be lost in his own desire for happiness, self-evident as the sky. And that would mean another round, at the very least. And was that even fair, fair to her?

"I'll tell you what the thing is. I think the line to thine own self be true and then you can't be false to anyone is wrong in a way. If you're true to yourself you'll always be untrue to everyone else. The moment always comes, and you have to choose. That's why I come and go with you."

"You don't think it's because people can't stand the happiness of love?"

"It could be that. In the end it could be."

"It is for me," she said. "I always found reasons to turn away. Whenever I felt it really coming at me, it was too much—I had to turn away. But with you there have been times . . ."

She took a sip of water, and when she was facing him again, a wet glint drew his attention to her lips—their fine, encoded striations.

"Well, just forgive me in advance, is all I can say," he said.

"I have some new wine at home, Petit Sarah."

9 The guard looked at the photograph

on Yuri's pass, squinted hard at Yuri, and then looked down at the photograph again. The same potato nose, the same scraggly beard, but because Yuri had blinked when the flash had gone off, his eyes were not visible in the photograph. The guard was new and taking his responsibilities seriously. Yuri could feel his blood stimulated by the poisons of shame and guilt, which he still could not shake, though he knew what he was doing was both inevitable and right. Something about the guard's youth, the care and seriousness he gave his job, brought on the little attack. Finally, the guard returned the pass with one last hard look in his eye—was he checking to make absolutely certain, or was it a glance of disdain for the nerves that had not been able to bear the instant of the flash?

Yuri nodded and proceeded to Wing 3, tilting a little to compensate for the weight of his briefcase, vaguely worried that the handle, worn and already patched several times with leather glue and electrician's tape, might give. What a wonderful luxury such mundane worries seemed now.

The corridors were mostly empty that morning. A technician disappearing through a door, a secretary clattering past with an armful of files and a brisk nod. Two old mustachioed Georgians stood by the Gerontology Department, chatting in their fierce and sexual language. There was something different about the background noise that morning, and at first Yuri couldn't quite understand what it was. He paused for a moment. He recognized the sound in the foreground: it was the automatic shufflers that shuffled the cards for the ESP tests that would begin in half an hour. There was, as well, the usual clack of typewriters, the ringing of phones, the hum of computers, and the murmur of voices behind frosted-glass windows. Then he caught it. A sound neither machine nor human. The cry of some deeply worried animal. And then he remembered. The animals were to have arrived that weekend—everything from dogs to chimps—and their voices had now been added to the chorus of science.

Perhaps it was only his mood and his having been a bit jangled by the guard, but that morning there was something vaguely menacing about those sounds, the automatic forward motion of science, which was so confident of itself and yet always admitted that it had no idea where it was going. To calm his mind, he had been reading Fyodorov again; saintly Fyodorov, who had slept on a trunk, because he found even a bed a foolish luxury; Fyodorov, the only man in whose presence Tolstoy had ever felt humbled. Fyodorov had said that the goal of science and all human endeavor was the resurrection of the dead, all our dead ancestors. Probably it was centuries too early for anyone to take him literally, and maybe he never intended to be taken literally, but metaphorically Fyodorov was absolutely clear—science should serve the highest good of human life, and what could be a higher service than rescuing our fellow creatures from hated death? And what was science that did not serve the good? An armaments factory of one sort or another. Oh, please, give me the courage to stop justifying myself, thought Yuri Trofimovich.

When Yuri turned the corner and saw Kovalyov talking with Andrusha by the door to the lab, he missed a step, his foot coming down flat and sticking for a moment. Not quite a stumble, but enough for Kovalyov, who had an eye for such things. Kovalyov gave no sign of having noticed anything as he turned from Andrusha to Yuri with an official smile.

"Good morning, Yuri Trofimovich," said Kovalyov with a heartiness as official as his smile had been. "I was just saying to Andrusha here that I hoped your increased budget had not gone to your head and turned you into one of these temperamental types that only show up when they feel like it."

A crooked smile appeared in Yuri's beard. He looked over at Andrusha, who threw him a comic expression of long suffering that made Yuri's smile real. There was something so likeable about Andrusha—his merry eyes; his hair, black and curly like that of an angel on a Greek icon; his complexion, the sort known as blood and milk—Yuri almost always felt better just to look at him.

"Well," said Yuri to Kovalyov, "we're spending government funds carefully and there is no personality cult here, I can assure you."

"You don't have to assure me, Yuri Trofimovich. I am here to assure myself."

"Which means?"

"Which means that I will, for example, be present at today's experiment, and in general will be making something of a pest of myself."

"Fine. We welcome your presence today. I am sure I don't have to remind you that the interests of science will be best served if you confine yourself to the role of observer and do what we ask."

"Of course, of course," said Kovalyov, "in there you are the boss, Yuri Trofimovich. But first I would like to ask one specific question."

"Please."

"These special film magazines you ordered for Andrusha's camera—what exactly is their purpose?"

"That's easy enough," said Yuri, relieved. "Most of our experiments seem to produce results within twenty minutes of the new serum's being injected. A standard magazine of film is good for about ten minutes, isn't it, Andrusha? But we have to be able to shoot for at least twenty minutes continuously to record the experiment without interruption."

"Is it so burdensome to change magazines?"

"No, the point is that the film, to have any value as a scientific document, must be one continuous, unedited strip shot from the same angle, or it might appear faked."

"But are such elaborate and expensive precautions necessary when these films will only be seen by our own scientists?"

"That is the scientific method, and Soviet science demands the highest standards," said Yuri conclusively; then he turned to Andrusha. "Is everything ready?"

"I may want to fool with the lighting a little more, but otherwise yes."

"And Marya Nikitovna will be here at ten?"

"They called in to say she might be a little late."

"Let's check the room, and then I'll take a look through the viewfinder—which you might also wish to try, Comrade Kovalyov."

"Thank you. And I would also be grateful for any explanations you might be able to provide. My own education was, you know, interrupted by the war."

The three of them entered the room, which was bare except for an ordinary wooden table and chair and a clock on the wall.

"Where's the camera?" asked Kovalyov.

"Up there." Andrusha pointed to a small square opening a few feet from the ceiling. "Most people get nervous when a camera is pointed right at their face. We'll observe from up there, too."

Kovalyov looked up at the large rectangular pane of glass

beside the camera slot. "One-way?" he asked. Andrusha nodded. "And what will we see today, Yuri Trofimovich?"

"Perhaps something very interesting, or perhaps nothing at all. Wouldn't you prefer a surprise?"

"I don't like surprises."

"Excuse me," said Andrusha to Kovalyov, "but I wonder if you could do us a favor."

"Of course."

"Could you sit at the table while Yuri Trofimovich and I take a look at you through the viewfinder to double-check on the shadows?"

"Of course."

As Kovalyov walked to the table, Yuri and Andrusha headed across the room toward the small door flush with the wall. On the staircase up to the observation room, Yuri whispered over his shoulder: "That may not have been a good idea."

"Why not? We're rid of him for five minutes."

"Still, you know how these psychic types are—they pick up everything in the atmosphere, and I can't believe Kovalyov's vibrations will be of any help to Marya Nikitovna."

"You worry too much, Yuri. It may actually be better if the test fails today; maybe that way they'll get off your back and give you a little room to breathe."

"True, true," said Yuri, half relieved by the thought. He wished he could be more like Andrusha, more devil-may-care.

"What a monster!" said Andrusha.

"Who, Kovalyov?"

"Him, too, of course, but I meant that," said Andrusha, pointing at the ungainly black plastic magazine on top of the camera. "Have a look through."

Yuri walked over to the camera and stood on tiptoe, since the tripod had been adjusted for Andrusha, who was a good five inches taller than he. Squeezing his left eye shut, he looked down through the viewfinder at Kovalyov, who was stifling a yawn with his fist.

Yes, thought Yuri, it is all much less interesting than they suppose. Besides, it's only the results that interest them, the rockets, the sputniks, the lasers. What a pleasure if this were a rifle scope instead, thought Yuri. Taken aback by the ugliness of his own thought, he switched his attention to the matter at hand. Kovalyov's torso cast no shadows on the table. "It should read nicely," said Yuri, pulling his head back and coming down from tiptoe at the same moment, aware of a slight muscle burn in his calves.

"You don't think it should be a hair back?" asked Andrusha, pulling out a cigarette and offering it to Yuri. Yuri turned the cigarette slowly in his fingers. "We have found a way" had been written on it lightly in pencil. Yuri put it in his own pack.

"No, it looks fine to me," said Yuri. "But better double-check yourself."

Andrusha looked through the eyepiece. Trying to act for the good of Soviet science, Kovalyov was already uncomfortable, however, and cracking his knuckles. Good, let the bastard squirm for a while, thought Andrusha; we squirm enough for them. "Yuri," said Andrusha, "go down and hold up the case. I want to check that all the writing's visible. You can send Kovalyov up for a look now."

Andrusha watched Yuri speaking to Kovalyov, who nodded and then walked out of the frame. There were many good reasons to hate the system, and he was feeling them all at once today. There was the weight of men like Kovalyov on you; you carried them all your life. There was the pain of men like Yuri Trofimovich, which was becoming more evident in the jagged lines around his eyes, lines like scars from a broken bottle. There was his own lousy fate, which had him stuck here, doing service for the state, when he should be in Moscow, filming and directing his own script on the last year of Pushkin's life. There should be a bushy Negroid sideburn filling the lens as the camera pulled back to reveal the poet arguing with the frivolous beauty who was his wife, a fireplace to one side of her.

Andrusha could hear Kovalyov's heavy steps on the stairs as Yuri held up the case, which contained a simple wooden spoon. The document attached to the case, printed in large letters so that the camera could pick them up at a distance, certified that the sealed case contained an ordinary wooden spoon, as attested by three scientists, Yuri's name first among them.

"Have a look. But be careful," said Andrusha to Kovalyov.

As Kovalyov looked warily at the camera, Andrusha was again happy to see him timid and hesitant. "Like this," said Andrusha, showing him how. Not to be outdone, Kovalyov strode decisively over to the camera and took the viewing position.

Kovalyov saw Yuri still holding the case, read a few words of the document, then shifted his eyes back up to Yuri's face. So much depends on such people, so much. And who really knows what they care about, what they think? Is he nervous about the experiment, or because I'm here? I don't feel at home with either of them, and that's always a bad sign. "Thank you," said Kovalyov, straightening up again. "Very interesting."

"Have a seat in the next room," said Andrusha. "We'll be starting in a short while." Then, pushing a button on the intercom, he said, "Reads fine, Yuri, just fine."

After Yuri came back and took a chair beside Kovalyov in the observation room, there was a long moment of silence. Yuri was hoping that the waiting and the boredom would have dulled Kovalyov's curiosity at least enough to keep the questions general, not probing.

"We can smoke here?" asked Kovalyov, glancing at the gray metal ashtray on the floor; emptied but never cleaned, its sides were coated with ash.

Yuri nodded. He was about to pull out his own cigarettes but, suddenly realizing that Kovalyov might offer him a light, let his hand fall back to his lap. Yuri knew what Andrusha's childishly clandestine note meant—they had found a way to send large quantities of information out of the country.

"Not smoking?" asked Kovalyov.

"I'm trying to cut down."

"You should do what Brezhnev used to do."

"What was that?"

"He had some scientist make him a special cigarette case that only opened every . . . I don't remember exactly . . . thirty minutes or something."

"Did it work?"

"The case worked fine. But Brezhnev bummed cigarettes from Podgorny, Suslov, anybody," said Kovalyov with a laugh.

Though Yuri was repelled by the idea of personal chitchat with Kovalyov, it was better than having the conversation return to the experiment itself, and so he kept it going. "What are you smoking these days?"

"Rossisskies. I like the pack—they look almost the same as Marlboros—and they taste good, but somehow a little dry."

"Let me try one," said Yuri.

"You, of course, probably prefer foreign cigarettes?" said Kovalyov, offering him the black flip-top pack decorated with traditional Russian folk designs.

"I should be patriotic about lung cancer?"

Kovalyov snorted, half in appreciation of the joke, half in acknowledgment of the rebuke. "Anyway, tell me what you hope to see today, Yuri Trofimovich. But keep it simple. I hate it when scientists use too much special jargon. There's something insulting about it, like when the doctors are talking about your own body and you cannot understand a word and they even seem to be enjoying your ignorance."

"I'll do my best," said Yuri, exhaling and glancing up at

the wall clock, which read ten to ten. "You see, there's one basic problem with parapsychology. On the one hand, its existence is certain, because even under the strictest conditions it will appear much more often than chance would allow. Of course, our concepts of chance and statistical probability might be off the mark too, but that's another matter. On the other hand, these parapsychological events, which we call 'psi' for short, display none of the predictability or the regularity of the physical universe. So, in a certain sense we're caught in a very interesting middle ground, if you see what I mean." Yuri looked over at Kovalyov, whose eyes were glazing over from the abstractions.

"What I asked you," said Kovalyov coolly now, "was what you hoped to see this morning."

"And without a certain amount of background," responded Yuri, with the precise amount of sharpness his position allowed him, "you would not understand what you saw."

"All right," conceded Kovalyov reluctantly, reaching forward to tap the ash off his cigarette.

"And there's another problem. We could call psi a talent, but it is unlike any other talent—unlike, say, a violinist's ability to play. Even though he may sometimes be more inspired than at others, a good violinist can always turn in a good performance. But psi seems to elude conscious control."

"If it can't be brought under control, what good is all this?" said Kovalyov, waving his hand disparagingly.

"I know," agreed Yuri with a sigh of smoke. "But for some reason psi resists the control of the rational intellect. Or perhaps it is the other way around. In America they did a very interesting study on the Mensa organization, whose members represent the top two percent of the population in terms of IQ. When they tested the Mensa people for psi abilities, they found they had significantly *less* than would have been statistically probable."

"And so that is why you are always dragging in those fat, hysterical peasant women with cow shit on their boots?"

"You could say that."

"So, I repeat, what do we hope to see today?"

There was no way around it: to prevaricate anymore would be too suspicious, and Kovalyov was looking right at him. "We will see Marya Nikitovna, a peasant from this district who seems to possess the ability to make objects move —how exactly we don't know. Before the experiment she will be given an injection that will both relax her and, we hope, increase her abilities. The serum in that injection has been synthesized from chemical traces found in her blood and that of other people with parapsychological abilities. The chemicals are present in their highest concentrations just before and during the eruption of those abilities and are accompanied by changes in brain waves, which are observable on an EEG machine. Marya Nikitovna will be hooked up to an EEG which will read her brain waves and at the appropriate moment activate the needle in her arm, which will begin to draw blood."

"And from that blood we will make stronger drugs to make these abilities even stronger and more controllable; is that the idea?"

"Yes," said Yuri, now hoping that Marya would have a good session today and make the wooden spoon move. The more successful the psi experiments were, the better a cover they were for the more interesting experiments that could begin now that the animals were here.

"But there is one other thing I do not understand, Yuri Trofimovich. Here you are working in the best conditions, the very best of conditions, making excellent progress, from what you tell me, and maybe on the verge of presenting the motherland with a scientific breakthrough. A normal person would expect you to be beaming with enthusiasm and excitement, and yet what do I see? A very morose and melancholy person. That has to strike me as odd, Yuri Trofimovich, very odd."

"You mistake concentration and nervousness for melancholy."

"Perhaps."

The conversation was interrupted by the arrival of Marya Nikitovna, brought into the test room in a wheelchair. She was already hooked up to the EEG and had a needle in her left arm from which a thin clear tube rose to a small plastic bottle. There were three attendants, one pushing the wheelchair, the other two rolling the stands for the EEG machine and the bottle. They helped Marya into the chair at the table, making certain that the equipment was moved into place at the same time.

As Yuri walked to the stairs, Andrusha shot him an inquisitive look, but Yuri did not respond. He told himself that he was probably doing fine, that it was like those lectures he sometimes gave that passed in a cloud of nervous fear suddenly dispelled at the end by strong and sincere applause. He told himself that Kovalyov was not being any more suspicious than usual and that it only seemed that way to him because he had lost his footing in himself, lost the gravity of being real. But, thank God, the task at hand required him to be calm and fatherly, to reassure that good woman.

Marya Nikitovna smiled shyly, as if embarrassed that Yuri could see her arms bared up to the shoulder by the hospital smock she wore. Her eyes had no squint of mistrust.

"Good morning, Marya Nikitovna. How are you?"

"I should have listened to you, Yuri Trofimovich, I should have listened to you and spent the night with my sister in town, because, wouldn't you know, as soon as the car pulls up for me, my Volodya falls off the chair. I told Tanya to watch him, but talking to her is like talking to a post. I should have taken them both in with me and stayed with my sister, Yuri Trofimovich. And there was Volodya's nose bleeding away, and them outside honking for me. So I'm sorry I'm late, Yuri Trofimovich, but what could I do?"

"It's all right, Marya Nikitovna, it's perfectly all right."

Then a great sigh filled Marya Nikitovna's chest, lifting her large breasts against the smock, and Yuri realized that the injection had just taken effect. Ashamed before her, he lowered his eyes for a moment.

"Now I feel better, Yuri Trofimovich, now I feel pretty good. I'm ready to start. Maybe today I'll have a little luck."

"Good."

"So, tell me one more time: I pick up the case and then?"

"Then count to ten slowly, open the case, and take out the spoon. Put the spoon wherever you like, but put the case on the floor. That's important, Marya Nikitovna. Then just keep your hands under the table at all times."

"Yes, wherever I like, fine. The only thing is, I never told you this before but sometimes, just before it happens, I get so scared, Yuri Trofimovich, so scared, I don't know why, it's like I might just burst. If I'm doing it at home with a pencil, I start thinking it's going to move—the pencil's going to move—I know it, and I get so scared. So you know what I do sometimes? Sometimes I sing a little, just to help myself along when I start to get that feeling. So what I was wondering was whether it would be all right to sing here a little, too, I mean, if I feel like I really need it?"

"Of course, it's all right to sing here if you want to."

"It is? Here?"

"Certainly."

"Thank you, Yuri Trofimovich."

Andrusha's voice came over the intercom, asking that the EEG machine be turned a little to the right.

"Whose right?" asked Yuri.

"Marya's."

Yuri waited by the door until the attendants had left the room, then gave Marya a smile of encouragement.

"Buzz in five seconds," he said to Andrusha on the way to the observation room.

"What do you think?"

"God only knows."

Yuri heard the buzzer just as he sat down beside Kovalyov, who had glanced up neutrally at him. Marya held up the case. Good, good, that's it, thought Yuri, talking her through it, and he himself began counting. He reached ten before she did.

Marya Nikitovna opened the case with deliberate, ceremonial slowness, as if breaking bread at a wedding banquet. She placed the case quite carefully on the floor, keeping an eye on the tube that led up from her arm to the clear plastic bottle. Then she positioned the plain wooden spoon so that its handle faced her directly. Andrusha had done his job well: there were no shadows falling across the table. Yuri looked beneath the table and saw her calves, large as Indian clubs.

Kovalyov was smoking again, blowing the smoke out of the corner of his mouth so it would not interfere with his vision.

Marya stared at the spoon for nearly two minutes without any perceptible change in her expression or posture. Kovalyov pulled hard on his nose several times. Yuri let his hands relax over the edges of the arms of the chair.

"You found yourself a good hefty cow there," said Kovalyov.

Yuri grunted something that could pass for agreement, but Kovalyov clearly respected Yuri's professional need for concentration, because he turned away after a second. They were more than three minutes into it now. Marya's brows were furrowed and her shoulders had risen slightly. Though it was extremely rare for anything to happen in the first six or seven minutes, he had seen tests where phenomena manifested nearly at once and then gradually receded. There was simply no knowing, no predicting, whether it would happen and how it would behave if in fact it did happen. It was outside the will; Koestler had been right, thought Yuri, to compare psi to erection and orgasm—perfectly normal, perfectly common human experiences, and yet quite beyond the reach of the will. Even shy of it; yes that was the word, "shy," just at Marya Nikitovna had been shy about her bare arms' being seen.

Five minutes and thirty seconds. Marya Nikitovna's right knee had begun to bob up and down as if she were working a treadle.

Yuri glanced up at Kovalyov, who was sitting to his left and about a foot in front of him, so that Yuri saw mostly the skin at his neck creased by the starched white collar of his shirt. What did they think about? Kovalyov was getting along in years—he must be sixty-five—but those old crocodiles lived forever. Maybe his thoughts were completely commonplace, maybe he was dreaming of his pension, his little *dacha,* going fishing with his grandchildren, or writing a little book about his war experiences. Where would they all be if they didn't have their war experiences to lord it over you with? But somehow the worst of it was that these monsters who ruined everybody's life were human, too.

Suddenly Yuri realized that success today would not be good. It would bring too much interest and attention too soon.

Fail, Marya Nikitovna, fail, thought Yuri. Let's hope that shy little spirit inside you is intimidated by all these machines and blank walls and retreats deep inside you, that little spirit that can sometimes read another person's mind or see what's written in a sealed envelope or tell the future in a dream, that little spirit that confounds all our modern arrogance, that little spirit that is so scared by all our noise and machines that it practically never shows itself anymore. Fail, fail, fail— don't do the one wonderful thing you can do.

Now, calmly and with a certain malice, Yuri took out the cigarette Andrusha had given him, with the words "We have found a way" penciled on it, and lit it quickly, before Kovalyov could be distracted by his movements and thrust his lighter at him. He enjoyed the first puff immensely. There was a way out, one little narrow chink in all that great Soviet armor, a loophole in that steel mesh of border control. He didn't know what it was yet, and maybe he would never know, any more than he knew now how his letters got back and forth from Farb, though they now were in close correspondence and it had never taken more than a week each way for their letters to travel. Happy with defiance, Yuri glanced down at the cigarette, which he let dangle over the right arm of his chair. The words "a way" had already turned to ash. "We have found" was all that was left, and Yuri's next drag took "found" away.

"You don't want the ashtray?" asked Kovalyov, turning around suddenly.

"Shhh," said Yuri, tapping the ash onto the palm of his hand.

Marya Nikitovna's head was now swaying slightly from side to side, as if she were trying to coax the spoon into moving. Yuri took another drag, bitterer than the last; perhaps the lead from the pencil had mingled with the other poisons in the cigarette. Now only the "we" was left. We, who are we? A young devil-may-care cameraman, a few scientists scared of their own shadows, a few exalted souls disappearing in the oblivion of camps, prisons, psychiatric hospitals. We.

Fourteen minutes in. Time was moving slowly, viscously, but would seem to make sudden spurts. The eighth, ninth, and tenth minutes had been an agony of dry boredom, and then suddenly they were fourteen minutes in. With a sudden updraft of elation, Yuri knew they would fail today. He would shake his head, feign all the usual gestures of disappointment, and patiently explain to Kovalyov that that was how science proceeded, by trial and error, test after test, experiment after experiment.

Kovalyov would be unhappy. Failure didn't interest them.

Now Yuri's attention was drawn by a sound that, for a moment, he could not identify. An odd low hum reverberating metallically in the intercom. It was Marya Nikitovna humming. Oh no, he thought, oh no, don't hum, don't sing.

It was like a lullaby without words, the way a mother sings to a child who is almost asleep, rocking him the last little distance into the world of dreams. Even Kovalyov's foot had begun to tap lightly in tune to the humming, which was becoming deeper, stronger.

Yuri leaned forward and stared hard at the dancing green light on the oscilloscope. Nothing unusual yet.

"Is everything all right?" whispered Kovalyov.

"Fine," Yuri whispered back. "Just checking the scope."

"And if the film runs out and then she does something, then what?"

"We'll repeat the experiment in a week's time," said Yuri, feeling that everything he said to Kovalyov was an awkward lie, an attempt at the language that Kovalyov spoke with native fluency.

"And she is paid?" asked Kovalyov, irritated now and overriding the enforced, irksome silence of science.

"Of course."

"Whether she succeeds or not?"

"Of course."

If she's humming, she's scared, which could also mean that she's still upset from this morning. Fail, Marya. Fail, Marya. Fail, Marya. He repeated this to himself, half closing his eyes, gathering his mind around his will. Fail, Marya. Fail, Marya. Your son fell off the chair again, your son fell off the chair again, he's bleeding, he's bleeding, you'd better go home, he's bleeding, go home.

Now her humming was edging into words, almost becoming a song. Yuri glanced beneath the table. Her knee had stopped bobbing. In fifteen seconds there would be only two minutes left.

Fail, Marya, fail.

She began singing, very softly.

> Meadow larks, meadow larks,
> dark above the green,

when the sky is blue with dawn
and when the day is done.

Your son is bleeding, go home, go home.

When the sky is blue with dawn
And when the day is done.

Fail, Marya, fail. . . . But Yuri broke off his incantation. It was never a matter of will—hers, his, or anyone else's. The will was puny, the will was nothing; what was the will against the forces that mattered?

She had stopped singing. Eighteen minutes, forty seconds. Almost there, almost there.

Yuri shifted his eyes from the clock to the table. And just as he was focusing on the plain wooden spoon, it suddenly sprang up on end, spun around twice as if following the contours of a mixing bowl, and then shot off the table and clattered to the floor while a long red line of blood leaped up the clear plastic tube to the bottle.

"Fantastic!" Kovalyov exclaimed, slapping his thigh. "Fantastic, Yuri Trofimovich. Congratulations!"

Yuri stood and stared at Marya Nikitovna, who had collapsed onto the table. Kovalyov rose and hugged Yuri, who had no choice but to submit to the embrace.

10   In the front room of Karen's loft,

                              the red dregs of the
Petit Sarah were slowly coagulating on the glasses, whorls
and streaks from which, in some country, fortunes might be
told.

In her bedroom, too dark for even the outlines of their
bodies to be seen, their fingers read slowly—elbow, lip,
nipple, the newly blind just mastering Braille. Her hands
asked: Are you there? Is this good? His answered: I am. It is.

He knew what was happening, and part of him was
resisting it, standing by the bed and mocking him, saying:
Oh, my God, there you go again; why rant about quack-
quack nature and plastic baby seats if you're just going to get
trapped in flesh and pity again?

Feeling his body twitch, she wondered what fear had just

run through him. Her hand asked the side of his chest if he was alright, and his sigh said that her touch gave him freedom.

Then he began to remember something that can practically never be remembered, except in the form of desire. He began to remember the place, the chamber in the heart of life, the loving freedom at the heart of life. The reason for life, the source of life, the place you could never be in alone and never be alone in. He felt them becoming as naked as their bodies, as they did the step-by-step dance of perfect trust on the sheets. Until excited joy swept over fear and they could move freely to each other, him with her on her side, her with him on his.

In an errant slant of silver-gray city light he could see her face changing as it rose to kiss him, changing after each kiss, as if all her selves were rising to the surface of her face to be kissed like river maidens suddenly freed from a spell. The face of an astonished girl, the face of a woman, selfish in pleasure, and all the faces of the women she might yet become, faces sad and radiant. Now the skin of her face was becoming transparent, and he could see through it to a face of sculpted light. Her.

11 Farb had been arguing

with his sister, Raisa, lately, and with her it didn't matter whether he won the argument or not—he always ended up feeling he had lost. She thought him a fool for allowing himself to enter into correspondence with Yuri Trofimovich, not to mention some long-distance and clandestine collaboration with him. She absolutely refused to hear what the nature of the project was: "It doesn't make any difference. It doesn't make any difference to me, and it won't make any difference to the rest of the world, either. It's too late for the world to change. And I can tell you what'll come of all this—trouble, trouble, and more trouble."

"Stop taking red lights!" Farb had yelled at his sister as she gunned her big Oldsmobile through a light just turning red. "You'll hit some pedestrian, and that'll be trouble, too."

Raisa had merely grinned at him and stepped on the gas, as if demonstrating something perfectly obvious to him about the world.

He could never understand his sister's odd combination of vitality and negativity. All that energy, all that unhappiness. And it was infectious. Soon enough he would feel it in his own thoughts as he accused himself of having a shallow heart. At some point after their fights, she would weep and talk about their parents and the times they had sat in the apple tree together as children, and beg his forgiveness for her outburst. And Farb would forgive her: he wanted peace, he loved her, and his heart, unlike hers, could not bear rage and hatred for very long.

A few days with Carolyn had also helped matters. A bubble of a weekend, kissing in taxis, laughing in bars, strolling through the monumental tranquillity of Manhattan on Sunday morning. But after a few days with Carolyn, it was time to return home. Carolyn was a terrible cook and their friends were so dissimilar that they would never be able to have much more than a small, private world of their own. Raisa had said nothing when he returned—that too, was part of their ritual—and Farb wondered whether she had known he would be returning that night, since she had clearly shopped for two.

He put Yuri's latest letter, the fifth, down on his desk without opening it. There was no getting out of this now. Farb's only regret was that his involvement with Yuri had deflected him from what would have been the pharmacological sensation of the century. But the logic was absolute. Yuri's research seemed to be leading to discoveries that should not be the exclusive property of the Soviet authorities. Therefore, the data must be sent out. He was the only person who had been involved in the project from the start and was now outside the country; therefore he was the obvious next link in that chain made of onionskin letters.

He opened the letter.

Dear Yasha,

I am going to keep this letter short and to the point. I have been working like a madman and I'm completely exhausted. But the preliminary results have been marvelous. The synthetic we have been injecting into our study subjects works, to put it as simply as possible. Psi abilities are significantly increased. But—fortunately, I guess—they still remain out of our control. A subject given an injection will have a longer and more intense psi experience if he has one at all, but absolutely nothing may happen.

We also tried injecting the serum into people who have no background of psi, to see if we could stimulate such abilities. For the most part we failed. Then one of our new assistants suggested we test for other reactions—physical stamina, problem solving, basic intelligence, spatial orientation. That proved to be a brainstorm, because all the tests we have run so far indicate that this serum enhances mental abilities to a significant degree. The Mahler-Wein test was used. Scores consistently increased by a factor of 10–60 percent! We have not, however, run sufficient tests yet, for the simple reason that we want those who take a practical interest in our research to continue to believe that we are attempting only to find practical applications for psi-type abilities.

A series of tests run on our rather extensive menagerie has also produced significant data, to say the least. The serum is lethal if the proper dosage is exceeded (I will not discuss the formula for determining dosage at this point). The serum produces no great changes in stamina or physical ability, but, in all the lab animals we have tested, we have observed an increased ability in problem solving, especially interesting in the primates, who now seem to be actively groping toward symbolic communication with us. The one physical change we have observed in all the laboratory animals is a potential life-span increase on the order of 40 percent!!! These are, of course, projections based on observed developmental changes— an increase in the length of the "youthful" stages of mice, rabbits, dogs, etc. The Gerontology Department is marked by more personal ambition than conscience, and so it becomes more imperative than ever to share this information with the United States. The Gerontology people are, however, not aware of the full implications of our work, that is, they are unaware that similar minute endocrine traces are found in those with longevity and those possessing psi abilities. The key word here is "similar": there are differences, and the formulas for calculating them are extremely important. But, in any case, the implications are obvious—a substance that both dramatically accelerates the mental powers and increases the life span by 40 percent would create a new order of man, of human life. It is now time to begin preparations for the last phase of this *correspondence. My next letter to you will indicate the exact means we will use to send all the relevant material out of the country.*

Please confirm receipt of this letter, as usual.

Incidentally, Yasha, as an old Polonophile, you'd be interested to know that the few of us in the lab who really know what's going on have nicknamed the serum "Stolat"; if man's normal life expectancy of seventy or so could be increased by 40 percent, the hundred years of life that Polish toast wishes us would be a wish come true.

Think of it—every man his own century.

Now, if we could only live better . . .

Farb replaced the letter in the envelope and was about to put it in the drawer along with all the others when he decided to take it home with him and read it to Raisa, whether she wanted to hear it or not. Even Raisa couldn't resist this. Farb reached inside his sweater and placed the letter in his left front shirt pocket. He had better be careful with it—take it home tonight and bring it right back tomorrow.

It was Tuesday night, Farb's traditional night at the Baltyk restaurant, and now he looked forward to his meal with a sudden appetite that caused him to speed up the final motions of closing his office for the day. He made sure that he had his key and the desk drawer was locked, checked that he had his wallet and that Yuri's letter was still in his shirt pocket (a faint crinkle assured him that it was). While checking his pockets, he found a phone bill that he should have mailed a week ago, and noticed as well that Raisa had forgotten to write their name and address in the upper left-hand corner of the envelope, as you were supposed to. Farb decided that the telephone company might be angered if he failed not only to pay on time but did not even take the trouble to write his name and address on the envelope. Perhaps they were even looking for that envelope, so that they could take his name off the lists of those to be canceled. But the one pen in Farb's pocket didn't work, and somehow it seemed wrong to write his name in pencil. Was it worth getting out his keys, unlocking his desk drawer, finding a pen? All right, all right, he would do it.

He printed their name and address very neatly, for he was never quite able to believe that a real American would be able to read his handwriting. Stuffing the bill back in his pocket, he locked his drawer and office door and darted down the dark corridor toward the elevator, Broadway, and his dinner.

Tuesday night was Farb's night at the Baltyk for several reasons: Raisa taught a class in extension school that evening; he would usually have spent the weekend and perhaps part of Monday with a woman and so was ready for a little break by Tuesday; and an old émigré, a psychologist whose writings Farb had always admired, had advised him to establish some regular habits right away in America to offset the profound sense of cultural disorientation that was bound to follow the initial elations of freedom. It had seemed like a good idea at the time, but rather quickly Farb had realized that he was going to like it in America and dropped most of the synthetic habits. The few exceptions, like Tuesdays at the Baltyk, were ones that had proved to be more pleasure than chore. His American girlfriends loved the place. Once. Or even twice. But to make a regular, weekly habit of eating there was literally more than they could stomach. Carolyn's pure fresh tummy, cultivated on quiches and salads, could not withstand the black bread, the vodka, the borscht, the heavy meat. He couldn't get that kind of food at home. Raisa had become entirely American in her eating habits and had none of his "foolish nostalgia for the cuisine of anti-Semitism."

Feeling ebullient, righteous, and somehow even rich, Farb decided to take a cab, even though it would cost around ten dollars.

"First and First," he said to the driver, bending his ungainly frame into the cab.

"How do you want me to go?"

"Down Broadway."

Farb smiled to himself at life's little coincidences—the primariness of First and First, the fact that he was on his way to a Polish restaurant having just learned that the fruit of their work had been given a Polish nickname, Stolat. Was life always making such patterns, with only a few of the more obvious ones available to us, just as only certain bands of colors were? Or was life only intermittently patterned, and otherwise random, free, chaotic, whatever you wanted to call it? Racing down Broadway, looking out at the great apartment buildings moored like ocean liners at the dock of the street, with the city's lights throwing their all one more time against the cold cobalt of the night sky, he somehow felt so deeply in accord with it all that he didn't even want to know.

There were some six or eight people waiting for tables. The restaurant had recently been written up, and now people were busy discovering it for themselves, which meant that, along with the usual neighborhood Poles, Ukrainians, and Punks in their khaki paratrooper pants and Hawaiian shirts, adventurous eaters from the Upper East Side were now competing for the vinyl booths and semilegible menu.

As he waited, Farb heard a young woman in purple plush pants saying to the man beside her, ". . . and he was so strung out on coke at the screening that . . ." He caught Janina's eye over their shoulders, and she beckoned him to the little table by the wall that she always saved for him. Farb smiled into her eyes as he excused himself through the unhappy and inquisitive line. Habitually flirting with Janina, he had pleased her without the least offending her womanly dignity, and it had been her idea to keep the table reserved on Tuesday for him.

Flirting, Farb believed, was like tipping: a small but useful social art that paid good dividends in ease and convenience.

He touched his shirt pocket to hear the letter crinkle as he slid himself onto his chair.

"You look very nice tonight," he said to Janina in Polish, with playful politeness.

"I do? I feel terrible."

"Sometimes it happens that way—you feel awful and you look fine."

"I know. Strange." She had the slight whine in her voice that Polish women use both to complain and to entice.

"What's good tonight?"

"The czarnina came out good this time."

"All right, the czarnina, a salad with lots of beets, and a beer, Krakus."

Janina brought him bread right away, served in a little basket and wrapped in a piece of filigreed linen. Farb always liked that sacramental respect for bread, so completely lacking in America. He liked the odd, vanity-free shapes of the men at the bar, looking at the TV above the flowers that surrounded a photograph of the Pope, shrinelike over the liquor bottles. Those were Slavic shapes, just as the distant buzz in the background was Slavic speech. A few vodkas, he thought, and he could probably become sentimental for an hour or two. But then his eyes met those of a man at the bar who was swiveling on his bar stool, and the look of gloating contentment in those eyes, Farb knew, was the glimmer of a certain organic anti-Semitism he despised.

Farb averted his eyes just as Janina brought the duck soup, whose dark, gamy fragrance entranced him and erased the unpleasant sensation of the previous moment.

"The salad in a minute," she said, replacing an errant lock of hair.

"And the beer."

"And the beer."

The soup was just right, Farb's highest praise. Food could be elegant, exquisite, marvelous, but Farb preferred it to be just right. Some things were ruined by becoming too good. The soup was brown and black, vaguely cinnamony, rich with the thick taste of duck. It made him think of rainy

Polish meadows and a woman with whom he had once driven to Gdansk. He had loved her, but they had remained loving friends, because he had been unable to unlock her sexuality, which was somehow too elevated, too Catholic, Polish, romantic, whatever.

The beet salad and the beer came.

The beer was good and cold, and he smiled with gratitude at Janina, who he knew had taken the trouble to feel at least three bottles to find the coldest for him. They were wonderful—all through his life they had been so wonderful to him—women. Had he been wrong never to marry? That was what they all seemed to want, and yet, more often than not, it turned out to be the worst thing for everybody; perhaps he had truly acted as their friend by refusing to take that step with them. Or had he just been an erotic maniac who had used them for his own selfish pleasure and spat them out like a piece of gum when the flavor was gone? No, he didn't believe that of himself, especially since none of the women hated him, were always glad to see him, and would still, all of them, take the extra second to show their love in little ways, like squeezing the necks of beer bottles to find the coldest.

It was in Moscow that he had first discovered the secret whose rarely kept promise brings men and women together, at the Hotel Ostankino, of all places, where he had been staying during a conference. At first he had been surprised at finding himself so strongly attracted to Lydia, a woman whose face, aside from a touch of the beauty of life, was plain, and whose body had no single line or charm that fixated him in fascination. But it was with her that he had learned for the first time what temperatures sexual alchemy could reach.

He lifted his beer and tipped it slightly in a toast to her. A hundred years to you, Lydia, wherever you are. But wasn't she in California? He had heard something about her, even tried to find her name in the Los Angeles directory at the library, though without success. It was strange. All those people who were once right there with you in your life— where did they go? Back into their own lives, of course. But the distance between lives could be so immense, almost frightening to consider. Lydia somewhere in California, perhaps sitting beside one of those horrible little blue chlorinated pools or pulling into a supermarket parking lot wearing some brightly colored dress and sunglasses. Her eyes had always reacted strongly to the light.

The check came to a little more than seven dollars, and so, strictly speaking, the tip should be a little over a dollar. If flirting was like tipping, the converse was also true—too much would be like overfamiliarity. Eight-fifty, he decided, would be fine.

As he put on his coat, he remembered with a grimace of irritation that he still hadn't mailed in the phone bill; what he *couldn't* remember was whether there was a mailbox between the restaurant and the subway. He touched Janina on the shoulder on his way out, and she wished him a good night, holding a steaming plate suspended for a moment in either hand.

The night was brisk, and Farb pulled his coat closer

around him. Pausing for traffic, he watched a tall, thin young man threading his way between the parked cars. The young man, who seemed to be losing his hair in clumps, had the look of someone just out of the hospital. There was a stack of posters under his arm. Posters for what? Farb wondered without much interest.

DON'T WALK changed to WALK. First Street was largely deserted. Farb stopped at the island in the middle of the street, just to make sure no cars would come flying out of nowhere. There was a couple to his left on the island, discussing something—arguing, actually; Farb caught the word "relationship." That's what they were always arguing about, their relationships. Just to think about love with that word guaranteed that nothing could ever go right, he thought, listening to the angry misery in their voices while waiting for a large truck that had been double-parked and had now started down the street.

". . . people who are such babies that they can't take one drop of constructive criticism, and then they wonder why they fail at everything," said the woman who had albino-blonde hair.

"Me? Fail? At what?" responded the man, potbellied with defeat.

"Try life, love, work, and whatever else's left."

"Oh well," thought Farb and stepped off the island.

He became aware of something moving quickly to his left and, turning, saw a small man wearing a short, dark jacket who looked as if he might run into him. Farb stepped back up on the island.

The short man stopped in front of Farb, and Farb looked down to see what he wanted. The man pulled a pistol from inside his jacket. What did he want, what was he saying?

"OK, man, you give me your fuckin' wallet right now."

Aha, so now it was even going to happen to him too. All right, then, Farb thought, less confused, less terrified, even vaguely amused. He reached into his pants pocket, placed his wallet in the small, impatient hand, and watched it disappear into the pocket of the man's dark blue pants.

What was he waiting for? He had what he wanted. Maybe Janina would loan him the money to get home; he probably didn't have enough change, but he would feel sheepish asking her for part of his tip back.

He was going to shoot, he was going to shoot! Why? He had the wallet.

The first bullet felt like a bee stinging his heart.

PART TWO

12 Dressed in a mixture of the somber

and the gaudy, with a receding hairline which gave his head the domed look of an artillery shell or a Churchill cigar, Solly Altheim of the New York Police Department, Homicide, entered the university building where the deceased, Yakov Farb, was supposed to have maintained an office. His nose crinkled up at the lack of any real smell, the smell of office buildings, dust and wax, lavatory soap and carbon paper. Solly's assistant, a sergeant named Apollon Yanopolis, was already busy checking the wall directory for Farb's office number. Yanopolis—dark, wiry, in his late twenties, always dressed in last year's swinging styles—was making a great show of efficiency for Solly's benefit, running his finger down all the names slowly enough to appear careful but quickly enough to seem on the ball. Yanopolis was in deep trouble, and he knew it. His knack for being in the wrong place at the wrong time, for losing scraps of paper with important information, and for expressing hilariously stupid opinions had caught up with him, and his status was, at the moment, shaky, to say the very least. "See what you can do with him, Solly," the captain had said. Yanopolis did have his virtues—he was nearly tireless, he was willing to handle all the boring details any normal person would be glad to shirk, and he was not personally or physically offensive. Solly said he would see what he could do, as long as they didn't expect any silk purses back.

"Not listed," said Yanopolis, shaking his head in angry disgust to let Solly know how much he cared.

"But his sister said he worked here," said Solly, and he touched the pocket that contained the plastic bag holding the keys found on Farb. The university's switchboard had been no help. There were two Farbers, one Farbloss, but no Farb.

"What did she say he was again?" asked Yanopolis.

"A pharmacologist."

"Is that anything to do with agriculture?"

"Are you kidding me?"

"No," said Yanopolis, looking away with the peculiar shame of the stupid.

"A pharmacologist is a guy who thinks up new medicines."

"Oh."

"Like pharmacy, drugstore."

"So, then, let's call the Pharmacology Department," suggested Yanopolis.

"Good idea. Do it," said Solly, glad to redeem Yanopolis from his shame.

Solly watched Yanopolis stride over to the row of pay phones. The old kind were better, thought Solly: you had privacy, you got to sit down. Now they were somehow like urinals. Yanopolis returned, fuming. "They talk to you like they were doing you a favor."

"I know the type," said Solly. "Anything there?"

"They never heard of him."

"Wait a second; I think I know what the trouble is."

Yanopolis took a step back and tried to look as eagerly interested and respectful as he could, all the time hoping that he would understand what he heard and be able to remember it for future reference.

"His sister said he works in this building, so let's say she's right. She also said that he was a pharmacologist, but her English wasn't too terrific, and maybe she didn't say the right word. We can't call up every department in this place, but since he worked here, that means he got paid here. So, call Payroll."

Yanopolis beamed a look of pure admiration at Solly, but admiration had turned to gloom by the time he reached the phone booth again. He was a stupid person. He should get out while there was still time. Maybe his cousin George would take him back in the business. They already had four restaurants, and two coming. But maybe, maybe, if he just kept at it, just kept trying . . .

From Payroll Yanopolis learned that Farb was employed both as a half-time researcher and a half-time instructor and was probably using Professor Philip MacDonald's office in the chemistry building. MacDonald's secretary said the professor was on sabbatical, and though she knew of Farb she was certain that he had not taken MacDonald's office, because she herself had moved in there for the interim. She seemed to remember hearing something about Farb's being given space over in Engineering and was sorry that she could not be more helpful.

"So?"

"He works for the Chemistry Department. And his office is in this building, but the secretary doesn't know just where."

"We'll give it another ten, fifteen minutes," said Solly.

He wouldn't have bothered going there in the first place if he hadn't wanted to take Yanopolis back over some of the basics, and if the victim's sister had not insisted that her brother had not been the victim of an ordinary street crime but the target of a political assassination.

"You don't know what they're like! You Americans have no idea! If they killed a Bulgarian diplomat in London with a poisoned umbrella, they could kill my brother in New York!"

Solly had told her that, unfortunately, in his opinion, what happened to her brother happened every day in New York, every day of the week.

"But it isn't every day that an important Soviet scientist is murdered in the streets of New York!"

There was something to that. And there was something to the fact that Farb had been shot with a .22-caliber pistol, which was the favored weapon of assassins working up close. But the little evidence there was all pointed in the other direction. Two witnesses had seen a short dark man, probably Puerto Rican, run past. They had been arguing, and by the time the shots had drawn their attention, the short man was already running away and the victim was already on the ground, half on the island, half on the street. His wallet had been taken, and they had been able to identify him only by the return address on the phone bill they found in his pocket.

Yanopolis was talking to an Indian who was shaking his head, wrapped in a bright pink turban.

"Nobody ever seems to have heard of this guy," said Yanopolis.

"The famous Soviet scientist," sighed Solly. "Go see if you can find a janitor."

Yanopolis started down the empty corridor to the right, but then, suddenly deciding that the equally empty corridor to the left would have been the better choice, he wheeled on his heel and passed Solly without looking at him.

As long as he doesn't get lost, thought Solly. And how come there's never any place to sit down in these colleges? he asked himself, looking around the lobby, which contained nothing but a hotel-type ashtray and a bulletin board shingled with mimeographed announcements—rides needed, apartments needed, jobs needed.

A few students walked by, but Solly didn't bother to ask them about Farb. The slight, red-headed man in the leather jacket, however, did not look the least bit like a student or a professor, and for some reason he didn't look much like an

American to Solly, either. Solly stopped the man, identified himself, and asked him if he knew Professor Yakov Farb.

"Of course I do," answered Sapozhnikov after a moment's hesitation. "I am right now delivering a letter to him. Where is it? Ah, here."

He showed Solly the envelope as if he expected him to be able to read the Russian words. In pencil someone had marked "Eng. 508" in the upper right-hand corner, where the stamp would be.

"You're a mailman?"

"No, I drive a van."

"So what are you doing delivering the mail?"

"How can I explain? Some letters have to leave the Soviet Union but not by regular mail, you understand me. So, some letters are carried out and some are mailed from normal countries, like Austria or Italy, and some are hand-carried all the way."

"You mean the more important ones?"

"I don't know. I only deliver them. I don't read them like they do over there. There's one other thing."

"Yes?"

"My van is double-parked."

"Don't worry. If you have any problems we'll take care of them."

"If they tow, it's a nightmare. They smash your car and then tell you to fill out three hundred forms."

"As soon as my partner comes back, you'll show us Farb's office, and then you can be on your way. They don't tow that fast up here. What's he like, Farb?"

"Farb? A nice man, very nice, very honest. One time I left my wallet in his office and he came running after me with it."

Yanopolis was returning down the corridor with a reluctant janitor in tow. The janitor, a Jamaican with short dreadlocks and a gold front tooth, was dragging his broom unhappily behind him.

"He no believe I," said the janitor. "I just clean."

"Forget it," said Solly. "Mr. . . . ?"

"Sapozhnikov."

"Mr. Sapozhnikov knows the way."

They rode up the five floors in the constrained silence peculiar to elevators, then followed Sapozhnikov to 508, whose milky glass window was dim in the autumn light.

Solly tried three keys before finding the right one.

"He's not here?" asked Sapozhnikov.

"Not today," said Solly. "We'll take care of the letter. Thank you. Yanopolis, you escort the gentleman back to his van. If there's a ticket, we'll take care of it. And," he said, turning to Sapozhnikov, "please give my assistant here your name, address, and phone number in case we need any further information from you."

"My pleasure to help the American police."

"You're a good citizen."

Solly looked through the file cabinets and the wastebasket but found nothing of much interest. The locked desk drawer turned out to contain four other envelopes that matched the one just delivered. Solly slipped the letter out of one, saw that it was typed in Russian, then slipped it back in. The other drawers contained only odds and ends, paper clips, elastic bands, a tin of aspirin.

It made him sad for a moment, the little things that people leave behind.

Solly sat down at the desk. The room smelled like chalk dust.

It was probably nothing. Sure, the victim was from the Soviet Union, but New York was full of them now, and sooner or later one of them had to get himself killed. Maybe he was even a big shot over there, but he couldn't have been doing much of anything over here, because look how hard it had been just to find his office. OK, he received smuggled letters, but that went on all the time too: the people over there weren't allowed to complain about the weather.

And, of course, the sister wanted her brother's death to be more than just another street crime. Who wouldn't?

Using Farb's phone, Solly called Raisa Farb and told her that they had found four other letters like the one that her brother had been carrying.

"So, can you translate these letters for us so we can see if there was anything going on?"

"Me? My English is inadequate. No. These letters will be read by important government officials. What we require is the services of a professional translator, but we have to be very careful to find someone who is known to be reliable person. I think I know of such a one. He is translator of my friend's memoirs. You are where?"

"At your brother's office."

"You can stay five minutes there?"

"I can."

"I'll call you right back. Wait."

Solly hung up. These political types, they were all a little soft. They reminded him of his Aunt Rose from Trenton. What was it she was? A Trotskyite. Every time something happened in Europe, she put her head in the oven. Anyway, it was simple. If the letters were important, they'd be turned over to the FBI; if not, the police would do what they could to catch who did it, which was about a hundred-to-one shot.

The phone rang.

It wasn't Farb's sister but a woman who introduced herself as Karen Cooper, an editor at the publishing house of Gander and Kuhn.

"Do you have a pencil?" she asked.

"Go ahead, shoot," said Solly.

She gave him David Aronow's phone number and address. "There's one problem with him though," she said.

"What's that?"

"He doesn't like to answer his phone. So, you can either leave a message on his answering machine or drop by. He's practically always there."

"He's good?"

"Very good."

"What do they usually get, these guys?"

"David gets about sixty dollars per thousand words."

"Sixty. Thanks for your help."

Solly put the keys back in the plastic bag and paper-clipped the envelopes together. Now it was only a matter of waiting for Yanopolis to return. Solly glanced at his watch, fought off the temptation to smoke, and began tapping his fingers lightly against the gray steel of Farb's desktop. It was the same rhythm he had been tapping since he was a little kid, some song he had learned in grade school, but what song, what grade, he had forgotten long ago. He was rarely even aware of that habit, except when it would get on his wife, Adelle's nerves and she would say, "Solly, you're doing that tapping thing again."

Hearing footsteps in the corridor, Solly went to the door and opened it enough to see Yanopolis, a parking ticket in one hand, stopping in front of every door, knocking hesitantly.

13 From the park bench

Yuri Trofimovich spotted Andrusha in the distance, a crimson scarf around his neck, breathing frosty clouds of exuberance as he stopped to photograph the early-fall landscape.

After they had pantomimed mild surprise at running into each other, Andrusha asked if he could take Yuri's picture, saying it would make for a good Russian fall scene.

He framed Yuri so that there were a few birches in the background, white against the darker trees whose leaves were going red. The only elements that clashed at all with the timeless Russianness of the scene were Yuri's jacket—a sporty European affair, beige, with a dark-brown knitted collar—and his cowboy boots.

"You have a nose like Lev Tolstoy's," said Andrusha. "I never noticed before."

Then Andrusha sat down beside him on the bench and accepted a smoke. He looked wrong smoking, thought Yuri, too fresh, too healthy; he didn't smoke with the sinister satisfaction of the true nicotine addict, but puffed and blew like a child.

"Without going into a lot of details, Yuri Trofimovich, here's what happened. I brought the materials we photographed to Moscow last week. As you know, it came to quite a lot, but we have someone there who's brilliant at this sort of thing. The material has been covered with a special coating that makes it look like ordinary film leader and has been attached to the fourth reel of *Apples of Ryazan,* which is the official Soviet entry in the New York Film Festival and will be shipped directly to New York on the third of November. Allowing time for customs and all that, the film should be at Lincoln Center by November fifteenth. Then Farb will have to figure out some way of getting hold of it, but that really shouldn't prove too hard. You must admit, it's daringly brilliant, Yuri Trofimovich."

Yuri smiled. Andrusha was such a child sometimes, he seemed actually to enjoy it all, hoodwinking the authorities as if they were school principals and not men with the power of life and death.

"Yes, quite brilliant. If it works."

"It's even the safest way, because they're doing all the work themselves," said Andrusha, laughing.

"So, I must inform Farb immediately."

The letter had gone out the same day.

Then the days became days of waiting. Even though Yuri

was busy with scrambling the data in their computers so that it would take months to reconstruct, time still seemed like some transparent, viscous, tasteless substance that he had to chew his way through. Arising exhausted, he would force himself through the motions of being Yuri Trofimovich. Any harsh or sudden sound startled him, delays and errors irritated him tremendously, and food seemed hardly worth the trouble of eating.

On Thursday morning, the guard took Yuri's pass and, though he had been doing so for quite some time, gave no hint of recognition, no little pleasantry to oil the machinery of the moment. As usual, he checked the face against the photo, but this time he did not return the pass; instead, he ran his finger down a list that Yuri could not see. Yuri knew his name was on it. All right, so it had come, thank God, thank God, he could live again, even if it meant disgrace for his family and the ruin of his own life. The main thing was not to tell them anything for five days, until the material was at least out of the country. But could he hold out that long?

"I have been ordered to confiscate this pass," said the guard, who, also as usual, gave no indication of what he was feeling or what he knew. "You are to proceed directly to Kovalyov."

For a moment, Yuri could not make his feet move. Even though a moment before he had desired an end to all the tension and duplicity, now that the end had come he couldn't go the final steps to meet it.

But then, somehow, he broke the spell of inertia and made his feet move as if he were a father teaching his little child to walk—one foot in front of the other, that's the way, that's good.

Kovalyov did not come out from behind his desk. Since the successful experiment with Marya Nikitovna, Kovalyov had been treating Yuri with something approaching deference, but there was nothing deferential in the way he rose and offered his hand. His greeting was neutral and businesslike, which Yuri would have found reassuring had he not been certain that it was the cover from which Kovalyov would pounce. The muscles in Yuri's upper back were now knotted and raised as if he literally expected Kovalyov to end up on his back, clawing and snarling.

Yuri sat down, wondering if he would be arrested immediately or if he were in fact already under arrest and this was to be the first in a long series of interrogations. Perhaps they thought that they could get more out of him here than in a prison, that he might not have realized the game was up.

"Yuri Trofimovich, the Committee for State Security has required us to institute much stricter security on the psi-pharm project."

"I noticed."

"Since you have been the project coordinator, I want to give you a little background. This project has now been given the same security classification as work in lasers, for example. But, of course, there's a difference here. We have been using people, outsiders, for our experiments, which makes for a lot of coming and going. So far, all our subjects have been chosen on the basis of one factor alone, but we must now add another characteristic."

"Namely?"

"Political reliability. We must be as certain as possible that our subjects are not engaging in any loose talk about what they've seen going on here."

In a way, he was grateful to Kovalyov: the idiocy of their move was itself almost guaranteed to bog the experiment down. How many politically reliable psychics did they think were wandering around the Russian countryside? Good—let them strangle it with their own paranoia, their own mistrust of freedom; there was a certain perfect justice in that. Still, weren't they in a sense right? After all, security had already been breached. And that was what Kovalyov would be getting around to soon enough.

"You have to realize one thing," said Yuri. "Our choice of subjects is going to be more limited now, and that can throw our entire timetable off. You can't press me for results on the one hand and then cut off my subjects on the other."

"That difficulty was foreseen. New software will be arriving this week that will enable you to locate suitable subjects from all over the Soviet Union. Not only that: those subjects will be brought here at state expense and kept in a small hostel, which will be available within the month, as soon as we renovate Building Three. Wouldn't that seem adequate compensation?"

"In principle, yes, but let's see if it works."

"There are many things that need to be seen to, Yuri Trofimovich. We have to worry about the reliability not only of the subjects but of the people in here as well."

"What does that mean in practice?"

"I'll show you," said Kovalyov, bending back and sliding open a desk drawer. "This," he said as he showed Yuri a small, dark blue book, "is the new pass to be given to all those able to work on the project from here on in. There will be new photos, and the pass will have to be stamped on the first working day of every month to be valid. Not only that, it will be valid only from eight to eight, Monday through Saturday. No more dropping in on Sunday as if this were a chess club or something. If anyone needs to come earlier or stay later, he will require a special stamp in his book, which can only be obtained from me or my deputy."

Yuri felt a surge of relief; his shoulders relaxed, and the muscles in his face seemed to thaw. They weren't going to arrest him. Otherwise, they wouldn't waste any time explaining all this to him. They weren't on to anything, but had just overreacted with security procedures, as usual. Kovalyov was only trying to put a little extra fear in him, dangling the passbook in front of him like a bone in front of a dog, expecting him to bark and beg.

"I will miss the old atmosphere," said Yuri. "You know, a lot of the best ideas come at the oddest times. Off moments."

"There is always a certain price," said Kovalyov. "Now is the time for a certain frankness, Yuri Trofimovich. Do you think that you would be able to render the project the fullest of your abilities in the current situation?"

"I'll be frank, too. The new regulations will hamper my work. The software and the hostel are fine, but using the local population has advantages. People are more relaxed in their own environment. Travel produces stress, disorientation. I have no idea how that will affect things here."

"But once you are satisfied that you are able to synthesize whatever it is successfully, the need for subjects will more or less drop away, won't it?"

"It will."

"Certain staff changes will have to be made. Yakutina, for example, will have to be transferred out. If there is any further photography work to be done, inform me ahead of time and I will arrange for a cameraman."

"And Andrusha?"

"Andrusha will be given work in another department. He's a very nice young man, your friend Andrusha, but somehow he doesn't smell quite right to me."

"I never like changing horses in mid-stream," said Yuri, after a moment's pause.

"In general, that is a sound principle. But no one is indispensable—cameramen are not, security officers are not, and neither are project coordinators themselves."

"Yes, that's true, no one is indispensable."

"Now, with our continuing frankness, Yuri Trofimovich, one last question. I said that this project is moving toward a phase in which security is as important as hard work. We have passed the point of needing, say, Farb's genius at original ideas, or yours at implementing them. What we need now is a man who can both finish things up and who understands that security is not an old man's obsession but a shield that keeps the arrows from your throat."

Yuri didn't understand the game. Clearly, Kovalyov wanted a declaration of loyalty from him, a declaration offered face to face so that he could read Yuri like a Geiger counter. But is that what he really was after? Either they had his scent or they didn't. If they did, why waste time on all this nonsense? Kovalyov should be shouting by now. It could only mean that they knew nothing of any substance.

"I must say," began Yuri, "that I think you have misunderstood my objections to the new security regulations. To my mind, a strong Soviet science means a strong Soviet Union. But too much security sometimes means that we lose time in implementing the discoveries made in the West."

"It is too bad that you weren't old enough to serve in the war, Yuri Trofimovich. Then you would have had a clearer idea of the West. Underneath it all, the West is Napoleon, Hitler."

Kovalyov paused, extending it for maximum effect, and then nudged the passbook across his desk toward Yuri.

"This will be your passbook, Yuri Trofimovich. Report to Room 308 for a new photo. Since we've already used a good deal of your valuable time, I won't require you to return here for a stamp; that would be the normal procedure, but I'll stamp yours right now."

"I appreciate it," said Yuri, watching Kovalyov press the little stamp hard against the stamp pad. He had survived.

Just as the passbook was in Yuri's hands, Kovalyov looked up and said, "Oh yes, there is one other thing."

"Yes?"

"Security again. Tomorrow a commission will arrive

here from Moscow. They'll be checking all the computer entries, readouts, log books. There have been some disturbing rumors lately—people fiddling with data, that sort of thing. Probably nothing. In any case, they'll be working through the weekend and finish up sometime late Monday or early Tuesday. So, in the meantime, Yuri Trofimovich, I must ask that you confine your work to the laboratory."

14   "Your cousin own this one, too?"

Solly asked Yanopolis
as they entered the pizza parlor, which had a faded, framed
review in the front window.

"Not yet," answered Yanopolis with a certain melancholy pride.

They decided to split a plain cheese. Yanopolis went to
call in.

As the waiter set their drinks down, two cans of orange
soda and two plastic cups full of crushed ice, Solly's attention
fixed on the young waiter's forearms, which reminded him
of his father's. Solly remembered watching his father shave,
rinsing his razor in the sink, the muscles playing under the
freckled skin of his forearms as he adjusted the faucets. Solly
could remember practically everything about his father, how

he moved, how he dressed, the exact color of the skin on his arms, but all Solly's memories were silent. He could remember things that his father had said, such as the time he had put his hand on Solly's head and said to another man, with a look of warm sorrow, "This is my little Kaddish-sayer." He could remember the words but not the voice, and lately that had been driving him crazy. He tried not to think of it, but sometimes he couldn't help it, and then that blank silence made him want to get violent.

The pizza arrived, followed a few seconds later by Yanopolis.

"Anything?" asked Solly, wiggling out a wedge.

"There's a couple of developments."

"For instance," said Solly, exhaling his words to cool the mouthful of hot pizza.

"The lab's done bleaching the blood out of the letter that was in Farb's pocket. So now somebody could read it except for the hole where the bullet went through."

"How many words could that be? So, go call the translator."

"I already did," said Yanopolis, proud of himself.

"And?"

"Just his answering machine."

"All right, so we'll swing by the lab and then go by his place. Is that it?"

"No, there was another thing, too. The other thing was that a charge came in on Farb's Visa card. A sweater."

"It was bought after?"

"Yuh."

"How much?"

"Must have been under fifty. They don't call in if it's under fifty."

"How about the size?"

"Size?"

"Sweater size. Small, medium, large."

"I didn't ask."

"I'd be curious if it was a small. This pizza is horrible. Try it."

"It's horrible, I should try it?"

"No offense, but personally I liked it better when the Italians made the pizza."

"My cousin's places are good. Next time we're in the neighborhood, we'll stop by."

"Naturally, the sister doesn't want the brother murdered so some Puerto Rican can have a new sweater."

"You're right," said Yanopolis, "the cheese is like rubber."

"I'll tell you something about cases like this one. It's like looking for an apartment. You do all the right things, you look in the paper, you go from one place to another, you do everything you're supposed to—and nothing happens. Then, when it looks like you're never going to get to move, somebody calls you up out of nowhere with two bedrooms, heat included."

"The dough is like cardboard."

"Save your drink to the end, to wash the taste out."

"OK, Yanopolis, question time," said Solly an hour later, at the counter of a Chock Full o' Nuts as their coffees came.

Yanopolis looked worried.

"Don't get worried," said Solly. "We were in there with Aronow about ten minutes. I want to know what you noticed."

"One thing I did notice was the way you put the envelope with the letters down on his side of the desk so that it would be harder for him to say no."

"There's hope for you yet. That was a little trick, plus homework. Everything was all written on the envelope. If I had to start writing things on the envelope there, that wouldn't have been good. So when the moment came and I wanted to say something about getting in touch with the sister if he had to for any reason, I could pull out the envelope and say, Here's her number."

"Did you think he wasn't going to want to do it?"

"It was just in case. I didn't want to waste time looking for another translator, especially since I don't think there's anything to this. I wouldn't say a hundred percent, but I'm just about sure nothing's going to happen with this one. So make it a learning experience, Yanopolis; that way, if it's a waste it won't be a total waste."

"I also noticed that he got a little pissed because you knew what his usual rate was."

"That was homework, too. I hate to waste money—you feel like a jerk wasting money, even if it isn't yours. So, what else did you see in there?"

Yanopolis looked away for a second into his memory.

"Well, I could see that you were very smooth and polite, the way you acted with him. You made that look easy, but I know it's not easy."

"Well, when you go in to see a guy like that, you don't

want to make him nervous, and you want to let him know you're sorry to be bothering him because of course you know he wasn't sitting there hoping the police would come by and ask him to do a little work at less than his usual price. How about the guy—what can you tell me about the guy?"

"Well, he was about five nine, a hundred and, I don't know, seventy pounds, gray at the side of his hair and beard, light-colored eyes—what would you call them—hazel."

"Where do you think he was from?"

"I didn't hear any accent."

"I thought I caught one of those Harvard Yard *a*'s."

"Now that you mention it."

"You see, that tells you something, too, because right away I know the guy is a Jew. How do I know that? I don't know. But Jews have a special thing, they can always tell when there are other Jews, and they can always tell what kind of a Jew the guy is. I'm not too sure about this one. I mean, would you say he was a nice guy?"

"He seemed like a pretty nice guy."

"That's true, he seemed like a nice guy, but I'm not so sure. And I'll tell you why. Because the most important thing for him was to let me know how brilliant he was, which, by the way, I didn't appreciate too much. It was the way he told us that the letters didn't really have to be translated—he could just read them and tell us if they were worth translating, and that would be quicker and cheaper. He was right, but I don't care about that, I care about the way he said it. Are you following me? But then I say to myself, Right, I thought I heard that Harvard Yard *a*, and so that has to mean that the guy's a Boston Jew, and that explains a lot to me about why he's acting the way he is. You see, up there, they never had too many Jews like in New York, so they were always like a fort without enough soldiers in it. You got to know how to pick up those little things about people, everything; sometimes something like that comes in handy, those little things make the difference. You wouldn't think so, but they do."

"You think he was queer?"

"No. A little strange, maybe. The thing you got to learn better is how to talk to people. You got to learn how to talk to each person the way that person has to be talked to; that's how you get the most out of it. If you look around, what do you see? People talking to each other. Look around this place; if there's two people together, they're talking. Everything is mostly talking, Yanopolis—talking, homework, and a couple of tricks."

"Talking, homework, and a couple of tricks," repeated Yanopolis dutifully.

"So, did you learn anything?"

"I did, I really did."

"Good. So then you pay for the coffees and let's go."

15 Moscow's connoisseurs of rumor

declared that the one concerning Evgeny Shar's imminent forcible exile was, in all probability, true. In part, this reaction came from old, honed instincts, which did not require reasons or proofs but could simply tell by a rumor's vitality, its resonance, how much reality it contained. Still, proofs could be offered, and were. Shar's works were well known in the West, where he had even become something of a cause célèbre, and the Soviet government was under pressure to do something about him. One variation or another of forcible exile had been the means used most frequently in recent times to deal with such problems. And there were other, supporting rumors—that Shar had been defiant in the camp and was frequently placed in solitary was more than rumor, for there were reports from people who had been with him in the camp and h... been released. It was also being said that someone ha... nessed Shar being driven under guard to Moscow. The prin... cipal rumor had a certain ubiquity about it, and had already been so thoroughly accepted that people no longer simply repeated it or asked if it had any basis, but were now more interested in speculating on future developments. When would he be exiled? To what country? What country would he choose to live in? Switzerland? Germany? America?

As is rarely the case with rumors, this one was entirely true. That had been seen to by the appropriate departments, which made sure that, of the prisoners released ahead of Shar, some would be sure to talk, and that the rumor itself was kept alive and developed at the Writers' Union, the Gorky Institute of World Literature, Peredelkino, and elsewhere. It had not taken long for those rumors to reach the ears of the better-connected foreign journalists, and notices had already started appearing in the foreign press. There was yet another advantage to all this: those who were known to have been the first to spread the information would now be considered reliable sources, for, of course, events would soon prove them correct.

Shar was in a special section of Lubyanka prison in Moscow, where he was improving his English and putting the finishing touches on his poem, which would soon make its way into the world of *samizdat* and *tamizdat*. And so Vinias was feeling especially satisfied with himself, and, as if to prove that fortune were smiling on him, his knee had not given him any problems for nearly two weeks. Perhaps the

...een receiving from the bioenergetic healer
... The man did have remarkable hands; they
...around his knee. And the report on the New
...ad also been more than satisfactory. The case
...ated as what, to all appearances, it was and
... already back in Soviet Armenia, which was a
bit outside the New York police's jurisdiction. The only
questionable aspect had been the witnesses. He knew that,
strictly speaking, he should not have included that detail: it
was the obvious point at which something could go wrong.
But he had been convinced that witnesses were the best
disguise. Their absence would have made for a certain void
that would invite speculation, and that, he had decided,
would be worse.

Details could be well chosen or ill chosen, but that was
not what Vinias feared. There were always the slippery random factors, a door sticking, a watch battery dying, a sneeze.
But there was nothing you could do about life's perverse
quirks except to be aware that they could happen. No, what
Vinias feared was the god of pure malevolence. Like a great
snake that slept on a dry rock but was aware of everything
that went by, the spirit Vinias feared was at the heart of
existence could, like death, strike at any moment, but was
worse than death, because it preferred to ruin its victims
rather than annihilate them. There was also something Vinias
feared in himself, a certain taste for disgrace, as if all his
successes were only the buildup to the disgrace he had been
so avidly desiring all along, the disgrace he had so brilliantly
constructed for himself. He did not believe this of himself,

but he feared it as a possibility because there was no denying it was there in himself like any other taste or desire. But it could be contained and controlled like any other taste or desire.

What Vinias could not control was his immediate superior, Malanov. Stupid Malanov, still worrying about that stupid new Finnish table of his, still worrying about leaks from the psipharm unit, which had gone from obscurity to importance with unusual speed. It had been Malanov's idea that Shar make some casual contact with Raisa Farb, who would, no doubt, be honored to meet the hero-poet and would have every reason to trust him. Shar could sniff her out. It made a certain sense, of course, but Vinias had been absolutely opposed to the idea: "Why confuse the issue? Shar is too important!"

"I disagree," Malanov had answered. "I don't want to slight you or your work. Disinformation is very important, an art. But it is not an end in itself; you must never forget that. In the end it is only a smoke screen to cover the real job, which is getting the goods. In the end, when the smoke clears, all that matters is who's got what."

Vinias leaned forward in his seat and looked out the rear window of the Zhil that was taking him to Lubyanka for a last meeting with Shar. He was not looking for anything special, or even to see how far they still had to go, but he needed to observe the world for a second, the color of the sky, buildings, cars, people, trees. A little light snow was falling. People hurried about their business. He leaned back.

Tomorrow morning at five o'clock, Shar would be spirited from Lubyanka to Sheremetyevo airport and flown to Frankfurt, Germany. The press campaign against him had already been prepared. Vinias had liked the "bacteriological" line taken in the article written for *Literaturnaya Gazeta:* it was a basic life response for healthy organisms to expel foreign bodies. And Shar and his poetry were foreign to the Soviet organism; those dreams of a Christian Russia poisoned the will, and clouded the mind with dangerous illusions. Like the drugs they were so fond of in the West. But Soviet society was not going to stand idly by and watch its children be drugged with poems about a Christ child born in the Warsaw ghetto who flees to Russia after his parents are killed, grows up on a kolkhoz, and, in time, becomes a cosmonaut. In outer space he has a religious vision of a repentant and reborn Russia. No, that was not the sort of thing that children who had to master the real world of genetics and space and computer technology, not to mention politics and agriculture, needed to prepare them for life. The children must be protected.

Communication with Shar was excellent; that wasn't the problem. But there was still some problem with Shar that Vinias couldn't quite put his finger on. Was he worried because so much of what he had conceived, planned, and constructed now depended on Shar for its realization? The writer and the director can be as brilliant as they want, but it is the actor who goes out on stage. All actors had the strange, irritable vanity of those who are used, but Shar did not seem to suffer from that ailment. Didn't Shar harbor any resentment against his fate, against being the one who is told not only what to do, but who to be? Shar had had to spend time in a labor camp, although his frequent trips to solitary had been designed both to further his reputation as a rebel and to provide him with a little ease and comfort in what had been very hard service. Shar had been struck violently that last time; there was still a discoloration around his left eye. No one in their day and age could be so loyal to the Soviet Union as to suffer all that gladly. This wasn't the Revolution, this wasn't the early twenties. Well, then, what was it that kept Shar so apparently content? Was he just biding his time to be sent to the West, where he would defect, rid himself of an identity he had come to hate, and reveal himself as the agent of Vinias's disgrace? That was not out of the question, because, Vinias realized as they pulled in, he could not really fathom why Shar did any of it and so could not predict what he might ever do. And Vinias took that fear with him from the car into the large ocher building on Dzerzhinsky Square.

"Twenty more," said Shar by way of greeting, his feet hooked under the bureau, performing his sit-ups rapidly with a hard side-to-side twist.

Vinias smiled vaguely and nodded.

Shar watched Vinias walk by, his view of him chopped by the fast corkscrew sit-ups. Vinias wasn't limping. Vinias looked worried, a cloud around his forehead. Something was going on.

"Eighteen, nineteen, twenty."

Shar hopped to his feet, his hair mussed, a light sweat on

his upper body, beaming like a strong young son insulting his father with the fact of his vigor, a form of love.

"I have beer," said Shar, wiping his chest with a towel, which he then threw in the corner. "Heineken, Kirin, or Zhiguli?"

"Kirin."

Shar pulled on a light-blue T-shirt and walked to the small American-made refrigerator in the corner.

"How is it that our enemies make such good beer?" asked Vinias, accepting the bottle without quite looking at Shar. Now he knew what he was afraid of—what he might see on Shar's face when he told him of the addendum to his assignment.

"By mistake the Americans bombed them into the Space Age," said Shar, looking to see if Vinias was going to laugh.

Vinias laughed. "Yes, those wonderful capitalist bombs."

"The knee is better?"

"Much better, thanks."

"I noticed you weren't limping."

"I've been receiving treatments from a healer, would you believe it. Something makes his hands red-hot."

Vinias took a swig of his beer. He didn't like it that Shar had reminded him of his weak knee. Didn't Shar have any real sense of what had been done for him?

"Your eye looks almost back to normal," said Vinias, to remind Shar that he, too, was physically vulnerable, and saw Shar wince involuntarily.

"Yes, the cameras may not even pick it up."

"But still, a little real blood goes a long way. A report

of that beating has already reached the French press and will be published in a day or two. There's a very nice line in it about the poet standing there bloody but unbowed. An old cliché, but one that works if the blood is real."

"I realize that."

"Good."

"By the way, while we're on the subject, here are your sleeping pills. A hundred. And we'll keep you supplied. But you should really try to break the habit."

"Some day I will," said Shar lazily, without conviction.

"The pharmacist was very concerned; he thought they were for me. He said they were very strong."

"Very strong," said Shar. "I was told that five could be fatal."

"So, limit yourself to four," said Vinias with an uneasy chuckle.

"Don't worry."

"I worry. I worry about you in the West. I know you've read about it and seen movies and all that, but it's different once you get there. I was there quite a while myself. It will tempt you, Evgeny. It tempted me. It can intoxicate you with possibilities, but they're all illusions, and I'll tell you why: because you're just the same as me, Evgeny. The only place for people like us is right here, doing what we're doing; otherwise we'd just become third-rate versions of ourselves. The one thing we need, the West can never offer us. The most important thing in life is to occupy the exact position you were born to occupy, or you feel forever at sea."

Shar smiled at the length and the sincerity of the lecture.

"Don't worry about me. I'll be coming home."

As Vinias smiled back at Shar, he realized that their eyes had still not met directly.

"And the poem?" asked Vinias.

"I'm almost done copying it down. I've made a few changes, nothing very significant."

"You left in the part about Walt Whitman?"

"Yes."

"Good. The Americans will like that. They'll probably write articles saying how ashamed they are that a Soviet poet's faith in freedom was kept alive by lines from *Leaves of Grass,* when Americans themselves barely know the book. They really have no poets anyway, the Americans. They have people who have written good poetry, but you really can't be much of a poet if nobody's listening."

"Not like here."

"Not like here, is right. You used to fill stadiums, but that was of course before bourgeois propaganda filled your head with all those slanderous anti-Soviet notions that have gotten you in such trouble."

Shar laughed.

Now, sensing that the time was right, Vinias said, "There is one other thing, Evgeny."

"I'm being sent back to the camp," joked Shar, taking a slug of beer to resist the urge to look up: he knew that Vinias was now going to tell him the most important thing.

"Hardly. I'll leave you some material to read on this, but what it comes down to is that one of our research units seemed to be coming up with some results. The project head had a friend in New York, a Jew who emigrated, who had been involved in everything from the start. There was a concern about leakage. But then, fortunately, the émigré fell victim to a street crime in New York, which cost him his life."

Vinias paused so that Shar would have a moment to realize not only that the street crime had been one of his little dramas but also that a similar scene could be written up for him.

"Now the question is: were we just being a little overcautious, or was there actually something going on?"

"And you'd like me to sniff around a little?"

"No more than that. Remember this, only to the degree that it does not interfere with your main task. You'll have a contact in New York named Vaska, a cab driver; he knows the city very well. Anything you have, you pass on to him."

Without quite meaning to, Vinias found himself looking up at Shar at that moment, and he suddenly realized this was a mistake, too late to correct. Now he knew that it wasn't what he would see on Shar's face that had frightened him but what Shar would see on his.

Shar, however, had chosen that moment to take a long pull on his beer, and when Vinias caught his eye the expression on Shar's face became apologetic for having slipped into pleasure at a moment like that, but what could you expect from someone who was still green and had not seen the world?

"Don't worry. I understand the priorities. The émigré— was he married?"

"No, he lived with his sister. You can read it all."

"Is there a lot of material?"

"A fair amount."

"Should I stop working on the poem to read it?" asked Shar, very curious to hear the answer to that practical question.

Vinias paused, then answered almost curtly. "Of course. The poem is already in your head. You can finish it in Germany. You'll be there tomorrow," said Vinias with a hint of wonder in his voice.

"So, it looks like I have work to do."

"Yes, I'll leave you now."

"Thank you for everything, Anton. Believe me, I know what you've given me."

Vinias nodded, suddenly relaxed and relieved. Or had Shar just played him like an old tune from start to finish?

16   "I am listening,"

said the woman's voice in Russian.
"Is this Raisa Farb?" said David in English.

"It is," she said, switching to English, the voice becoming
a bit less certain of itself.

"This is David Aronow."

"David Aronow who is translating Irina Petrovskaya's
memoirs?"

"Yes. I would like to have a little talk with you."

"You have read the letters?"

"Yes."

"When?"

"Yesterday."

"Yesterday, I see."

"They're . . ."

"I don't want to go into details on the phone, Mr. Aronow."

"I can come out there."

"No."

"Let's meet in the city, then."

"Fine. I will pick you up in one hour. Where do you live?"

"Fourth Avenue, between Tenth and Eleventh. East side of the street. A big yellow-brick building. It's a short block, and mine is the only building on that side."

"One hour."

"I'll be out front."

"My car is a 1973 Oldsmobile. Dark blue."

"See you."

"Yes, see you, Mr. Aronow."

As soon as he hung up the phone, he gave his full attention to his memory of her voice, wanting to go through it again while it was still fresh in his mind. He was going to ask her for something, and there was only one answer he wanted from her, so it paid to know as much as he could about who he'd be talking to in an hour.

He had felt the grief under the surface of the words and in the rawness of her throat. It was the voice of a strong woman. Her "Mr. Aronow" was forcefully correct. And she had asked him a question he had not been prepared for—"When?" But that had not been the dry intelligence that lives on the body like a parasite on the flank of a good-natured host. That had been a flash of vital intelligence, even though it was also clear from her tone and diction that she was a member of the intellectual class. There was the usual well-founded dash of paranoia, but that didn't tell him enough. There was something else he needed to know: who she really was.

And which language should he use with her? It would be his lead. To speak your own language gave you power; to speak someone else's always put you at the disadvantage. But that was also delicate, for if he put her too much at a disadvantage she might feel threatened and then become defensive. It might be smarter to speak Russian, because then she would feel more in control and at ease. But then, sick of conniving, he decided to decide on the spot.

He watched the Oldsmobile pull up, feeling that he had been seen and evaluated through the dusty windshield that reflected the sodium yellow of the streetlights. He waved in what he knew was unnecessary acknowledgment and started toward the little corridor between two sets of bumpers. He glimpsed her face through the murky window of the passenger door as she nodded, her hair black and Judaic, flecks of red lipstick on hard white teeth.

Now, inside the car, he saw her more clearly. The face slightly chunky but attractive in the way that chunky jewelry can be attractive. The eyes were too dark a brown to see into. A touch of the steppes in their shape.

"Dobry vyecher," he said.

"Dobry vyecher, but we should speak English," she said.

"All right."

"Let's go for a drive," she said with a glance at the rearview mirror, pulling smoothly into the traffic, which was light and fast.

He watched her maneuver in the traffic, saw that she enjoyed driving, enjoyed knowing she was good at it. She had already decided the language and the itinerary, he thought. He knew the type—imperious through an excess of energy; submissive with men, but with a submissiveness so passionate it was like an undertow.

"You haven't read the letters?" he asked.

"No."

"I brought them with me."

"I don't want to hear them."

"I understand."

"But I do want to know what is in them."

"All right."

"By the way, have you delivered your translation to Mr. Altheim yet?"

"No, I wanted to speak with you first."

"I see."

What did she see? he wondered, noticing that they were heading for the West Side Highway.

"The man who was writing to your brother . . ."

"His name was Yuri. Yuri Trofimovich."

"He signed the letters Vanka–Vstanka."

"That was what Yasha called him. You know what that means?"

"It's a kind of a doll that you knock down and it stands back up. We have something like them, too."

"That was Yasha's nickname for him, because once Yuri got an idea he would never stop until he saw if it worked or not. Yasha liked to have ideas, but he hated the day-to-day drudgery. That's why they were such a good combination, those two. A terrific combination that got my brother killed!"

He paused for a moment to let the passionate, grieving sarcasm of her outburst subside.

"Apparently your brother had a series of ideas, and apparently Yuri has come up with some results. As I understand it, they started doing research on the physiology of ESP, what they call psi over there. They found some unusual endocrine traces during peak psi experiences. People working in gerontology found similar endocrine traces in people living past a hundred. Yuri began experimenting with synthesizing the two, varying the mixture, until he finally came up with something that was adding forty percent to the life span of laboratory animals and making them more intelligent as well. Oh yes, and the serum is nicknamed Stolat, because if it works on people we'll all live a hundred years."

Now they were on the West Side Highway, approaching the George Washington Bridge's tons of steel, air, and lights.

"I can probably figure out the rest," she said. "Yuri, of course, decided that he couldn't give this discovery to the Soviet Union—that might mean the end, the great Soviet victory. It's one thing to love Russia, another thing to help make a Soviet world. So, he decided to smuggle out his findings, and so, of course, he picked my brother, because he trusted him and because he was part of the whole thing from the beginning. His only mistake was to forget that they would know just how he'd think, who he'd trust, who he'd send those letters to. And so they killed my brother, Mr. Aronow, either because they already knew, or because they weren't sure and didn't want to have to worry about it. That's what I tried to explain to that policeman."

"If that's true, then why didn't the killer take the letter from your brother?"

"Maybe he didn't know, maybe there wasn't time. Besides, they make mistakes, too."

"There's one other point."

"Yes?"

"They're shipping out all the information on a piece of tail leader."

"Tail leader?"

"A tail leader is a strip of something they put at the end of a film so that it goes through the projector."

"That sounds like something Andrusha would have dreamed up."

"Who's Andrusha?"

"Doesn't matter."

"Anyway, the information is on the tail leader, which apparently the Soviets will be shipping out themselves, because it's coming here for the New York Film Festival on a film called *Apples of Ryazan.* That's the basic story."

As they pulled onto the Cross Bronx Expressway, she said, "I live in the Bronx; not the famous burned-out part, just the regular part."

It didn't seem to be a statement that required any response. He had started to grow a bit worried about her, about getting what he wanted from her. She could be so definite and then suddenly list with some irrational gust, and neither quality appeared to be in his favor. Except that he had known from the moment he had entered her car that she was one of the women who would by nature want to make him happy.

"And now, Mr. Aronow," she said, "perhaps you would like to tell me your idea."

"How do you know I have an idea?"

"For two reasons—no, three. First, when I saw you standing there on the sidewalk and when you got into the car, there was something about you that reminded me of my brother."

"And the second reason?"

"And the second reason is that you haven't sent your translation to Mr. Altheim yet."

"Good thinking."

"Thank you. And the third is that you waited a day to call me."

"You're doing so well so far, maybe you want to tell me what you think my idea is?"

"Well, if my brother was an American, his idea would have been to retrieve the film, check the data, and then announce the greatest discovery since the splitting of the atom at some press conference at the United Nations."

David smiled.

"Was I right?"

"No. Fifteen years ago that would have seemed a good

idea to me, too. I still believed in Mankind and the World fifteen years ago, Civilization. I still care about them, of course, but not like before, not enough that it matters."

"Well, I would say that that's a good sign, Mr. Aronow. Because the idealists cause too many deaths. The world was bad enough when it was just the brutes who did the killings, but then the idealists joined in. And there's the kind like Yuri, who get people killed without even knowing it. Yuri, who forgot that if he had found this thing forty years ago, Stalin would still be alive today. Dunderheaded Yuri Trofimovich, he's probably in a camp already!"

"I'll tell you my idea," said David. "I think Yuri was right. Better that the Americans have it than the Soviets, if it works. But that's not the problem, that's not the interesting part. I mean, there's the question of who gets it. Do you give it to prisoners serving life, so they can be punished for another thirty years? Do you give it to welfare mothers with eleven children? Do you give it to the retarded, the crippled, the blind? And if you don't give it to everyone, then who decides who gets it? But if everybody knows about it and not everybody's getting it, there're going to be other problems too, so the first smart decision is to keep quiet about the whole thing. For a long time, probably. And what does that mean in practice? It means there're going to be some people who are out riding horseback and making love in the afternoon when they're eighty, and I'm going to be dead or getting my breakfast through a tube in my arm. And to make things even worse, I'm going to know what I'm missing. *You're* going to know."

"Interesting so far. And so?"

"You know what checks and balances are?"

"No."

"You better learn it before you apply for citizenship," he said, slightly ashamed of himself for prodding what had to be a point of weakness with her. "That's how the American system of government works. Its different parts are supposed to counteract each other so that no individual part becomes too strong."

"I knew that," she said. "I just forgot how it was called."

"So, my idea is really very modest, and in the best American tradition. I just want to create a little check and balance of my own. Yes, I do want to pick up the film, and I have a friend in Boston who can deal with the technical and scientific end of things. We'll keep a few copies, then we'll call Information and find out the FBI's number and turn it back over like good citizens. But we'll have leverage; they won't be able to cut us out, and if the thing works, we'll collect our fee—thirty extra years of life."

"I don't want thirty extra years of this life."

For a moment he could think of no answer.

"But the only alternative is dying, and dying is no good."

"My life has not been so very wonderful, Mr. Aronow, that I would be attracted by the idea of prolonging it."

"Thirty years is more than ten thousand days. Ten thousand days."

"Ten thousand days without love is a horrible prospect to me, Mr. Aronow. Yasha was the last person in the world I loved. Now there is no one. Why should I get excited?"

she said, braking the car and pulling over to the corner of a suburban street where the large dark brick houses looked like banks closed for the night.

"I respect your grief," he said, "but life is all we have now, the only real value we have left. And, for now at least, the best we can do is just get more. And there are times that are so perfect, like eating outside on a summer evening as the stars are coming out."

She smiled at him, softly, a little sadly, but not without her pleasure.

"Do you know where we are?" she asked.

"No."

"Riverdale."

"Riverdale."

"And you see that gate?"

"I see it."

"That's the gate to the Soviet compound. They bus them back out here every day, the UN people, the consulate people. They bus them back out by eleven o'clock each night so they won't get contaminated by America. But that's not the important thing. The important thing is what goes on in there. They monitor telephone conversations from in there; espionage operations are carried out from there. I am certain the compound played some role in my brother's death, Mr. Aronow. I'll tell you something else. The night my brother was killed, I came out here. I parked right here, hoping that some Soviet big shot might be returning late. I was going to ram his car. I waited two hours, but no one came by. My luck is never very good."

Her utter seriousness caused a ripple of fear in him.

"I won't say this again. Your idea is interesting and intelligent, but it's a bad idea, Mr. Aronow, a dangerous idea."

He smiled, nodding his head slightly. He knew how women agreed.

17 Yuri Trofimovich

took his daughter, Olya, up onto his lap, rejoicing in the lightness of her bones. He smiled down at her little red leather sandals, beige knit leggings, and checked dress, the pale ribbon coming loose in her lightbrown hair. She played with his beard as she always did when first on his lap, winding little ringlets around her finger or nosing the blind, pink worm of a finger through the thickest parts, where there were tiny tunnels and tiny chambers where tiny creatures she called bearders lived.

When life had still been normal—had their life there ever been normal?—when things had still been more normal than they were now, he had often regretted having only one child, even though, with all the running that had to be done simply to stay alive, one had sometimes seemed like a lot. But now he knew that it was of course better. He told himself not to remember that this was their good-bye; it would be better for both of them if it were just like any other night.

"Papa, tell me more about Boba and the planet."

"All right, let me remember what happened. Boba the cosmonaut had landed on the planet. . . ."

"Sladkoe—don't you remember?" Olya squirmed on his lap.

"Oh, of course, I'm sorry. The planet Sladkoe. And so Boba made his way across the North Pole, which was all made of vanilla ice cream, and all the penguins had vanilla-ice-cream restaurants where they served ice-cream borscht and ice-cream cutlets, and if anybody said that everything tasted like vanilla ice cream, the penguins would all get very angry and start squawking and slapping their flippers against their sides, which is what penguins do when they are very angry. And so Boba had vanilla-ice-cream borscht and a vanilla-ice-cream cutlet. Then Boba decided that he would like some dessert. He was hoping that they might have something special for dessert, thinking that maybe they did everything backward there and gave you meat and vegetables for dessert. 'What do you have for dessert?' Boba asked the penguin-waiter. 'Today,' said the penguin-waiter, standing at attention, 'we have ice cream.' 'Do you have any borscht-flavored ice cream?' asked Boba. 'Ha ha, what a funny idea,' laughed the waiter. 'You just had borscht. Why would you want it again?'

" 'Oh, oh,' thought Boba. 'Well, I'll take ice cream.'

" 'Very good, sir,' said the penguin-waiter. 'What flavor would you like?'

" 'What flavors do you have?'

" 'We have vanillocolate, vanillberry, and vanillerbert.'

" 'I'll try vanillocolate,' said Boba.

"A minute later, the penguin-waiter skated out with a dish of vanilla ice cream.

" 'But that's vanilla!' said Boba.

" 'Are you trying to hurt my feelings?' said the penguin-waiter, and began flapping his flippers against his side. Then all the other waiters in the restaurant began flapping their flippers, too, because penguins, and especially penguin-waiters, are very sensitive, and if you hurt one's feelings they all get excited. And so . . .' "

He looked down at her face, which was turned up to his, her eyes giving his a perfect welcome.

"And so Boba couldn't stand all the noise, and he ran out of the restaurant and walked and walked and walked"—he knew she always wondered how many times he would say it, twice, three times, and sometimes, but only once in a very great while, even four times—"until he came to a mountain, not a regular mountain but a volcano mountain, with a lake on top of it. Boba walked up to the top of the mountain.

"When Boba was at the top of the mountain, he saw that the water in the lake was boiling and bubbling from the fire of the volcano under it. Then he saw an old woman throwing big bales of something that looked like grass into the bubbling water. Boba called across the lake to her: 'What are you doing, old woman?'

"The old woman looked up and said, 'Making tea.'"

"Olya, come to bed, right this minute," came Marina's voice from the other room.

"Papa didn't tell me about Boba having his tea."

"He'll tell you tomorrow. Now, Olya."

She kissed Yuri quickly, damply, on the cheek and slid off his lap before he could give her a hug.

"Oh, I forgot," she said, and came back to him for his good-night hug.

"Olya!" called her mother.

At the doorway, Olya looked over her shoulder and said, "Papa, look." And then she went off into the next room slapping her sides like an angry penguin.

But as soon as she was gone, the moment of self-forgetting was gone as well, and, like a man who had stopped to admire the evening sky while taking out the trash only to remember that he had been diagnosed as suffering from a terminal illness, Yuri came crashing back into the reality of his own situation, which he himself had diagnosed as terminal. He sank back in his chair and took a sip of his tea, now cold. He turned on the radio to blot out his thoughts, to buy another five minutes of peace, but the radio only irritated him with its static and self-importance, and he switched it right back off. There wasn't much time left; he had better be clear and cold with himself.

The film had been shipped; that had been confirmed. The five-man control commission had arrived late on Friday and had begun work at once. He hadn't been summoned in on Monday, because the commission was running a little late, but now it was only a matter of a very short time before they realized that the data had been purposely scrambled, and who was responsible. After that, everything would be quite automatic.

"You're spoiling her with those stories," said Marina on her way to the kitchen, her face pale and harried. "Now all she thinks about is ice cream and candy."

"This is the time for that," said Yuri Trofimovich very softly; he knew he had been heard, even though she didn't answer.

Then, aware of himself in his chair and hearing the water jet out of the faucet in the kitchen, he felt the true horror of it hit him, soaking the roots of his hair and causing the blood to fall away from his mind. He would never see Olya again, not for a billion years; he would never hear water come out of a faucet again. But it was an unavoidable step, produced by all the other steps he had taken, a staircase that led nowhere, a staircase whose steps disappeared behind you. Only he knew what had been done to cripple the information, only he could reconstruct the experiments quickly, and that meant that he was the only person who could undo what he himself had done. If he walked in tomorrow and confessed everything, how would that make things any better? He would be a self-confessed traitor, and his wife would be the wife of one and his daughter the daughter of one, and their lives would be ruined, and he would merely be forced into working for them again, for he knew he could resist their direct pressures but even the merest threat against Olya would be more than he could bear. And since she was the obvious point of his weakness, it was better that she have no father.

The tiny phial of 881 (he always preferred that name to Stolat) had been in his possession for a week now, a dose perfectly gradated to take the life of a man of his weight and metabolic type in under ten minutes. For a time he had hesitated between three choices—at work, in the woods, or at home. Part of him had so much wanted to die at home, to have home be the last thing he saw and felt, and not to have to go out into nature or the world, which, whatever they were, were not home. It would be death by cardiac arrest, but they would of course perform an autopsy and find the traces of it in his blood. Better that Marina get a phone call from outside, hear the terrible news that way, than find him slumped in his chair or be unable to wake him in the morning. No, it had only been a final, fearful selfishness on his part to want to die at home. It was supposed to have been that night, but now he knew he couldn't. So, tomorrow. He would either get off the trolley in the birch woods and go for a walk, or take it while at work, having first smuggled it back into the wing, another minor irony in a great web of them.

Now that this was at least decided, it somehow felt a little odd to know that he would not be dead in the morning—in the early morning, at least. He took down a volume of Pushkin from his shelf and lovingly rubbed the brown cover with its gold-stamped profile of the poet. He fanned through the pages, feeling their faint breeze on his face, inhaling their special warehouse musk. He was forty-five, and Pushkin had died at thirty-seven, a fact he had remembered more than once with a strong sense of shame—to be older than Pushkin and to have done so little. He read through "October," which he had always loved for its beauty, but then turned to the poem "Whenever I wander the noisy streets," where Pushkin wonders which day will be the anniversary of his death and how that death will come to him. Finally, the poet accepts the inevitability of his death, his only request that young life play by his grave while indifferent nature shines with eternal beauty.

Yuri returned to the opening stanza.

> Whenever I wander the noisy streets,
> Or walk into a crowded church,
> Or sit among wild young men,
> I give myself to that fantasy.

Perhaps he could talk about that poem with Marina, somehow obliquely let her know.

He went into the kitchen. Marina handed him the dish towel, her face steamy, the corners of her lips twitching with the day's nervous exhaustion. After a minute of silence, he said, "I was just reading Pushkin's . . ."

"Yes, while I was doing the dishes. You could have at least come in and cleared the table. I worked all day, too, and I stood in line for the fish and I cooked it and I'm doing the dishes. The only poetry in our life is in the books, and the books can wait but the dishes can't."

He dried the dishes alongside her in silence, hoping to lose himself in the domestic ritual, but a dish slipped from her hand and clattered on their nerves. She cursed, pushing a wet lock of hair off her forehead.

They took that silence to bed with them: even though they had broken it to exchange a few practical sentences, it was still silence. For her it was just an ordinary night, an ordinary bad evening. When Yuri touched her back gently, inquisitively, she flinched away. A few minutes later he heard the soft, even sound of her breath in sleep, and his solitude was complete.

18 It was an ugly piece of paper.

David Aronow looked at paper all day, and this sheet looked worse than the stuff that came out of the Soviet Union. It had probably been run off on some overworked NYPD Xerox machine with soot in its ink supply. The word "interpreter" had been crossed out in ballpoint and replaced with the word "translator." Altheim had done that, telling him that "if anything happens and we go to court, you'll have to be sworn in, but for now this makes it official." A simple piece of paper with a dotted line where his signature would affirm that he had to the best of his ability provided a true and faithful account of the original.

The physical effort required to sign was no more than it took to scratch a minor itch between his shoulder blades. But he knew that no matter how he scrawled that signature, it would be his, forever recognizable as his; experts would have no problem agreeing that it was. The document would be filed in some ill-painted, bulging storeroom, would be microfilmed, and then eventually, after some officially determined period, destroyed to make room for other such documents, which in perhaps one case in five hundred thousand would prove useful.

But none of that mattered; none of that was the real point. The real point was that as soon as he put his name on that dotted line on that poorly Xeroxed sheet of paper, he would have made a little definite turn, a change of angle that would increase in time as the two lines forming that angle —that which had happened and that which had not—began to spread away from each other.

Was there any question of his not signing? he asked himself. Did he have to go through all that moral fandango just to end up where he knew he was going to end up anyway? He couldn't tell Altheim to hire another translator, explaining that he was sick or too busy. No, that would mean someone else would read the letters. And so, the only other choice was to translate the letters as if they contained only tedious political harangues and sign the paper that he had been faithful and true to the original. But that wasn't the only other choice. There was also the truth. As a last resort, you can always tell the truth.

And what would that mean? A handshake from Altheim, a check from the city for a hundred and twenty bucks that would probably take two and a half months to come, and back to the memoirs, the endless memoirs of people from countries where nothing ever worked out well.

How could the situation be so constricted, he wondered, that there could be no other choices?

The phone rang, and he was glad. Not that the piece of paper wouldn't still be on his desk when he hung up.

"Hi," said Karen. It was her special "Hi"—sexy in a lazy sort of way, funny, kidlike. "Working?"

"A little."

"The memoirs?"

"Are you my editor or Karen?"

"Both."

"That may be too much."

"It's because Irina called me today, worried about them. She's afraid she's going to die before she sees them in print, and that's all that's keeping her alive."

"Some Russians like to get excited," he said, remembering Raisa in the car, her skin sallowed by the streetlight, her hair Turkish black. There had been some transaction between them in those moments of silence.

"She *is* eighty-something."

"There's only a few chapters to go."

"So, what are you working on, then? Is it that thing from the police?"

"Yuh."

"What is it, anything?"

There it was. Sign, not sign, tell her, not tell her, he loves me, he loves me not.

"It's a headache from bad Xerox and a hundred and twenty bucks that'll come when you don't really need it."

Liking sarcasm for the same reason she liked hard liquor, she laughed at the remark.

And then her voice became quieter as she said, "David, let's see each other soon."

"An hour is soon."

When he hung up the phone, he was, as he had known he would be, alone in that room with the piece of paper that was still neither signed nor unsigned. Nothing was definite and final, he was still free to choose; the lie he had told Karen could still be absorbed or dissolved by the truth.

It was, as always, a choice of lives. That was serious business especially since the new life required lies and forgeries right from the start, not the best sign. But he already belonged to that life through desire, through Raisa, through the actions he had already taken. He loved Stolat, he worshipped it. It was not a god but it was close, a Holy Ghost of science come to make Annunciation of the Third Millenium.

To choose against it would be like turning down a chance to travel in space and behold the Earth. For what? For a few moral luxuries, a speck of happiness?

But then why did his hand hesitate? He knew why. Others would be dying and he would be living only because he possessed a certain scrap of knowledge. He would have been glad to feel the presence of a god who could inspire him with moral love, the strength to refuse to sign that paper, he would have been glad to sense in his flesh that the universe was not a cathedral of magnificent absence, and at that moment, in a burst of angry desperation, he gave that god one last chance to show himself.

Now, if there's anything, now!

19 Adelle Altheim looked

from the television to her husband and knew that if she spoke to him Solly might not even respond. He had eaten dinner with her as if he were sitting alone in some cafeteria. Now she was alone in front of the television, with someone else there, someone who looked like Solly.

She returned her eyes to the screen, where men in black masks were firing rifles into the air while bagpipes played and people wept in an Irish cemetery. As she reached for her cigarettes, there was a sudden pain in her right side, so sharp for a moment that she couldn't get her breath. Then it passed. She clicked open her cigarette case and slid out a cigarette, bending her head away to light it so as not to distract Solly. Maybe it was connected with work; maybe he had seen something terrible and he didn't want to talk about it with her because he was worried it would upset her too much, or maybe something wasn't going well at work, or maybe he himself had done something wrong. Or maybe, she suddenly realized, it had something to do with the Yahrzeit candle. She had come into the kitchen a few weeks back and found him staring at the Yahrzeit candle on the kitchen counter. At first she had thought he was looking for something to eat, but then she saw he was staring at the candle. "I should've lit candles too," he'd said, when he became aware of her presence, "but you can't just start after ten years." "Why not?" "No," he had said, and just shaken his head. She would bet that it had something to do with that, because his father's Yahrzeit was coming, November 11. Well, whatever it was, she'd get him out of it, or it out of him, when they had their usual coffee after the news. And she'd do it so well and so skillfully that he might not even notice it was happening or have the sense to thank her for doing it. But that was all right, too; she wasn't doing it to be thanked.

Two women began talking in the politest possible terms about personal hygiene, and Solly's attention, which had only been vaguely focused on the news, slipped away from the screen and back into himself. What did he care that there was nothing to the Farb case? Wasn't that what he had been saying from the start? So, then, why had he been pissed off when Aronow had called to say he was sending the translation over by messenger but wanted him to know that there was nothing unusual in the letters, just some grumbling about the injustices of the Soviet system.

He had called the sister when he had received the letters back from Aronow and said he was sorry and would she like copies of them. He had expected another tirade from her—that policemen were idiots, they didn't know what the Soviet Union was capable of, maybe there were more letters, maybe the letters were really some kind of code, some sort of cockamamy nonsense like that—but she had just sounded tired and indifferent and said, "Yes, please, send me the letters." So there wasn't going to be any more pressure from her, which was just as well, he supposed. Still, it was frustrating—dead ends always were—but at least it had turned out to be a short street.

He had read through the transcripts of the two witnesses again, fifteen pages of next to nothing because the two of them argued over everything: how tall the killer was, how many shots, what time it had happened. The only chance they had was that the prick who shot Farb would get himself caught doing something else.

People were being murdered every day, and how many of the killers were ever going to get caught and be punished? One out of ten, if you were lucky. That was his job, and lately he hadn't been doing it all that well. They were getting away left and right; people were killing other people and then going out for Chinese food and laughing at all the underpaid schmucks like him who were supposed to be doing something about it. The world had gone nuts. It used to be that the numbers racket was a serious crime, but now the government had taken it over. It used to be that abortion, prostitution, divorce were disgraces; now they were rights.

If he didn't get an ulcer before he retired, it would be the miracle of miracles.

Adelle returned to the living room with the little tray containing the coffees, the half-and-half, the sugar for him, the Sweet 'n Low for her.

"I went to the nursing home and saw Anna today," she said, knowing the important thing was to get a conversation going before you steered it around to what you wanted to know.

"Anna," he said, "how's Anna?"

"I'll tell you, Solly, she's a remarkable woman for eighty-seven. The life in her. If it wasn't for her problems with her eyes, she'd still be living by herself and baking and going visiting. But it's the eyes."

"The eyes."

Good. She had gotten two sentences out of him.

"You remember how she used to bake?"

"Nobody could cook like her. I remember when I was a kid, sometimes the women would ask me who the best cook was, and I'd say 'Anna' like if you asked me what color the sky was I'd say 'blue.' Sometimes they'd laugh, but sometimes they'd get a little angry too. They wanted me to say it was them."

"She asked for you."

"I'll go there with you. I'll go there with you one Sunday."

"She'd be happy to see you. She gets plenty of visitors, of course, but she likes to see the people she knew way back."

"She was tough too, Anna. I remember at the hospital

186

with my father, she was always there. Every day. I remember her grabbing people by the arm and saying, 'Get in there and say good-bye to Barnie, don't be so chickenhearted.' That's the expression she used, 'don't be so chickenhearted,' " said Solly, taking a slurp of coffee.

She was about to tell him not to slurp his coffee but restrained herself, thinking it would only get them off the track.

"The anniversary is coming up. Eleven years on the eleventh," said Adelle, who didn't need a Monthly Minder to remember all the important dates.

"I know," said Solly, looking away.

"Solly, I'm going to say something. Every year it comes and you start feeling bad because you never did anything about it and then you tell yourself it's too late to do anything about it and that makes you feel even worse, and some years, I have to say it, you get like a wooden Indian, a golem, I don't know what, but it can drive a person a little crazy, Solly. I'm telling you for your own good: it's not too late. Buy a candle, go to temple, say a prayer, visit your father's grave. That's all anybody can do, and what does it matter you didn't do it before—you do it now, that's all."

Solly put his coffee down on the table and scratched the side of his face.

"Can you remember your parents' voices?" he asked.

"Of course I can. Why do you ask?"

"You see, the thing is," he began, "I can remember my mother's voice, I can remember the things she used to say to me and just how she used to say it, little things, even like how she said 'hamburger'—she used to say 'humbuggah'—but I can't remember my father's voice, Adelle. Sometimes I sit there and I try. I can see him, all right, but I can't remember even one word of his voice. I hate that. It drives me crazy."

For a moment neither of them said anything. When there was something important, you had to let a silence follow; otherwise it didn't get a chance to sink in.

"Solly, listen to what I'm telling you. At least you go out and buy a candle."

"I should this year, really," said Solly, picking up his cup. She watched him becoming distant again and knew that he would have to be reminded more than once to buy the candle and she would have to work to keep him from slipping away like that, which was the one thing she couldn't stand.

"And don't slurp your coffee," said Adelle sharply.

There was a sour fire in Solly's stomach as he slammed down the phone. "Son of a bitch," he hissed to himself, then looked up and saw Yanopolis standing in respectful silence in the doorway.

"Yanopolis," he said, "you should have been a waiter."

"You're telling me," said Yanopolis with a crinkled smile, hoping to discharge some of Altheim's enmity. "We may have a break on the Farb murder."

"Is that a fact?" said Solly sarcastically—not only because he was already sure that one had gone down the drain, but also because Yanopolis, in his zeal to please, was always too optimistic. Nothing, of course, ever worked out well enough to match the expectations Yanopolis would raise, and people always ended up angry at Yanopolis. Solly had once even tried to explain all this to Yanopolis, who, after listening in respectful silence, had said, "I know." "Then why do you do it?" "I can't help myself. I forget till it's all over." They hadn't spoken of it since.

"Yes," said Yanopolis, "a witness has come forward."

"Are you shitting me?"

"No."

"OK, what does that mean, 'come forward'—did he call up, leave his name, what?"

"He's out front."

"Now?"

"Yes."

Solly scowled at Yanopolis threateningly. "He better be."

They went down the hall to the waiting room and looked through the pebbly glass window. An old black woman with a shopping bag by her feet was sleeping peacefully on the bench, and beside her was a tall, thin young man who looked as if he was losing his hair from some disease.

"Which one?" whispered Solly.

"The guy."

"And you're sure it's about the Farb case?"

"On the basis of what this individual said."

"What the fuck does that mean?"

"It means yes."

"All right, then, let's see."

Solly introduced himself and extended his hand, which the young man took lifelessly, without rising.

"Let's talk in my office. There's less people coming in and out. So," said Solly as they entered the hall, "my associate here tells me that you may know something about a crime that we're investigating."

"I think so."

"In here, please," said Solly, showing him into his office and at the same time giving Yanopolis a this-is-going-to-be-quite-a-character look. Yanopolis smiled, glad for the sign of friendship, and closed the door behind Solly with a slightly exaggerated care which Solly noticed and found irritating.

"I just have to get the usual information down," said Solly, looking with almost voracious curiosity at the young man sitting across from him. Now he could see that the hair had been cut to look that way, as if it were falling out in clumps. He hadn't seen that one before.

"So, your name; just first and last is all right."

"Thomas White."

"OK, Thomas, and your address."

"Twenty-four St. Mark's."

"Oh yeah, twenty-four, that's down by Avenue A."

"Right."

"I used to go to the Kiev down there."

"The Kiev is still there. It's good."

"Yeah, good, you like the Kiev. And the phone."

"The phone is . . . well . . . the phone is 643-2019."

"Anything special with the phone?"

"You see, I work nights and so usually you'll only get the answering machine. But I pick the messages up."

"So you work nights?"

"Yes, I'm a musician."

"You in a band?"

"Yeah. Radiation Sickness. Ever hear of it?"

"No, but you can't go by me."

"We only do songs about nuclear war. We've got our first single out: 'Kiss the World Good-bye.' It's getting some local play," the young man said, and then broke into laughter.

"What's so funny?"

"It's hard . . . I mean, to me it's already all over. . . . Maybe it won't happen until Thursday, but that's just a detail, you know; things always take a little longer than they're supposed to. And here I'm glad that my record's getting a little local play."

"I know the world could go up," said Solly. "But in the meantime, what can you do? Besides, maybe we worry about it too much. Maybe it's like driving—you don't know any of those people, but you're figuring that they don't want to get into an accident, either."

"Yes, but there's lots of accidents."

"That's true," said Solly, finding himself enjoying the conversation. The young man was decent and intelligent and had probably been to a good college. Still, there was something creepy about him, the deathly-white skin and the hair cut to look as if it was falling out and the name of the band, Radiation Sickness; you felt it just looking at him, but Solly guessed that was the idea.

"So what did you actually see?"

"Well, I was putting up posters for our next gig. I usually go as far as First and First. That's far enough. So, I crossed onto the island, at the far end, and I was putting one up around a streetlight. I wasn't paying much attention to what was going on. I just took one look to make sure nobody too dangerous-looking was around, and I started putting up the poster. Then I heard two shots. I looked up and this short guy ran by me and for a second we even looked in each other's eyes. I was scared that he was going to turn around and shoot me, but he didn't, he just kept running."

"Can you describe him for me?"

"Well, he was about five six. He looked young by his clothes, but when I saw his face I could tell that he was in his thirties—anyway, not in his early twenties."

"Could you tell what nationality he was?"

"Again, by the way he was dressed he looked like a Puerto Rican, but he might have been Iranian or something like that."

"You think you could identify him from a photograph?"

"I could try. I always wanted to look through those books."

"We can take a look right away. Can I just ask you why you waited until today to come over, Thomas?"

"Well, there was a period there when I kept getting that feeling, kept bracing myself, you know, bracing myself for the impact. And every time I thought of coming over here, it seemed ridiculous. I mean, what if the whole world was wiped while I was on my way over here? But today, I don't know, for some . . . I mean, you can't think about it all the time."

20 The cab moved slowly

up Commonwealth Avenue as the driver checked the street signs.

"I think it's a little ways yet," said David Aronow to the driver, who was leaning away from the wheel and looking out the passenger window.

He was getting tired now. It seemed a long time since he had first caught sight of Boston that morning, the line of eighteenth-century red brick along the cold blue river, the gold dome of the State House flashing like a higher value against a second city of glass and steel.

The area around MIT had not changed much. There were still all those Oriental students wearing chinos and white shirts, their breast pockets stuffed with ballpoint pens, their brains packed with equations. His friend Jim the biochemist was glad to see him, and glad to help when the time came, and wished he could be more enthusiastic about the whole thing, but the problem was that his mother had just had a stroke and he was dreading picking up the phone and hearing his father's voice say, "Jim, your mother's died." And so they ended up spending less time together than David had figured on, which gave him a couple of free hours before Abram, his second visit, would be home.

He thought it might be interesting to have a look at his old neighborhood—more than that, to feel himself as he was now against that background, where his life had started. But he did not stand in front of that U-shaped red brick courtyard for very long. Somehow, knowing that the site of his childhood had gone condo—the word itself containing all the heartbreaking human-all-too-human cheapness of the age—was enough to sour the moment.

The polyurethane of modernity had been brushed over Brookline Village as well. Where Jew-hating Irish street gangs, wearing their big brothers' hand-me-down clothes, their heads shaved for ringworm, had once sauntered, there were now bakeries featuring *pain au chocolat.* And that, too, was somehow ridiculous. He thanked God that he had held out for something that delivered him from the vicious ridiculousness of that life that was everywhere now.

He passed the library where he had learned to read. It was unchanged, a solid, graceful structure from the days when the city had been serious about its municipal buildings. They had played their little part, all those biographies of great men. There had been a whole series, he remembered, with tan-colored covers; he had read them all—pioneers, heroes, inventors, patriots, explorers, athletes. Now there were probably progressive librarians with M.A.'s in communications recommending real-life stories about a young girl whose parents are divorcing and so there is no one to tell that she's pregnant from Ramón, the Hispanic hotshot strung out on drugs who's worth saving if only everybody wasn't so wrapped up in their own problems they had no time to care. He'd take one quick look at his school, he thought, and get the hell out of there.

The Pierce School, where he had learned the letters, the numbers, the colors of the rainbow, the days of the week, and the months of the year, a great urinously yellow Victorian train station of a building had been replaced twenty years before by what was then the latest thing and had now begun to look embarrassingly "modern." He had seen the new one a few times already, and so there was no real shock except for the realization that he could no longer clearly visualize what his school had looked like in the second half of the forties, and was afraid that if he saw pictures of it, they would still somehow not look right.

"Turn right here," said David suddenly, recognizing Abram Luntz's street.

There was a wheelless car up on cement blocks, its axles rusted the color of iodine, in front of Abram's building, and a half-squashed Pepsi can on the high front steps. For a moment David wondered about that Pepsi can. Why it hadn't been squashed all the way? Hadn't the child been strong enough, had some other child called him away to play?

David stepped into sorrow as he moved toward Abram, who was waiting in his doorway, looking where he thought David would be. It was only in the instant before their bodies locked into a hug that the light of awareness flashed across Abram's face. They squeezed and pounded. Then David followed Abram back into the apartment, marveling at his outfit —well-worn slippers, dark-blue sweatpants held up by suspenders over a bright yellow shirt decorated with little red crowns.

They began their ritual at once. Ferocious, irresistible Russian hospitality had, in under a minute, a kettle of water boiling, refrigerator doors opening and closing, jam scooped out of jars, cookies and raisins set out.

"Before I forget, Abram, there is one favor I'd like to ask of you," said David.

"Anything, if it is in my powers."

"I need a letter sent to the Soviet Union."

"Give it to me right away and I will put it someplace safe. I am afraid to leave it on the kitchen table," said Abram with a look in that direction. The table, as always, was covered with mail, magazines, Russian newspapers, books, manuscripts, dishes, teacups, Soviet knickknacks; this time it was also graced by a rabbit-shaped piece of chocolate wrapped in blue-and-white foil with Bugs Bunny's face on it.

Abram took the letter, removed his glasses, and held the envelope up close to his eye. "Should be all right."

"But now I'm worried," said Abram, coming back into the kitchen. "Sometimes I hide things so well I can't find them afterward."

"Well, tell me where you put it, so there'll be two of us who know."

"In volume three of Dahl's dictionary."

"Volume three."

"But that's not all I am worried about."

"What else?" said Aronow, with the poker face of the straight man.

"America! And to say 'America' means the entire West, not to mention what is sometimes known as civilization. For example, I can't believe it, I can't believe it!"

Abram whacked himself three times on the head as if trying to wake himself from a nightmare. Three resounding whacks, loud enough to scare a child into crying.

"The intellectuals . . . the American intellectuals . . . they ought to be taken out and . . ." Suddenly Abram looked sheepish, as if he had realized that he was about to make one of those remarks that confirmed all American suspicions about the abiding authoritarian nature of all Russians. "Not literally . . . but they . . . the kettle is boiling."

Glad to have a reason to pause, Abram went to the stove.

"Please pour for yourself," said Abram, handing David the kettle. "You know . . ." he paused and then said with a certain horrified amazement, "I cannot see."

Pouring his own tea, one finger in the glass to tell him when it was full, Abram re-erupted into fury as some inner flange opened again. "American intellectuals wasting their time getting murderers out of jail so that they can kill more people—that is their idea of social responsibility! And those lawyers with all their little cunning tricks—how can people stand for it! My brain wants to explode!"

"But a man is innocent until proven guilty. Proven," said David, happy to be turned into a liberal against his will so that they could perform their routine, their vaudeville. And this time he wanted to give Abram something, not only for the favor he was doing him but because David was all too aware that he was keeping his secret from Abram, the secret that had turned him into its keeper.

"Yes, I know, proven, proven. But they could show a movie of someone killing someone and then he even confesses that he did it and then the lawyer will say that the movie wasn't properly subpoenaed and that the confession was forced out of him and the next thing you know he's back walking around with the rest of us and then one day somebody says something to him he doesn't like and so he takes out a knife and sticks it in a person's heart!"

Tiny, wrinkled, luminous, wearing a blue terry-cloth robe, the grandmother (Aronow was never quite sure of her name, for she was always called Babushka) came into the kitchen. Her presence was so smooth, even silvery, that the kitchen quieted at once; even Abram was changed into a young person, awkward with impatience.

"I was sleeping," she said, her eyes smiling. "I'm sorry I couldn't make you tea."

She took a glass of water from the tap and left the kitchen. David remembered that he had never seen her eat anything, or drink anything but water, and he wondered if she had reached some stage beyond the actual struggle of life, where water was enough to subsist on.

Abram was just gathering force to continue the tirade when Babushka's voice, itself plain and pure as tap water, came from the other room: "News."

"Let's watch," said Abram with enthusiasm, even appetite. "I am now a devoted fan of Channel Four."

They went into the living room, where Babushka was sitting on a chair with her feet up on a footstool, sipping her water. The room was dark except for the glow of the television.

Abram sat close to the screen, the blues and oranges playing on his face. Babushka sipped her water and made comments: "Him I don't like." "This one is good." As usual, David was thrown into the role of translator, answering Abram's questions: "Will they sell the planes to Israel or not? I don't understand." "The President will address who?"

"Did you see that?"

"What?"

"You know, now they have little previews of the news to come, so you won't change the channel, and it said, 'Soviet poet exiled.' "

"It must be Shar. I heard rumors. I only hope he will not become part of all that Russian-genius-celebrity-in-exile apparatus that your media have dreamed up."

"Shhh, here it is," said David four commercials later.

Frankfurt airport. Mike in hand, the reporter said that today the Soviet Union had forcibly exiled the dissident poet

Evgeny Shar. The camera shifted to an illegible crowd flickering in the light of flashbulbs. Then Shar filled the screen. Handsome, exhausted, the hair milky blond. Shar leaned forward slightly toward the cluster of mikes and said, in English, "Soviet Union is a country that prefers to cut its own throat than to hear its own voice."

PART
THREE

21 Shar unpacked.

After two days in a cyclone of flashbulbs, champagne, and questions, he had been spirited away to a small ski lodge in the Bavarian Alps. The eminent German writer who was in charge of Shar's welfare had thought this the ideal spot for him to get his long poem down on paper, since the snows had not started yet and the area was still very quiet. Shar agreed readily. He was feeling a little raw, as if he had just come out of anesthesia, or woken in a stranger's house after too deep a sleep.

Rich in gifts and telegrams, he was now the owner of a portable typewriter with a bilingual keyboard, which, at the flick of a gnurled plastic switch, went from the Roman alphabet to the Cyrillic. He owned a leather briefcase and a Pelikan pen. Women were drawn to his blond heroic charisma, his bruised face, his deep reedy voice. He had already been attacked by the German extreme left, which said that he would be used by the capitalist revanchists and that, in any case, he was a religious reactionary. Shar did not accept any of the offers that were made him, either by the women (after all, who knew who they really were?) or by the universities or even the Russian Book Fair in Exile in New York (thank you, but it was too early). It was better not to make any serious moves until his reflexes were again in sharp focus and he had had time to gauge the systems operating around him. There were so many little things. For example, how to say good-bye to Europeans of a certain class and social level, like the prize-winning German writer and his wife (which one gets kissed? whose hand do you shake?). Of course, no one expected him to know these things, but it made for awkward moments and kept him at a certain disadvantage. The only thing he could do now was exploit his awkwardness until he perceived all the little rules of the game. And perhaps Vinias, who, for all his genius, was a bit of a clod and a desk warmer, had simply underestimated the difficulty of sending someone so far out into the world, into its brightest and best-lit areas.

He had set up his typewriter on the table by the window with a view of the mountain. That was appealing—to stare out at that large, simple thing and get all those words onto paper. Two or three days would be plenty. But after that, the sooner he got out of Germany the better. The Germans made him nervous. They were so cozy and hearty and nice, enchanted by prosperity into forgetting what monsters they were. Now he could see what a danger the two Germanies were, for one day they would, of course, want to be reunited, and then, one arm chained to the West, one arm chained to the East, they would at last succeed in pulling the world down with them. Really, they had been right about genocide. But exterminate the Jews? Jews were absolutely essential to the world. It was the Germans who should have been wiped out once and for all.

Though he had not met many Americans yet, he had already spotted two types: intelligent boys with gray hair, and sharp-eyed farmers who would make good soldiers and were very practical men. But both types seemed somehow odd, futuristic, light, as if some component were missing from their makeup, as if the weight of the past had been lifted from their shoulders. So light. He had read that Americans were always moving, taking new jobs, new wives, buying new houses, new cars, and now he could see why—their soil was rich only in natural vitality and had not been thickened with the blood of historic battles or seasoned with fifty generations of bones. No wonder they had gotten to the moon first.

He sat down on the bed with the telegrams, vaguely regretful that he did not have a woman with him, one of the compliant kind who could fit her personality to his tastes and desires, who did so by nature, without stress or artifice, would be honored for the hour, for the memory, the distinction, and would then, with a minimum of fuss, vanish back into the nowhere from which she had emerged.

It could be a decent business, observed Shar, totaling the figures mentioned in some of the invitations. Two thousand dollars to speak for an hour. Do that fifteen times and you could probably drive away in a Mercedes. Besides, he should live it up, to have material for his book. This assignment would, if everything went right, take three or four years, after which he would return to the Soviet Union. Then, except for an occasional statement, Evgeny Shar the poet could, for all practical purposes, cease to exist, and he could move into a new phase. That was what Vinias had promised him. But he could not conceal a touch of panic from himself, the panic accompanied by the thought that Vinias might have moved him into a position from which there was no exit, so that he would be trapped in that carefully cultivated mask for the rest of his life, gasping for air as the mask grew into his face and began closing the nostrils.

The beige telephone on the night table buzzed softly, discreetly.

"Allo," said Shar.

"I am sorry to disturb you, Herr Shar, but the gentleman you were expecting, Herr Zygmunt Bauer of the German Press Association, is here."

Shar checked his appearance in the wardrobe mirror and flicked a lock of pale-blond hair onto his forehead. There was a knock at the door, soft but definite.

"I am Zygmunt Bauer," said the man at the door, puffing —tuckered out by the little hill from the inn to the guest cottages. His face was flushed with dark blood and he had the slightly apologetic air of the short and fat when they speak to the tall, lean, and athletic.

"Please, come in," said Shar. "I am sorry I have nothing to offer you here, but we can have something sent over from the main house, if you like."

"For me nothing, thanks," said Bauer. "My doctor has put me on a strict, very strict regimen. Bauer, he tells me, you must lose fifteen kilos or your heart will go pop like a balloon. Not a very pleasant prospect."

"No," agreed Shar.

"Your English seems very good. Would you prefer to do the interview in English or in Russian? I can speak OK Russian, but afterward we make German translation in either case."

Shar smiled at the chubby Bavarian, who was folding his coat over the arm of a chair. "Russian, I think," said Shar. "Russian is my language."

"Perhaps we can work at your desk?" said Bauer, switching to Russian. "Excellent view."

"Of course, I'll just move this chair."

Bauer lay his briefcase on the long table and sat down. He unzipped the briefcase and pulled out a small Sony tape recorder and a long cord, which he plugged into the socket under the table.

"The most horrible thing," he said, "is when the batteries have run out and you are not aware; then you go back to the studio and listen to thirty minutes of stupid silence, and that makes you so mad your heart wants to pop. This happened to me when interviewing Sartre; can you imagine? All right, then. Testing—one, two, three; allo; testing—one, two, three."

He pressed the REWIND button and the tape went screeching backward with a metallic mouselike sound.

"Allo; testing—one, two, three."

Shar was watching with the amused, patient dignity of the celebrity.

"Now you, please. I just want to get the right microphone distance."

"Raz, dva, tri," said Shar lazily into the mike.

"Raz, dva, tri," echoed the tape, his own voice clear and recognizable yet strange.

"Good. Sounds fine. Now we begin. Mr. Shar, you have only been in this country, I know, for a few days, and under very unusual circumstances, yet I would still like to hear your initial impressions of the West."

"The problem is," began Shar when the mike was pointed in his direction, "that there have been so many impressions and so little time to put them in any order. And you must remember that I do not come here just from the Soviet Union but, rather, from a labor camp—not the worst of them, to be sure, but hardly like this cottage in the Alps, for example. So, one week ago, I was grinding glass for television screens in Mordovia, and today I am being interviewed in rather luxurious surroundings. I feel like a man who has been underwater for months and months in a submarine that stinks of machine oil and human bodies; then suddenly the sub surfaces and he is in some exotic foreign city."

Shar paused to look over at Bauer, who was nodding his head and then smiled to let Shar know that it had been a good answer and could be used, though of course in a somewhat shortened form, for their newspaper.

"Just to be absolutely one-hundred-percent sure, I am going to play the entire answer back. Do you mind?"

"Not at all."

Bauer lay the microphone on the table, rewound the tape, and pressed PLAY. Then he reached into his briefcase and pulled out a child's magic slate and a thin red wooden stylus.

He looked over at Shar, who nodded.

"The problem is," said Shar's voice on the tape, "that there have been so many impressions and so little time . . ."

Setting the magic slate down on the table between them, Bauer quickly traced out the message: "Head psi project suicide. Data tampered with. Leak certain. This now principal objective. Additional information to follow. Proceed New York at once."

As soon as he was done writing, Bauer looked to Shar, who nodded with a quizzical frown. Bauer lifted up the plastic sheet and the words disappeared; then he scribbled over it and lifted it again. Reinserting the magic slate into his briefcase, he said, "At the end, I would like a picture of you at your typewriter, by the window with the mountain in the background; would that be all right?"

"Of course," said Shar. "A good idea."

———

Shar stayed in the doorway, enjoying the feel of the quick mountain air, which had sudden cold places in it like lake water, and watched Bauer pick his way almost daintily down the hillside. The German turned and waved one last time before disappearing around the corner of the main building.

The assignment had shifted; a peripheral task had become central. And that meant that Vinias had been shoved aside. Orders would continue to flow through Vinias, but now that was only a matter of form. In a way, Shar even felt sorry for Vinias. He must hate this defeat—the worst kind of defeat, defeat by an inferior. Because everyone was inferior to Vinias, by definition; Vinias's definition. Not that he was arrogant. He even made a show of modesty, but there was no disguising that odor of superiority around him.

Then the thought of Vinias's humiliation filled Shar with an angry hatred for the man, the same angry hatred he had felt that day in the cell, with the taste of blood and vodka in his mouth. The same certainty that he had to elude Vinias's grasp if he was ever to be more than a clever toy designed by an old man with a game knee.

But Vinias had given him a life, a life in the world. He shouldn't forget that, or what he probably would have become without Vinias—a Red Square hustler, a ladies' man, a pathetic Russian criminal with some grandiose nickname and nowhere to spend his money.

Then the sound of a car motor sputtering in the rarefied mountain air broke the spell, and Shar returned to his room to finish the poem.

He unscrewed the cap from his Pelikan pen, a present from his German publisher, and opened his notebook. There were only about forty-odd lines left to jot down, polish, then type. For a moment, watching the tracery of ink following his pen, he wondered how poets could stand that life of sitting, solitude, silence. A life for a man with no life in him, someone close to the end. But he might be close to the end too, if he kept on seriously considering doing something independent, something that would break Vinias's hold on him. Now he understood Vinias's point in telling him about the émigré murdered in New York. Not only for his information, and not only so that Vinias could crow about his latest success.

Suddenly death did not seem some distant event that would come in the course of time, like the end of the century. A tingle passed down the hair on his forearms. It was in the room with him!

Impulsively, he flipped the pages of his notebook to the rear, away from the other poem, and wrote in block letters: DEUTSCHLAND.

He paused for a moment and then watched his hand write:

> Death is here in Germany.
> Death is in this room with me.
> Death would gnaw my rib cage here,
> another mammal full of milk and fear.
> Death is here in Germany.

He stopped and grinned. The start of his first real poem. But was it really his? Or was it his teacher speaking through him, reminding him of the limits of the game, as exact and jealously guarded as the border?

22 Yasha had been happy,

thought Raisa as she returned his framed photograph to the table, and he had always rebuked her for being unhappy, but how could any sane person with a heart not be unhappy in this world? Yasha had a heart, though not a very great one—a heart that was selfish in its way, too fond of its own happiness—and he had been too much the visionary ever to be what she would call sane.

But people didn't understand her. Yasha had really never understood her, either. She was not morose, not unwilling to enjoy life; her appetites were healthy. It was just that she was too realistic not to be unhappy. It was too late for people ever to be happy again after everything that had already happened. Only children, fools, and criminals could be happy now.

And she was no child, no fool. But that David Aronow

had turned her into something of a criminal. Though of course she had let him do it even against her better judgment. Why? Because Yasha had been taken from her and now she had no one. Because Yasha's death had brought David Aronow to her and she had felt at once that he was her recompense. The look of him, the feel of him, right from the start. And there were all the obvious practical reasons too. He was American and could bring her the rest of the way into that country and its life, but not so American that the Russian in her would always remain a stranger to him. She had done her duty, watched over her foolhardy brother just as she knew their parents would have wanted her to. Cooked for him, cared for him. But he was dead now like all the other people she had loved. Perhaps she could have a little life of her own now. Perhaps even eat outside on a summer evening as the stars were coming out.

You couldn't force these things to happen but you could give them a few good chances.

It was only after she had dialed David Aronow's number and heard it ringing that she noticed it was after eleven. It didn't matter. She had the right. Besides, he might find it intriguing.

"Mr. Aronow, this is Raisa Farb."

"I was going to call you tomorrow."

"You have been away to see your friend?"

"Yes. Can we get together tomorrow and talk?"

"What time?"

"Whenever's good for you?"

"Well then, how about four-thirty?"

"Four-thirty is fine."

"Where?"

"There's a coffee shop near me. The Broadway. On Fourth Avenue and Eighth."

"The Broadway. Fourth and Eighth. I'll be there."

"Fine, see you then."

David knew that it must be at least quarter past eleven because the anchorwoman had just wrapped up the local news and the weatherman was promising an update on the weather after the commercial. Late for her to call, he thought. Maybe she wanted to back out. Maybe reminding her that she was not a citizen had been a wrong move, and now, after a little reflection, she did not want to do anything that would get her in trouble with the authorities. The fears and tremblings of the stateless.

At the time he had thought of lying to her about the way the material was being shipped out of the Soviet Union but had decided against it; a good idea because later on the police had sent her copies of the letters.

She had the power. One call and it was all over. One call and he was a translator again.

And it would be weeks, weeks, before the film arrived.

The weatherman predicted it would rain in the morning and clear up in the early afternoon, somehow taking an equally toothy delight in both forecasts.

He snapped off the set. Weeks!

When he first saw Raisa coming toward his table, he knew that it was she but at the same time he didn't quite recognize her, having only seen her that once, going in and out of the dark as they drove under streetlights. Because visual etiquette did not permit two people approaching each other from a distance to look constantly at each other's faces, David shifted his eyes to see what she was wearing. She had on a plaid pleated skirt (certain émigrés favored that look, the most American of the American) and high boots of the sort that had once been popular with long suede coats, though he knew she wore them mainly because Russians loved and needed fur and boots. She was wearing a pearl-gray blouse that looked like silk but probably wasn't, though it was always interesting to know just how much extravagance a woman allowed herself. He was glad to see that she had not fallen for the blouse style, favored by women professionals, featuring an abstract tie that struck a socially-acceptable balance between femininity and ambition.

"Hello," he said, rising.

Raisa gave David a little nod and a little look but did not say anything.

Now, as she sat down, he saw that she had some of the usual female appeal—the gloss of the hair, the touches of art on the lips and around the eyes, the small earring piercing the lobe. But her face was so entirely united with who she was that it seemed irrelevant to make an aesthetic-sexual judgment about that face. And those very dark brown eyes—you could never penetrate them the same way you could light-colored eyes.

"They said it was going to rain in the morning and clear up in the afternoon," said David, "but it just kind of stayed half-lousy all day."

"I'll never learn English; I'll never be able to say, 'it just kind of stayed half-lousy all day.'"

"I know how that must be."

"Some mornings I wake up and I'm afraid that I've entirely forgotten my English, just like I forgot geometry."

"But your English is good. Anyway, important as it is, language isn't the worst of it."

"And what do you think the worst of it is, Mr. Aronow?"

"Well, it's the difference in the way people are. I mean, Americans will tell you everything about themselves, everything, but they won't be intimate with you. Russians will tell you practically nothing but they *will* be intimate; they can't help being intimate."

"That's exactly right, David," she said with a laugh of delight, noticing at the same time that she had called him David and wondering if he had noticed, too.

But he was busy recalling that he still did not know the real point of their meeting, what new intention she might now announce.

"So, tell me about your trip to Boston. Is it a nice city?"

"Well, I was born there, and so for me it's more like a relative than a place, but I guess a person could visit for a couple of days."

"But I'll tell you one thing that worries me."

"What's that?"

"You see, you live in a country where if you want to fly to the city where you were born, all you need is the money for the ticket. Capitalism is so intelligent. And I am a person who cannot even live in the city where I was born, let alone visit it. And so that makes me wonder."

"Look, I don't pretend that I have your experience. But you can't pretend that you have mine, either. Even if America is a jerky country in a lot of ways, we're as mysterious as the Nepalese, and it takes some time to learn our rituals and games, to learn them just right. Once that film clears customs, it'll be an American game. And we'll win."

Against her better judgment, she had to smile at his easy audacity—itself proof that there really was such a place as America, where people were easy and audacious.

"Look, so far so good. The detective—what's his name, Altheim—probably looked at my translations of the letters, shook his head, and stuck them away someplace. That's one. I talked to my friend in Boston, and he said he'd do what he could when the time came. That's two."

"And what's three?"

"Three is making arrangements with somebody at Lincoln Center."

"Have you done that?"

"No, but it shouldn't be too hard. That's the world of the cultural elite, and the elite is small by definition; I must know somebody who knows somebody."

"Yes, David. If we had three I would feel better."

"And to make us feel even better, we'll celebrate with a good dinner, agreed?"

"Agreed. I know how I am: I always foresee disaster. Maybe I am trying to do magic, to ward it off by imagining it with so many details. Maybe I'm really looking into the past all the time. I have too much past. It's like a pit I can't crawl out of; the sides keep caving in. The past came and got my brother, too."

"But there was a line between Yuri Trofimovich and your brother that they could trace."

"And that line goes from my brother to me to you, David, to this coffee shop."

"And do you think someone is busy tracing that line?"

"Past experience tells me yes."

"Then we'll be more careful about meeting. We'll decide today which restaurant we're going to and when we'll meet."

"David, don't, please don't misunderstand me. I hate it when people don't understand me. I think about Stolat, too. More and more now. I find that I am very charmed by the idea. I keep imagining things clear and bright as a movie. Sometimes I see myself standing on a balcony overlooking the sea. It's late evening. My shoulders are bare. A little breeze comes up. It makes me shiver a little tiny bit, but it's delicious. Then I go back to the party, where people I love are enjoying themselves. And I'm smiling because I should have been dead for twenty years already."

David spent a few moments flipping aimlessly through his address book—every name a snapshot in ink—sad and curious to see that he had at last forgotten a certain woman's phone number. Still, it was a pointless exercise, for the obvious person to call was Marty. Marty had the connections and would do him the favor. He was one of the few old friends David had retained, though they didn't tend to see each other very often.

"You can't be calling me all the time, Aronow," said Marty, who nearly always spoke in pure sarcasm, the English almost incidental. "I'm a busy guy now."

The sight of the bookstalls on the sidewalk in front of the Strand bookstore reminded David of Berkeley, the evenings—half-lonely, half-fun—he and Marty had spent in bookstores and cafés. He remembered that they had been together when Sproul Hall was taken over. Joan Baez had been on the front steps playing her guitar and singing, her hair Apache black, a tiny gold cross against her wine-colored sweater. Liberty leading the citizens on to the revolution and the great new world. Inside the dimly lit corridors scared, indignant office workers were scurrying out to safety, armfuls of files pressed to their chests, the way girls used to carry books.

Balding, bearded, with a potbelly that came in the winter and left with the spring, Marty greeted David at the door with a bear hug and more wisecracks. "What happened, did your building burn down?"

"It should have, but it didn't."

"I heard of a good place in Tribeca. There's some key money, but there's almost five years left on the lease. Four and a half."

"Thanks, but I'm not looking."

"Thought I'd ask. So, what do you think of the office?"

"Great. What's that, a Reuter's machine? Two computers *and* a word processor. You must be doing all right."

"Not too bad. I made a little on T bonds, I lost a little on silver. But it's not the money, it's the excitement. This is where the action is. If Hemingway was alive today, he'd be trading commodities."

David told him the story, more or less. Farb was left out entirely; no one liked to hear about people shot dead on the street, especially when their cooperation in the same venture was being solicited. He just said that his contacts in the dissident world had asked him to retrieve that piece of film or leader or whatever it was exactly, and they said that it was important and they would tell him what it was when they found out themselves.

Marty made a face that said it sounded interesting but irritatingly vague. "So, what do you need, then?"

"I need to talk with someone connected with the festival who'll give me five minutes alone with that film."

"That's Naomi."

"Naomi?"

"Naomi Rosen. You never met her? She used to work for ABC, did some documentaries with the famous woman producer, what was her name; then she went on to make a couple of docs on her own. Good stuff—one of them got a prize. Wait a second, I got her number here someplace."

David watched his friend's index finger do its seven-step dance, seven more little steps on the way.

"Naomi?" said Marty into the phone. "Listen, I've got this character here named David Aronow. I can't get rid of the guy, he's been bugging me for over twenty years now. So, do me a favor and talk to him, will you? What's it about? Better ask him yourself. OK, thanks a lot, 'bye. All right, David, Naomi will see you today at four-thirty. Be on time —she's got a screening at five sharp."

"Thanks. You should run for mayor one of these days."

"I'd love to."

"I'll talk to you," said David at the door.

"When?" asked Marty. "In two years?"

Small and dark, Naomi seemed to be hovering with a hummingbird's intensity above a tremendous exhaustion. Yet it was clear that she was competent, that the work piled on her desk would be done well and on time.

"Thank you for seeing me," said David. "I'll tell you what the story is."

"Please do." She lit a long, thin brown cigarette. "Marty sounded so mysterious over the phone, but he's always fooling around, that one."

"It *is* a little mysterious. Some of the details I shouldn't talk about, some I don't know, but what it boils down to is this: some Russian dissidents will be—are—smuggling certain important information out of the Soviet Union. It has to be on a special kind of material—don't ask me why, I'm a technical moron. Anyway, they hit on a way of getting it out. They've disguised it as tail leader and attached it to the fourth reel of the film *Apples of Ryazan,* which, as I'm sure you're aware, is the Soviet entry in your festival."

"And it's coming here?" she asked, blowing the smoke from her cigarette up close to her face.

"And it's coming here."

"I love it. And what do you want me to do?"

"To let me know as soon as it's here. Then get me to wherever you keep them. For five minutes."

"But don't you think there could be trouble?"

"They're slipping it out right under their own noses."

"But there's always some trouble, isn't there?"

"Five minutes. How much can happen in five minutes?"

"I like it," she said, "but something tells me not to."

"That means you're helping them."

"I've got to get going," she said with a sudden worried glance at her watch.

"Do you want time to think it over?"

"No, if I think it over I'll just say no. So, the film should be here sometime around the middle of the month. Start calling me around the eighth. Call before eleven or after three, three-fifteen. I've got to run. This is all I needed."

"Stolat," said David, pouring the last of the wine into Raisa's glass.

"Yes," she said, "stolat."

When they set their glasses down, she asked him for a cigarette.

"I didn't know you smoked."

"Sometimes. After a dinner. Or with wine."

She took the first drag very deliberately, as if not quite remembering how to smoke.

"Isn't *stolat* what they used to yell to Lech Walesa during the Solidarity days?" asked Raisa.

"That's right."

"Poor Solidarity."

"Raisa, this is a celebration."

"David, are those men going to play music?" asked Raisa, pointing to an area that had just been lit to reveal drums and music stands. Five black men in red jackets had just entered, nodding slightly to acknowledge the crowd's ripples of applause.

She looked from the stage to him with a look of wild, almost frightening happiness. "What kind will they play?"

"New Orleans."

"New Orleans! That's what I love best! How did you know?"

"Everybody loves New Orleans jazz except the Politburo."

The trumpet player began blowing some old notes from his last performance out of his horn. The drummer was at his stand, twitching his shoulders. The bass player was talking to the trombone man, who was sitting, his head back, smiling as if he were looking up into sunshine. The leader had his clarinet at his mouth; his cheeks were out, a vein was twitching on the side of his forehead.

The band was from New Orleans, and they didn't waste any time. The bass began laying the foundation, while the clarinet was giving hot little calls like a woman just starting to get excited, and that made the trombone laugh because it had seen it so many times and it was always good. The trumpet was starting to insist on something, the drummer using his brushes, building his trance.

Raisa clapped her hands, once, in glee, not applause.

David leaned over the table and said in a whisper, "Welcome to the U-nited States of America."

She laughed to the music.

23 Andrusha dropped

the balled-up waxed paper into the public trash basket and watched it fall. It made nearly no sound as it fell onto the other paper at the bottom.

He wiped the crumbs from the corner of his mouth. Since Yuri Trofimovich's death, officially described as heart failure, Andrusha had been in a state of constant panic. Often he would find himself staring too long at things, like the falling paper, trying to escape, if even for a moment, the fearful certainty that sooner or later he would be brought in for questioning. A creak of the floorboards was enough to wake him from sleep. Everyone connected with the project was being questioned—technicians, research people, computer operators—and he knew that the only reason they had not gotten around to him yet was that he had not been associated with the project's latest phase, and they were working backward from the present.

He started walking down Victory Street toward the trolley stop. He had no choice; he had to go to work each day and continue filming through microscopes for an educational film called *The World Within a Drop of Water*. Sometimes he could lose himself in the exacting technical requirements of the work, sometimes the savage profusion of life forms could cause him to forget his own anxiety for a moment, but, just as often, the sight of one microscopic creature being consumed—eaten alive!—by another only accelerated his dread. The horrible nonchalance of one living thing's devouring another. Somehow the lack of malice made it even more terrifying.

The old women were sweeping the sidewalk on Victory Street, using brooms made of long, dark twigs. Their movements were brisk and energetic, as if they were positively at war with dirt and disorder. They did, however, stop to watch a young woman walk by. She was wearing jeans, heels, and a long striped Italian sweater, and she looked as out of place on that sidewalk as would a cosmonaut in a silvery suit. As she passed Andrusha, she looked right into his eyes and smiled, half to be rid of the judgment she had just felt on her and half because his face was both handsome and touchingly bewildered. In a second she passed and was gone. Andrusha resisted the force that was swiveling his head around to watch her go. It was too depressing. Would he ever be with a woman again? Would he ever make a film, a real film, the way only he could make it, or had all this stupid business wrapped itself around him like a chain that was now dragging him down to the bottom, where he would be devoured as casually as any other living creature?

He took a deep breath. The air was raw and tasted like sorrow. Maybe he could make some sort of deal with them. Why shouldn't he? Was any of it worth it? Would Yuri Trofimovich say it was worth it now, if he could see his wife and daughter? What difference was one more invention going to make? The Americans invented the bomb, but then the Soviet Union got hold of it quickly enough. But, then, could he stand himself? And how would people look at him? Even if they didn't know what he had done, they would still somehow know; there was always a certain smell that people could sense. And he didn't know if he could stand having that smell inside of him, in his mouth and nose. As long as they didn't do anything to his eyes—that was the one thing—as long as they didn't do anything to his eyes . . .

Then he hated them because they would do anything to get what they wanted. But what could he resist them with, what did he believe in that was so strong that it could stand up to them?

He was no Christian, with a set of beliefs that he would walk into the fire for; he just wanted life to be half-decent, to serve some cause that was noble and exciting, and to make films that would astonish people with their grace and beauty. And he wanted some of the silly things of life, knowing they were frivolous and vain but wanting them anyway—travel, applause, interviews, festivals. He had always been a curious mixture of the frivolous and the sincere, and now he could not help hating that plodding, earnest part of himself, that crumpled and bearded Yuri Trofimovich in him, that stupid conscience that had prodded him into risking everything and given him nothing in return, not even some sort of heroic inner calm to face the inevitable questioning. If he had been so noble, then why did he feel like a rat in a closet? He didn't know if he could stand another night of watching the street sweeper's headlights flash across the walls and ceiling of his room.

As he turned the corner onto October Boulevard, he saw the trolley at the stop. The line of passengers was still long enough that he could make it if he ran.

A black Zhil sedan sped past him and came to a stop just before the end of the block. Andrusha saw the door open and a man in a dark blue raincoat and a brown felt hat emerge and hold the door open. He was looking right at Andrusha. Andrusha felt a few drops of rain touch his face. As long as they didn't do anything to his eyes.

The man at the desk was in his early forties, and his civilian clothes were well tailored. He clearly belonged to a different generation from Kovalyov, who was sitting by the wall looking ashen and murderous. He rose and introduced himself: "Colonel Yarov."

Andrusha took the seat indicated to him. As soon as he had seen the rear door of the Zhil open, even before the man in the blue raincoat had come out, he had lost all sense of being in control of himself. He could move only if told to, speak only when spoken to. He tried to struggle against the gravity and pull of that power, but he felt like a man in the water, his clothes becoming heavier and heavier.

"Do you know why you're here?"

Andrusha moved his head from side to side, afraid to hear himself say the word "no" aloud.

Yarov exchanged glances with Kovalyov.

"And you cannot even guess?"

Andrusha shook his head again.

"Then what are you so afraid of?"

"To be stopped . . . on the street . . ."

There, it was over, he had spoken.

"I understand. It can be shocking. But let me be frank, that was a very mild shock. It can be the first and the last, or the first in a long series; that is totally dependent on you. So, I have several clear, direct questions, and I want clear, direct answers. You knew Yuri Trofimovich?"

"Yes, of course, we worked together."

"You never saw him outside of work?"

"Only by chance."

"It was only by chance, for instance, that you met with him in Varny Park on the twentieth of September, took his picture, and sat talking with him?"

"I go out and take photos every Sunday."

"And was it by chance that you ran into him a few weeks before that, outside the museum?"

"It was. He was my colleague, and of course we stopped to chat."

"And what was Yuri Trofimovich working on when he died?"

"The last I knew, he was working on drugs to increase psi. The last time we worked together we photographed an experiment. Comrade Kovalyov was there. . . ."

Kovalyov twitched in his chair and made a movement to interrupt Andrusha; he repressed it immediately, but his panic had already been felt in the room. Andrusha realized that Kovalyov, too, might be in trouble. That gave Andrusha a toehold on himself. There were other fates involved, other forces. And maybe they did not have anything specific on him. Perhaps that was why they were being careful with their questions, so as not to reveal anything to him if he proved not to be involved.

The colonel took a Marlboro from the pack on his desk, rapped the tobacco end against one knuckle, and then lit up slowly.

"You have been to Moscow twice recently."

"I'm trying to get a position with Mosfilm."

"Very hard to crack into, I understand."

"Yes," answered Andrusha, aware that that was the first remark from Yarov that was on the direct track.

"The Americans have a nice expression, they call it 'the carrot and the stick.' A donkey can be made to go either by dangling a carrot in front of him or by beating him with a stick. I happen to be something of a film enthusiast myself. And it would be pleasant to discuss the cinema with you sometime over a glass of vodka. As for Mosfilm, I know some people there, and not the least important ones, either. So, please tell me, then, who do you think were the people that linked Yuri Trofimovich to his military contacts abroad?"

For a second Andrusha did not answer.

"As far as I know, Yuri Trofimovich devoted all his time to his work and his family."

The colonel ground out his cigarette with controlled exasperation, as if some pet theory of his had been disproved. Then he glared over at Kovalyov for a moment, as if to assign part of the blame to his initial failures.

"Frankly, I am always surprised," said the colonel, "when an intelligent person refuses the carrot."

Alone in the small cell, Andrusha tried to analyze his situation to see if it offered any hopes, any possibilities. Now he realized that he must be a principal suspect, because otherwise they would simply have called him in at work. They must also have been fairly sure that he would not respond to their initial questioning, and so they would want to be able to imprison him directly. To be able to do whatever came next. But it was hard to think. Stupid thoughts kept coming into his brain. Would he be out in time for his brother's birthday? What was Liza's patronymic? Though he forced himself to concentrate, the cell and his situation were like death, too real to be thought about.

He lost track of time, which had ceased to have any quality of motion. Halfway through a set of push-ups he decided that he did not want to feel his body flushed with energy and health—he wanted to have as little awareness of his body as possible.

They would do something to him. They would do it until he told them what he knew or until he died from it. But he wouldn't die from it; too smart for that, they would keep him on the edge of life. It was only a question of how long he could keep his silence. Now his entire life had been resolved into a simple, abstract equation made of silence, time, and pain. Time would equal pain, and the greater the pain and the time, the smaller the silence, until at last the silence would become the zero of a mouth, a mouth through which everything they wanted to know would come howling out. That would shift the equation, and then the pain, too, would start falling toward zero.

Now he should begin emptying himself and not torture himself with the memory of the woman in the Western clothes, or even let himself spend a minute yearning for the simple peace of walking down a sidewalk on a dreary morning watching old women with their brooms. No, there could be absolutely nothing in him now but silence. But the greater the silence, the more time it would take, and the more pain there would be. Silence, time, and pain.

If he could just keep his hatred strong, that would protect him, be his first line of defense. Remember your hatred, remember what these people have done to life, what they will do to your life. Those shits that made life shit.

Now he felt strong in his hatred. There was something in him that could stand up to them—not a belief, not an ideal, but hatred, beautiful hatred, strong, brave, beautiful hatred.

He heard footsteps in the corridor.

People were coming.

What could be worse.

24 The man lying on the blue

linoleum floor had been shot in the back. Solly squatted down and then rolled him over to get a look at his face. It was his father! Someone began pounding on the door. Solly opened the door and Raisa Farb went racing by him. She knelt down by his father and began giving him mouth-to-mouth resuscitation. Between each breath, she would raise her head and scream: *"Vyiskidal. Vyiskidash!"*

Solly woke up, saw the windows bright with day, and smelled the aroma of coffee wending its way from the kitchen.

Now it was giving him nightmares. When he was awake the case gave him a headache and now it was giving him nightmares.

It was his day off, but he was waking up thinking about it. He had had it all planned—lounge around in the morning with the paper and Adelle, work out and steam in the club in the afternoon, then out to dinner and the movies. Be a little human for a change.

He knew if he called in and found out there was something going on, that'd be the end of the day. He'd have the taste of work in his mouth.

Yanopolis was on today, standing in for somebody, trying to look good. When he ought to be out with his girlfriend.

Solly had met the girlfriend the other day. She turned out to be very pretty, well dressed, and pleasant, and seemed to think she was the luckiest girl in New York to have found Apollon Yanopolis. As his mother used to say, for every pot there's a cover.

He called in. Yanopolis said that somebody who might match the description Thomas White had given had been arrested, and they should get White over there for a look. Solly said he had White's phone number and address and he'd deal with it. Yanopolis reminded him it was his day off. Solly thanked him for the information.

He spent some time with Adelle, but it wasn't the way it would have been if he didn't have Thomas White on his mind. An hour later, as he was leaving, she reminded him that while he was out he could buy a Yahrzeit candle, and he said that he would.

———

Solly called Thomas White from the lobby of a coffee shop. The answering tape clicked on, followed by a burst of what sounded like music coming through a broken radio. Then Solly heard a voice he recognized as White's singing:

> Kiss the ground, kiss the sky,
> You better kiss the world good-bye,
> Because they're coming,
> Maybe today, maybe tomorrow.
> Hey, what's those white streaks in the sky?

"Hi, you've been listening to the voice of Tom White and the Radiation Sickness Band. We're not in right now, but if you leave a message after the beep, we'll *probably* get back to you." Then the voice was followed by a long, macabre laugh and a beep. "This is Detective Altheim. We have a suspect we'd like you to see. Call me or Sergeant Yanopolis at 348-3694."

Back on the sidewalk, Solly walked over to a newsstand where an old man's face was framed by an iconostasis of girlie magazines. Solly bought a *Post*.

He'd put a note on White's door, he'd lean on his doorbell, thought Solly, taking the first downtown bus that came.

After settling into a seat, he unfolded the paper. Two famous movie stars were going to marry each other for the third time. Is that love or confusion? Solly thought, and turned to an article claiming that the Soviet Union was far ahead of the United States in developing space weapons, especially laser weapons, that could destroy America's spy satellite system. It sounded like the sort of junk kids watched on television, but of course it was real and he could see it, he could see them starting to shoot down from the sky at each other; why not? So no wonder young kids like White were nervous. And it couldn't be good for taxes, either.

A story on the FBI's annual crime statistics indicated that crime was on the increase in every major category, with violent assault showing a particularly sharp rise. The article went on to break the statistics down into regions, which did not interest Solly very much. He looked out the window almost as if expecting to see a crime being committed.

Of course, people had the wrong idea. They read that there was a crime every thirty seconds or one of those cute statistics and they expected to get mugged every time they turned the corner. They were so worried about themselves, they forgot how many millions of other people there were walking around. But, in another way, crime was everywhere, the fear of it.

There'd probably been a few dozen crimes since he sat down to breakfast. A woman's neck left bleeding where a gold chain had been ripped off, somebody with a bread knife going after the husband or the wife or the girlfriend, cars being hot-wired in parking garages, prostitutes taking their first calls of the day—sure, it was almost eleven— little cocaine deliveries being made to the jerks on Madison Avenue, a naked fag covered with blood and found hand-cuffed to an iron bed in a warehouse, and maybe some

Puerto Rican dancing to the sound of the radio and pulling on the sweater he had charged with a credit card from his victim's wallet.

Thomas White's hallway was dim and smelled of piss and ammonia. Solly leaned on the bell for a good minute, then waited. He didn't like waiting in that hallway; it was too small, and he didn't like not knowing what was happening behind him. After he rang again, he stuffed a note in White's mailbox.

Since he was in that neighborhood, Solly decided to walk down to First and First. He peeked into the Baltyk restaurant, which was very quiet. The street and sidewalk at the corner of First and First looked normal, but Solly knew that this spot wasn't innocent anymore. When the DON'T WALK changed to WALK, he went out onto the island where Farb had stopped and been killed. A little to the left, that horrible couple had been standing and having their horrible little argument—they were probably still having it—and Farb had been standing there after dinner at the restaurant and heading for the subway. Now, why does the Puerto Rican stop and pick him? It was probably one of those instinctive things: he looks at Farb, sees that he's a pigeon type, and decides to go for a fast couple of bucks, and maybe there's some problem between the PR's English and Farb's English, and the next thing you know the gun goes off.

All right, then, so what would it be if it wasn't that? The Russians hire a Puerto Rican to shoot a scientist for receiving smuggled letters full of political crap? That wasn't reality.

On his way back from the island, Solly passed a young man with a Mohawk dyed green and a tattoo on his head, and thought to himself, "Compared to White, this guy's already old-fashioned."

As he was approaching the Second Avenue Deli, Solly's attention was caught by a cab parked at the corner. The cab driver was reading a little book and kissing the page tenderly every few seconds. Solly could not see his face, which was obscured both by the angle and by the man's light-blue golf cap.

He called White again from inside, but as soon as the song came on he hung up and looked around, wondering if there was anyone there he knew. A man with a concentration-camp number on his arm told Solly to take any table he liked and handed him a menu.

There were two bowls on the table, one full of pickles and the other full of green pickled tomatoes. His father had loved those green pickled tomatoes, and it had made his father sad that Solly hadn't liked them. He ordered a hot pastrami on a roll, and coffee.

The restaurant, according to the back of the menu, which he glanced at while waiting for his order to come, was now billing itself as a sort of museum of the past where you could eat. It was probably a smart idea, he thought, because that way you got the nostalgia business, the guys dragging their kids in from the suburbs to see where Daddy used to eat before he made all the money and bought the house with the grass.

Solly ate slowly. He thought of the women he knew—

the model, the lawyer, the Chinese singer. He was tempted. It made him feel bad that he wanted other women and that he didn't feel that way about Adelle much anymore. But what could he do? You couldn't tell your hand to like touching something it didn't like to touch.

As he was paying at the cashier, Solly saw the owner, Marky Stein, talking to a short man he recognized by the blue golf hat as the cabby he had seen outside. Solly gave Marky an I'll-talk-with-you-in-a-second wave of the hand while watching his change being counted back to him.

"Marky, you're looking good," said Solly.

"What are you talking about, I look terrible. I've got eyes. I own a mirror. Solly Altheim, this is Jack Vizner, a friend of mine."

Smiling, Solly shook hands with the gentle birdlike man with the light-blue golf cap.

"Solly is a detective with the New York City police, Jack. And Solly, let me tell you about Jack. Jack's been coming in here for years, and for years he's been telling me I shouldn't be open Saturdays, and for years I've been telling him what's the difference. Then, one day, for some reason, I said to him, All right, I'm going to start closing Saturdays. At first I'm losing a little money; then I start getting all sorts of business from the people who wouldn't set foot in here before because I was open Saturdays, and so now I'm open one day less and I'm actually making more than before. And that was from Jack."

Jack nodded happily in agreement. "And tell him what you do now on your Saturday off."

"Sure, you know what I do, I go to temple over in Brooklyn and I sit there and, I'll tell you, it feels good."

"We've got a wonderful temple," said Vizner. "We've got old people, young people, people from Israel, Russia, Iraq even."

"Come by," said Marky. "You'll see people you haven't seen for years."

"Here," said Vizner, "I have a card with everything on it. See—my name, phone, the address of the temple. I'm the beadle, so I had cards printed. Little things count. For want of a nail . . ."

"Thanks," said Solly, slipping the card into his wallet. "Marky, I'm down here looking for one of those screwball musician types. He doesn't answer his door and he doesn't answer his phone, and so now I'm thinking he may be out somewhere having a late breakfast. Is there any place you know besides the Kiev where they like to eat around here?"

"There's a place over at Second and Seventh, the northwest corner—not right on the corner, a couple of doors up—you see them in there sometimes. I forget the name; they call it Nick's, but the sign says something different. Anyway, you'll see where I mean."

But Thomas White was not in either the Kiev or Nick's, or any of the coffee shops on St. Mark's Place. The note was still in his mailbox, the song was still answering the phone, and Yanopolis was out to lunch when Solly called in.

Relaxed from weights, steam, and a massage, Solly returned home around four-thirty, looking forward to their evening out. It was only after he had hung up his coat that he remembered with an angry snap of his fingers that he had forgotten to buy the goddamned candle!

25 Shar returned to his seat

with a fresh pile of magazines. Dinner and the movie were over, and most of his fellow passengers were already asleep. Leaning up against the galley and stifling yawns, even the stewardesses were starting to look pasty.

He liked the American magazines; the worse they were, the better. *Time* and *Newsweek* were like little toys, interesting until you figured out how they worked. He didn't actually focus on *The New Yorker,* enjoying instead its perfume of wealth, the paper glossy as a rich woman's dress. He looked hard at the pictures in *Black Enterprise,* wondering to what extent the blacks there really were a race apart, though, judging from the pictures, it would seem they were as American as anyone. *Esquire* he couldn't understand; he simply could not imagine the actual person who was supposed to read the magazine. He smiled remembering the odd look the stewardess had given him when he asked, "*Playboy* isn't available?" But he had seen someone reading one. Ah—the man must have bought it himself. An interesting distinction. American hypocrisy.

People magazine amazed him and was in some way his favorite. The indulgence of personality on a scale he would have been unable to imagine—what a best-selling writer has for breakfast, anchormen talk about their "personal fears," everyone divorced and "rebuilding their lives." Perhaps America was not a nation at all but just a swarm of two hundred million lonely personalities with a government. In any case, he found *People* the most useful of the magazines, for it provided him with concrete clues on how to act in the spotlight of publicity; after all, he was now part of that elite club of the famous and wonderful, the Mercedes Benzes of humanity.

He looked out the window, though he could see nothing but darkness and did not even know what darkness he was looking down on—the darkness of the sea or of the clouds.

Shar had also purchased some Russian-émigré journals in Frankfurt and had been presented with several others by admiring editors, journalists, writers. The same old terms, the same old arguments—Lenin, collectivization, Hitler, Stalin, Molotov-Ribbentrop, the Gulag, the meaning of history. He had liked one article, which said that the principal trauma of the twentieth century for the Western democracies was the unimpeded rise of Hitler. That was the specter haunting the

Western mind as it attempted to make the most significant perception of the late twentieth century—was the Soviet Union another danger on the order of Hitler's Germany, or just one state among others that could somehow be lived with? Other than that, he found nothing that he hadn't seen before in one variation or another. But it was important for him to hear the exact tone of the polemics, to sense the divisions in the little camps that had formed, the positions that had hardened like old men's arteries.

He reached into his pocket and pulled out the sleeping pills Vinias had brought him in Lubyanka. White, they sometimes seemed to have a faint greenish tinge. He hesitated for a moment between taking one or two, then settled on one, which he washed down with the melted ice that still tasted of whiskey in his plastic cup. Then he closed his eyes and slipped back into himself, like an amphibian returning to the water.

Everything that had happened to him since the guard struck him across the face in the camp seemed to want to fit into a pattern. The magazines he had just read, the plastic glass on his fold-down table, Vinias's look when visiting him in Lubyanka—it was all a message that kept appearing and disappearing like the message on the fat German's magic slate.

The question was, was there any other life for him but the life he was in now? Was Vinias right when he said that a person was lost outside of his proper place? Where else could he go, what else could he be?

But Vinias was not right about everything; they had

shifted assignments on him, and someone with more power than Vinias had decided that it was more important to retrieve that little piece of hard science than to perform an extravaganza of disinformation. Of course, there was no question about it—something that could give a person thirty years of life was worth immeasurably more than any virtuoso performance. Who wouldn't want to live an extra thirty years, to have a life that spanned a century? People would kill for that; people already had. And if they would kill for it, they would certainly pay for it. Americans paid billions of dollars each year for drugs, legal and illegal; what would they pay for something that gave thirty more years to gobble down life's pleasures?

America was still hours away, but already it was making possibilities percolate in his mind. For example, if, instead of obeying orders he kept the information himself, went underground, produced the drug himself, and sold it on the black market like cocaine or heroin, he would be rich and powerful in six months. No one could touch him, and he would be doubly protected from Vinias's revenge—first by American society (not much protection but something) and second by being out of sight in the criminal underworld. After all, what was crime but politics without the excuses, practically his business anyway.

Things were happening quickly, too quickly. The guards unlocked the cell door quickly. They dragged Andrusha quickly down the hall. Then they pushed him into a very large room and shut the door quickly behind him. The floor, walls, and ceiling of the room were covered with gray mats which made it look like a deserted gymnasium, though Andrusha realized that they were there to muffle screams.

Toward one end of the room, a small man in a blue suit was sitting at a desk. He did not look up from his writing, but some message came from him, some slight movement of his head (bristly with a hedgehog haircut) informed Andrusha that the man was aware of his presence. In the far corner of the room was a large man—Andrusha could not tell how large because of the distance. The man was wearing gray sweatpants and a dark-blue sweatshirt. Concentrated, he seemed in a world of his own.

Andrusha stayed by the door, resisting the temptation to go to the empty chair in front of the desk. Now his own thoughts were coming too fast. Should he march to the chair? Or should he wait to be told what to do? But that was the feeling he wanted to shake, the feeling of utter passivity, waiting to be told what to do.

The man at the desk looked up and smiled with the corners of his mouth, as if aware of exactly what Andrusha was thinking. But he made no gesture, said nothing.

Andrusha began walking across the room. He knew that it had already begun, that the man at the desk had intentionally requested that Andrusha be shoved through the door so he would be left in a moment of confusion; this was all part of the process of softening him up. Well, fuck them, he would walk right in. As he approached the desk, the man behind it came into sharper focus. Now he could see that his blue suit was in fact pin-striped and that the light plastic frames of his eyeglasses were transparent. And with a quick glance at the face, which from a distance had looked thin but closer up was pale and fleshy, Andrusha remembered the type from school. He was the one that no one had ever liked, and now he had made a career of it.

Andrusha sat down.

The man continued writing for a second, his eyes squinting in the lamplight. When he looked up at Andrusha, his face seemed happy.

"You are here," he began, "because you did not cooperate upstairs. You realize that you will be charged with treason. Every state has the right and the obligation to protect itself against treason. As I am sure you are aware, the traditional punishment for treason is death. In that sense, you are, for all practical purposes, a dead man. Right now is your very last opportunity to change that situation. Tell us what we need to know and you will at least remain among the living."

He had said all this hurriedly, blandly, even with a touch of boredom, simply to get it over with.

Andrusha took a deep breath. The room smelled mildewy.

The official smiled. "Good." He took out a stopwatch from his desk drawer and spent a moment adjusting it, then tried out his pen to make sure the ink was still flowing. Satisfied, he made a series of quick notations and looked up at Andrusha almost apologetically.

"You may be interested in this," he said. "Lately I have started keeping records on interrogation times—how long it takes to achieve success. We would like to be able to establish some sort of predictability, but of course it's very hard; the material varies so much, you'd be surprised. Sometimes they bring some old woman in here, and it takes forever—their obstinacy is nothing short of amazing. Whereas, on the other hand, a young, healthy man like yourself may take one look around and fall to his knees, beg the Soviet state's forgiveness, and cooperate fully. We'll be starting in about a minute and a half, Edward," he said to the large man in the sweatpants. Then, looking back at Andrusha: "For some reason, I like to start right on the quarter hour."

"Go fuck your mother," said Andrusha.

"By the way, Edward prefers it if you resist. Let's start in ten seconds, Edward. Legs first, knees, shins. Ten, nine, eight . . ."

Edward did not move, but his concentrated attention seemed to shift from some space only he could see to Andrusha. Though Andrusha looked for his eyes so he could at least stab them with the hatred in his own, there was no contact. Hatred, remember that, he told himself; your beautiful hatred for them is your wall.

"Five, four, three . . ."

Edward began running across the room, picking up speed at a horrifying rate, his head and shoulders down. Andrusha braced himself. It had begun. A terrible collision of flat, hard bone threw him over onto his back and half out of the chair onto the mats, which were harder than they looked. All right, the first blow; he was still with them. A hard, pointed shoe kicked his shin, and a heel came down on his stomach. Then he was being lifted to his feet and pressed to the wall. The hard toe was kicking his shins.

"All right, stomach, face, stomach, then put him back in his chair!" commanded the man at the desk.

Everything was happening too fast. The pain was too great already. He would hate himself if he could hold on only for some cowardly, short period of time.

Back in his chair, he knew that he would have to beware of gratitude.

"Relatively speaking," said the man at the desk, "that was nothing. Just a shade under thirty seconds. Call it thirty."

On the way back to his apartment, David stopped Raisa under a streetlight and looked at her with the too-happy eyes of lust. She pushed him away lightly, and they walked the rest of the way in silence.

She was modest until she was naked. Then she became dangerous, the danger greater for being contained, as they circled each other bristling with wariness.

For a brief moment he was afraid that he might not be able to make love to her, that he might not be excited by her all-too-human body, the thin calves, the gravity-defeated breasts. She put one knee on the corner of the bed, and then it no longer mattered what she looked like or didn't look like. There were no thoughts in his mind now, no words in his throat.

He walked over and stood across from her, a corner of the bed between them. It became a game to see how long they could stand the terror of desire, who would move first. Her body was a dare; his pleasure was in resisting his pleasure.

He pushed his hand through her hair, which felt dry and ignitable like straw, and yanked her head back. She yielded with voluptuous cunning, then clawed his ribs with her fingernails, making him laugh in pain and surprise.

Side by side on their hands and knees, they bit at each other's necks and ears. Sounds came from their bodies, groans of organs and loins, along with their smells, which mixed at once.

She fell to her side. He pushed one shoulder and she was on her back, passive as a trap. He reached under her thighs and pulled her toward him, entering her at the same time, jabbing as if there were a membrane to puncture. She came up and around him, stomach and thighs, the hair between her legs tickling between his like a little fur tail. For a moment he could feel every vein and ridge on him and inside her, profiles on a coin.

At first they fucked almost lazily, with regal leisure, like lions. He was up on his hands, head back, until he started to feel that he was not far enough inside her, that there was some dynamic emptiness drawing the point where he was concentrated, glowing orange like a burning stick.

But there was still something in the way; tattered strips

of mind and personality were keeping them caged in themselves. Now love meant only one thing—to claw through all
those tattered strips until there was nothing left of each other.
And they had to work for an hour in the joy of that murder.

26 Evgeny Shar

became a logistics problem at Gander and Kuhn, his publisher, when he cabled them to announce that he had changed his mind and would accept the invitation to speak at the Russian Book Fair in Exile and would they arrange accommodations for him and, if possible, send someone to meet him at the airport.

The problem stemmed from the belief that Shar's English would be inadequate at best, which meant, of course, that he should be met by someone who knew Russian. Unfortunately, one of the two editors who qualified already had a luncheon appointment with the Greatest Living Russian Poet (referred to as GLRP around the publishing house, and sometimes as Glurp); this luncheon date had already been canceled once before, and to cancel again, especially for another poet, was asking for trouble. The other editor was Karen, and there was a problem there as well.

A meeting had been called. Someone suggested that the editor and the Greatest Living Russian Poet go to the airport together to greet Shar: it was a sort of historic occasion, wasn't it, and two birds would be killed. The suggestion caused a flare of enthusiasm, which faded to nothing as soon as someone pointed out that it was all much too spur-of-the-moment, and some mysterious Russian cultural protocol was bound to be violated. All these suggestions and counter-suggestions were, as Karen well knew, simply detours around the obvious—that she should be sent to the airport. She did Russian books, knew some Russian, and was the person who, after all, had gotten Shar's poems published on the Op Ed page. But she had spoken very sharply to the owner of the publishing house at a previous meeting when he remarked that Russian literature was ceasing to be a viable commodity because that story had been told, and it might well be wiser to start scouting around for Central American novelists while they were still cheap. When Karen suggested that they might combine several trends and come up with something like Guerrilla Secrets for Thin Thighs, the silence that followed was, to say the least, colossal.

The publisher was avoiding looking at her, and she wondered exactly what he was thinking. It would be very bad if he didn't send her out to meet Shar. Not that she wanted to go. She was never very good at that kind of thing, for it tended to bring out the girlish, admiring side of her, which she had spent years learning to guard against.

The publisher was irked that such a problem even existed, irked that there were such things as different languages which made it impossible for people even to speak with one another, and irked that the prestige of the house demanded that Shar be met by someone from their staff, at least an assistant editor. But if he sent Karen, that would indicate to everyone that he was willing to swallow the humiliation of their last encounter.

"Well," said the publisher, "does our last contract with whoever it is that represents Shar give us the right of first refusal on his next book?"

"It does, but what does that mean these days?"

"Has anybody read the poem?"

"Nobody's even seen it."

"Well, he'll be arriving here broke," said the publisher. "He'll need money." Suddenly it was all quite clear to him. He would send the editor who was having lunch with the Greatest Living to the airport, and he personally would take the Greatest to an excellent restaurant. Or at least to a very good one. He was just about to announce his decision when he glanced over at the editor in question and knew it was a stupid move. A man who has just spent three years in a Soviet labor camp would not be entranced by being met at the airport by an aging homosexual.

"Karen, I would like you to go to the airport and meet Shar," said the publisher, swallowing his bile for the sake of the house. "Not only that; why don't you see if you can get hold of David Aronow and take them both out to lunch? Whatever that poem is, it has to be translated well or it'll go right to the library like that monstrosity of Solzhenitsyn's, *Prussian Nights*. Yes, if Aronow and Shar hit it off, that could help matters along. Take them someplace nice. You still have a company credit card, don't you?"

Stung by the last remark, as she was supposed to have been, Karen rose from her chair and said, "I'll call Aronow right now."

The efficiency of her steps controlled the distress she felt as she walked down the hallway to her office. Now the remark she had made to the publisher seemed childish to her, a self-destructive rage disguised as high principle that had fooled no one but her. Suddenly she felt juvenile, unformed, damp at the core, as doubt after doubt rose to hypnotize her into believing she had acted not from natural courage but from that skein of old neuroses whose prisoner she would forever be.

David Aronow sat by his one window. It was hard to sleep very late unless he had had a lot to drink. Now he was only waiting for the film to arrive, and the taste of waiting was in everything he did. It became worse after he started calling Naomi. Before, it had felt as if he was only waiting until the eighth came and he could start calling her as they had arranged. But once the eighth had come and he could call, then he was waiting for the film itself to arrive, and that was almost unbearable. His conversations with Naomi were always short; there were only so many ways she could say that they had not been notified by their broker that any new shipment of films had arrived. He could detect impatience and irritated regret creeping into her voice, and since the last thing he wanted was to encourage any second thoughts in her, he kept his side of the conversation as positive and brief as possible, never responding to any of the little signals that could develop into a change of heart.

Abram Luntz had called the night before to say that he was coming to New York to participate in a conference called the Russian Book Fair in Exile at the Public Library. He had been asked to prepare a short statement for the press (Oh, my God, the Russian idea of a short statement, thought David, who knew what was coming), and would David mind translating it? It was important that it be done right. David said that he didn't mind, hoping that the sheer obligation of it would force him to concentrate.

Abram had the latest news. After refusing, "like Caesar," Shar had decided to accept the invitation to speak at the conference and must be due to arrive in New York very soon because the conference was only a couple of days away. The Shcherbatinskys were getting divorced. Semyonov had just sold his novel for sixty thousand dollars!

David had made the usual expressions of interest, regret, pleasure, but in fact all that belonged to his old life, whose reality had begun to thin, as does that of a house when you have made up your mind to move.

Raisa would be in his new life, Karen would not. He would have to do something about Karen; he didn't know exactly what. But life required a period at the end of a sentence, a good-bye, some tone of conclusion; as his friend the dour psychiatrist had once put it, no experience was ever complete without its own anticlimax.

In her office, Karen let her hand rest on the phone, thinking what a terrible combination love and business were, especially when they both were going badly. The hateful sister-self that was always with her now reminded her that it was her fault that David had turned away from her. Had she forgotten that she was unworthy of love and that any love she got was at best a temporary error?

But she was wise to that part of her now and could sometimes ride out those rapids on the skimpy, transparent raft of consciousness. She told herself that David was just acting the way he had acted before. Staying close was impossible for him. It wasn't her, or it wasn't only her, it was him. Things could change in a minute, they had before, why shouldn't they again. She had never met anyone without crippled emotions, so what was the big surprise.

David looked at the ringing phone, thinking he might not even answer it. There was nobody in the world he wanted to hear from at that moment; the only calls that interested him were his calls to Naomi.

He picked up the phone, his "Hello" that of a man woken or interrupted.

"Hi," she said, more to identify herself than as a greeting.

"Hi, how are you?"

"Good, you?"

"Good."

"Good. David, I don't know if this'd interest you, but

I'm going out to meet Evgeny Shar at JFK around one o'clock."

That would hardly be a situation in which he could say anything to her. Still, he felt that he should go with her, out of pity for her—the executioner's pity.

Besides, maybe she would just feel it and he wouldn't have to say anything.

"Sure, I'll go."

"I'll come by in a cab around twelve-thirty, even though his plane'll probably be late."

"I'll be out front."

"Oh, by the way, did you see the *Times?*"

"Not yet."

"There're some excerpts from an interview Shar gave in Germany."

"I'll check it."

"See you, David."

"See you, Karen, 'bye."

David leaned against the front of his building and un-folded his *Times.* The article on Shar was not in the back with the book reviews, film ads, and crossword puzzle, but on page 3 of the front section, where it had been appended to a larger article on the recent Soviet peace offensive. There was a picture, Shar against a window with a mountain in the background.

He looked up to see a cab making an abrupt yellow diagonal across Fourth Avenue.

The driver stepped on the gas the second David slammed the door shut.

"How are you?" he asked, looking over at Karen, who was fumbling through her pocketbook with an energy that verged on panic.

"You're not going to believe this, you're going to hate me," she said.

"What?"

"I meant to go to the bank on the way to work, but then I figured I'd go after lunch because I was a few minutes late as it was and there's always those lines, and, besides, I'm in enough trouble there as it is, and, David, I've only got six dollars—no, seven."

"Don't worry, I've got some cash."

"And I can't even remember how to say 'Welcome to America' in Russian."

Before he could supply her with the correct phrase, she was already crying and leaning toward him. For a moment she seemed to hesitate, then let her head fall against his chest. He stroked her back—a doctor, a father, a friend. This was not what she wanted, he knew, but she had to feel every nuance in his fingers; maybe they could do without all those clumsy, frustrating words.

He was surprised to see iron gray glints on her glossy brown hair. He reached out to rub her hair, but he caught himself and brought his hand back. If he touched that hair, if his hand began to trace the form of her skull, if he touched the back of her neck with his fingers, her love for him would stream into his fingers through her hair and her neck. And then he would have to fight off that love.

Wondering why he had not touched her hair, Karen sat

up and began drying her eyes with a piece of Kleenex from her purse.

"A lot of it has to do with work," she said, so that he wouldn't think it was all him, and then told him the story of Guerrilla Secrets for Thin Thighs.

"The problem with you is that you've got this wonderful pure courage, not to mention wit, but then you tell yourself a whole different version that makes you look like a neurotic dope."

"Well, some people are complicated."

"It's such a relief to be a crude brute, you can't imagine."

The cab pulled hard up onto the on-ramp that led to the airport, pressing them back against the seat.

"But wait," she said as they slowed in front of the terminal, "how do you say 'Welcome to America' in Russian?"

"Dobro pozhalovat' v ameriku."

"Of course, I knew that, *dobro pozhalovat' v ameriku.*"

Shar's plane would be twenty minutes late. When they had taken up a position by the customs gate, David went to get coffee and call Naomi.

Naomi was not at her desk.

They're never at their desks, he thought angrily on the way back with the coffees.

After a few sips she could no longer sit there making small talk with him and jumped up to call the Algonquin Hotel, to make sure there were no foul-ups with Shar's reservation. David watched her disappear into the crowd, telling himself that's what it was going to be like to lose her.

A white-haired couple trotted, suitcases in hand, past two black marines sleeping in purple plastic chairs, duffel bags at their feet.

Just as she returned, a voice that came from nowhere and was suddenly everywhere announced that flight number 889 from Frankfurt had arrived.

About half the passengers had cleared customs when they spotted Shar, who kept glancing back at the porter behind him like a nervous dog-owner checking that his pet was still at the end of the leash.

"Mr. Shar!" called Karen.

Shar looked about for a moment in confusion, then spotted her, smiled, and, tossing off a quick playful salute, began striding athletically toward her, a new crackled leather briefcase in one hand.

David had the odd sensation he always had when he saw the famous, a photograph walking toward him in the flesh.

"Dobro pozhalovat v ameriku," said Karen, getting it out too fast to make any mistakes.

"Thank you, thank you very much," said Shar in English. Setting his briefcase down, he took her hand in both of his and bowed slightly.

David felt a twinge of complicated jealousy at seeing her beam in admiration. Then his attention was caught by Shar's eyes—transparent gray around dark blue—and by his nose, which looked as though it had been carved by a folk artist who had finished off the tip with a single cut. But as Karen turned to introduce him, David became aware of Shar's after-shave lotion, a cheap, too-sweet, very Soviet smell that softened the jealousy.

"I am so happy to meet you, Mr. Aronow," said Shar, extending his hand, which was large and dry.

"My pleasure," said David.

27 Andrusha felt trapped in the scream

which seemed to rise from deep inside him and rush toward the surface, where it would break into sound. He did not want to return to the surface—he wanted to stay down where it was murky and safe—but he could not resist the upward rise of the scream, which burst out of his mouth and made his teeth, eardrums, and skull vibrate for a moment. Then he was back in the room with the small man and Edward.

The small man looked up from his desk with approval.

Andrusha saw that he was naked, his hands and feet tied to the chair. It was horrible to be naked in a room with them. Now they could do anything they wanted to him. There were little places in the world where people could do whatever they wanted to you, and he was in one of those places.

For a second he thought of the weekend he had spent with Tanya at her parents' *dacha*, and how she had said naughtily, like a little girl on her birthday, "And now we can do anything we want." He forbade himself to think of her or anything like that. But did he still have that power over himself? Did he have any power left at all? He could not even resist screaming, though it had brought him back to this room. He had to find something he could bite his teeth into, as people did in the old days when doctors sawed off their legs.

Were they going to use electrodes on him? He had heard about them, read articles denouncing their use by South American fascist regimes, but of course they had to have them, too. They always liked the latest in everything; Russia hated to feel behind. And that's why they could do anything they wanted to him: they knew he had helped them fall behind, and that was the worst thing anybody could do to them, and so they would do the worst things to him.

"I have a set of needles in my desk," began the small man. "Some of them make you lose consciousness, some of them make you regain consciousness. We can turn your mind on and off like a light bulb. So blacking out is not going to do you any good anymore. Now you will have to stay here, wide awake, with me and Edward."

He didn't know whether to say anything or not. Letting them do all the talking made him feel powerless. But when he spoke, it established something with them, brought him closer to them, and that, too, gave them more power over him, in a different way. It didn't matter what he did, because whatever he did gave them power. That was how the room was set up.

But he could choose to keep silent or to tell what he knew; that was still his choice. That took a little bit of their absolute power away from them and turned them from gods into people, one of whom even had a name, Edward.

How could a person with a name, how could a person named Edward, do those things to him? That was what he couldn't understand. It was some sort of misunderstanding, and it would be cleared up any minute. How could they be human and not realize that what they were doing was wrong and that he was a person too, even though he was tied naked to a chair and they could do whatever they wanted to him?

He forbade himself any of those stupid hopes. There was no misunderstanding; they knew what they were doing. His bones were hot with pain, and he hated having a body: see what people could do to you if you had one.

"Some people are happy as children, some people are happy as adults," said the man at the desk. "I can see that you were happy as a child. The women loved you—they stroked your hair and kissed you. And the men liked you and took you places and listened to what you said. And maybe you even had a nice nickname. And now look how badly you've ended up—a traitor to your own country who won't even cooperate when everything, or nearly everything, is known about him and the only useful thing he could be doing with his miserable life is to help the country that gave him birth and reared him from a child. One treason leads to another. But we must look on the bright side of things as well. I did not have a happy childhood. No one was ever glad to see me coming. No one gave me any nickname; nobody called up to my window from the street. But I've done very well as a grown-up, you see. I do work that I thoroughly enjoy. I have good companions. Edward, for example, can be very humorous after he's had a few drinks and relaxed.

"The only way out now for you is to die, and we are not going to let you die. We are going to get it out of you. That is one-hundred-percent guaranteed. Think of that for a moment. One hundred percent. You are fairly strong; you might be able to resist us for five to eight days, but certainly no longer than that. Then you will tell us what we want to know. You think it makes a difference. It makes no difference if you resist. The only difference is the amount of pain that will have to go up your nerves and into your brain. It must be truly terrible. I myself am very sensitive to pain. I hate to even cut my finger on a piece of paper. So, this would be a very appropriate moment for you to tell us everything you know about Yuri Trofimovich's clandestine activities in be-half of the American military establishment. Don't you agree that this would be a very good moment for you to tell us everything about Yuri Trofimovich's clandestine activities in behalf of the American military establishment?"

Andrusha was swimming through a rushing inward emptiness like a man about to vomit.

"No? You're shaking your head no? Then I'm going to tell you something about yourself. You think that you are a good person. You are not a good person. A good person does not betray his motherland. A good, healthy person does not invite pain. A healthy person tries to avoid pain. Those are very fundamental things. You may think you are a good person, but you are not a good person; you are a traitor to your own motherland, and you are a person who likes pain and makes—yes, that is the truth—makes other people do painful things to him. That is the kind of person you are, and so, of course, a person like me will get angry when perverted traitors like you make him do things, painful things. Now, tell me everything you know about Yuri Trofimovich's clandestine activities in behalf of the American military establishment."

They said he couldn't last more than five to eight days, but how long had it been already? He had been there several times, yet, when they threw him back on the bed and he slept for a few hours, there were always nightmares, and the nightmares always took place in that room with those two men. And since everything was exactly the same in the nightmares as it was in that room—the same sorts of things were done, the same sorts of questions were asked—he didn't know how many times he had been in that room. He could not tell his memories of his nightmares from his memories of that room.

Maybe he had a weak heart or a weak artery or something that hadn't shown up in any medical examination, some weak vein in his brain that would burst and make consciousness, horrible consciousness, swim away like the picture fading on a TV set. Everything that you loved in life was bad in that room—keen senses, good health, consciousness, those were his enemies in that room as much as the man and

Edward were his enemies. Again he was awestruck by their magical power, which, in that dingy room that smelled of mildew, could transform everything that was good in life into something bad. That awe was followed by a sudden despair: if they had so much power that they could turn life inside out, then, of course, they had power to spare when it came to making him say what they wanted to hear. How could he be such a fool as to resist them for a single second? He who had never done much of anything, how could he resist people who had the power to change everything in life? But at that point he realized they were getting inside of him, they were in him sniffing around for that little room where he was hiding in silence with his secret, and now they were even hypnotizing him into opening the door himself, from the inside. Fuck them.

Andrusha blinked his eyes and saw the room very clearly. Dark gray mats with darker gray stains on them. A man at a desk writing as if he were in an office at a bank. And Edward washing his hands with a pitcher and basin.

Edward had not said a word yet, and Andrusha realized that he would be frightened to hear his voice. The man at the desk was angry at Andrusha today. Now he had started to feel personally offended by Andrusha's resistance, because it said that he couldn't do absolutely everything that he wanted, that he, too, was just a person, with limited powers like everyone else. That meant that when they got started, they would be worse to him than ever before.

"Finish up now, Edward. I want to start in a couple of minutes."

Edward was drying his hands on a towel very slowly, as if for some reason his skin had a tendency to stay wet.

"In two minutes," said the man at the desk, "we will be starting. Once I start, I like it to run its natural course; otherwise it leaves me all keyed up. And so now, more than ever, is the right time to tell me about Yuri Trofimovich's clandestine activities in behalf of the American military establishment."

Andrusha said nothing, busy locking all the locks on the door to his little room of silence.

"You think we're so afraid of the Americans and all their technology? We don't need their technology. Do you see any technology here? We don't need expensive machines that break down and need to be repaired and sit on the shelf for a week while someone tries to scare up a spare part; we don't need technology. So don't think that your silence about the technology Yuri Trofimovich gave them is going to make any difference in the end, because technology is not what counts, and I am going to prove that to you right now. Edward, take your position."

Edward came from the corner of the room and walked past Andrusha, his face distracted like that of a speaker on his way to the podium, checking his lines one last time. Then he was right behind Andrusha. Andrusha could feel Edward's breath on him; it smelled of tobacco and eggs.

Now, for the first time, the small man was coming out from behind his desk. Andrusha could see that he was limping, and for a second he thought with contempt that the man was a cripple taking his revenge on the world. But then

Andrusha saw that he was limping because he had only one shoe on. The other shoe was in his hand.

"What's going to happen now is my own little invention. I call it the shoe and the eye."

He held the shoe by the heel and flapped it rapidly several times in the air. The sole was very thin and flexible.

"Now, Edward, show him why we call it the shoe and the eye."

Edward's hands came around Andrusha's face, the thumbs and forefingers forming ovals around Andrusha's eyes and then opening like calipers to keep them gaping. Now the force of Edward's chest came down on the back of Andrusha's head, forcing him to look down at his naked thighs and genitals.

"Do you understand now?" said the man coming closer and slipping the shoe under Andrusha's genitals like a spatula. "Then what I don't understand is why you won't take this last opportunity to tell me about the nature of Yuri Trofimovich's clandestine activities in behalf of the American military establishment. Still no? I can't understand that. But, to tell you the truth, there are many things I cannot understand. For example, I could never understand why a man would want to put *that*," he said, slipping the shoe out from under Andrusha's genitals, "inside of a woman. What a truly disgusting idea, don't you agree? DON'T YOU AGREE!"

28 "You know what I would like

more than anything?"
said Evgeny Shar, putting his whiskey and soda down on the
table in the lobby of the Algonquin Hotel. "More than lunch.
More than seeing New York. What I want more than anything is to go to a Xerox machine."

"To copy your new poem?" asked Karen.

"Yes," said Shar. "There is only one copy in the entire
world."

"I can have it copied for you at work." Karen knew
immediately, from the expressions of disapproval and disappointment on both Shar's and Aronow's faces, that she had
somehow said the wrong thing. Since they had left the airport, their little group of three had already been through
several mutations. Sometimes she had felt left out, when Shar

and David conversed fast and free in Russian, her mind always two or three sentences behind before it finally gave up. But then David had been odd man out as she listened, too admiringly, to Shar's impressions of Germany and the West.

"You understand, David?" asked Shar.

"Sure."

"So explain."

"You know in the Soviet Union you can't get near a Xerox machine."

"Oh, right, of course, I knew that," she said, angry at David for acting superior and European.

Still, she had to be fair. It had been a stupid mistake. It was one thing to read their books and support their struggle, but it was somehow hard to remember that this all occurred in a daily life with its own very different and quite specific details.

"Yes, you see," said Shar, "to do it myself, that would be the entire pleasure. I don't want to say anything against the great publishing house of Gander and Kuhn, but to make the copies myself, to have that power, that freedom—no, you could never imagine that. And so, Karen, don't feel bad that you offered out of goodness to do the work for me. That was goodness, and goodness is the most important thing. So," said Shar, lifting his glass, "to goodness and Xerox."

"To goodness and Xerox," said David, smiling at Karen, who had just come out of her cloud of self-recrimination and took a healthy slug of her whiskey, which impressed both of the men at the table and once again changed them into a group of three.

"There's a Xerox machine in the library," said Karen. "That's about the nearest one I can think of."

"How many pages is the manuscript?" asked David.

"Thirty-seven."

"And how many copies do you want to make?" asked Karen.

"Oh, for right now, say ten."

"That's a lot of dimes," said David.

"There's a bank on the corner of Fifth," said Karen.

"So let's go," said Shar, reaching to finish his drink.

"I'll make one quick call," said David, rising and heading for the phone booth, which he had been watching for some time, waiting for it to be vacated by the large woman in the lime green coat who was now emerging, a several-stage operation—pocketbook, hip, torso, head.

The texture of the situation, so rich in details—Shar's Slavic brogue, Karen's lustrous hair and nervousness, the dark oak paneling, the peanut skins' salty tickle at the back of his throat, the liquor pinching his stomach—all that richness had suddenly turned gray and transparent, for he had once again remembered that all he was really doing was waiting to call Naomi.

There was a vague aura, a sort of powdery warmth, left by the large woman, which David became aware of as he closed the old-fashioned hinged door. But did *he* have a dime? That was the question. He didn't, but he had two nickels. A dime was somehow preferable. Two nickels doubled the chance for mechanical error.

"I'm sorry, Naomi is on the other line," said the voice

of her male secretary, who dressed with too much humor.

"Let's go to Xeroxland," said David, returning to the table and finishing his own drink on his feet.

"Xeroxland? What is Xeroxland? I thought you said we were going to the library?" said Shar.

Karen and David laughed, which brought them together again, Americans.

"A real temple of capitalism," said Shar, stopping to savor the bank's marble and hush. "We get in line?"

"Yes," said Karen.

"Aha, here too."

It seemed somehow foolish for all three of them to stand in line, and so David separated himself and went over to the chair by the ashtray. He lit a cigarette, his face grimacing from the sulfur, shook the match, and dropped it into the clean metal ashtray.

For some reason he thought of the way Naomi smoked, blowing the smoke up close to her face.

He glanced over at Shar and Karen, who were almost up to the teller. Their heads were close as they talked.

What if Karen went from him to Shar? he thought. It could happen. In the cab she had felt what he would not give her, the simplest assurance of his love. On jealousy's vivid screen he saw her hands on Shar's ass as it shuddered like a motor that wouldn't stop even after the key was turned off.

"Dimes, dimes, *New York Times*," said Shar, grinning boyishly, a little pyramid of green-rolled silver on the palms of his hands.

"Dimes, dimes, *New York Times*—I like that," said David.

Then all three of them picked up the refrain and chanted it on the way out, both to defy the solemnity of the bank and to affirm the happy specialness of their little group; it reminded David of the trips he had made to Europe in his early twenties, when he would return to the hotel late, drunk and laughing with people he might love for five days and never see again for the rest of his life.

It was sunny on Fifth Avenue, and the sidewalk was crowded with people and shadows, the street so sparkling and unreal in its wealth that even the pretzel vendors and the blind men with their tin cups and dogs seemed more the inspired touches of some urban artist than actual suffering people who, at the end of the day, returned to rooms where they counted their change, spooned soup from cans, and fell asleep.

David and Karen grinned in appreciation of the delight on Shar's face as the first copy slid into the bin. He pulled it out and stared at it with a wonder and pleasure that made them ashamed of their American lives, in which such things were only noticed when they failed to perform properly. David hated to feel so American, that better but lesser state of being.

"Look, in some ways it's even nicer," said Shar. "The letters are darker, and the paper is whiter. It just doesn't feel as good. And, of course," he said, sniffing the paper, "it smells different."

Soon the air around the machine was warm with a damp, chemical smell. Shar seemed indefatigable and hummed to himself as he slipped dime after dime into the machine. Left to themselves, David and Karen began talking softly at first, so as not to distract Shar from his joy.

"He's wonderful," whispered Karen.

"He is," agreed David.

"But somebody's going to have to tell him about that cologne of his."

He was glad she had noticed. But then he could see her and Shar naked in her bathroom, her hand stopping his as he reached for the bottle of cologne. With her other hand she pinched her nostrils together, and then they both burst into laughter.

"I'll be right back," said David. "I have to make a quick call."

He was out of dimes, he remembered on the way, and turned back to ask Shar for one.

"Take three, take four," said Shar. "I am a millionaire of dimes." David took three.

First Naomi. He got the other secretary this time, the young woman with the bland face and alert eyes. Naomi had gone to lunch. She wasn't expected until after three.

"All right, I'll call her back then," said David. "No, no message."

Then he had to call Raisa, if only for a minute. To hear her voice. To be sure she existed, that that other world really existed.

He could hear the smile in her voice as she said, "Hello, David," and then added, "Are you at home?"

"No, I'm in the Public Library. With Evgeny Shar."

"Evgeny Shar is here?"

"Yes."

"What is he like?"

"I'll tell you when I see you."

"When will that be?"

"Do you teach today?"

"No."

"Let's have an early dinner, then."

"Fine."

"I'll meet you at the corner of Seventh and Bleecker at seven. There's a lot of good places around there."

"Bleecker and Seventh at seven."

There was a pause in which both of them wished to say something more but neither of them did.

His third call was to his answering machine. In a voice made strange by the recording—thin somehow, or hoarse—his friend Jim from Boston said that it was very important that they talk.

Not wanting to borrow another dime from Shar, David moved to a blue credit-card phone. What was the problem, he wondered? Was Jim going to back out?

"Listen, David, you remember that I told you my mother wasn't doing too well," said Jim. "Well, she's had another stroke. We're leaving in about an hour. I don't know how long we're going to be down there."

"I'm sorry to hear that."

"Thanks. I thought I was prepared for this after the last

one, but you're never prepared. It's a shame, too—we were just starting to get through some of the old bullshit and really talk, and now it's too late."

"Too late," repeated David, the worst phrase in the language.

"Listen, I'll give you my number down there just in case, all right?"

"Sure."

Then the voice that would soon be thanking people for their condolences recited ten numbers, area code first.

Shar and Karen were stacking the manuscripts when David returned.

"Look, a first edition of Sharizdat," punned Shar. He pulled out his large black Pelikan pen. "And now my first dedications. Should I give one to the two of you, or one each?"

Before David could react, Karen had shook her head and said, "Better make it one each."

"All right, then," said Shar, uncapping his pen, "but this costs a poor Russian émigré an extra three dollars and seventy cents."

He looked off for a moment and then wrote, "To Karen, who welcomed me to the land of freedom in my own language. With gratitude." He handed her the manuscript with a little bow; she accepted it with a playful curtsy, then, pragmatically, blew on the ink.

"And now for you," said Shar to David.

"To David Aronow for his genius translation of 'To My Daughter.' "

Shar looked up and was glad to see the same expression on both their faces, that of a person pleased not only by the gift but by its rightness.

Then the pull of their individual lives overcame the force that had bound them together. Karen had to get back to work. Shar had to rest. And it was time for David to return to pure waiting undisguised by errands and talk.

Karen hailed a cab while David explained to Shar what the lighted signals on the roof meant. Then, after one last wave through the rear window, she was gone in traffic.

"While you were making your calls, I told Karen that I had prepared a little speech for the book fair, and she offered to translate it for me," said Shar. "I didn't want to bother you with it."

"I'm sure she'll do a good job," said David, relieved.

"But you know, David, I'm really a little nervous about this speech."

"I'm sure it'll go fine. And I'll give you some free commercial advice. Don't sell your new book until after the fair. You'll probably get a lot of publicity, and that will drive the price of Evgeny Shar up."

"Everybody is a company here?"

"You could say that."

"Dimes, dimes, *New York Times*," said Shar, but more wryly this time, as if he had gotten a whiff of the essential sadness of American commerce, gleam though it might.

"By the way," said David as they were shaking hands, "thank you for your dedication, but you can't use the word 'genius' as an adjective in English."

"Why not?"

"You just can't."

"Still, it was the work of a genius."

"That you can say," said David with a laugh.

As David walked down Fifth Avenue, deciding to pass a few bus stops since it was such a lovely day, he thought he heard a scream pierce the cloud of noise from the street. His head spun around, but the sound vanished at once, and he was not sure if he had really even heard it or, if he had, whether it had been real or just some teen-agers horsing around.

29 Solly felt like a jerk.

As soon as he walked into the temple lobby, he knew he had made a stupid mistake. He had always hated being in temple, and though it had been years, it still felt exactly the same. Knowing he had to be in Brooklyn, he had thought of Vizner's invitation and impulsively called him. They had arranged to meet at five-thirty. And now there was no getting out of it, for the face he had first noticed in the cab outside the Second Avenue Deli kissing the little book had just parted the wine-colored curtains.

"I'm so glad that you could make it, Detective Altheim," said Vizner, pleased to address a man by his title.

Solly smiled, nodded.

"Have you got five, ten minutes? I'd like to show you around. Ten, fifteen years ago this place was going to seed, but then the community all of a sudden got a shot of new blood, young people, Jews coming over from countries where they wouldn't even allow them to bake matzo—from Poland, where they kicked the last of them out, can you imagine," said Vizner, making a little gasping sound and looking away for a moment.

Solly followed Vizner over to a large, well-polished oak box containing yarmulkes. On the small brass plaque on the box, Solly caught a glimpse of the words "In Memory." Vizner kissed his yarmulke and put it on.

The guy kisses everything, thought Solly as he selected one for himself. The silkiness of the yarmulke made him feel oddly lightheaded.

Vizner held the door open for him. The silence in the temple, as large and domed as the building itself, made Solly pause at the door.

"You see how big it is," Vizner whispered. "On the high holidays you can't get a ticket. We have to turn people away. We hate to, but what can you do. Look how it's cared for, look, every little piece of brass is kept shined, the benches are polished once a week."

"Very nice," said Solly, wondering what was the minimum polite time he could stay.

"Let's sit down here for a minute," Vizner said, and slid onto one of the long benches. Solly sat down beside him, glancing at the prayer books in the slatted containers on the back of the bench in front of him. "It's a funny thing about America," said Vizner, still in a half whisper. "There's everything here—freedom, a living—and yet, for some reason, the

Jewish people here have drifted away from their religion. Explain it to me. And our fathers, they came here from countries where they killed you just for being a Jew, but they would go to temple at the risk of their lives. My own father, *ohabei shalom,* was from Lithuania, he told me. Was your father born here?"

"No," said Solly, ashamed that he was not going to say a word of blessing when mentioning his father as Vizner had. "No, he wasn't born here. He was born over there. In Russia. Near Kovno."

"Kovno is Lithuania, too!" said Vizner, delighted by the coincidence. "But I noticed that when you spoke of your father—I don't mean to pry into your business, but is your father alive?"

"No. He died eleven years ago."

"Eleven years ago. You lost him young."

"You see," began Solly, "I was never much for religion myself. My father was, but I just wasn't. But I always did feel bad that I never said Kaddish for him."

"You never said Kaddish for your father?" said Vizner with a gasp.

"No."

"That's . . ." Vizner began, but was unable to complete his sentence.

"So now I feel like maybe I should, if it isn't too late."

"No," said Vizner softly, "it isn't too late."

"So what should I do?"

"You should talk to the rabbi. But for the time being, I think you better start learning the prayer for the dead; that's the most important thing. Here, let me show you." Vizner reached forward for one of the prayer books and flipped through the pages quickly till he found the prayer. "Can you read Hebrew?"

Solly looked at the page, which for some reason reminded him of a piece of matzo. The only letters he could still recognize were aleph, lamed, yod, and shin. "No," he said, shaking his head.

"Then what we do is, I write the Hebrew words for you in English letters," said Vizner, pulling out a ballpoint pen and clicking it. "Would you happen to have a piece of paper?"

From his inside jacket pocket Solly pulled out a sheet of orange paper that someone had placed under his windshield wiper. One side advertised a new car wash in Bensonhurst, but the back was blank. He offered it with an apologetic shrug to Vizner, who took it, saying, "When you get home, copy it onto something better."

"Sure."

"All right, then, how would you say this word?"

"*Vyiskidal.*"

"That's right, very good. The first part means, 'May His Name be magnified and sanctified.' It won't be hard. You've probably heard it many times before already. And this one?"

"*Vyiskidash,*" said Solly.

After three hours of suspended-animation sleep, Shar walked out the front door of the Algonquin and headed across town toward the East Side. It was the second time that day he had walked the half block from the hotel to Fifth Avenue, and now it actually seemed a bit familiar to him, even though he was noticing obvious details, like the melted marble around a club's windows, for the first time.

Some things were the same everywhere. People loved to be strong and hated to be weak; they all ran about pursuing goals invisible to others but usually easy enough to guess. But the differences were interesting. The atmosphere here was like their Iowa black earth: anything could grow in it. And people seemed both weaker and more hard-edged than at home. More convinced of the importance of their individual lives. Even proud of their realistic selfishness. Busy, busy. Like Karen and David.

Karen was more American than David. He must have had a grandfather from Russia; he was easy with the language and its ways. She was more or less what she seemed to be, but he wasn't, though what his secrets were might be of no interest to anyone. They could both be useful.

Then he spotted what at first looked like a modern sculpture made of rags and junk but which, on closer inspection, proved to be a woman sleeping under a cardboard blanket in a doorway, surrounded by plastic bags. He noticed that nine out of ten people paid her no attention, yet somehow they were all aware of her. He squatted down beside her for a closer look at her face, which was no longer that of any definite person. A little smile at the corners of his mouth, he pulled the last roll of dimes from his pocket and let them fall from the green tube onto her chest. Though she stirred as they chimed lightly onto her, she did not wake.

He envied the soundness of her sleep. Crossing Madison, he felt the dynamo of the city subside somewhat. Fifth Avenue must be the center, he thought. And Wall Street.

It would be easy to disappear in a city of ten million where people did not even have to register with the police.

A woman of incredible beauty in a fur coat smiled right into his eyes over the top of a Mercedes, then disappeared inside, the tinted glass forbidding him any further view of her.

The cab was waiting at the corner of Second and Forty-sixth.

"I hope you will not refuse me your services," said Shar to the dark-eyed driver with bushy muttonchops, whom he recognized as Vaska from his photo in the file. Vaska, an American success story: four years ago a poor émigré and now the proud owner of a taxi medallion.

"My services have just become available again," said Vaska, clicking off his OFF DUTY light.

Shar got into the back of the cab, which was tidy and well kept.

"Where to?"

"First Wall Street," said Shar, "then later on I would like to see the area called Brighton Beach." Brighton Beach was Vaska's territory: he was the KGB's man, the *rezident* there, overseeing the smuggling of opium from Soviet Asia into the United States, obtaining valuable hard currency by selling drugs through the Russian Mafia.

"We might hit some traffic downtown," said Vaska.

"I'm in no hurry today."

"All right, then."

"Are all cabs here as clean as yours?" asked Shar.

"Thank you," said Vaska. "I just cleaned mine thoroughly this morning."

Good, thought Shar, that meant they could talk, but for the moment he was more interested in looking out the window at the young black man running from car to car trying to sell a set of wrenches in a red plastic case. No one was buying.

30 Late the following afternoon, Shar

called David and
invited him for a drink. David accepted the offer, more like
a challenge than an invitation. They arranged to meet the
next evening, at Shar's hotel room, around eight; Shar remarked that he had already noticed that Americans believed
in being on time, whereas for Russians eight o'clock was an
impossible ideal that life would of course never allow them
to fulfill. David laughed and agreed.

After hanging up, he looked over at the Xerox of Shar's
poem. He hadn't even glanced at it yet! And, naturally, that
was exactly what Shar would want to talk about. Now he
saw that Shar's invitation implied that David would already
have put everything aside for the golden opportunity to read
a Shar-Xeroxed, Shar-autographed Shar original. Well, he
hadn't, and he wouldn't.

He tried Naomi again. To his surprise, he got right through to her, but then the connection turned bad, and by the time he had redialed her number she was on a long-distance call; would he try back in about half an hour?

Half an hour later, she was just away from her desk for a few minutes, which meant that she had gone to the bathroom.

He called back in five minutes. At first, the raw irritation in her voice screened out the significance of what she was saying.

"We got notification that a shipment of films is going through customs tomorrow and will probably arrive here sometime the day after."

"Did they say which films?"

"I've told you everything I know. One minute," she said sharply to someone else. "Call around eleven. Thank you, David."

Why did they always say "thank you" in New York instead of "good-bye," especially when they meant "thank me"? thought David, infected by her tension.

That was it for today. He went to check his answering machine but found only one message—from Abram, announcing his arrival in New York and leaving a number at which he could be reached.

When the person who answered the phone went to search for Abram, David knew from the background roar, the clunk of something tipping over followed by laughter, that an epic Russian party had already begun to gather steam.

"Khai."

"Khai. Where are you?"

"Not so far from you. In Greenwich Village. You must come. Everyone is here—Volodya, Borya—and, besides, I have a letter for you."

"Give me the address of the party."

Abram gave it twice, first in English and then in Russian, the numbers never substantial enough in a foreign language.

"And I would like to remind you of that little talk of mine that you promised to translate, if you still don't mind."

"No, fine, you can give it to me there. By the way, I saw Shar yesterday."

"Yesterday? You did? Where?"

"Here. He arrived yesterday. Seems like a nice guy. He's at the Algonquin Hotel, if you want to give him a call."

"I would very much like to talk with him and even give him some warning about American-mass-media-celebrity-making machinery, which in fact conceals man's own true image from himself."

"I don't think Shar's the type that'll be ruined by success. He seems modest, a bit of a hick in the big city."

"Hicks get ruined the fastest. What does he say about the new poem?"

"He gave me a copy, but I haven't looked at it yet."

"You haven't?" said Luntz, almost stunned into silence.

"Would you like to see it?"

"Would I-I-I like to see it?" Abram began to sputter, flabbergasted that such a question could even exist. After a moment of silence, he finally settled on an answer: "Yes."

"Then I'll bring my copy with me. You can give it back

to me at the fair, though maybe we should check with Shar first."

"Bring it. We'll call him. Come," sighed Abram and hung up.

David turned to the first page of the Xerox and glanced at the opening of the poem.

> When the walls of the Warsaw ghetto
> were smashed like the tablets at Sinai . . .

The phone rang. It was Abram.

"I did not mean to hang up without saying good-bye, but the idea of having in my hands that manuscript, no, you simply cannot imagine."

"Well, it won't be long now."

"Come as soon as you can. This is official good-bye."

Swept away by a tide of Russian hospitality, David had ended up on a couch holding a glass of vodka and a plateful of food, sitting beside a tall scientist with a Solzhenitsyn beard. A debate was raging in the little group sitting in a semicircle around a coffee table in front of the couch. One man drove home his point by tapping it into his opponent's knee with his index finger.

"But I have to ask this question, because it's been troubling me and I want to know if I'm alone in this or not," interrupted the scientist with the rimless glasses and the Solzhenitsyn beard. "When I first came here to America and for years afterward, whenever I spoke of Russia, the Soviet Union, I always said 'we.' *We* should never have gone into Afghanistan, *our* literature seems to have improved. And then, maybe a week ago, I realized something—I had started to call Russians 'them.' "

All the people around the table suddenly fell into silence, a powerful silence, for what the scientist had said was not an opinion to be countered at once but a simple truth that, it turned out, belonged to nearly everyone.

"Yes, I know, it's the same for me too, but I still do not find myself saying 'we' about America," said a large woman on a small chair.

Just then David noticed that Abram was striding quickly across the other end of the room as if he were late for an appointment but then, suddenly realizing he had no destination at all, came to an abrupt halt and, smiling and squinting, began looking for someone to talk to. David squeezed his way over to him.

After the greetings, hugs, apologies, Abram said, "You brought the manuscript?"

"Sure."

"Good. Don't give it to me yet."

"Why not?"

"I'll read it."

"So?"

"It would be impolite to lock myself in a room when

there are people here who want to be with me. That's it in your hand?"

"Yes."

"Let me see."

"No."

"Just the opening lines."

"The opening lines are: 'When the walls of the Warsaw ghetto were smashed like the tablets at Sinai . . .'"

"Now I have to read the whole thing."

"But maybe Shar doesn't want anyone reading it yet."

"We'll call him."

They squirmed through the crowd, in which people rubbed up against one another as unself-consciously as seals on a rock, and on the way to the bedroom they nearly collided with a white-haired comic novelist who, a glass of vodka in one hand and a cigarette cupped in the other, was searching the crowd with his hot brown eyes for something to enjoy.

"Here it is a little quiet," said Abram, closing the bedroom door. "Call."

At first David didn't recognize Shar's voice on the phone, and it was only when they had said a few words that he was certain he was actually talking to Shar.

"Of course I would like to speak to him, and of course you may show him the poem."

Abram took the phone from him as if it were something else (although David wasn't sure just what) and invited Shar to the party, thanked him, warned him, advised him, and wished him all the best.

"He seems very nice, as you said. He may come here,

even though he's very tired from everything he's been through," said Abram. "No problem with the manuscript, which, since I now have official permission to read, I would appreciate your giving to me."

"But then you'll read it."

"What can I do?"

"All right, but first the letter and the translation you want me to do."

"I have both," said Abram. "Letter, and little statement."

The statement was on top, a single-spaced mass of Russian letters webbed with corrections.

David pulled the envelope out from beneath Abram's manuscript.

"Abram, this is the same letter I sent."

"What?"

"This is the letter I sent."

"It came back?"

"Apparently."

"Let me see."

David handed him the letter. Abram lifted his glasses and held it up to his eye.

"You're right," he said. "I saw the name Yuri Trofimovich on it, and I thought it was from him, so I put it away for you."

"But are you sure that you gave it to somebody to take over there?"

"One-hundred-percent sure. I gave it myself to . . . it doesn't matter who I gave it to, but I did. I'll ask him what happened."

It was clear that Abram was telling the truth, yet David had certain lingering doubts about Russians and efficiency, their vitality including a predilection for chaos.

"OK, if you say so."

"It is one hundred percent," said Abram, waiting to be released so he could begin reading.

The elevator operator nodded respectfully to Shar, and the people riding down with him looked at him for an extra second, trying to place him. He had the look of fame now; he could feel it in the way people's eyes approached him.

Partly because he felt a bit chilly and partly for the pleasure of buying something in an American store, Shar purchased a royal-blue jogger's sweatshirt that had white stripes down the sleeves and on the small collar. He decided to wear it under his suit jacket. "Usually people wear them for running, jogging—you know what I'm saying?" said the salesman as he made change. It was an odd game, this playing store. The customer was flattered and coddled, yet was considered a sucker who needed to be relieved of the money in his pocket. And the customer, strutting with his own importance, was aware of the game, too, but, like a woman with her favors, could prolong the courtship to his satisfaction or, as others seemed to prefer, do it quickly and get it over with: "I'll take this, I'll take that," pulling out cash and counting it quickly, or scribbling a check and tearing it with a crisp snap from their checkbook, or fuming while the salesman ran the credit card through the little machine.

Back on the sidewalk, he consulted his map and chose to follow the downward-sloping sidewalk toward Times Square, which seemed to be the closest point of interest. Besides, he wanted a taste of the American street at night. Now the sidewalks were crowded with people hurrying to their pleasure. Shar could sense a drastic shift in atmosphere as he entered Times Square—a dark place, for all its light and color. He saw who was leaning up against the buildings, he saw the eyes that moved through the crowds nimbly as a pickpocket's fingers, he saw the increasing numbers of whores. And so many black people; he had not expected so many loud and insolent Negroes.

A display window caught Shar's eye, for among the chrome tripods, cameras, fake Persian rugs, video cassettes, and watches was a small display of knives and daggers. Shar was shocked to realize that anyone could simply walk into that store, pay his money, and return to the street a minute later the owner of a bone-handled, six-inch hunting knife. Were Americans absolute idiots? They allowed large numbers of poor Negroes to congregate in a public place where alcohol and knives were sold. What a cocktail! And then they wondered why they had such a terrible crime rate.

Shar went into the store, looked down at the knives in the display case, and selected a long Finnish fishing knife that came with a nicely tooled light-brown leather sheath, all for under fifteen dollars. He noticed with interest that the salesman could just as easily have been selling him a pair of socks.

With the knife transferred from the bag to his pocket,

Shar felt more secure walking down Forty-second Street. Black men kept separating from the walls to approach him, hissing offers he could not understand, but there seemed to be plenty of policemen around, walking in twos, beefy, comically well equipped, some with surprisingly long hair and mustaches.

Wanting to see one of the porno emporiums, he chose a large, well-lighted one on the corner of Eighth Avenue that, like all the other businesses he had passed, displayed its promises in the window and praised itself shamelessly. Inside, the atmosphere reminded him of a men's room in a train station. The magazine rack, which was quite extensive, had been arranged by categories; the amount of space given each must be in proportion to the pace at which it sold. Shar was surprised to see so much homosexuality and perversion represented. The man to his left, whose quickened breathing Shar was aware of, returned his magazine to the stand with vigorous disgust, as if he had just sworn off his vice forever.

At the base of the racks were newspapers where prostitutes advertised. Each ad contained a price, a picture, and a phone number. Shar admired the efficiency of the system. As he moved past the racks, his eye was caught by a woman digging her high heel into the back of a man's neck; a woman bound to a desk with a red rubber ball in her mouth, her eyes bulging with terror; men with breasts. The images of normal sex seemed out of place, touching, old-fashioned.

As Shar turned, he saw a tall, young black man with an Afro comb in his hair shift his eyes away from his. Shar didn't like that and quickly drifted into the interior of the store, where men were going in and out of little booths, a forced blankness on every face. Janitors were mopping the floors and the vacated booths. The air reeked of sperm and ammonia. Shar watched a segment of a film, and when his quarter ran out he inserted another. Yes, of course, it worked—the bright flickering image of the woman taking the man so greedily into her mouth. A dime for a Xerox, thought Shar, cigarettes a dollar, and this a quarter.

In another area, the dropping of a quarter caused a metal screen in the booth to rise and reveal a little theater, a man and a woman both naked and dark-skinned, on a worn red-velvet couch. Only in capitalism could fucking be a job, thought Shar, deciding he had seen enough of their famous sexual freedom.

Prostitutes were waiting on the sidewalk and came up to Shar as he unfolded his map. Shar smiled down at them from his height and shook his head. They persisted for a moment, then flocked to the next man out, like park pigeons to a handful of bread crumbs.

He decided to walk down Seventh Avenue toward Greenwich Village and the party. With his map folded up neatly and slid into his inside jacket pocket, he touched the knife in his right pants pocket and then set off down Eighth Avenue, intending to cut over to Seventh Avenue after a few blocks.

Suddenly it was darker and there were many fewer people. Shar realized that knowing the city meant knowing where the people and the light were at night, because that was what created the sense of safety.

He could hear the sound of footsteps behind him, a man's shoes scraping on the sidewalk, but he did not turn.

"Hey, brother," came a voice from behind him.

Shar stopped, turned around slowly. It was the young black man with the Afro comb in his hair, signaling downward with his eyes to the muzzle of a pistol held close to his mustard yellow imitation-leather coat.

"I know how you white folks get nervous when you see a nigger pointing a gun at you, so just give me your money before I start getting nervous my own self."

As Shar reached into his right pants pocket, containing both the knife and his money, he realized that the gunman was left-handed. He extended the money straight toward the gun and watched the flicker of confusion in the black man's eyes who hesitated then used his right hand to reach across for the money. In that second Shar grabbed the barrel of the gun and, corkscrewing it, snapped the finger in the trigger guard like a twig. The small revolver fell to the street. Shar slammed the black man against the wall, his knee punching his groin and solar plexus. The Afro comb fell from his hair as he slid to the ground. After sending the gun clattering down the street with a long soccer kick, Shar bent down to pick up the Afro comb.

David didn't like it that the letter came back. Why had it come back? Had they tried to deliver it over there, or had it never left America for some reason? He needed more information, feeling certain, or at least hoping, that information would assuage his sudden uneasiness. As he walked through the party, it occurred to him that all those people were there, talking and talking, only because of the great force that had hurled them across the globe, and it might well be that same blank wall of force that his own letter had run into while traveling in the other direction.

He moved close to a little knot of people, one of whom was saying: "Yes, all right, I accept the metaphor of world politics as the Olympics, and yes, of course, it's typical that the Soviets always win the super-heavyweight weightlifting medal, but perhaps the international arena could be better compared to a hockey rink, where the action keeps shifting and the puck is always being passed, and if we accept that metaphor, then we would do well to remember that American hockey team, made up of street kids who could probably not even read and who defeated all those well-trained, well-fed Soviet professionals, because they dazzled them with the freedom of their moves—do you understand that, Alyosha? —there was absolutely nothing in the Soviets' experience that could have prepared them for the freedom of those moves!"

It was then, slightly entranced by the passion and metaphors of the speaker, a man with choppy brown hair and thick glasses, that David noticed Raisa at the other end of the room, holding her glass high to maneuver through the crowd.

In a moment of voyeuristic freedom, he not only saw her but himself, saw that he was afraid of her in the same way he was afraid of life when it became too specific and too real.

But he willed himself past that vague drift of withdrawal in the muscles, pushing his way through the room until he was only a hand's reach from her back.

"Hello, Raisa," he said, reaching out and touching her back.

Raisa spun around, a drink in one hand, an unlighted cigarette in the other. She seemed slightly embarrassed to be seen enjoying herself.

"Hello, David," she said.

"You seem to be enjoying yourself."

"I am. I've met this crazy American who's half convinced me that life can be all right."

"You shouldn't get involved with that sort of people."

"I'm sure you're right," she said with a laugh and then moved her cigarette forward slightly.

Glad that the match had struck the first time, he brought it up to her cigarette, now in her mouth. She bent toward the flame, holding one side of her hair with her free hand, her eyes looking into David's for a moment on the way.

"How long have you been here?" he asked.

"Not very long. Vera Zaslavich told me at work that there was a party."

"I called you, there was no answer."

"I came straight here from work."

"Raisa, I want to ask you about something. You remember the letter I sent Yuri Trofimovich. I don't quite understand how, but the letter has come back."

"Get me another drink, would you please, David?"

Reaching for an open bottle of wine, David found himself thinking that it might have been a mistake to have asked her that question: she had seemed almost to shudder.

"Let's walk out of the crowd," she said as she took her filled glass. "Maybe the hallway is better."

Except for a bald man sleeping with his head against the wall, the hallway was deserted. They walked past him toward a little telephone table with two chairs.

"David, now listen," she said after they had sat down, clearly making an effort to control herself. "The letter coming back means that Yuri is no longer reachable. And that means that Yuri's secret is no secret anymore. By now they must know everything. The experiments, who Yuri was sending the material to, the film."

"But I was informed today that a shipment of films is clearing customs right now, and it might contain the one we're waiting for. You may be right, but it's a little late for them."

"David, if I had to bet on anyone to get hold of that film, I would have to bet on them."

"You know, I was listening to a conversation earlier, a Russian talking about the U.S. hockey team—just a bunch of crazy boys that probably couldn't even read, as he put it, but they skated circles around the Soviet team because the Soviets couldn't anticipate their free moves; the Soviets had nothing in their training or experience that would have allowed them to anticipate those free moves. Because, by definition, you can't anticipate free moves. It's like when jazz men are improvising, they don't know themselves what note they're going to blow next."

"David, this isn't jazz, this isn't hockey."

"I know it isn't, and you know I'm just making analogies," he said, something flat and hard about his voice now to counter the mounting hysteria radiating from her shoulders. "We don't need a lot of time, Raisa. Just enough to pick up the little piece of film, a cab to La Guardia, the shuttle to Boston, a cab in from Logan. The first thing we do is start making copies, and every copy increases the odds in our favor. And then we get the FBI's number from Information and give them a nice copy of their own. One very uptight day, two at the most."

"David, sometimes you fool me because you speak Russian and you know how to act with us, but really you're such an American. Don't you see, we're just two little rabbits in the bushes, and their dogs can already smell us. Two little rabbits against all those dogs and shotguns—don't be silly. If you have any sense at all, pick up that telephone and call that detective and tell him everything!"

He could feel her emotion loose in the air around him, unsettling him, making his own anger rise.

"And that's the last we ever hear of it. And then what do we do, try to go public with our story? Two crazies with some Xeroxed letters in Russian with a Xeroxed bullet hole in one of them? And what do we do, picket government buildings, give interviews to the *Enquirer,* go on TV programs about the weird and the incredible? No!"

"David, they monitor calls from that compound in Riverdale. They may have been monitoring my brother's calls since he got here; they may have heard every conversation you and I have had by phone, and they may have noticed that all our calls started around the time my brother was killed. Did you hear what I just said—when my brother was killed, by some Uzbek pretending to be a Puerto Rican. No!" she shouted, rising from her chair. "They killed him, and now you're going to let them kill me and you. I didn't come to America to be killed by them here because some American needs a reason to live; I didn't lose my brother so they could kill you next. I believed you that there could be a new life, but you're offering it to me with one hand and taking it away with the other."

"There is no new life if we call Altheim."

"David, they're going to kill us! Make them stop!"

Now she was weeping hysterically, her face in her hands.

But when he went to comfort her, she wrenched her shoulder away from his hand, turned, and ran down the long hallway back toward the party.

He was not going to go after her. There was nothing more he could say to convince her, and she was not going to allow him to console her because he was not willing to do the one thing that would in fact console her. And suddenly he knew that he had to get out of there, away from that alien taste, that dark Russian stew salted with grief.

Shar paused on Seventh Avenue in the upper twenties to consult his map by the glowing orange light of a hot-dog stand.

A strange city, he thought. If you looked up, it really was

magnificent, but at street level predators and lunatics cruised the filthy sidewalks; the eyes he could look into were blank with fright.

Replacing the map, he became aware of the Afro comb's alien ounce in his pocket. A comb spattered with a street criminal's fingerprints—a perfect detail, blindingly local. Vinias would approve.

He had knelt to pick up the Afro comb just as he had when anointing the bag lady with dimes. Now he understood who those people were, why they existed. To mark one end of the scale, the depths implying the heights, the ten-dollar pistol parodying real power, utter failure demonstrating the skyscraper reach of success.

The range was intoxicatingly vast, irresistible; the American air, ionized with endless possibility, was getting into him too. He could feel it though he wasn't sure how much he liked it. There was something undignified about quick changes which seemed to be the main promise of that atmosphere. And yet, he had to be honest, he was a customer for it too, he wanted a change and, like anyone else, he wanted it quick. He wanted to cease to be Lieutenant Shar, immediately subordinate to Lieutenant Colonel Vinias, and become a great figure in the history of crime, to grow rich and powerful from black-marketing life, for that was exactly what selling that wonderful drug would be. Of course he would have to spend the rest of his life guarding against attack from all his enemies, Vinias chief among them, but that was better than working for Vinias, being his puppet, taking his slaps in the face.

It would need more time, more thought, but now a light rain had begun falling and he had a party to get to.

It was a deceptive rain. Falling in fine streaks, it seemed gentle and refreshing after the cattle pen of the party, but after a few blocks David felt a damp chill moving through his coat toward his body. His blood shrunk away from the surface of his skin towards his bones which had already begun to plead for warmth.

Warmth, the simplest desire. And now Karen was the only one person out of all the four billion who would give him that warmth.

And he had made it the condition of his life that he could not be with her. Because he could not be with her without telling her the truth. There was no love without truth, that was a law stricter than gravity. Because the body was like an animal, innocent of guile and fiction. The body would submit and submit, or else, suddenly enraged, might attack but it would never lie, simply because it did not know how to. He had seen that clear enough on the night he had spent with her after signing the form for Altheim. His cells had been locked as tight as safe deposit boxes and his skin had the anesthetized clamminess of a wet suit. And it broke his heart to know that he had taken the truth from her life because she had to be thinking all the wrong thoughts of why he had turned away from her.

This was all too sophisticated for the body. His body

wanted to be with her, it could be happy with her, it could fall asleep beside her in peace. And as it fell asleep to the sound of the rain outside, all the world would fall away, all the cunning watchfulness, molten ambition, and crude stupid danger. Then all that would be left was body and soul, flesh and dreams.

And to not go there now for that—what did that really mean, he asked himself, he wasn't stupid, he knew how to think about that sort of thing.

It mean to choose again what he had already chosen. What he would have to keep choosing until there was no choice left.

But what the hell was he thinking? Raisa would get over it. Her rage would pass, her tears would pass. She loved him now, she was hooked, she was in it to the end. In a day or two or three, he would be back with her. The shipment would arrive, he would remove the tail leader from reel four, he would take the tail leader to Boston, Jim would do the hard science, and then it would be his. It was very simple. That was all that he had to remember. But it could seem so faint a thing when a cold rain was falling, steadily now, and his bones were pleading for warmth.

Evgeny Shar sat in the kitchen relating the story of his forcible exile to a group of admirers that, he had already noticed, included Raisa Farb.

He had just finished the story of the young intellectual

who had been stabbed by a criminal known as Venya the Swan when he first noticed her, dark-haired, traces of recent agitation around her eyes, in the second or third rank of those sitting and standing around him in a little impromptu amphitheatre.

"More and more of the scientific intelligentsia seemed to be under attack just before I left. I don't know why. Just before my exile one of them was sent to our camp—not in very good condition, either. Yuri Trofimovich Kovshin."

"I knew him," said the tall man with the Solzhenitsyn beard and rimless glasses, who had found himself in a position close to Shar.

"He was a friend of your brother, wasn't he, Raisa?"

"Yes, they were friends." Then she paused and looked directly at Shar, who nodded slightly. "You say he wasn't in very good condition?" asked Raisa.

"No," said Shar, "he wasn't."

"And will he survive the camp?"

"It all depends," said Shar. "If they don't want him to, they will assign him to grinding glass permanently. That's the worst job at T-52."

"T-52?" asked a blonde woman with disorganized hair who was a reporter for one of New York's émigré magazines.

"T-52 is where we worked," said Shar, shifting in her direction. "We made televisions for the Soviet consumer, who still has to wait years to be able to hear lies about the very people who made him the set."

His remark produced a few smiles of bitter pleasure.

"And do you intend to remain in this country?" asked the reporter.

Shar sighed. "Let me say that I am very tired and don't know the answer to any question right now. I'm sorry. I just want to be with people and have a few drinks and go to sleep."

Embarrassed, the woman reporter put away her little notepad.

"Really very tired," repeated Shar in such a way that those around him would know that the audience was over and that he needed to be left to himself. People started leaving the kitchen or began conversations of their own.

"So, you knew Yuri Trofimovich?" said Shar to the scientist with the Solzhenitsyn beard.

"My first wife was a cousin of Yuri's wife. I can't say that I knew him, but we met a few times, we talked. I was sorry to hear what has happened to him. He has a child, I know."

"Yes," said Shar, "he misses her very much. We became close, Yuri and I, in the short time we knew each other."

"And what was his sentence?" asked Raisa Farb, who had now pushed her way through to Shar.

"Five years of corrective labor, three of exile."

"Did he say why he was arrested?"

"As I said to the other woman," said Shar somewhat harshly, rising to his feet, "I don't want to answer questions right now. Questions tire me terribly. There have been so many questions lately—you can't imagine. But I'm sorry I spoke sharply. It's nerves, fatigue. Let me bring you a drink."

"Thank you," said Raisa, accepting both the offer and the apology. "I'll go with you," she added, realizing that the odds were against his making his way back to the kitchen in under half an hour with all those devoted fans and adoring women out there.

"My name is Raisa," she said as Shar poured white wine into her plastic cup. "Raisa Farb."

"Oh, I'm sorry," said Shar, whose hand had lurched when she said her name, the wine splashing onto the edge of the cup and her hand.

"What's wrong?" she asked.

"Is Yasha Farb your brother?"

"Yes. And so?"

"I read that the American critics faulted *Dr. Zhivago* for having too many coincidences in the plot, but that only shows how they don't know Russian life, doesn't it? I mean, after all, here everything is nicely arranged and people make appointments to see each other. But in Russia it's one chaos or another, and things are always flying around and making the most improbable combinations. One day you're polishing television cabinets, the next day you're in Germany, and a week later you're drinking white wine in New York."

"Yuri mentioned my brother?" she said. "Oh, I'm sorry, that's a question."

"That question is important, really too important for me to answer with all these people around. Can we get some air?"

A moment later, plastic cups still in hand, they were out on a quiet West Village side street. The rain had left puddles in the places where the sidewalk had given. An almost refreshing coolness had come into the air.

For a certain time they walked without saying anything.

Raisa was now angry at David for yet another reason, for not realizing how small the world was. A stupid American for all his intelligence, he didn't even have a sense of the actual size of the world. The Soviet Union and America were neighbors now; the Soviet Union was very close, as close as the compound in Riverdale. One day Shar could be talking to Yuri Trofimovich about her brother in Mordovia, and a week later he could be in Greenwich Village with her. Shar gave himself airs too—Pasternak, Zek romanticism, the "specialness of the Russian destiny"; there was nothing so special about it. The world was small and the people booted out of Russia did not have far to go before they landed. But if Russia was close, that meant the past, the common grave of the past, was also close; it kept reaching up for you, so that every time you thought you saw the blue of the sky up above, bones and roots would wind around your ankles. And now this man, too, was somehow connected to her through her brother's death. No one was connected to her except through one death or another.

"So, the answer to the question you asked back there is yes, Yuri spoke of your brother. More than that. Should I go on?"

"I am listening."

"I have an important message for your brother from Yuri."

"It can't be delivered."

"Why not?"

"Because Yasha is dead."

"Your brother died?"

"Officially, my brother was the victim of an ordinary New York street robbery, a 'mugging,' as they call them here. But I never believed that. I always thought it was them—it had their smell."

"Now what should I do? I'll tell you what the problem is. Yuri was sending your brother certain scientific information. Later on he found out it was not entirely correct. Some serious side effects had shown up in the tests they were doing. But it was too late for him to warn your brother. Since I was supposed to get out in a year, Yuri asked me to memorize about seven pages of new data. Which I did. Neither of us expected that I would be getting out so soon. Ordinarily that would have been a favorable development. . . ."

"Yes, ordinarily."

"The problem is that just now I've been having trouble retrieving it all from memory. I don't know if it's the shock of being here or having to write down my whole poem or what, but there's about three-quarters of a page that I can't retrieve. I keep writing it all out to keep it memorized and hoping that the missing part will come back, but it hasn't yet."

"Do you keep what you write down?"

"No, it's best not to. Even here."

David was such a fool, she thought—he would have gone running off with information that was incorrect and dangerous. Because Yuri hadn't had time to send out his revisions. Because poor Yuri had ended up in a camp just as she said he would. They must have observed Shar talking with Yuri in the camp, and David was with Shar today at the airport, and they must know about David by now. It could only end in a disaster for all of them. She could smell a disaster coming, the way she used to be able to smell snow hours before the sky even turned gray.

But if she called Altheim that was the end of her and David; he'd made that clear enough. It was up to her to decide, all of it.

She looked over at Shar—tall, his shoulders stooped against the cold, tieless, his shirt buttoned to the top like any immigrant. How could she trust him? In the end he was the same sort as her brother and David, drunks, quixotes, who never noticed what happened to the one who had gone before him.

"I paid absolutely no attention to my brother's follies," said Raisa, her lips tight with anger at all of them—Yasha, David, Yuri, Shar.

"But Yuri Trofimovich told me he was a wonderful person, your brother, Yasha."

"Yes, he was a wonderful person."

"I must ask you for this favor," said Shar, his voice soft. "I must ask you to help me. Just find out who I should give the information to. I'll be at the Algonquin for at least a week. I promised a good man in a Soviet labor camp that I would see that this information was passed on and I intend to keep my promise," concluded Shar, his voice rising and strong with moral intent.

"At the Algonquin Hotel for at least a week," repeated Raisa, so that she could respond without committing herself.

For a moment Shar could not help admiring Vinias: this formidable woman beside him doubted him for all the wrong reasons. And the exact contours of her deception and Shar's knowledge of it suggested Vinias's presence, like those silhouette drawings in which the space between two goblets suddenly becomes a face.

PART FOUR

31 "It's here," said Naomi.

For a moment David couldn't say a word and wasn't sure if he were going to feel elated or somehow let down.

"I'll be right over."

He replaced the receiver on the pay phone. People, cars, and buses were moving through a fine drizzle that seemed not so much to fall as to condense out of the air.

"It's here," he thought, stepping off the sidewalk, his arm in the air, knowing that the rain would make the competition for cabs nastier than usual.

The back seat had come a little loose in the cab he managed to flag down, and the thick plastic barrier separating driver and passenger forced David to holler the address a second time, which he found irritatingly inappropriate.

He looked out the window at the world, which had not changed even though his life now had, or almost had. Buses with ads, the cheap pink of celebrity faces, smiling, endorsing. Something evanescent, Assyrian, about that gray brown city in the rain. A woman's hat red as a blood red tulip against beige stone. A black woman at a corner holding a newspaper over her head made him feel ashamed of himself for a moment. He was only blocks, minutes, dimes on the cab's meter away. Then he withdrew his gaze to the window itself, where raindrops paused and quivered until, regaining energy, they streaked transparent lines to the bottom of the glass. It would probably hit him later, he thought; like a death in the family or winning the lottery, it took time to sink in.

"Five-forty," said the driver, flipping back the rocking tray.

"Keep the change," said David as he slipped a ten into the tray.

"What?"

"Keep the change."

"Hey, thanks, have a nice day."

Naomi's assistant told him that Naomi was expecting him and would be with him in a minute; would he have a seat on the couch?

He sat down and glanced at the coffee table in front of him. The film was in the building and he was going to have to stare at magazines and an amber ashtray full of squashed-out butts.

His eye moved from a news magazine whose cover displayed a missile blasting off, the words NUCLEAR BLACKMAIL stenciled in large red letters on it, to a film journal whose feature story was "Sam Talbot: Saint or Snake?," and finally came to rest on a copy of *Variety* that was open to the top fifty grossers of the week.

"Naomi will see you now."

She was leaning back in her chair, smoking one of her long brown cigarettes and squinting, either because the smoke was getting in her eyes or because she was taking one last critical look at him.

"I just got off the phone with a Mr. Fedorenko from the Soviet delegation to the UN," said Naomi. "They want *Apples of Ryazan* for a private screening tonight. What chance do you think there is that's just a coincidence?"

He had not anticipated any more obstacles and needed a moment to throw his mind into operation.

"Let's take a worst-case approach. They know. But what they can't know is when and where that little piece of tail leader disappeared. It could have been over there, or at the airport, or at customs, or on the truck coming into the city. They can't know any of that. They're probably not even sure it's on the film, either. What did you tell them?"

"I'll tell you what I told him," said Naomi, giving no sign that David's words had made any impression on her. "I told him that I would need a letter on his stationery messengered up to me, and then I would messenger the film down to him."

"So, good."

"I'd like to know what's on that piece of leader."

"I'll tell you what."

"What?"

"Once I know, I'll take you out for a very good dinner and tell you everything," said David, aware that for the time being she should not know anything, for the sake of her own safety, and that really he could probably never tell her anything, because she would want it for herself and the people she loved and there would be no end to that.

He saw her face relent as she blew a column of smoke out of the corner of her mouth. "I hated his voice on the phone," she said, leaning forward in her chair.

Both secretaries nodded as Naomi said, "I'll be back in about twenty minutes. If anyone calls, just say I'm out of the office."

David had trouble keeping up with her in the corridor and on the cement steps of the stairwell. When they reached the basement door, she stopped and looked through the chicken wire of the window at the corridor.

"Let's wait till they go past," she said over her shoulder. He saw a blur of faces; then, looking down, he noticed that she had separated one key from the bunch in her hand. She must have done that on the stairs.

They were in the hall for only a few seconds: the storage room was the second door from the stairwell. As soon as she flicked on the light, she tried the door to make sure it was shut. The room was low and very long and smelled of dry concrete. Film cans were stacked in iron racks the dark green color of school lockers.

"Where is it?" he whispered.

"I don't know. Nothing's been sorted yet. We'll just have to hunt around."

"I'll start from over here," David said, and headed off past a rewind table to one far corner.

He found a musical from Brazil, a French film titled *Nostalgie de la boue*, *The Shriek* from Sweden (hadn't he heard something about that one?), a Samurai epic from Japan, films from Australia, Germany, Yugoslavia. Wheels and wheels of images.

But where was it? he wondered with a sickening fall in his stomach. It wasn't there. It wouldn't be there. Nothing ever worked right. There was always the stupid hitch, the rub, the fuck-up. The truck bringing the film in from the airport had been delayed till almost three o'clock because of a broken fan belt, but this was a fresh situation with its own built-in trouble. There he had been, convincing Naomi to overcome her final hesitation, and the film probably wasn't even there. Maybe the piece of leader was never attached to the film in the first place, and they hadn't been able to give notice of the change in plans because something had gone haywire with the chain of communication.

He began to check the racks again, this time stopping in front of each can and touching the title label with his finger. He was just about to touch *Nostalgie de la boue* when Naomi called out in a loud whisper, "I've got it."

He ran to her. She was standing waiting for him with two film cans at her feet. For a second neither of them said anything.

"It's the tail leader, reel four—that's what you said, right?"

"Right."

She picked up one of the cans and carried it briskly to the rewind table.

"OK, let's see," she said, flipping open the can. There were two reels of film in it, the empty spaces stuffed with newspaper. David's eyes went automatically to the Russian words and picked out "cosmonaut," "glory," "crisis."

"They should be marked," she said. "Right, this is three so that must be four. Which it is." She nodded at the large strip of duct tape on which an oversized "4" had been marked in black. "And the film is heads out, which means that I'm going to have to rewind."

Naomi placed the reel on one rewind, snapped together a split reel for the other, then undid the little piece of red tape holding the film. She stretched the film across the table and, using the same piece of red tape, attached the film to the yellow plastic core on the empty reel. The leader at the head was black-and-white film with a clocklike image counting down from ten to one.

Positioning herself in between the two reels, Naomi began cranking the handle on the take-up reel harder and harder, then let it fly free; when it started to slow, she caught it and cranked it hard again.

"We used to have races in film school," she said over her shoulder. "To see who could rewind the fastest."

"Did you use to win?"

"Sure, sometimes," she said, and gave the handle another vigorous crank, as if to demonstrate her style.

"The film won't break?"

"Not if you do it right."

He looked over her shoulder at the black blur of the film. Her hair had a sort of lilac smell to it; the hair on her neck looked like lines drawn in fine charcoal.

Suddenly she slowed the spinning wheel with the flat of her hand.

"Went past it," she said, and began cranking it back, peering closely to see where the leader had been joined to the film.

He remembered that feeling of absolute impatience combined with a sense of utter uselessness from his one night in the waiting room with the other fathers-to-be.

"All right, then, we'll just break this off. Come on, you little sucker. There. All right, now I'll wind it off for you."

She took the reel of film off the rewind and replaced it with another small yellow plastic core. Once she had found a piece of tape on the edge of the table, she attached the leader to the core; only two cranks were required to send the leader flapping around the yellow core.

"There's not much there," she said. "Maybe a hundred feet or so. But it might be a good idea to return this piece of tape to the Russians." She plucked the tape off the leader and pasted it onto the table, reached up to one of the shelves above the bench to fetch a plastic bag, blew it clear of dust, dropped the leader on its yellow core into the bag, and handed it to David. "Here," she said, "it's yours."

Then it was in his hands, a specific object, a few ounces of synthetic materials. For a moment he stood without moving, cradling that object in his hands with exaggerated care, then quickly slipped it into the inside pocket of his old

327

corduroy jacket, saying, "I admire your courage, Naomi."

She nodded in acknowledgment. "What I think I'll do now," she said, "is put the tail leader from reel one on reel four, and then find a piece of leader on some other Eastern European film. I think they all use the same type."

"Good idea. Naomi, I should go. I'll be in touch soon."

"You better be—you owe me a good dinner." She turned back to the rewind table.

David paused at the door to let a man in gray chinos pass and vanish down the hall. Taking one last look back, he saw Naomi's right arm rotating furiously, the reels spinning and spinning.

32 Solly couldn't find the grave.

"Lot 94A, spaces 1–4,"
read the little ticket in his hand. Only as he checked it did
he realize that the man in the information office had expected
a tip for looking up the location and writing out the little
ticket, which he had done with the flourish of someone who
wanted you to be aware he was performing a service for you.
Solly felt ashamed for being so thick.

He walked along a row of grave markers, not needing
to look very hard for the name, which he knew would leap
up at him when he came to it. He read some of the names
and dates out of idle curiosity. Arthur Fein had lived from
1893 to 1961. How much was that? Sixty-eight, not too bad.
Bessie Lowenthal had done better: she had lived from 1889
to 1970. Eighty-one. Eighty-one, you could see your grand-

children grown up, you could be there at their weddings, you could hold your own great-grandchildren, even though they would never remember you. But Gerald Mandel had been born in 1940 and died in 1959. He didn't get to see much, and Solly wondered what took him—a car crash, some disease, or maybe the kind of thing he was used to seeing, a knife in the chest on the way back from the store.

The cemetery looked like a vast golf course in the hanging mist. The grass had already started to go the color of iodine, and the ground was hard under the mucky grass as he kept walking. A black Cadillac hearse stood on top of one hill, but there didn't seem to be a funeral going on. Looking at the outlines of the city through the drizzle and the dark branches, he had a sudden urge to be back there among the people, the cars, and the noise.

He didn't like this kind of weather—the low masses of pale grayish clouds and the drizzle that came and went, the yellow leaves pasted to the sidewalk. It made his kidneys feel like two little potatoes rotting in the ground. In the ground, everything ends up in the fucking ground.

He quickened his step, hoping to find the lot marker to confirm he was in the right place. There was no one to ask directions from. The groundskeeper who had been working when he had pulled up in his car was nowhere in sight now, and no one was laying wreaths or flowers. He thought he had listened carefully to the directions at the office, but how well could his brain have been working if he hadn't even had the sense to realize he was supposed to tip the guy? He couldn't go back there.

It started drizzling again. He felt that he would never find the grave today, that something was keeping him from it. It was too late; he had waited too long.

Seeing the back of the white sign on the picket, Solly started toward it, glad to have a destination that took him away from his thoughts. He was in the wrong lot. It must be the next one up. But how was the place arranged? And why did they have to call them lots? That wasn't the right word for it.

A shiny new compact car with an old couple in the front seat went by, its tires hissing vaguely on the drizzle-dampened road.

The next lot up was the right one, and he found the grave fairly quickly. His father's name, his father's numbers. Solly was there, standing over him. It was hard to think of it, but the man he had watched shave was down there now. The ribs were still probably on the rib cage, though the fingers would have separated like pieces of chalk that had fallen to the floor and broken.

Solly had thought that something was going to happen there, that he was going to feel something he hadn't felt before, that the silence in him, the knotted silence of his father's voice, was going to open and speak. But it didn't feel like that at all. He had the same blank feeling he always got when he looked down at the dead. Blanko.

The drizzle had started to condense on the sleeves of his coat.

For a moment he began to feel very angry, but then he reached inside his jacket pocket and pulled out the orange sheet of paper folded in quarters. It opened to the side that advertised the car wash, so he flipped it over to where the words of one language had been written in the letters of another.

33 Now it had started to hit him;

now it was sinking in. As he stood in the bathroom and taped the plastic envelope to his chest, he could feel a certain nervous excitement in his fingers and in the muscles at the back of his legs, a tremulousness that combined fear and exhilaration.

Though his chest muscles were relatively large, the hard plastic core still rose a little above them, but it would not be visible through his shirt. Removing the tape would be painful, he thought: the nerve roots would wince as the tape scythed away the hair, gray and brown in the same mix as his beard. He reminded himself that it would hurt less if the tape were ripped off fast.

Back in the studio, he found himself gathering up a few indispensable things—cash, credit cards, watch, pen—and suddenly realized that he had begun making preparations to flee his apartment before he had even quite consciously decided to. As if he were in some tacky made-for-TV thriller. And who was kidding who? He couldn't run three blocks without panting, and guns, in the end, belonged to the same world as metric wrenches and power tools—you had to know how to use them. If it came to running and guns, he knew he didn't have a Chinaman's chance. And there had been some bad signs and bad luck. The letter's coming back and the Soviet delegation's wanting to see *Apples of Ryazan* tonight were bad signs, and Jim's mother's dying was bad luck, for it meant that Jim wouldn't be back in Boston for at least two days, and that meant that David's boast to Raisa that the whole thing would require one or two uptight days at the most had now been rendered somewhat hollow.

His fear told him to be a smart rat and do the cab-plane-cab routine right away, to go hide in some Boston motel watching television until Jim had buried his mother. Everything else could wait; nothing else mattered.

But the exhilaration in him demanded its due as well. It asked for one night in New York, it wanted to smile across the table at Raisa as he told her the news and tapped his chest as if swearing to the truth, it wanted to keep his appointment with Shar.

He called Raisa, letting the phone ring half a dozen times before he remembered that it was Tuesday, the night she taught in extension school.

He glanced around his desk, at first automatically but then as if saying good-bye to that piece of pine where he had spent so many hours of his life. All the typed paper, the ink —it struck him now as a wintry world, black and white, the endless snow of paper, the bare black boughs of sentences. Not a single dot of color. And he had so loved to draw and paint and color as a child. It had always been his secret regret that he had not chosen to become a painter. To live in a world where blue was important.

But the unfinished translation of Irina Petrovskaya's memoirs now seemed to be regarding him with a dubious, reproachful look. Would he have to finish them? There was always that dreadful carryover, like the work he would lug with him on vacation during his married days. And conscience demanded that he not jeopardize Karen's already shaky position with the publisher. He thought of the moment when Shar had asked how many copies they wanted and she had quickly answered, "One each."

Besides, he would need money in his new life; there was no escaping money.

Before leaving to walk up Sixth Avenue through the early-evening crowds, he checked his answering machine. Excited, vehement, Raisa said, "David, I must see you tonight. Come to my place; it doesn't matter what time—you must come tonight!"

34   Alone in her office, Naomi screamed

"Shut up!" at the
phone, which seemed to be ringing with a special insistence,
as if the caller knew she was there. But the day had been too
much—a hundred phone calls, two screenings, the business
with David Aronow, and then Mr. Fedorenko, who had
come from the Soviet delegation for the film. There had been
something creepy and infuriating about Fedorenko's dullness
—an aggressive, superior dullness—and she had taken pleasure in making him wait while her secretary typed out a form
releasing the festival from responsibility if there was any
damage to the print or the print was lost or not returned in
time for its scheduled showing.

It was ten past seven and she was hungry, but she decided
to resist the easy temptation in favor of a swim. The half of
an oatmeal cookie stashed in her desk drawer took the edge

off her hunger. Hating the feeling of walking alone through the building at night, Naomi was glad to run into Jeremy Salt, even though she knew he was more company than protection. She found herself making good conversation with him in the elevator, comparing the fear of riding in elevators generated by the film *Dressed to Kill* with the other great terror generators *Psycho* and *Jaws,* which of course raised the question of the filmmaker's ethical responsibilities. Jeremy said it sounded like the basis for an interesting article, and why didn't she try her hand at it.

Naomi surprised herself in the pool by swimming nearly three-quarters of a mile, having figured she would be lucky to do half a mile after a day like that. But once she had ground out the first twenty laps by pure will, she had gotten a second wind. As she swam she looked up through the glass roof above the pool and watched the skyscrapers slide past, propelled by her strokes. There was even a star or two sparkling in the damp black night, and once again she knew why she stayed in that city, that job.

She could feel the poisons evaporating out of her in the steam room, her blood clearing and brightening, even the surface of her eyes beginning to relax as if some transparent net of tension had tightened over them in the course of the day. She sat there for nearly ten minutes, lulled by the voices that emerged from the steam, partial and edgeless like the shoulders or toweled thighs of other women entering or leaving. And she laughed to herself as she heard one voice saying that swimming had liberated her from needing sex— not wanting it, needing it.

As usual, the scale had harsh news. Not a pound had been

lost. She had run around all day, barely eaten lunch, and the goddamned thing wouldn't even give her half a pound. She took a hard, evaluative squint at herself naked in the mirror. Incipient saddlebags but holding up, was the verdict. She promised herself to swim three times a week no matter what, two at the very least.

Naomi went to dry her hair, hoping there would be someone fun to talk to over the sound of the dryers. At that moment she decided not to go out and eat but to heat up the spinach pie in the fridge; with a little salad it would be just right for dinner. Was there enough lettuce left? She couldn't remember.

As soon as Naomi opened the door to her apartment, a hand in a white gardener's glove came around her face and went right into her mouth, which had opened to scream. Another hand caught her waist in its vise and lifted her from the floor. Though the lights were off, she could see another figure by the window, and that figure began moving toward her, its hands spread apart, holding something about three feet long which she knew would be used to strangle her. Now the hand in her mouth was wriggling out of it, stuffing the glove into her mouth at the same time. The figure from the window was now in front of her. He put his hands behind her head and then, moving very swiftly, wound the strip of adhesive tape around her head until the glove was secured in her mouth. With the tape covering her nose, she could barely breathe. The man in front of her reached forward and very carefully peeled the tape away from her nose. Then he clicked on a small pocket flashlight. She could see that he was wearing a black-and-red lumber jacket and his face was covered with an ace knee bandage in which slits had been cut for the eyes and mouth.

"If you can understand me, nod."

She nodded.

"In a moment I will hand you a pencil and paper and you will write down the name and address of the person you gave the tail leader on reel four to. Nod if you understand me."

She nodded.

He handed her a pencil and a small pad of paper, then shone the light on the pad.

The first time she tried to write, her hand was trembling so badly that she could only produce a sort of seismic scrawl. The man with the flashlight reached out and tore off the sheet of paper, crumpled it in his hand, and put it in the pocket of his lumber jacket.

As she wrote David Aronow's name the best Naomi could do was to change the spelling of his last name to Aronov and to put "New York City?" as his address.

After a moment the flashlight clicked off.

The man holding it said something to the man keeping her off the ground. It must have been the order to let her go, because she felt the arm loosening at her throat. There would be time to warn David, stupid David. Then the man in front of her reached forward, grabbed both her legs, and raised them parallel to the floor. Just as carefully as he had peeled the tape from her nose, he now pinched her two nostrils together, and then Naomi knew what the most horrible thing in the world was—to want to be able to breathe.

35 David was surprised to see

a bottle of vodka leaning in a bucket of ice, and a table gleaming with covered dishes, for he had assumed that they were just going to meet in Shar's room and then go find a bar somewhere.

"I hope you don't mind," said Shar, "but I decided that I couldn't stand any more stimulation, especially with tomorrow coming. I think I am suffering from jet shock and culture lag."

"It's the other way around, jet lag and culture shock," said David, "but I like your version, too."

"Thank you. I'll remember, jet lag. But you can't imagine how strange it feels to be living in somebody else's country, speaking somebody else's language. It's like wearing borrowed clothes."

"I know the feeling a little," said David. "Whenever I speak Russian, I automatically feel twenty-percent stupider."

Shar laughed. "Exactly. Twenty percent. Minimum."

David felt his own chuckle stopped by the band of tape around his chest.

"Well," said Shar, "I am boycotting Stolichnaya, and I'm not even sure if I will drink Polish vodka, either, for isn't that really just putting money into a different part of the same pocket? So, I ordered Absolut. You know it?"

"Yes, Swedish. Good, not Slavic, but good."

Shar removed the cap from the vodka bottle, poured out two glasses to match some exact inner sense of measure, then whisked off the metal covers with a Chaplinesque flourish to reveal herring in sour cream, cold cuts, pickles, and a little basket containing slices of black bread. Then he glanced over at David.

"Looks great."

"I am happy you like it."

Shar paused, glass in hand, then said: "I want to drink to the health of David Aronow, who lives at the border of Russian and English and helps smuggle poems across that border. If a poet's work is his true life, then, to some extent, I exist on this side of the border thanks to you."

They both exhaled, Shar's head bolting back as he took his drink, David tilting his back like a bird. They both grabbed bread, bit off a piece, and exhaled vigorously, as the ritual prescribed.

David felt something right away, like an ocean wave breaking on his dry chest, a stinging chill. He had come there in a state of elation, and it would not take much to put him over the top.

"But I'll tell you, Evgeny," began David, "sometimes I feel that all of us—poets, translators, painters—we're a dying breed, dinosaurs thrashing around in a tar pit."

"I don't believe that. Poetry is too basic; poetry is language with a heartbeat."

"So you think in a few hundred years people will be living in orbital satellites slurping dinner up through a straw and then slipping off to some quiet corner to write poetry?"

"Yes. I have to believe in poetry or I couldn't live. I have to believe in the powers of invention."

"I wish I could, but I think the future is going to be quite horrendous. Not that I wouldn't be glad to see it."

"Yes, we get to see so little. And fame is no consolation."

"Fame is the only immortality, real fame."

"Fame is stupid," said Shar. "Fame means strangers can walk up to me on the street or bother me on the phone. I would prefer real immortality."

"Who wouldn't? But maybe we can't be immortal until we feel that we deserve it."

"That's true, we don't feel we deserve it. Part of me always feels unworthy. Now more than ever, I feel like an unworthy fraud."

"Of course, because you aren't the person you read about in *The New York Times,* you're really just Zhenya or whatever you call yourself when you talk to yourself. What *do* you call yourself when you talk to yourself?"

"Zhenya."

"So, let's drink to Zhenya."

Shar smiled and then filled their glasses again, this time with a bit more abandon than precision. They prepared their appetizers beforehand—Shar wrapped a pickle and a piece of salami in dark bread, David scooped his bread into the herring and cream sauce, fiddling until he had gotten a slice of onion on it—then clinked glasses and two seconds later slammed them back on the table.

"Yes, we may break the record tonight," said Shar.

"We're off to a good start."

"Let's sit down and take a little break," Evgeny said. "I like to drink two glasses quick, then wait a little, and then do a second series, three glasses, but with more time between them."

On his way to the chairs arranged around a small coffee table, David's eye paused for a moment on a copy of *The New Yorker* tossed on the bureau and Shar's blue-and-white jogging top hanging from a doorknob, the only disorder in the room.

Just as he settled in his chair, a streak of white energy traveled up David's spinal column, making one shoulder after the other twitch forward.

"You're feeling it already," said Shar, setting the glasses on the coffee table. "I hope I can feel something, too. I still have this sort of anesthetized feeling. Yes, I had a Russia amputated from my life."

David laughed. "A serious operation. I'll tell you something, Evgeny, I love to talk like this about the world, but only with someone who loves to talk about it the same way

I do. As naturally as two housewives discussing the cost of bacon."

"So, here we are, two housewives," said Shar.

"Yes, and what with the cost of bacon today . . ."

They laughed like people who are becoming fast friends.

"But we were talking about time. My three years in Mordovia were horrible because I only lived each minute to be done with it. But now, when I look back, there's nothing there."

"Yes," said David, excited to be brushing close to his own secret, "it's insulting that we only live 70.4 years or whatever it is."

"And what can I be here?" Shar sprang to his feet. "What is a Russian outside of Russia? The idea makes no sense at all. A Russian is only a Russian in Russia. Outside Russian air he is just a caricature. I saw that at the party last night."

"So you went?"

"For a little while."

"I was there earlier."

"That smell in the air, that aroma of melancholy."

"Aroma of melancholy—that would be a good name for a line of émigré perfume."

"It would, it would. But, David, that aroma, that *toska* —there's no other word for it—that feeling that the most important thing is elsewhere, I don't want to live like that," said Shar, looking away for a moment into memory, not to the memory of the party but of the hour he had spent with Vaska in Brighton Beach. They had gone to the Golden Palace, a restaurant that re-created a Soviet hotel in style, size, and atmosphere—the little out-of-date combo blaring away, the dance floor packed, the tables roaring. Thick throats, overripe women, gold teeth. There had been a certain moment of horror and revulsion as he had seen that, no matter what, he would become a version of them, a Russian hick gangster in big-city America, always outlandish, forever awkward, and, no matter how successful, ultimately absurd. His dream was a blind alley, childish, unworthy of him. And the revulsion also came from the nearly palpable feeling of Vinias's hand on him, moving him about the chessboard of Manhattan and somehow even bringing him to that restaurant to demonstrate that the jump he was contemplating led to a corny nightmare, a crowded nowhere.

"Yes," said David, "all that melancholy got to me, too. But I know a good antidote for it."

"You do? What?"

"The second series."

"You're right! It's time to begin the second series."

They brought their glasses and food back to the coffee table.

"Well," said David, "being a Russian is more dramatic than being an American. My melancholy has a fancy imported name like *malaise* or *Weltschmerz;* theirs—yours—is exile. But the trick is to carve out a little place for yourself, a place that would never have existed unless you made it; that's the only way people like you and me can ever start to feel at home in this world."

Now they drank greedily, no longer having to overcome the inborn timidity of the epiglottis.

There was something to what David said, thought Shar. The fact that the émigré world he had seen at the nightclub and the party was so dreary did not mean that he would share that fate. He had never shared those people's fate when they were in Russia. He never shared anyone's fate.

"That's an interesting idea," he said. "I wonder if it's possible—I wonder if it's really possible to invent one's own life. I would believe it, if it were not for one thing, the one thing you Americans always seem to forget about."

"And what's that?"

"It's the problem of evil, which is really the theme of my new poem."

" 'When the walls of the Warsaw ghetto were smashed like the tablets at Sinai,' " quoted David, glad to remember the opening lines and now a bit guilty that he had read no more than that.

"Yes, exactly," said Shar, "with the difference that Moses went back up and got the moral law from God a second time, but no one has gone back up for us. And no one will. And so I have come to believe that though life is good, the world has been abandoned to evil once and for all, abandoned to evil."

Stunned by Shar's passionate conviction, David could not reply for a moment. "You really believe that?"

"It seems obvious to me. Sometimes I am called a Christian poet by the critics who never get anything right. Yes, I use Christian symbols; they still have a little life in them. But when I look at the people out on the streets of New York at night, I can see that they exist in a world where no one has ever been before, a world where the old symbols do not reach. That's why I was glad to leave Russia, because not only is there plenty of evil there, but they want you to sing happy songs. And that doubles the evil."

"But don't you think it will all pass and in a few hundred years the Soviet Union will be as dead and boring as the Hapsburgs? Even evil isn't perfect; it destroys itself. Look at the Nazis."

"Fascism is very different from communism. People think they have made a great discovery when they detect similarities between communism and fascism, but what they have really made is a great mistake. Fascism is evil, of course, but it passes quickly. Look at Germany, Greece, Spain, Portugal, Italy—torturing yesterday, voting today. Fascism is adolescent. Of course, it broke the tablets of Moses, it broke new ground, medical experiments on people. But communism is very different. Communism is mature, conservative evil. Establishment evil. It doesn't care about all those adolescent uniforms and death's heads. It only wants real power. It is the most perfect system ever devised for getting and keeping real power. Torture today, torture tomorrow, torture forever."

"But the beauty for me, Evgeny, is that I don't care what happens to the world. I care about my life, my existence."

"But what happens in the world tells you what really is."

"Not quite. Nothing is ever quite what we think it is."

"That's true, too," said Evgeny, no longer excited. "Time for another, I think."

The room was quiet now, except for the background

buzz of hotel machines maintaining light and heat and running water.

After the next drink, David could feel the vodka melting into his bloodstream like snow. He had a sudden impulse to share his secret with Evgeny but struck it down at once, telling himself to beware of that impulse, which might rise again as he got still drunker.

The phone rang. Shar frowned and rose, comically missing a step on the long way across the room.

"Hello?" said Shar in a reluctant voice.

"Evgeny, this is Raisa Farb."

"Hello, how are you?"

"Thank you, fine. Are you alone?"

"No."

"Then I'll be quick. Bring whatever you can put down on paper to the book fair tomorrow. You understand what I mean?"

"Of course."

"I will meet you there at one o'clock."

"Fine."

So quick, thought Shar, so easy. But that also meant that he would have to be quick about finally making up his mind. He would need help, he would be going into action, and there could be no second thoughts when he was in action.

"Not bad news, I hope," said David, noting the quizzical frown on Shar's face.

"No, just a woman wanting me to write something for tomorrow."

"For the book fair?"

"In that connection."

For a moment David sensed a grayness in the air, as when you had to leave a party to run to the store.

"Interesting woman?" he asked, to dispel that atmosphere.

"I'm not interested in women now. In the camp I thought I would be, but I'm not now."

"Either they're all you think about or else you wonder why exactly you were supposed to be so excited."

"We need more vodka!" Shar exclaimed, and poured four long splashes into each glass. More than anyone could take at once. The ante had been raised.

"David," he said very seriously, "I really have to decide about my life quickly. I can't stand this having to choose. Sometimes I even wonder why people want to be free when it's so painful to choose."

"To be or not to be, Roquefort or French, for here or to go," said David to introduce a little levity, an effort that failed.

"So, let's drink to my solution, to my decision. Will you drink with me to that, David?"

"Yes."

For a moment, as the vodka ran coldly over his teeth, David could feel the northern lights start to come on in his mind.

"So, what exactly is the problem? We can solve it right here, tonight, I'm sure of it," he said.

"The problem is that I don't want to be that stupid person, Evgeny Shar, Soviet poet in exile. Those boring parties, those unhappy people, those little magazines arguing, arguing, arguing."

"So, then, be something else."

"Like what?"

"Like whatever you want. You could become a rock star or a lobster fisherman or a cowboy or whatever. This is America. We're so free we don't even have to be who we are!"

"That's the question. I know a man who believes that personality is only a fiction, and yet he also believes in occupying the right place in life. So, if he's right, it's not a question of who you are but where."

"Give me more vodka, I think I'm getting an idea," said David. They drank quickly this time, without toasting or eating. "The real problem is that you can't make an important decision without really knowing about life. But nobody knows about life. There's disagreement on every point. Nobody knows. So we have to make up our own version, our own myth, to live. Maybe our myth turns out to have significance for the whole world, or maybe it's just an experiment for ourselves. Jesus died for our sins, but we die for them, too."

"I think about heartbeat again, David. The heartbeat is too important to be under our control—we'd die in our sleep. Maybe all these choices are just nonsense to keep us too busy to meddle with important things like the heartbeat."

"That's a reasonable doubt, but what good does it do you? Does it satisfy you? Is that the answer you were looking for?"

"No."

"That means we really have to push now."

"You mean, the metaphysical housewives are actually about to purchase some bacon?"

David laughed. "Here's the question," he said. "The question is not whether God exists or not. Of course God exists —God the living universe, God the mystery of existence. That's not the problem. The problem is us. People. What are people? Persons, that's what we are, persons. Of course, we're animals that shit and die, but we're also persons. We're the only persons in nature. That's the main thing about us, the boring mystery of us. How can there be something called David Aronow, something that calls itself David Aronow? Stars, OK; whales, OK; but me? So, then, the question is— is there anything immutably real about us, any divine structure to our personalities, or . . ."

"Or are we just pathetic mammals deluding ourselves with little stories before we're clubbed over the head?"

"Right."

"How can we find out?"

"Not by talking."

"That's true, too," said Shar. For a moment he sat without moving or speaking; then he poured them each a very small shot, which they drank offhandedly. "I know what to do."

Shar rose and marched off to the bathroom, to return a moment later with his shaving kit, brown European leather with a gold zipper. "Let's sit together on the couch," he said. "I want to show you something."

When they were side by side on the couch, Shar emptied his shaving kit on the coffee table—razor, deodorant, a small plastic container of pills.

"These are my sleeping pills," he said. "I sleep well, but for some reason I have great difficulty in falling asleep. These little pills are very strong. I was told that five taken at once would certainly be enough to kill me."

He poured the pills onto the table, making them click faintly.

"It seems odd that something so little can kill you," said David, not sure what the point was.

"So," said Shar distantly, a lock of hair over one eye, the outline of his jaw more visible under skin more sallow now, "so, let's be scientific. Let's conduct a scientific experiment. Let's take pills—two, three, four—let's push ourselves to the edge and take a look over, let's find out once and for all what we're made out of and what the hell is going on here. What do you say, David, good idea?"

David hesitated, not having expected a challenge of that order. He touched his shirt lightly to reassure himself with the hard presence of the reel. But then, suddenly, he loved the idea—to gamble freely between life dramatically extended and life dramatically shortened.

"All right," said David, "I'm game."

"Good, I thought you'd be," said Shar, his voice still distracted as he removed his wristwatch and laid it on the table. "They take about ten minutes to reach the bloodstream."

"Ten minutes."

"Until then, you can still puke them up."

Feeling himself sobering up with fear, David poured himself a quick shot and drank it down. Shar smiled.

"Now," said Shar, separating the pills like a pharmacist with his comb, "let's start with two to prove we are serious people."

"All right."

"Two for you, and two for me. I will make the toast." Shar's face came back to life, his eyes grew moist and clear. David was glad to have him back. "So, now we'll drink with pills for *zakuski* instead of meat and pickles. I want to drink to the health of whatever's really inside us, because if you're in there and you're anything more than fear and ganglia, we're going to make you come out and be with us here tonight."

David glanced slit-eyed over the top of his glass to make sure that Shar was taking both of his pills. He was. David felt one of his click against a tooth as it was washed into him with vodka.

"Good toast," said David, moving a bit away from Shar to be better able to face him. "My first thought is that I'm being terrifically stupid and I'll end up destroying brain cells or damaging my liver or something like that."

"My thoughts are running like that, too. But we're still in the safe zone; we can make ourselves throw up, we can call the hospital."

"It reminds me of one time in Idaho—it's a wonderful state, you should go there if you get a chance, Evgeny. I had rented a little house in the mountains. One night I went outside, and there were so many stars. I could actually see billions of them, and the darkness was so deep I felt I was looking down into it and might even fall into it."

"And so?"

"And so I went back inside."

"Aha."

"So, that's us now. Still close to the house. But looking."

"Yes, I'm having a twinge of panic now, too," said Shar. "I know the feeling. Once I got caught in a riptide and I was way out; I could see the little people on the shore just over the top of the waves, and I was afraid I couldn't make it back in."

"You're not supposed to swim against a riptide—you're supposed to swim at an angle to it."

"Now you tell me." Shar laughed. "But I still don't feel any riptide in me."

"Let's take the third one," David heard himself saying.

Evgeny glanced at him with curiosity and respect. "You make the toast."

"I'll drink to this pill, pill number three, which puts us in the danger zone, far from the house, far from shore."

They washed the third pill down with desperate matter-of-factness.

"Yes, now it feels different," said Shar. "Now it's interesting. Now I feel that with all the vodka and everything, there is a chance I could go under."

"But do you want to?"

"No."

"Neither do I."

"Are you saying we should stop?"

"No, I'm saying that we're both starting to really feel that we don't want to die."

"But maybe that's just the practical common sense of the body and its survival systems."

"Maybe. But, look, it's not only a question of the body. Would you want to be kept alive as a body by machines if there was no chance of ever coming out of a coma?"

"No," said Shar, "I wouldn't."

"So, that means that we want to live not just as bodies but as persons. And that means there is something in us."

"Now we are starting to produce results. But I am not convinced by what you say. It's only the ego pretending it's the soul, because the ego by definition does not want to cease to exist. Nothing does. But people die easily and peacefully in their sleep, when there is no stupid ego to say, I want to live, I have important things to do in life."

"Let's not talk for a little while," said David. "Let's close our eyes and not talk for a little while."

"All right," said Shar, leaning back against the couch.

David closed his eyes and for a moment felt he was lurching, as if he had lost his balance. The day's events, the vodka, the elation continued to elevate him, but now he could feel a dark gravity at work in his bloodstream, magnetizing his consciousness away.

Put your fingers down your throat and hold them there until you puke up all that stupid poison, you idiot, cried a voice in him, almost causing his eyes to snap open. But he held on. It was worth it. It was worth it to really know if there was anything to it all besides metabolism, panic, vanity.

If there was anything there at the very center, he wanted to touch it—now, tonight, right there.

He had gone too far away, he could see that, too far away from everyone, which, by some law he could not fathom, meant too far away from himself, the person he was, the boring mystery of him, familiar as the taste in his mouth. He was slipping away from himself, going under, far from shore. Families were laughing on the beach and he was drowning alone in the waves. Not alone. He was with Evgeny.

"Let's take the fourth one," said Evgeny. "I don't feel anything."

"I don't know, I'm starting to feel sick."

"Let's take the fourth one, let's give it five minutes, and then, if nothing happens, we can stop. I'm taking mine," said Evgeny with wild insistence. "Stay with me. I know we'll get there, David."

"Five minutes, not a second more."

They waited until the second hand was at the twelve and took the pills.

Their faces were damp and pale now, like those of people who had been driving much too long. Evgeny was nodding as if in inward agreement with something, but then David realized he was nodding off.

"Evgeny!" he shouted. "Wake up! We're dying!"

"No, I'm all right. Something was starting," said Shar slurrily.

"No, we're going to die from this! Stay with me, don't drift away!"

Shar reached out and took David's hand in both of his,

smiling. "David, that's it. I had something strong and definite for a moment. For a moment I did not want you to die. I didn't care about me, but I cared about you, because you had come that far with me. And now I know there's something there—whatever it is doesn't matter. But that means that the place is not what counts, that means I can be free, that means I am not trapped anymore. And you helped me find that; you are my brother now; let me kiss you."

They kissed each other hard on both cheeks and then sprang wobbily to their feet.

"I'll call Room Service for coffee," said David. "What's the room number?"

"Nine-oh-six. I'll open the windows."

"Room Service?" said David. "This is 906. We need a pot of black coffee right away. Someone's sick. Nine-oh-six. Right away."

David ran into the bathroom, fell to his knees, and puked *zakuski,* pills, and bile into the bathtub.

"Come to the window," called Shar, as his own throat gagged with vomit.

David staggered to the window next to the one Shar was at and braced his hands against the sill, afraid of blacking out.

They both inhaled vigorously, greedy for oxygen.

"We'll be all right," said Shar.

"We'll be all right," repeated David.

Cars were honking. The lights from windows and car headlights dissolved on the damp surface of his eyes. It was crazy, too crazy. But they would live.

There was a knock at the door.

"I'll get it," said Shar.

"That was fast," said David, continuing to inhale the too-moist night air. He threw a quick glance at the door and saw the black-and-red-checked sleeve of a lumber jacket, then turned back to the window.

With his eyes Shar indicated to Vaska that he was not alone.

"What is it you want?" asked Shar.

"If you would sign this," said Vaska, handing Shar a copy of *Icons*, which he opened to reveal the piece of paper on which Naomi had written David Aronov, New York City. Shar took his pen and wrote on the flyleaf, "He's with me now. Wait and follow him."

Furious that he had fallen for all that nonsense, all that metaphysical blab, with a person who would already be dead if he had invited Vaska into the room, Shar slammed the door angrily. There was no new life, only this one.

Still gulping the night air David looked over and saw Shar's face come through the other window frame and toward him, pasty white, a look of fury softening into bemusement.

"Can you imagine," said Shar, "in the middle of all this, an autograph hound?"

"Grotesque," said David with a little laugh. "But funny too, in a way."

"Yes, funny too, in a way."

The next knock was Room Service.

"I forgot to order two cups," said David as the waiter set down the tray.

"Get the glass from the bathroom."

The waiter crinkled up his nose at the smell of vomit. Even the ten-dollar tip did not dispel his disgust.

David came running back in with a water glass wrapped in a washcloth. "Pour," he said to Shar. "Quick."

Shar poured David's glass, then his own cup. David was already fighting the heat of the coffee when Shar raised his cup in a final toast and said, "Well, as the Jews say—to life."

36 Solly didn't catch on right away.

"Hey, you musta done a good job on that Yanopolis. I didn't think he could find the sky with a flashlight," said Moran, the desk man, who had an odd way with words.

"Yuh?"

"No, I mean it. It makes us all look good for a change."

"What does?" asked Solly.

"Him getting the killer of what's-her-name Rosen in less than twenty-four hours. You mean you didn't know?"

Solly took the stairs two at a time. That was the final fucking straw! He had been under a hex since the Farb case —everything he did turned to shit, and some of the younger men had started giving him the hey-you're-starting-to slip-a-little look and then that dickhead brings in the killer in under twenty-four hours. It was too much. It couldn't be right. If it was Yanopolis, there had to be a mistake somewhere.

"Where's Yanopolis?"

"In 301, questioning the suspect."

Solly opened the door gently to hear Yanopolis saying, "That's right, you have the right to remain silent, and we have the right to question you until your fucking eardrums collapse."

There was a sneer on Yanopolis's face that didn't entirely vanish when he turned to Solly.

"I told you I was going to get this animal. I worked through the night on it," said Yanopolis, whose face was pasty with fatigue, the rims of his eyes the color of Bloody Marys.

"Good job," said Solly, looking over at the black man in his late twenties wearing a mustard yellow imitation-leather coat. The suspect's left index finger was in a splint, and there was a large bandage on the side of his head. He let himself be looked at with indifference.

"So, what's the story?" asked Solly.

"We got a pretty quick match off the prints on the Afro comb. I got a warrant. I went looking, I found him, and here he is."

"And what's he have to say for himself?"

"So far, nothing," said Yanopolis, reluctant to tarnish his victory with any admission of failure.

"What's his name?"

"Jackson. William R."

"Previous convictions?"

"Drugs. Breaking and entering. Two street assaults."

"A bad guy. Nothing in the sex department?"

"Nothing except that we know he hangs around Playland, over at Eighth and Forty-second, but if he's putting out women, none of the other pimps seem to know anything about it."

Yanopolis didn't like answering Solly's questions: a minute ago, he had been the one doing the asking.

"I don't want to interfere here," said Solly. "You just go right ahead."

"All right, Jackson, it's simple," said Yanopolis. "The prints on the Afro comb are yours. The Afro comb was found in the murdered woman's apartment. You got no alibi. Put it all together and it spells life in the joint, where the big guys are going to fuck your stupid ass."

Solly smiled to himself as he watched Jackson twitch and then nonchalantly pull out a pack of menthol 100s.

"And of course she struggled, which accounts for the busted finger and the head injury. You're going to rot away in there, Jackson, like the piece of garbage you are."

Jackson lit up and exhaled languorously. "Man, you're so lame it's pitiful."

"Solly, you better take over," said Yanopolis. "Otherwise I might do something unconstitutional here."

David did not know where he was. For a moment he did not even know how old he was, and thought he might be at his grandmother's summer house. A terrible fear hit him —he was lying naked in the lobby of the Algonquin Hotel. Then he began to remember walking thirty blocks until he was sure he would live. Raisa in her doorway yelling at him. Bouncing the hard plastic reel against her chest as they fucked. And so that meant he was still in her bed. Now he became aware of the smell of her sleep in the sheets. Without opening his eyes, he touched the taped lump on his chest and smiled.

There was some reason he had to get up. He could not remember the reason, but he knew it had something to do with the voice talking nonstop in the next room. It didn't sound like Raisa. No, it was a man's voice. He was talking about the Dow-Jones average. What friend of Raisa's would talk so much about the Dow-Jones? Then it was obvious. The radio alarm. He opened his eyes. A stringent blue-gray light came through the window. It was New York. Morning.

Shaky, elated, he had coffee and two bites of toast at a coffee shop in Raisa's neighborhood, then took a cab into Manhattan. One o'clock at the book fair; he'd be on time. She had even written two notes to remind him—one on top of the clock radio, the other scrolled into his shoe. But why was he supposed to meet her? Oh, right, some new information, some last-minute hitch.

He had the cab stop a few blocks from the Public Library at Fifth and Forty-second. It was only twenty of, and he couldn't stand the taste in his mouth, stamp glue and ashes.

The eyes watching David through the drugstore window smiled as David bought a pack of cigarettes and a roll of mints, which he started peeling open as he waited for his change.

"Abram!" shouted David a minute later, catching sight of Luntz, a bobbing dot about to vanish between the library's immense pillars. But David was still at the bottom of the steps, and the noise from Fifth Avenue snatched his voice away.

Mounting the steps to the library, David felt momentarily oppressed by the tons of stone and marble, the hundreds of thousands of books, which made being alive seem not only insignificant but even somehow impertinent.

David started to approach Abram in the lobby, but it was clearly not a moment to interrupt, for the man facing Abram was just saying, "What? You won't give me your hand? Why not?"

He continued past them without being noticed and followed the stream of people on the stairs to the second floor, where the fair was being held.

In the hallway that led to the ballroom, David paused briefly to scan the books displayed on a long library table. Russian books printed in Munich, Paris, Michigan. A few lucky works selected for translation, the American editions bright, the lettering catchy.

A three-man TV news crew came bumping by unapologetically, trailing a thick black cable. Two beefy, one scrawny, they all wore red T-shirts and moved with the special assurance of those who serve a powerful master. Two

New York Times reporters, wearing the pin-striped suits favored by serious men of finance, watched the TV crew with a look of amused disdain. But the men in the red T-shirts were immune to that and even seemed to loop the cable toward the reporters.

David went into the main room, a hive of gossip and body heat. Lights were being adjusted on the stage, and a voice was testing the mike—one, two, three.

"It's depressing," he heard someone say, "it's always the same faces."

But the only face he was interested in was nowhere to be seen. There was no high point from which he could survey the crowd; it was already packed fairly tight, though natural corridors kept forming for him, which he noticed with pleasure.

He ordered a club soda at the bar. A young Russian woman who seemed to enjoy startling people with her beauty, curious to see how they would react, asked him for a light. But what surprised him was the aristocratic style of her coquetry—had it somehow managed to survive under the Soviets, or had she relearned it in New York? Or was she one of those Paris Russians? His curiosity was never to be satisfied, for just as she was thanking him, a man moved beside her and said, "I've been looking everywhere for you," and David could hear the right to jealousy being exercised in his voice. She smiled to David over her shoulder as she disappeared into the crowd.

But he knew that her sudden appearance was no accident, and more than mere flirtation. The constellation of his great good fortune was in its perfect fateful alignment, and its effects were to be seen and felt everywhere in that crowd, that swarm of particles where his own charge drew the brightest to him and caused the rest to disperse.

Now he was glad he was there. It was important that he see these people, his colleagues—journalists, writers, editors, translators; it was important to see what he had almost become. Some faces pleaded not to be insulted, some lips were compressed against a pervasive sourness. Maybe it was just age.

But Sid Kohl was jaunty, freshly launched on a third marriage, crackling with savvy and opinions.

"You saw my response to Shapiro's review of my book?"

"I did," said David.

"The nerve of that *momzer.*"

"You see the Shar poems I did in the Op Ed?" asked David, to keep the conversation going, though at that moment he was incapable of taking the world of books and reviews seriously.

"Sometimes he gets a little too metaphysical for me."

"Socialist secular humanist to the end," said David.

"You betcha. I didn't spend ten years in California like you."

"Anyway, there're no real poets left now."

"What about Milosz?"

"Milosz is the last."

"Is it true he's a practicing Catholic?"

"I wouldn't know."

"Remember, keep your eye out for articles I might be

interested in—you know what I like," said Kohl, ever the editor, and he hopped back into the crowd as deftly as a body-surfer catching a wave.

David looked at his watch. Ten to one. Raisa would have better sense than to try to find him in that crowd, he thought. Of course, maybe she had lied to him; maybe there was no problem, no last-minute hitch. Maybe she had called Altheim when she ran from him at the party. But as he headed back for the door, the suits and shoulders continuing to slip past him, he could not believe that Raisa would jeopardize everything, everything, and that it was Altheim she was bringing there at one o'clock.

Solly pulled a cigarette out of his own pack but did not light it.

"Your full name is William R. Jackson, is that correct?" he asked, looking down at the card.

Jackson nodded.

"What's the 'R' for?"

"Roosevelt."

Solly grimaced and said: "Twenty-eight years of age?"

Jackson nodded again, a little curtly this time.

"And you reside at 116 West Forty-third Street?"

"Man, I already told the other guy."

"Just double-checking here."

"That's right, that's where I reside," said Jackson, pronouncing the verb with languorous humor.

"So, then, tell me—did you break into Naomi Rosen's apartment, kill her, rob her, and then sexually assault her?"

"No, I didn't."

"OK, Jackson, let's say you didn't. The law says you're innocent until proven guilty."

"I know what the law *says*."

"But we have to ask ourselves, If this guy is innocent, then how did the Afro comb with his fingerprints on it get into the victim's apartment? So, if you can tell us that one little thing, you're going to be in good shape."

"Afro combs, man, they're always getting lost, I go through a couple, two, three, a month."

"I can believe that, Jackson; I'm always losing things myself. But, you see, the difference is, say I lose a glove or my scissors, they just disappear; I never see them again, and they don't find my glove or my scissors next to somebody who's been murdered; you follow me on the difference here?"

Jackson said nothing. Solly was pulling on his cigarette to loosen the tobacco.

"When you go to court, you're going to have to make people believe that that comb fell out of your pocket in the middle of New York, some guy comes by and sees it and says, Hey, is this my lucky day, I found an Afro comb, I'm saving myself a buck and a half. So the guy sticks the comb in his hair without even getting a single one of his own fingerprints on it, and then he goes and kills a woman in her apartment, and *then* he sexually assaults her, and he loses his new comb in the process. But what does he care? He's got money now

—he can buy himself his own brand-new one. Is that supposed to be a real story?"

"It could happen."

"But it didn't."

"How do you know?"

"I don't have to. What I know is that nobody with half a brain's going to believe it, and that comb is going to cost you a lot of grief."

Jackson turned away sharply in his chair, the only escape the situation offered.

"Who fixed your finger?"

"Bellevue emergency."

"Did you give your right name?"

"No."

"So we can't even check. You see how honesty is the best policy, Jackson. What night was that?"

"Tuesday."

"You think anyone there might remember you?"

"I don't know."

"What was the doctor's name?"

"He was some black dude, but he talked like an Englishman."

"We can check that, but it might not make all that much difference, either. Being in the hospital Tuesday night doesn't mean anything; it's where you were Wednesday night that counts, Jackson."

"Like I already said, I was home recuperating in my bed."

"You weren't hanging around Playland?"

"No, sir, I was home in my bed."

"How come you put in so much time at Playland?"

"It's a free country."

"You putting out women?"

"No."

"You look like you do all right with the women."

"I do all right."

"I'm going to tell you the kind of guy I am, Jackson," said Solly, pretending to look through his pockets for a match. "I'm the kind of guy that goes by first impressions. I open the door here and I look in and what do I see? I see a young, good-looking guy, nicely dressed, intelligent-looking. So, right away I think to myself, Shit, this may not be the guy, because why would a good-looking, intelligent-looking guy who probably does all right with the women, I mean, why is a guy like that going to do what was done to that woman? But then we ask you questions that are for your own good and what do you tell us? Nothing. And so then I start to think, Hey, maybe I was wrong, maybe this guy is not so intelligent, and so I got to think if I was wrong about the guy's brains, maybe I was wrong thinking the guy does all right with women, too, and maybe this is the kind of guy that does do those kinds of things."

"You were right the first time."

"Well, OK, but one more question. It's a little personal, but you know how these things are. I mean, afterward, when you fucked her, did you get it up good, or was it one of those softies you have to pull at? Yanopolis, you got a match? I used my last one."

Solly turned away from Jackson and bent toward

Yanopolis, who had lit a match. Continuing to look at Yanopolis, Solly said, as if Jackson were no longer there, "You should remember that, Yanopolis: in most of your sex crimes, the guy can't get it up unless in some special way, if even then. I remember one telling me how horrible it was; he was crying, I almost felt sorry for him, except that his specialty was killing the little boys afterward so they couldn't tell on him. Now, of course, maybe they'll drag a shrink in on this one and the shrink'll say it was all Jackson's mother's fault because Jackson can't get it up for a woman that's alive. I don't know, maybe it is her fault; maybe they should put her on trial."

When Jackson began speaking, his voice was so controlled that both Solly and Yanopolis tensed involuntarily.

"All right, this is the gig. I hang out at Playland. I hang out by the magazines, I check out who's reading what. Then, when they walk out, I come up to them and tell them I've got just what they want. I get their money and they don't get shit. But that night I picked the wrong dude; he knew something—karate. I went down hard, but I saw him—I saw him kick my piece down the street and I saw him pick up the comb. Now, that's it, that's really it."

"And what did this guy look like?"

"Tall. Blond. Looked like an athlete. He was wearing one of those blue-and-white sweatshirts under his jacket, he looked like a foreigner, that's why I picked him."

"You could identify him?"

"Yeah, I could. You got him?"

"Any additional questions, Yanopolis?"

"Solly, I don't believe a fucking word this guy is saying, do you?"

Just then Sergeant Guerra's head appeared at the door. "Solly, phone for you," he said, his voice serious. "Your wife, you better hurry."

The corridor was nearly deserted now, except for the man straightening the books on the tables and two old Russian women quibbling about the date of Belinsky's death.

The men's room's heavy wooden door created a sudden peace and silence when it closed. David walked to the farthest stall, checking for shoes on the way and seeing nothing but a folded newspaper in the next-to-last stall.

The gray metal walls in the last stall had the usual drawings and curses. He rolled up his shirt to check the adhesive tape, which had felt loose when he was talking with Kohl.

He decided to try his luck on a crap, certain, though, that he would be knotted up at least until his plane was in the air. Automatically he reached out with his foot for the newspaper he had noticed in the next stall. The back page showed three horses in a photo finish.

He flipped the tabloid over and saw the black letters of the headline: SEX MURDER IN SOHO. There was a very strange second between seeing Naomi Rosen's face in the oval and putting the puzzle of words and pictures together, a clear but very somber second that suddenly turned hideous as his knees began bobbing uncontrollably, sweat seeping out of his thighs.

Suddenly his mind was full of too many meanings. It meant that Naomi was dead, and it meant that she had been killed by the people who wanted the film, and it didn't matter what the newspaper said, it was a disguise murder just like Raisa's brother's must have been. And that meant that Naomi had told them who she gave the film to, because anyone would, he would. And that meant that they knew about him, that they were looking for him that very second. They were there in the building, they were there at the book fair—they would be there anyway, but today they would be there for him.

The door to the men's room opened. They were here. They were going to come in over the top of the stall and cut his throat fast while he struggled helplessly, hogtied by the pants at his ankles, and he was going to bleed to death from the throat as they ripped the adhesive tape from his chest.

It was just one of them, he could tell from the sound of the footsteps. But one of them was enough; any one of them was enough for him.

He felt like a tree that had been struck by lightning

Then he understood why he was there. Raisa was one of them. She had told him to be there at one o'clock, and like a fool he had come. They had needed somebody to retrieve the film for them, some American stooge, and now that that was done they would just pluck it back from him. But this didn't make any sense, either, because why would they kill

Naomi if Raisa could have just as easily told them who had it? He realized that he was only capable of thinking terrified thoughts.

The footsteps had come to a stop. In the tiled silence he heard the sound of a zipper, followed by the usual melody of urination and flush. Zip, shoe leather on tile, faucet, brown paper towel, door open and door close.

It was just a guy who needed to take a leak, he repeated to himself, as if unable to believe the beauty of the simple truth. But nothing had changed—they were still out there.

There was no choice. He was going to have to make a dash for it, like a crab that had molted and was making a dash for the ocean before some winged scissors came swooping down on it.

He was afraid to look himself in the face in the mirror above the washstands as he splashed cold water on his face, grateful to the water for its coldness.

As soon as he opened the door, David saw Evgeny Shar illuminated by hand-held lights, speaking directly to a television camera. To the left of the small crowd behind him, Raisa was just taking Shar's picture with a Polaroid flash. When Shar glanced aside and saw David in the doorway, Raisa's eyes followed; letting the camera fall from her hands to bob on its neck strap, she ran over to David.

As he saw Raisa running toward him, he thought that maybe she had brought Altheim there after all, and it would be all over, thank God, it would be all over.

"Raisa, they killed the woman who gave me the film."

"And they'll kill us next."

"Do you have what you were going to give me?"

"No."

"Why not?"

"He needs more time. He could only remember half of it this morning. Another fool—he drank so much he couldn't get his mind to work."

"Shar?" asked David, in what was both a question and an exclamation.

"Yes, Shar."

"How?"

"They put Yuri Trofimovich in the same camp with him."

To the astonishment of the director, Evgeny Shar simply walked away from the camera and toward the man and woman at the end of the hall.

"I told him it was you," said Raisa as Shar joined them.

"The woman who gave me the film has been killed," said David.

"I see," said Shar, his face becoming grave at once. "All right, I can't get rid of these television people until later this evening. And I need some time to try to get the rest down on paper. Where can you stay until around eleven-thirty?"

"Not at my place," said Raisa. "They're probably tearing it apart right now."

"Your hotel?" asked David.

"No, hotels aren't safe."

"They must be at my place, too."

"Wait," said Shar. "What about Karen's?"

"I can go to her office."

"No, she's here, helping with the speech and the documentary. She went inside ahead of us. Is her building big?"

"No, very small, way downtown."

"Perfect. You see that man over there?" Shar nodded at a man with thinning hair, dark glasses, and a light leather jacket, who nodded when they looked at him. "That's Borya, my driver, a good man. He can take care of you until I come. He'll make sure no one gets into her building."

"Oh, Mr. Shar," called the director.

"Give Raisa Karen's address and phone number."

"Four-fifty Greenwich Street—Street, not Avenue," said David.

"Four-fifty Greenwich Street—not Avenue," said Raisa, writing on the back of the Polaroid photo of Shar that had just slid out of her camera.

As he gave her the phone number, David saw that she was smiling.

"Why are you smiling?"

"Dead people exchanging information; it's funny, don't you think?"

"Raisa," said David, reaching out to put his arms around her, whether to give her courage or to take courage from her, he wasn't sure.

"Go get the keys," she said and turned away.

Dazed, David began walking toward the main room. His legs felt like fluttering cords of muscle as he squeezed between the packed bodies that did not part for him now.

"After the Russian invasion of Czechoslovakia in August 1968," the first speaker was saying in rousing conclusion, his voice rattling metallically in the public-address system, "a

Czech writer remarked that the pen is mightier than the sword but not mightier than the tank."

The crowd responded with low, unhappy laughter.

The stage lights were still being adjusted, and David could not pick out any faces in the flashing glare around the stage.

"But we are here today," continued the speaker, "because of our belief that the pen is mightier than the sword, the tank, and the ICBM, that the human spirit is greater than the worst human history has to offer. . . ."

As he pushed and apologized his way through the crowd, David was aware of the speaker's voice somewhere at the side of his mind; it frightened him, for it lacked the fire of real conviction.

The next speaker, a former Soviet general, took the stand, his shaved head gleaming under the lights. He held the English text of his speech as though it might fly away if he slackened his grip for a second.

David thought he saw her to the left of the stage and began moving in a ragged diagonal in that direction.

"We must not forget those who are not here with us today," said the speaker, his sibilants hissing in the microphone. "We must not forget those in the camps, the prisons, the psychiatric hospitals."

Now he was close enough to see that it wasn't her. He'd been fooled by the hair.

"We must not forget Anatoly Marchenko, Father Gleb Yakunin, Yuri Orlov. . . ."

For a moment the litany of names calmed David: he was not alone; there were others with him, good people, brave people. But then he recalled that these were the names of people who had been caught and crushed, just as he would be caught and crushed.

"Books are being removed from library shelves in upper New York State," said the next speaker, a former state senator and labor leader. "Nobody has a monopoly on this problem."

The remark drew scattered applause and a few hisses.

As David began moving toward the right of the stage, he felt a hand on his arm and knew, with a sickening sense of relief, that it was all over.

"David, I have been looking for you everywhere," said Abram. "Here is Shar's poem I promised to return to you, here."

"Thanks," said David flatly, taking the envelope.

"There is one thing I must say to you about that poem, David," said Abram in a whisper that grew louder as he spoke. "Now I have read it three times. First reading, all right, pretty good, some new images, rhythm very basic but of course . . ."

"Shhhhhhh." A vigilante of public decorum turned around and stared at Abram, who for a moment became a shamefaced boy. David began to squirm away, having spotted Karen talking to a technician. Abram followed, holding on to his sleeve, whispering passionately: "But that is not poetry; I don't know what it is, but it is not poetry. What do I know about anything? I know nothing. All I know is poetry. All I can do is hear the exact person in the words, and I did not hear anything in his poem. Nothing."

"Abram, listen," said David softly, pronouncing each word precisely, separately. "I can't talk about poetry right now."

The doctor explained about Adelle's kidney stone, but Solly didn't care about the details. The only thing that mattered was that either she would pass the stone or they would have to cut. The doctor explained that the pain caused by a kidney stone was extremely intense, roughly equal to that of childbirth, which was why they had had to sedate her at once. She would sleep through the night now, and there was no real sense in his staying there.

He called in to the station. They asked about Adelle and told him he shouldn't come back but should go home, where the hospital could contact him if they needed him. Yanopolis got on the phone to say he had located the doctor at Bellevue emergency who had set Jackson's finger. The doctor had identified a photo of Jackson but, as Solly had said himself, that didn't mean anything, because it didn't matter what happened the night before.

"Right," said Solly, "but I wonder how he strangled her with a broken finger."

Even though it was only seven-thirty, he went home. When he closed the front door behind him, he felt as if he were entering a place that wasn't his. No voice on the phone, no sound of water running, no TV. It was a little like coming into a place where something had happened.

Something had happened. Adelle had waited for him to come home for her, because she didn't feel she could drive and she didn't want to ride in the ambulance alone. As Solly had been helping her on with her coat, her arm had leaped out of her sleeve to clutch her side. For a moment her lip had been lifted by a fishhook of pain that bared the whitish tops of her gums. Solly had flinched, repulsed for a second by the ugliness of her suffering, before he put his arms around her. He brought Adelle in himself, attaching a flashing light to the top of their car.

Now Solly poured himself a glass of whiskey and took a long gulp, enjoying its medicinal bitterness. What if she died? Then it would be exactly like this—him here in these rooms, coming home day after day. He could never marry again; he could never be with anybody who didn't know him from before.

He hoped the stupid stone passed by itself. He hated the idea that they would put her naked on a table, mark her, cut her open.

After another long belt of whiskey, he ripped the filter off a cigarette, thinking of the model he'd had a quick thing with—she used to rip the filters off. She'd been too young and beautiful to resist, and they'd gone at each other like two teams after the snap of the ball.

But what a crummy bastard he was, he told himself, spitting loose tobacco off his lips. The only woman in the world that could have stood him all those years, and her face gets twisted out of shape because of the pain she's going through and that makes him disgusted for even half a fucking second. She had always said he was good, but maybe even she didn't really know him either, because if she did then she would have seen what a lousy son of a bitch he was. If she had seen his face at the moment he was helping her on with the coat and the pain hit her, if she could see him sitting here thinking about that model, her phone number coming right into his mind like it was the most important thing he had to remember even though it had been almost a year since he had last called her—sure, he could remember that bitch's number, but he hadn't managed to learn the words to the prayer for his father and had to read them off that fucking piece of orange paper with the car wash ad on it.

He was nothing. Shit. A disgrace.

Time seemed to have accelerated. Every time David Aronow looked at his watch it was forty minutes later. Ten after nine.

He checked the front window. The car that had brought him to Karen's was still out front.

The terror had faded now but its aftertaste was still at the back of his throat. He even wished that the terror would return and relieve him of the dry moral pain that he did not have the strength to avoid before or to resist now.

He had helped in the murder of a human being—unwittingly, but that was even worse. Naomi would not be here with everyone else tomorrow.

And he had helped, actively helped in that, because he wanted her cooperation more than he valued her safety. He had not cared about her life. Which meant that he would be punished twice—once for what he helped make happen, and once for not having cared.

The only start of a salvation would be to pick up the phone, call Altheim, and tell him the truth, to remove the shroud of the lie from her murdered body.

He took out his address book, remembering that at one point he had jotted down Altheim's number in pencil, but uncertain whether he had already erased it.

It was there, seven faint penciled numbers that could change everything.

He dialed the number very quickly.

"Sergeant Yanopolis," said the voice at the other end.

David remembered him—the nervous, deferential assistant.

It was almost impossible not to say something into the phone, the humming void of silence calling the voice out of him.

David Aronow watched his own hand slowly hanging up the phone.

Solly aimed his index finger at the bottle next to his foot, but missed the neck of the bottle. His finger went in on the third try, and he pulled the bottle slowly up toward himself like a cautious fisherman. He looked from the bottle to the glass on the floor, trying to decide whether to drink the last of the whiskey from his glass or just straight from the bottle. Straight from the bottle, that's what he wanted, straight from the bottle. The whiskey still burned his lips, but now his lips didn't feel part of him; they were two folds of stinging rubber an inch in front of his face. He put the empty bottle down by his foot, where it fell over, and then, suddenly, Solly felt that he couldn't straighten back up. Gathering his strength, he slowly hoisted himself up until he could let gravity pull his head down against the upholstered back of the chair. He closed his eyes and fell into the world of drunken sleep, where Yanopolis was a choirboy dressed in white, kneeling under a bridge table and saying, "Our Father, Who art in Heaven." What the hell was Yanopolis doing there in a temple? Solly saw his father off to the side praying, his thin black hair combed neatly and shining like the white tallis around his neck. The chair was there in the temple, and the congregation was looking back over their shoulders at him for coming to temple drunk while his own father was trying to pray.

"Sol, now I'll teach you the right way to read the prayer for the dead," said his father in a firm and even voice.

He had spoken—after all those years he had spoken to him—and Solly could feel a knot of tears dissolving in his throat.

"You just don't know how, Sol," said his father. "I'll show you."

Solly felt unbearable love as his father approached, then unbearable sorrow as he disappeared behind him.

"I'm right behind you, Sol," said his father, his arms coming from behind the chair. He held a Bible in one hand, its pebbly black cover stamped with gold letters.

His father's hands opened the Bible, and the right hand began moving from the page on the right to the page on the left.

"See?" said his father. "See?"

Solly looked closer. The page on the right was orange and advertised a car wash, and the page on the left was pierced four times by a bullet hole and was written in a language that looked like Hebrew but was not.

"Sol, do you see now?" said his father with a touch of impatience. "You were never good at languages, Sol."

He opened his eyes. He was in his chair, the same chair as in the dream.

His father had spoken. But it was more than that. He had told him something. What was it, what was it?

His father had said that Solly didn't know how to pray. That was true. Or was it? Hadn't he prayed him back from the dead?

Why had he showed him that Bible? That wasn't a real Bible. You don't advertise a car wash in the Bible. And the other page had a bullet hole in it. How did that get there? He couldn't read that page. Of course, it was in a foreign language. He was never any good at foreign languages; his father had even reminded him of that.

Solly raised his hand slowly, then suddenly, angrily, snapped his fingers. That lying son of a bitch David Aronow was the blind spot! And the sister had to know too!

———

Hearing a horn honk lightly, David went to the window and saw the car that had been waiting by the door pull away, to be replaced by a Yellow Cab. Karen got out, turned around, and, bending slightly, said something to Shar, whose white-blond hair became visible through the rear window as he moved. She left the door open.

David tossed the key down to her in an envelope that twirled like a seed pod from a maple tree. Her arms reached up, the angle making her body seem oddly foreshortened. When she missed the envelope, she grimaced in frustration. He smiled, loving, for a moment, the spirit that had so wanted to catch the key.

His coat was on and buttoned by the time she came through the door.

"Evgeny's waiting," she said.

"I know. I have to catch a plane."

"Can you get a plane this late? It's almost twelve."

"There's a plane from Newark at one."

"If you don't make the one o'clock plane, come back here. Just call. Don't worry about waking me."

"I will," he said, to leave her at least with something.

"David, is everything all right?"

"Everything will be."

"When?"

"In a week at the most. Then we'll talk."

Their embrace was awkward, if only because he did not want her to feel the hard circle on his chest.

At the bottom of the staircase, which smelled of cats and dust, he paused to look through the front door at the cab, squat and ocher in the misty halo of a streetlight.

Fuck it, he thought.

The cab smelled of stale cigarette smoke and Shar's too-sweet cologne. That had never gotten mentioned.

"David, I'm sorry I'm a little late but those television people were like parasites," said Shar as the cab pulled away. "I was trapped in the spotlight."

David smiled. For a moment it felt as if they were back in Shar's hotel room. Then, with a nod of his head, David indicated the driver.

"Vaska is with us; Vaska is a good man."

David met the driver's dark, smiling eyes in the rearview mirror. "Where to?" said Vaska.

"Newark Airport."

"I wouldn't recommend it," said Vaska.

"Why not?"

"Too much open space, too few people this time of night."

"But you two can stay with me until I'm on the plane."

"Yes, but who'll meet you at the other end?"

"Listen to Vaska. Vaska knows," said Shar.

"I can't stay in New York. Do you have any ideas?"

"My idea," said Vaska, "is to drive to Connecticut. New Haven, maybe Hartford. We can spend the night in some motel. Then, in the morning, when it's light and there's plenty of people around, you can take a plane to where you're going. And that also gives us time to make arrangements for friends to meet you at the other end."

"Good idea, Vaska," said David.

Vaska nodded. The cab took a left and began heading for the West Side Highway.

David looked over at Shar, whose face was wan and tired, though there seemed to be some sad amusement at the corners of his mouth.

"It's a small world, isn't it, David?"

"Too small."

"Yes, it is when you're running."

"And you better be careful, too, Evgeny. I'm sure now they killed Raisa's brother. And so that means they must be watching her, too. You've got to stay away from Raisa. It's dangerous for you to be near her."

"I'm sure you're right," said Shar. "Connecticut is far away?"

"Not too far."

"Vaska, is anyone following us?" asked Shar.

"Too soon to tell."

David looked out the window. The stripped carcass of a wreck, its hood up, sat on its axles by the side of the road. They passed the George Washington Bridge which plunged away into a cloud of fog.

It was almost over. He felt almost good again.

"Would you like a mint, Evgeny?" asked David.

"Yes, thank you," said Shar. "My mouth feels like the bottom of a parrot cage, as they say."

They laughed.

"Were you able to remember all of what Yuri Trofimovich told you?"

"Nearly everything."

"And you have it with you?"

"Of course. And you have yours?"

David patted his chest.

"Going through the Bronx, I always put the buttons down," said Vaska, pulling a lever. All four door buttons snapped down at once.

David had lied, thought Raisa, there was no happiness. Shar had lied. She had lied. It was a world of liars. But now she had told the truth to the man with the tan shirt and the brown tie. She wouldn't have told it to the thin, ratty one who stood by the doorway, but it had been a relief to tell it to Altheim, yes, she had wanted to for so long.

Solly glared at Raisa, who was sitting by the wall in her nightgown and robe. The phone to his ear, he turned the Polaroid photo from the side where Karen Cooper's number had been written to the front, the picture of the blond-haired man wearing a blue-and-white jogging top. Jackson had been a good witness, which meant that Yanopolis had been robbed again.

Yanopolis was keeping his eye on Raisa but thinking of what Solly had told him on the way over about his dream. He's smarter asleep than I am awake, thought Yanopolis.

"About fifteen minutes ago?" repeated Solly. "With who? Evgeny Shar? In a Yellow Cab. Which way? Oh, your street's one-way. Newark Airport, the one o'clock to Boston? No, nothing's the matter."

"There's one more question," said Solly to Raisa, who nodded wearily. "Where do you think Shar would take our friend David Aronow?"

"I don't know,"said Raisa, thinking of the Soviet compound in Riverdale.

"Not Newark?"

"I don't know anything anymore."

"Let's get back into the city fast," said Solly to Yanopolis.

"Is she lying?" asked Yanopolis on the stairs.

"Everybody's lying on this one."

Solly slid in the ignition key but did not turn it. Just as Yanopolis was about to protest the waste of time, Solly raised a finger to his lips, then pointed to Raisa's window.

"Why is Vaska getting off the freeway?" asked David as they pulled onto a suburban street whose large brick houses looked like banks closed for the night.

"Vaska, why are you getting off the freeway?" asked Shar.

"We'll pick it back up in a while," said Vaska. "I want to cut through here to make sure no one is behind us."

"I told you that Vaska knows what he's doing," said Shar.

David found that his body had tensed, and he made himself relax against the seat.

"I thought there was someone following us," continued Vaska, "a big car—a Caddie, an Olds—but they passed us a minute ago."

"I'll make you a deal, David," said Evgeny Shar, softly but distinctly.

David moved his head slowly toward Shar, somehow very frightened by the inappropriateness of Shar's remark.

Now, when his eyes were in their clearest focus on Shar's face and eyes, David's stomach dropped as in an elevator and a wave of electrical revulsion discharged across the surface of his skin.

"Now you understand," said Shar.

"No, I don't."

"You understand," said Shar. "You just don't know the details."

David's right hand went up protectively across his chest like a man taking an oath of allegiance. But there was nothing left in the world for him to declare his allegiance to. The world had been reduced to a locked metal tube moving slowly through the suburbs, making full stops at every stop sign and blinking red light.

"It might help to think of it as the conclusion of our discussion, a valuable lesson in reality," said Shar. "There are two choices—see how wonderful America is, David, even here there are two choices. One: Open your shirt and give me the film. We'll go to the compound; you might have to spend a little time there, a week or two, but they'll let you go. Our people will find some way of compromising you into silence, your own government won't want the story known, and what newspaper would print such a story without any hard facts, documents. Two: I can cut the film off your chest with this knife." Shar opened his suit jacket and unzipped his jogging top to reveal the light tan sheath at his belt. "But if I have to cut it off your chest, David, I'll have to think you're a fool, and I'll lose all patience with you."

David knew that Shar was lying. He would never come out of the Soviet compound alive. His body would turn up in some shallow grave in Arizona and be counted among the victims of one of the mass murderers that rove the Southwest.

He knew that for all practical purposes his life was over. There was only one little square of life left, one move to make; he was checkmated either way, but he still had the freedom to make one move.

A choice between swallowing a sweet lie that contained a bitter death, and leaving the world in truth and bloody violence. Something perverse in him told him to choose the sweet lie, saying it fitted him better: he had chosen to lie so many times, had betrayed so much, the other way was only a cheap, desperate grab at redemption.

"Look," commanded Shar, pulling the knife up until it was entirely out, then balancing the point on the sheath.

There could not have been more distance between the idea of death and sharp, specific steel jumping in and out between his ribs. Still, David said, "No."

Shar looked surprised, irritated, even somehow betrayed.

David hoped that Shar knew what he was doing and that it would be over quickly.

Still balancing the knife point against the sheath, Shar moved a small hop closer to David, as if still threatening, giving him a last chance to see reason. Then Shar was brought up short by the look of wild amazement on David's face.

Life was too amazing, thought David. It made him choose his own death, and then a second later sent him another death instead.

When the car that David had seen hurtling at them struck the cab, everything became preternaturally clear. He saw every detail—Shar struck from behind, thrown hunched forward, the knife driven in above Shar's pelvic bone, then Shar's body propelled by a wave of almost visible energy across the seat, his head hard as a helmet striking David's ribs, which yielded in resistance before crackling like kindling, until suddenly everything was moving at a blurred, terrific speed that sent David's head slamming against the window, his pain fracturing the glass.

Then there was a very quiet moment in which David was aware of Shar writhing on him like a lover or an epileptic, and then the car struck them again. The cab seemed unable to decide whether to go up on its side or not, but then David felt the street skidding under his back. He had to throw off the burden of Shar's dead body to climb up that well to the hole in the window where he could breathe again. But he couldn't make his arms move and he was suffocating with that slaughtered deer dripping dark blood on his face.

He pushed his hands and arms from inside himself. His chest was pierced by knitting needles of pain until that heavy thing rolled off him. As he sat up, glass fell like sharp confetti from his hair, and the blood tipped from his eye sockets ran down his face. He pulled himself to the window.

First he saw red and yellow leaves lit by a streetlight, and then, lowering his eyes, the big car that had rammed them.

Its front end was smashed, smoke was pouring from the exhaust pipe. The crazy woman who had done it to them was coming out of the car now. She was wearing an unbuttoned coat over her nightgown. She looked furious. Why should she be furious? She had been the one to come crashing into them—what was wrong with that crazy woman?

But then, as she ran toward him and he heard the sound of an approaching siren, David remembered everything.

He ripped the tape from his chest, the pain playing lightly over other pain.

His head, one arm, and part of his chest through the window, he let the reel fall to the ground. Raisa made no attempt to catch it and did not even watch it fall.

They looked at each other for a long second. He had no more words in him, his eyes said what they could.

"Liar! Murderer!" she screamed, then stooped down and snatched up the reel.

"Run!" he whispered when he felt the arms tighten around his ankles, pulling him down. Something with hard feet went over his back, kicking his head as it wriggled out the window.

He pulled himself back up and saw Shar hobbling after Raisa, her coat and nightgown flying. Then Shar stopped and bent forward, howling as he pulled the knife out from above his own pelvic bone.

David grabbed the door handle on the right front door and pulled himself out onto the side of the cab as Raisa jumped in behind the wheel of her car, a red light flashing war paint on her face.

He looked to the source of the red light—the roof of the car that had just pulled up beside the cab.

Shar was almost to Raisa now, her door still open, his knife hand coming around like a windmill.

"Son of a bitch!" said the driver of the car with the red light. A short man jumped out the passenger door. David could not remember their names, but he knew who they were as he dropped to the street, pain ringing from his ankles to his skull.

Altheim was coming out of the door. Yanopolis was already on one knee.

The three loud stupid noises from Yanopolis's pistol, one after another, turned the back of Shar's suit into a flag whose symbol was three interlocked circles of red.

Raisa pulled away, her door slamming shut. Shar fell to his knees like a Moslem, facing East.

"Stop shooting, you stupid son of a bitch, you'll hit the gas tank!" yelled Altheim as Yanopolis continued to shoot at Raisa's car.

Her car went across the sidewalk over a front lawn and onto the next street. Then, as if bulldozed from the side, it went skidding to a stop against a mailbox. There was a very short stillness before her car erupted in a cloud of black-and-orange fire.

David started toward her, every step making more pain for the next step to overcome.

Raisa burst from her car, running from the torch on her back.

Now he was on the lawn, crossing the tread marks she

had left. She was running straight for him, her arms extended in sleeves of fire.

David knew there was only one important thing left to remember in the world—how you helped a person who was on fire.

He could smell the stink of scorched hair as they collided and he forced his arms around her burning coat, their noses smashing against each other's faces when he threw her down to the ground and rolled her over and over on the hard suburban lawn until they were a single rolling scream of flame and compassion.

PART
FIVE

37 Anton Vinias squeezed his knee,

hoping to resurrect some pain hot and specific enough to divert his mind from his disintegrating world. But that goddamned healer had done too good a job; except for an occasional incandescent twinge, the knee hadn't given him any trouble for months.

The faster his world disintegrated, the more desperately his mind tried to find exactly what had gone wrong. At first, Vinias stood apart from those automatic mental operations, which he considered as absurd as an engineer's rechecking his blueprints while his bridge collapsed under him. Yet he could no more will his mind to stop attempting to create order than he could will pain into his knee.

What else could he do while he waited for the machine to grind out its exact verdict? That would take time, maybe months. But he could already sense the change in the air around him. Now some people always managed to be reading an important document as he walked past; he had caught the smile of contempt in certain eyes, though a few still offered him tentative respect either out of inexperience or the smart fear that he might yet land on his feet. Besides, it was no secret that a rat was most dangerous when cornered.

Vinias knew that it was only a matter of time before his office and his desk and his chair evaporated as his position, his power, the magic of his authority already had. In a month, two months, three, he'd be transferred to a middling position in the Ministry of Fisheries or something infinitely humiliating like that. That would be his official hell, but he would not have to wait until then to feel the nauseating taste of disgrace saturating every cell of his body.

Despite everything, Vinias was able to find a furious courage, which he drew from his pride in the power of his mind. He had ceased to mock himself, ceased surrendering to his own obliteration.

At first his mind kept returning to the street where it had all happened. He knew the area from his own period of service at the United Nations: he could picture those American homes, the trees, the streetlights, the cars in the driveways. He had seen an accident map and read the sketchy newspaper accounts, and, until recently, other sources of information had been available to him. And all of it happening less than a hundred meters from the gate to the compound!

Maybe it was all nothing but luck. Vaska had been the

luckiest of them all. Knocked unconscious by the first impact, he would live to fight another day. Vaska had been supplied with a good lawyer and promised that he would not have to languish for very long in prison—he'd be swapped as soon as they could compromise some United States Embassy worker of sufficient rank.

To devise a story for Vaska had been Vinias's last official assignment. One last version of reality to invent, one last blurring of the issue. But it wasn't clear how much was actually known on the other side. Like many burn victims, David Aronow had experienced an hour of freedom from pain before he died, and Vinias could learn nothing of what Aronow had said. Clearly, strenuous efforts were being made over there to play down the story and keep it vague. And, as far as he knew, Raisa Farb remained in a coma.

The story that Vaska told, the story that was leaked to the media and to various grapevines, maintained that Evgeny Shar was not a spy—David Aronow and Raisa Farb were the spies—and Vaska should know because he was the KGB *rezident* in the émigré community. Raisa Farb betrayed her brother and tricked the New York police into hiring David Aronow to translate the letters, whereas in fact Aronow was Raisa's control. This, of course, meant that the letters would never go any farther. The problem was that Shar had new information (in this version, not from Yuri Trofimovich, news of whose suicide had now reached the West, but from Andrusha). So, it was Shar who knew too much and had to be kidnapped by Vaska and Aronow and taken to the Soviet compound. In fact, said Vaska, it was the Soviets who wanted to blacken Shar's reputation, thereby casting doubts and aspersions on the émigré community as a whole. When it came to certain specific questions—why had Raisa Farb rammed the cab? where was the strip of tail leader?—Vaska was necessarily ignorant: "Maybe she ran the stop sign in her hurry, I don't know, ask her. And the tail leader? You mean your science can't find it in the ashes?"

As he worked on that version, Vinias had been reminded of the Jewish engravers who had been forced to forge pound notes and dollars in a special department at Auschwitz, a slim usefulness separating them from extinction. His final task, a little coda to a failed work. But even knowing that did not prevent him from doing his best, if only because, now more than ever, he needed contact with his gift and strength.

After a while his mind stopped returning to Riverdale; what had happened on the billiard table of that street was not what really mattered. All that ever really mattered was the invisible vectors of force that ruled the world of human reality, just as the laws of physics and geometry ruled a billiard table. So, then, what was the angle of force in that final collision, precisely who or what had made that last shot that had propelled Shar, Aronow, and Raisa into their dark little pockets, scattered the others in various directions, and done what had been done to him?

For a time he blamed his superior Malanov—stupid Malanov, who cared only about getting the goods, about keeping his power, about his spacious office and that stupid new Finnish table, stupid Malanov who had assumed control of Shar and shifted the angle of Shar's assignment to the immediate needs of the moment—some stupid drug that might or might not work. But there were many good reasons to think that explanation correct but inessential, self-esteem not the least among them. But it was also his general view of reality that prevented him from seeing himself only as Malanov's victim, a sweaty little toad squashed by a boot heel. After all, he had remained in direct control of Shar; Malanov had merely switched the angle of the assignment. Vinias had accepted that switch, accepted it in the belief that Shar could succeed at both tasks, and would attempt to. And therefore he could not credit Malanov with his ruin.

That made no more sense than blaming the policeman who had fired the three bullets into Shar's back a hundred meters from the gate to the compound. The fact that the policeman had fired at his back and not his legs, the fact that the trajectories had proved fatal and not otherwise were not, ultimately, the coordinates that mattered. But, then, what was the element that had caused the havoc? Raisa Farb's passion, grief, and fury? No, they were just another volatile mixture, harmless until ignited. So what was the spark? Aronow must have been the spark. Shar had told Vaska that Aronow was one of those Western intellectuals who were too smart for their own good, and had ended up needing a reason to live.

American civilization failed to supply its citizens with anything more than an astonishing flow of goods and services, thereby alienating its intellectuals, one of whom happens on a lucky find that promises to put excitement and meaning in his life—could that bit of foolishness have caused his genius to be humiliated, his power taken away, his dignity and sanity placed under enormous stress?

No, that only explained why Aronow had acted as he did. But he, Vinias, was not a plaything of forces like Aronow, and the proof was that Vinias himself had created the force, Shar, that had destroyed Aronow.

Or had it been Shar? Shar had known that his assignment had been shifted but he had also known that the choice of keeping his cover remained with him. Vinias pitied him for his youth and his panic, for not being able to stand the suffocation of the mask, for needing that pitiful hour of freedom. He grieved for the loss of him, a son killed in battle on a distant front. But the gray of his sorrow was shot through with rage—Shar had betrayed him, risen against him. He should have known, how else could it ever be?

But if Shar had destroyed him, he had created that destruction in creating Shar, and in the end the responsibility came back to him.

But did that mean that he had been the author of his own disgrace, as he had always feared he would? That explanation simply did not ring true with sufficent intensity.

So, then, was it the malevolent spirit he suspected was at the heart of existence? The snake deity, indifferent to the workings of the world, that every once in a while demonstrated its ultimate dominion by striking lives at random. But to believe that was to believe that the world was ultimately devoid of logic and coherence. And he had always prided himself on his ability to merge his mind with the world, to think in realities. If the world was in fact insane, he would have no alternative but to surrender to the insanity that he now felt flooding all the compartments of his mind like cold rushes of water, obeying laws all the more meaningless for their regularity.

Something absolute, central, and irreducible in him resisted that. With a mixture of dread and blessed relief, he knew he was almost to the bottom of it.

He had not failed because human life was insane fluid chaos; on the contrary he had failed because life was always free to invent more form, law, and pattern than even a mind as great as his could grasp. His was the greatest of all possible tragedies because it had come in the greatest of all possible over-reachings.

Now he could see into the core of life where all knowledge became paradox and he understood that he could never have manipulated reality so skillfully all those years had he known what it really was, could not have lived that life had he known what life was.

A thrilling peace ran through him as the star of paradox grew clearer and clearer. Then he saw his own perfect paradox—what he now knew had saved him from disgrace, chaos, insanity, but there was not enough healthy tissue left in him to respond to that searing ray that either annihilated or revived; there was not enough love in his heart to rejoice in this knowledge.

He had seen the truth and it would kill him.